CHINA WIFE

RUTH MACNAIR

© Copyright 1999
Eleanor Macnair

The right of Eleanor Macnair to be identified as the editor of this work has been asserted in accordance with the Copyright, Designs and Patents Act 1988.
All rights reserved. No reproduction, copy or transmission of this publication may be made without written permission.
No paragraph of this publication may be reproduced, copied or transmitted save with the written permission or in accordance with the provisions of the Copyright Act 1956 (as amended).
Any person who does any unauthorised act in relation to this publication may be liable to criminal prosecution and civil claims for damage.

First published in 1999 by Falcon Books
An imprint of M & N Publishing Co. Ltd
P O Box 448 Northumberland Street
Huddersfield West Yorkshire HD1 4YA

Paperback ISBN 1 899865 64 0

Edited by Eleanor Macnair

Acknowledgement

My thanks are due to Monica Catling, who produced a legible typescript from the original hand-written letters.

Publisher's Note

When dealing with China, and indeed the Far east generally, spelling can be a problem. One has to decide whether to adhere to old forms or to accept the modern use of pinyin.

In these letters, Ruth uses the old forms, of course, but she also has a peculiar way with spelling of proper names. It has been decided to make changes where there are clearly spelling errors but to accept Ruth's spellings where these are part of her character. They display - as do all the letters - her charm and her intelligence.

Ruth was also a great one for neologisms of various kinds. Again, some are because of her sharp intelligence, while others are specially meant for her child, Eleanor. These spellings have been retained. So too have older forms such as Chinaman for Chinese, and Jap for Japanese. We could perhaps have changed these, to avoid offence where none is given or intended. The temptation has been resisted: political correctness is a form of fascism, with which we have no truck. And neither would Ruth Macnair. Read her wonderful letters, and you will surely agree.

Introduction

My mother, Ruth Macnair, was born in October 1898, the only child (apart from a brother who died in infancy) of Captain Edgar Dent of the Kings Own Scottish Borderers, and his wife May Sellar. Her father died when Ruth was eight, and her mother moved from Scotland to Burley in the New Forest in 1908. Here she built a house, Beacon Corner, which was to be Ruth's home base for the rest of her life, from which she married, and where two of her children were born.

Ruth's Dent forbears had been Shanghai merchants for several generations, (including opium trading, as she was to discover somewhat to her embarrassment), and she was to meet the current generations there in the course of her travels. Her maternal grandfather was Professor William Sellar of Edinburgh University (previously a Fellow of Balliol when Benjamin Jowett was master). His father, I regret to say, was the notorious Patrick Sellar, the factor of the Duchess of Sutherland during the Sutherland Clearances. In 1916 Ruth went to stay with her grandmother in Buckingham Terrace, Edinburgh, and to attend Edinburgh College of Art. This was her first time away from home, as she had never been to school, but had been educated at home by a series of governesses. On her grandmother's front doorstep she met my father, Ian Macnair, then a naval Sub-Lieutenant stationed at Rosyth. They fell in love at first sight, and in August 1918 it is no exaggeration to say that 'they married and lived happily ever after.'

Their first married home was furnished lodgings at South Queensferry, and later at Blythe, where Ian was standing by a submarine refitting at Cammell Lairds. In early 1920 Lieutenant Macnair was appointed to take the submarine L17 to Hong Kong, and in April Ruth followed him, setting off on her own for the first time for the long sea voyage to China. A second posting to China followed in 1927, and there were also tours of duty in Malta and Gibraltar (twice) to diversify the standard Naval round of postings to Portsmouth, Plymouth, Portland and Chatham. My parents lived in furnished rooms and later in rented furnished houses, apart from a short spell of house ownership in Alverstoke (near Portsmouth) before the Second World War. When Ian retired from the Navy they settled at Beacon Corner, Burley, where they celebrated their Diamond Wedding, in 1978, and where Ian died in 1980. Ruth survived him for another four years, but said that she felt she sad been 'cut in half'. Her happiest occupation in old age was recalling her early married life and travels.

While her mother was alive, Ruth wrote to her once or twice every week, and all these letters covering nearly half a century were preserved, making fascinating reading for the younger generation. It seemed that the letters from China in the 1920's, and the sea voyages out to Hong Kong, might be of interest to a wider audience.

Chapter One Voyage To China, 1920

Early in April 1920 Ruth said goodbye to her mother on Liverpool Docks, and embarked on S.S.TIRESIAS, a small liner carrying about 75 passengers, for the six week passage to China. The Royal Navy's summer time station in the China Seas at this time was Wei Hai Wei island in the north of China, leased by the British from the Chinese. Ian was already there with L7, and Ruth, after a brief call at Hong Kong, was to go straight on the join him. She was armed with various letters of introduction, including one to a ADC to the British Governor of Singapore. She sent letters home from every port of call, the first being Port Said at the entrance to the Suez Canal.

I have cut out some of the inevitably repetitive chat about fellow passengers, bridge hands, clothes and food (as well as personal and family messages), but hope I have left enough to give the flavour of the long weeks at sea, so unfamiliar to the present generation of air travellers.

I have retained Ruth's 'conversational' style of punctuation, consisting largely of dashes and exclamation marks. As regards the spelling of Chinese names, I have kept to the old Wade Giles usage which was in general use among foreigners at this time (Pekin, Canton, Nanking for Beijing, Guanzhou, Nanjing, etc.)

S.S. Tieresias
At Sea April 13th 1920

My darling Mummy,

It was too horrible for words seeing you grow smaller and further away on the jetty - and I felt so dreadfully cut off and forlorn - and especially sorry for you with all the flatness of being left behind. To occupy myself I began agitating about my cabin trunk - which however only made its appearance today. Then I unpacked my suitcase, had a most excellent dinner and went to bed. I missed you most dreadfully Mother darling. I do love you so much - and I'm already beginning to long to see you again. Take great care of yourself.

On Monday I got up at 8 and ate a large breakfast (still feeling strong) and went and walked up and down the deck and met and chattered to the Captain, also to the twins and their nice mother. At lunch time I didn't feel very hungry - then I went to bed - and for the next forty eight hours I did nothing but sleep and wake up at intervals to be sick - It <u>was</u> painful. My two cabin mates succumbed very soon after me - in fact the <u>whole</u> of Monday the stewardess said that there was only about one woman visible - and I'm told we had the most fearful crossing over the Bay. Certainly the ship heaved up and down as well as in awful spirals and we heard the sea breaking over the decks - and all our trunks jazzed round the cabin floor to the accompaniment of every sort of crash - bang and jingle. Everything was battened down - but even so half the cabins were flooded - mercifully we escaped this. At one time our door burst open and went bang - bang - bang - Each of us in turn tried to get up and shut it - but whenever we lifted our heads we were sick and we had to wait until a steward came along. I've got such a kind stewardess who fills my hot bottle at all unreasonable hours - also a very nice steward - it makes such a difference. One of my cabin mates the tall girl Miss Dunkley is really nice - and the fat one Miss Boys though not out of the top drawer, is quite inoffensive.

This morning I woke up feeling better - though there was still a terrific sea on. I struggled along to the bathroom (one had to go bare foot as the passages were about 6ins deep in water). I very nearly shot straight into the bath dressing gown and all owing to the roll of the ship. Dressing was a feat of some difficulty varied by being sick - but I felt better directly I got up on deck - it was quite exciting trying to walk round. I made friends with the twins and their mother and father who are certainly the nicest people on board. There is another nice looking party, a middle aged man and a very pretty young wife (rather like Mrs Steele) and a little boy - she is the daughter of Mr and Mrs Montagu Ede - the latter lady fascinates me - as in the highest gale she appears in a faultless coiffure and smart London hat perched immovably on top - no veil or anything - long pearl earrings and a high net collar.

This afternoon we got out of the Bay and the sea began to go down a bit. It was grey and cloudy - but appreciably warmer and I ate out on deck and we had a tentative tea brought up to us - I got my cabin trunk up and began Ian's socks. I've just come up from dinner now (my first meal since Sunday breakfast - if you except water biscuits which I never want to see again!) I'm feeling very strong though the sea is about the same as when we crossed from Dover to Ostend. Tomorrow we pass Gib: and there is a horrid rumour that a wireless message has come saying a southern gale awaits us!

April 14th

I'm writing this out of deck so please excuse pencil. I've forgotten to bring my fountain pen.

It's been a lovely day - warm and sunny and fairly calm, and I'm beginning to enjoy myself. It's a lazy life - it seems impossible to settle to any one thing.

This morning I had a huge breakfast - then did my unpacking and tidied up - then came on deck and played with the enchanting twins (I'm going to draw them later on). Then I solemnly took exercise round and round - and the Captain felt it incumbent on him to come and chat to me.

Then I was asked to draw the numbers in a sweepstake - and then came lunch. All afternoon I made gloves and attracted a large crowd.

Thursday
Such a lovely day - flat calm - and a half hidden sun. I secured a deckchair - put it on the top deck and basked there all day. At 11am we sighted land and at 1.30 passed Gib: The straits seems hardly any wider than the Sound of Mull - on one side was the Spanish Coast - low and rocky with patches of orange sand - on the other the splendid great bluffs and sharp peaked mountains of Africa - blue sea in between with a few sailing ships. The rock itself is very fine jutting out into the sea - the flat roofed white houses clustering round the base and on the far side extraordinary slopes of cement which constitute the water supply of the place (ask Cousin Byrnie to elucidate this) I kept rushing from side to side so as not to miss anything.

On the African side the great rock mountains suddenly go down into a flat sandy place with a town - Algiers I believe. (Ruth's geography was distinctly shaky!) I was thrilled at seeing porpoises playing round the ship - and every thing is very exciting and interesting and I'm feeling most awfully well (result of sea sickness I suppose) and the present temperature is heavenly. I'm going to wear a cotton tomorrow and I fished out my straw hat today. We have both our portholes and the door wide open and get a lot of air - A swimming bath is to be rigged up on the top deck which will be great fun. Tonight there is to be a meeting to choose a sports and entertainment committee. Last night we had a sing-song. Two men sang well and so did Miss Boys. One man played the violin - another recited (gr.r.r. - he was a Scot of Scotchest) and an elderly female sang Annie Laurie which was extremely painful!

I finished one glove - otherwise I did nothing all day but loaf and enjoy the warmth and loveliness - this evening it really was glorious, the sun setting and lighting up the snow peaks of the Spanish mountains. (Isn't Spanish a nice word?) I've read little - it is difficult when everyone is chatting or wanting to.

This is really a very good ship - such nice baths and very good food. Would you like to hear what I had for lunch? Lobster salad - boiled chicken and fried potatoes and oranges - for dinner soup, fish, roast duck, cauliflower, apple charlotte and dessert. The tea and coffee are horrible but we have excellent salt butter instead of the marge I feared. All the people are very nice and friendly. One of the elderly ladies has been telling me lots about China. She says Canton (90 miles from Hong Kong) is the place to go to to get glorious mandarin coats - real old ones - they are each only worn once for a ceremonial occasion - so I should think they would be quite clean. She says you <u>can</u> get them for 30 dollars - but that is great luck - jade she <u>says</u> is fearfully expensive except the light sort.

<u>Friday</u>

Yesterday was another 'blue day at sea' though as a matter of fact the Mediterranean hasn't quite come up to my expectations in the way of blueness. But it was very lovely - and the whole time we saw the African Coast a grey outline on the horizon. The day passed as usual. I made another glove - played quoits read and wrote and began Ian's sock and wandered about the ship and talked - and ate far too much! It is rather amusing to see the ship settling down into coteries - who all group their chairs together. Our lot consists of the Lapages (twin's parents) Mrs Beresford Stook (the N.O's wife) and Miss Dunkley (the nicest of my cabin mates).

Monday

Yesterday we steamed along all day in sight of Sicily, but about 40 miles away. It was very clear and one could just pick out the grass and the rocks and the sand. It's outline is low and undulating with the magnificent peak of Mt. Etna rising up at the back. In the evening it was quite beautiful the sun set dead behind us and we seemed to be travelling along a path of gold. The sea was pale like an aquamarine and the only land visible was Mt. Etna rising out of a low lying mist. Later on I went on deck after dark, the familiar stars were very bright - and down on the western horizon was one livid streak of yellow, the air was so warm and delicious.

I saw some swallows that flew round the ship. I wonder if they were en route for England.

Yesterday morning we had a very nice little service in the saloon - the very Scotch first mate read the lessons just like a Presbyterian minister. I spent most of the afternoon reading a book about China lent me by an earnest young man who is going to China for the first time and has got a perfect library of books on the country with him. It was very interesting. I've finished two pairs of gloves and written a lot of letters. For exercise we skip! and play deck quoits. I've been playing in a bridge tournament. You first draw for partners - I drew a certain Mr Button.

Tuesday April 20th

Yesterday was the hottest day we've had - but I still follow the sun round and avoid the shade - but we've got the awnings up.

The silk socks I'm knitting for Ian are becoming on of the jests of the ship! They are being unpicked for the 3rd time - but really this time because the needles are too coarse - I'm going to try and get finer ones at Port Said. I believe we only stop there for three hours. Then slap on to Colombo where we stop longer. I'm sorry there will be such a long gap between letters.

Heaps and heaps of love my darling Mummy. Please take care of yourself. I do miss you most awfully especially when I want to

share something funny with you. - because nobody else in the world sees certain things in the same way you do.
    ever your very loving
    Ruth

S.S. Tieresias
Suez Canal 21st April

    I've just discovered I can post at Suez if I hand this letter in tonight.

    I've got so much to say I simply don't know where to begin. We sighted Alexandria at about 11 am and got into Port Said at about 1. It was most amusing going in along the breakwater which has a statue of Mr de Lesseps on the end. There were a lot of orange sailed fishing boats about and directly we dropped anchor swarms of little boats came alongside laden with oranges etc. some had absurd little triangular awnings. There was one boat with a diver who went after pennies thrown to him from the ship. Then the passport people came on board and the mails!

    I was awfully damped at finding no letter from Ian - but presently a cable was handed to me! It contained one word 'Hurrah!' and was sent from Hong Kong on April 7th. It is a relief to know that he is expecting me. I cabled to him that I arrived at Shanghai about the 20th.

    Directly after lunch we went ashore in one of the little boats - with a villainous old scoundrel in a fez to row us - who said he would not put us ashore unless we gave him an exorbitant sum. However we had a man with us who knew how to deal with him. Our party was Mrs Stook - Miss Dunkley, Mrs Buzzard, Mr Stook (the young man with the Chinese books). We wandered about in twos and threes and bought things. (I only bought knitting needles!) Then we had tea at the Casino, Palace Hotel on the sea front and came on board again at 5 when we sailed.

The first glimpse of the East is very exciting - but curiously familiar somehow - after the first few minutes one quite ceases to feel wonder or surprise - and there is so much to take in that one's brain almost ceases to act. You see every sort and kind of nationality - weird people in long robes and turbans - oily gentlemen with fezes and striped cotton sort of night-dresses, dark coats and elastic sided boots. Sharp little boys and fat brown babies - but very few women - the Turkish ladies all wore dresses like one Ian sent me. The houses are square and flat roofed - many coloured and with ornamental verandahs and balconies - the streets are sandy and there are exotic twisty trees with great long pods on them. There was one house covered with purple bougainvillaea (I don't know how to spell it) - a most wonderful colour. There we came upon a garden full of palms and nasturtiums and marigolds and a beautiful hedge covered with many coloured flowers and a most exciting tree covered with huge scarlet flowers. It wasn't very hot - about the same as a hot summer day in England. The shops in Port Said sell the strangest collection of things and all very expensive though one can do a lot of beating down. I saw ostrich feathers and I mean to get some on my way home.

I wanted badly to have some delicious looking ice cream at the hotel, but Mrs Lloyd wouldn't let me - she was also very afraid of my losing myself. In the end we lost her and in waiting for her nearly missed the ship - though as we were such a large party I hope they wouldn't have gone on without us.

It is rather lovely as there is a tiny slip of new moon - but the stars are all out of place - the Great Bear is right overhead.

I hear now that we really had the most fearful passage through the Bay. The top decks were on a level with the sea and they had all the rockets up, ready to fire distress signals.

S.S. Tieresias
Red Sea April 23rd

It's going to be a proper scorcher today - and tonight we are going to take up our beds on deck. I've shed every garment I possibly can - but really I much prefer the heat to the cold, but it makes one awfully lazy.

I had to write you a very hurried letter about Port Said in order to post it at Suez. As a matter of fact I saw so many new things that they none of them have left much impression. The chief impression is of a scarlet boat pointed at both ends - laden with great big oranges and propelled by one of the forty thieves in a striped long garment, aided by a little brown boy in a blue turban. The water was a wonderful intense green and the whole thing was a glorious bit of colour. I hope I'll remember it enough to paint it. The other thing that stands out is the yellow house covered with purple bourgainvillia - a purple such as you have never seen before. The great palm trees were rather nice too, but everything was extraordinarily like what I expected it to be.

We started through the canal about 6 o'clock. At first there were sandy banks on both sides with sort of feathery palms and rushes and occasional date palms - beyond the banks sand and then sea and crowds of boats with coloured masts. There was rather a fine sunset and the night was beautiful - new moon and brilliant stars, and we had a searchlight on to light up the way. At intervals we tied up to let other ships pass. I was awfully sleepy so went early to bed - but I arose at 6am to see what was to be seen - chiefly desert - but very interesting, it was a dull orange colour and the canal was very green - on one side the desert was flat but ridgy - on the other there were rocky hills in the near distance. All along the banks of the canal there were barbed wire entanglements - dug outs and trenches and occasional working parties with camels.

Every now and again we passed stations - a few bungalows - palms and a flagstaff. The railway runs all along beside the canal.

We reached Suez about 11 and anchored for ½ an hour. Various sailing boats came alongside with fruit etc. There was nothing much to look at in Suez, just outside there was a huge camp.

Our first day in the Red Sea was very pleasant - and no hotter than a hot day in England. All the awnings are up and the boats swung out - so we have a lot of room. A lot of people bathed in the swimming bath - I alas had to look on only - we had iced asparagus and ice cream for dinner - and after dinner we went on deck and some of the boat officers gave us a concert - 2 mandolins and another instrument and we all sang. It sounded very nice out in the open. We were in sight of land all day - on one side we saw Mt. Sinai - and the mountains became increasing high and pointed and rocky (rather like very enlarged Coolins in Skye) when the sun set they went a beautiful purple on the shady side and rose colour on the other. Do you remember the lantern slides of Arabia at that lecture we went to in London? They were very good as that's just what the country looks like.

<u>April 24th</u>

If the heat is never worse than this I can safely say that I love the heat. We get up soon after 6 - bath and exercise on deck. After breakfast you put your chair in a nice shady place - with a breeze if possible - I read and sew and talk until lunch. After lunch you hump round with your chair and possessions to the other side of the ship where you stay until about 3 (we played bridge yesterday - I drew the same partner as before, Mr Button, and we made 2000 before our opponents made 600 - the opponents weren't good and we had wonderful cards. So now I'm in the semi-finals and only 'Lady' left so I hope I secure the ladies prize whatever happens!) At 3 I go down a change to the skin (not that I really get awfully hot - but I find its the best plan to keep two sets of clothes going and evening ones as well and I've a railing in front of the electric fire so you can keep them beautifully aired and anything you wash, dries in ½ hour.) But it is a disadvantage not being able to get any washing done. We may be able to in Colombo. At 3.30 we have tea on deck - then bathing which I'm looking forward to. Yesterday all the small children went in. It was most amusing to watch. The Boatswain (proper Treasure Island man in blue dungarees with a huge bowie knife on his hip) climbs down into the bath and lifts the children in - they all cling to him and shriek - but he is inexorable and under they go and eventually enjoy it hugely. After that we play deck games etc. and dine at 7 - sit up on deck in the moonlight for a bit and then go to bed early. We don't sleep out after all - as our cabin is really wonderfully cool.

When we were in Port Said we did look such a little tramp compared to the great P and O's, Bibbys and Rotterdam Lloyds - but everyone tells me who have done both that a small ship like this is far the most comfortable.

So far the only defects I've found with my clothes are that I ought to have had some blouses and dresses made with elbow sleeves. When your hands are hot and sticky it is so difficult getting into cuffs and they get so dirty when the rest is clean - besides everyone has short sleeves. The only thing is that everyone tells me that China won't be nearly as hot as this. The other thing is a Solar topee hasn't been necessary so far - all the men wear them but no females - a Panama with a chiffon scarf tied round it to hang down the back is quite sufficient with a parasol in the sun.

So far this journey has been as uncomplicated as London to Edinburgh - but I'm rather dreading Shanghai - I believe there is only a weekly service between it and Wei hai wei - so unless Ian got a fortnight's leave he probably won't be able to meet me - of course if I'm lucky I shall just hit off the day the ship goes or only have a day or two to wait - let's hope so as Shanghai is frightfully expensive. If Ian doesn't meet me my plan is this - hand over all my luggage to the agents (Robinson with whom I'm insured) and just take my suitcase - go to Cooks and get them to fix up my journey as expeditiously as possible - go to one of their hotels and more or less hand myself over to them.

Then go to the bank and ask them to help if I am in any difficulty. If I'm there a day or so I'll look up Mrs Lamond's friend and the Dent relation. Possibly even if Ian can't meet me he'll know of someone in Shanghai and I shall hear from him about it either at Singapore or Hong Kong. All the nice people in this ship are getting out either at Singapore or Hong Kong and only a few duds going on to Shanghai.

You will remember to ginger Miss Dudgeon up about Jardine Mathieson in the autumn when I go to Hong Kong - they are apparently all-powerful out there and I'm told if you have an introduction to them you can get anything done - I rather wish now I'd had the introduction to them in Shanghai as I believe they run one of the Wei-hai-wei boats.

I've been reading the official guide book about Wei-hai-wei. It sounds fascinating - the English town is mostly on the island - the native town is very old and surrounded by an old, old wall with gateways. There are interesting places all round to make expeditions to, the guide book says the scenery is beautiful and the climate ideal.

The captain invited me to his private deck yesterday to find out how I was getting on and if he could do anything for me. I said I was enjoying myself and had everything I wanted - then I questioned him about Shanghai and he says if Ian doesn't meet me he will look after me there - take me to the agents and fix up my passage to Wei-hai and show me where the bank is etc. He also says I can have my luggage on board and he will send it in a launch straight to the Wei-hai ship. I've enlarged my circle of acquaintances considerably since I last wrote, though I still see much the most of the people I told you about. There is a very nice

M. and Madame Birbosia - he is Belgian Consul at Singapore - she is English - They are very interesting and have been all over the world - to Korea and all sorts of out of the way places. We have also acquired one nice young man in the ship - he has planted his chair in our select circle (Mrs Stook, Miss Dunkley, Mrs Lloyd and Mrs Buzzard and me) in return for our agreeable conversation he moves our furniture and escorts us ashore (very useful this as he can tell off the boatmen and people) he also lends us nice books - he is a friend of Siegfried Sassoon's whose poems I've read in the Georgian poetry.

April 26th

Such a tragedy, we've lost the final in the Bridge Tournament by 50 points! It was a most thrilling game - I drew Mr Mallory - very good - our opponents were Mr Button(my late partner) and the Chief Engineer - both very good and all very much in earnest. I felt terrified - but I only made two really awful mistakes. We played in the saloon after dinner - it was like the Black hole of Calcutta - all the bridge enthusiasts came and sat round amidst tense excitement - my friends came and fanned me!

Yesterday it was very hot - I reduced my clothes to the rockbottom limit - viz.: a silk chemise - drawers - petticoat and dress. I'm so glad I got fairly substantial dresses - the blue one is a joy - you can wear so little under it without it looking bad - and it is nice and loose - the old yellow dress is good too - but the people who wear light voiles have to wear so many underclothes and you can see them all - so it neither looks nice nor is it really so cool.

I've seen the Southern Cross - it is a fine group of stars - but not so nice as the Great Bear - which is now right up overhead. Yesterday we passed groups of rocky islands - quite barren - but rather a nice orange red colour - today we pass Aden. Flying fish have been seen - but not by me.

April 28th

Who do you think I've discovered on board this ship? Kathleen Parker Smith's brother! He was the solitary passenger we picked up at Port Said and I didn't hear the name until the day before yesterday. I went up and asked him if he was any relation to Mr James Parker Smith in Edinburgh and when he said "son" I said it must be another one(I had quite forgotten that Kathleen had two brothers - and I knew one had been killed) also he looked far too old. However he identified himself and I apologised - and now I spend the day trying to lose myself - in a ship of this size a difficult feat. He is really nice but has what Uncle Edmund called "the cold grey eye of a bore" - he has been lecturing the troops in Egypt and lecturing has become a habit.

We reach Colombo early Monday morning and stop there 12 hours to coal. At Singapore we stop 3 days - rather a bore as I don't know anyone(except possibly Arthur Mallet) and we are recommended to sleep ashore as it will be fearfully hot and they will be working night and day unloading the cargo which will be a noisy business. Mrs Stook has offered me a share in her room at the hotel which I shall probably do.

I'm afraid the monsoon is breaking and we shall have an awful time after Colombo. Thank heavens we'll anyway be on dry land tomorrow. I hope it won't rain - as I'm looking forward to seeing Colombo. I wonder if there will be a letter!

S.S. Tieresias
Bay of Bengal 4th May

We had a lovely day in Colombo yesterday. I awoke up at about 6am to find the ship had stopped rolling and that we were just entering the harbour. At 7 the mails arrived - a lovely long letter from Ian written just after he had got my cable and very excited. He can't get down to meet me - but friends of Mr Stopford's are going to meet the ship at Shanghai and probably put me up and see me off again to Wei Hai Wei. Ian himself has been away from Hong Kong for 3 weeks as "L7" is in quarantine for mumps. Hence a good deal of delay in getting my cable. He says directly he returns to Hong Kong he was going to go to Holt's agents to find out this ship's exact programme. (Please excuse writing - the ship is rolling horribly and there is a big sea on covered with white horses - but the weather is much cooler.) I also had a letter from Major Norton (a neighbour of the Macnair's) saying he was very sorry he couldn't meet me as he had just been sent up country - otherwise he had arranged a very nice programme for me. The MacFarlanes were also away. Mrs Stooke and I decided to go off on our own - so we started directly after breakfast. When we landed at the jetty we felt rather like lost sheep - but we met Mrs Lloyd who told us various things to go and see and we agreed to meet her and Mrs Buzzard at the Galle Face Hotel for lunch. We got hold of the gharri (a sort of victoria) and after protracted bargaining with the driver he agreed to take us all round for the sum of 2 rupees (5/-) At intervals he stopped and thrust his head inside and tried to raise this charge - but Mrs Stooke was quite firm - she was as good as you were in Belgium. We clattered off in great style - slightly marred by the harness coming off and having to be mended with string! First we went through the main streets with covered in pavements and fine shops - then we got into the native quarter which was fascinating - if smelly. We drove through the bazaars, little low roofed booths selling every sort of funny thing - largely dried fish! The nicest stalls were the fruit stalls - mangoes and pineapples and coconuts all being in front - then there were tailors and shoe makers and silk merchants and shops that sold sweet meats and cakes that looked like fritters. The natives were mostly very smiling and pleasant looking compared to the villains at Port Said. The women are small and gentle looking except when they have heavy black moustaches! Men and women alike wear a skirt preferably of a bright check (pink and orange for example) the women wear a tight little white camisole on top of this frequently with a gap where it ought to join the skirt. The men wear nothing above the skirt and have beautifully polished looking backs. A great many have their hair long and done in a little bun at the back and a tortoiseshell comb placed like a tiara only wrong way round. The fat brown babies were rather enchanting. They were chiefly clad by having a piece of string tied round their middles! There was really too much to look at - carts drawn by humped oxen - and hooded carts made of palm leaves (the hood I mean) - men with great jars suspended on a long thick stick rick-shaws and heaps more things. It was a festival (Buddha's birthday) and all the native streets were hung with paper lanterns and streamers. We got out to look at a Buddhist temple - but didn't go inside as we objected to removing our shoes! It was a horribly tawdry looking place anyway - with a colossal plaster cast of Buddha in front of which were offerings of rice etc.

Then we drove on to the Cinnamon gardens through the residential quarter. Such nice looking bungalows with shady gardens and green lawns but awful Bournemouthy names! We got out again at the Cinnamon Gardens and walked about for quite a long time. They were full of gorgeous many coloured flowers and shrubs and trees - but not a single familiar one.

The Galle Face is a huge hotel on a sort of sea front - the rooms were beautifully cool and we had an excellent lunch. Asparagus omelette and wonderful chicken curry with about 10 things you ate with it and not at all like English curry. All sorts of fruits - pineapples - tiny bananas - mangoes and rather a nasty scented melon. The lunch was 3 rupees each (3/6 in ordinary times, 7/6 now). We drove back to Colombo in rick-shaws and did some shopping - mine was chiefly getting some picture postcards for the stewardess! Except for the Exchange things weren't expensive - but they looked to me mostly trash. You can get nice white hand embroideries and nice baskets but I'm going to do my purchasing on the way home. We met Captain Parker Smith who gave us tea and escorted us back to the ship at 4 o'clock when we sailed. Colombo is a good place - and it wasn't very hot.

When we got out to sea again it was fearfully rough - and rough all yesterday. I think I must have got my sea legs as it didn't worry me - but it restricts one's occupations. I've done a fairly successful portrait of the 18 months old baby - but painting is a struggle on a ship.

Last night the heat was so terrific that we simply couldn't endure our cabin, so we humped our mattresses right up onto the top deck and spent a cool and comfortable night there - at least, airy if not cool as I had a thick blanket over me - having been instructed that this was essential - I put my mattress on top of a long cane chair and it was as comfortable as a bed and I slept like a top. The only bore is at 6 o'clock the boatswain comes round and you literally have to take up your bed and walk as the decks are swilled down.

Today it was calmer - but very hot. We had deck sports which lasted nearly all day. I entered for practically everything and won one first prize in a telegram race. In this 6 letters were put up and you had to make up a telegram in 2 minutes, the letters were P.S.D.O.E.F. my telegram was "Please send Dromedary only, Elephant follows" As this got first prize you may judge the intellect of the rest of the passengers! There were potato races, cock fighting etc. and an awful race where your partner runs to you - eats a water biscuit, drinks a bottle of fizzy lemonade and whistles a tune which you have to guess - my partner Mr Stock got stuck in the lemonade. It was really great fun - but I shall be glad when this voyage is over now. It would have been the greatest fun in the world if you or Ian had been coming too. Still only about another fortnight to Shanghai a couple of days on - and then Ian - isn't it glorious!

Thursday

Cooler and fresher today - the only event being the distribution of prizes. I got a very nice black and gold penholder - and the Chief Engineer gave me the Bridge Tournament prize for being the only "lady" left in - even though I didn't actually win.

I'm awfully sorry that almost all the nice people are leaving this ship either tomorrow at Penang or on Monday at Singapore. I've been asked to stay with Mrs Buzzard at Bangkok (Siam) with Mrs Stooke at Kuching (Sarawak) and Madame Bribosie at Singapore, all on my way home - so anyway I don't lack opportunities of seeing the East! I shall miss Mrs Stooke particularly she is good company and really nice and an excellent person to go ashore with. I shall also miss Miss Dunkley as a cabin companion. I dread a tête a tête with the other one!

S.S. Tieresias
Penang May 8th

Yesterday Monsieur Bribosia came up to me and said with great solemnity "Remember - you can nevaire nevaire see the East again for the first time - so write down your impression while they are fresh - write - write - write" I think it is good advice - though my impressions are so chaotic that it is difficult to put them down.

A lot of people slept ashore last night at the hotel - the Captain gave me and Mrs Stooke permission to bring our mattresses on to his private deck under the bridge where we were very comfortable and safe from being disturbed. I fell asleep with the scent of the East strong in my nostrils. It is really a very unpleasant smell - but there is an underlying aromaticness which concentrates all the sights and sounds and conjures them up to you. I awoke at 6 to "the grey dawn breaking" it was lovely and cool - secure in our private perch we sat in our dressing gowns and ate oranges and watched the coolies in the boats alongside cook their breakfasts on a brazier and eat, sitting cross legged.

Penang is supposed to be one of the finest views in the world. The harbour is surrounded by hills covered with jungle - hills that in the distance might almost be Scotland - in the foreground are forests of coconut palms - the water was very green and covered with boats of every description - sailing boats with striped sails - (orange and red for example) and row boats pointed at both ends. Yesterday the sky was lovely - blue - with great banks of white clouds - some coming down onto the tops of the distant blue mountains.

We arrived about 12.30 - but it was too hot to go ashore until 3.30. Mr Stock invited us to tea. (I must here explain - that the inevitable romance is going on in this ship. Mr Stock who is an exceedingly nice young man, in fact the only nice one in the ship - has been very smitten by a certain Miss Williams - Mr Montague Ede's hospital nurse. She has only come to the fore since Mr Ede has been better. I must say she is rather attractive and much nicer than most hospital nurses - but being several years older than Mr Stock it probably won't come to anything. In the meantime the affair is being conducted on the most decorous lines - and Mrs Stooke and I play the part of heavy chaperones by invitation. Our party yesterday consisted of Mrs Stooke, myself - Miss Williams - Mr Stock and a Mr Cook - rather a bounder but with a useful knowledge of the Malay tongue.) After tea we all set off in rickshaws - very pleasant conveyances as you can't talk to your neighbours and so can give entire attention to looking - and I did look too! Every single thing I saw I wanted to paint - or more especially to make into woodblock prints. Do you remember the print of the "sword grinders"? Well at every turn there were scenes like that - and even nicer. The Chinese element is very strong and it attracts me much more than the Indian element in which there is a feeling of tawdriness. I love the great, bold decorative Chinese signs outside the shops and houses - done in red and black and gold. Then there are the temples with their huge lanthorns and funny little Chinese ladies in butterfly coloured dresses with wreaths of flowers round their heads. There is a romance and weirdness in this place which was quite lacking in Colombo - picturesque though that was. (Picturesque is a horrid word). After we had gone through the town and the residential quarter we went along the coast road, past market gardens and fields of sugar cane - and hedges of tapioca! until we entered a palm forest - all among the palms were the funniest little wooden houses built on stilts and thatched with palm leaves - like Peter Pan houses. As we were coming back, in front of one of these houses was a fire built of coconut husks which gave a pale clear flame - a crackling noise and a smell like incense - the blue smoke followed up the straight lines of the palm trees - disappearing into their great tops - tops that made beautiful shapes against the sky - still yellow from the sunset. Round the fire squatted dark nearly naked Malays. Oh I do wish I could paint it - but as yet I can't draw the simplest thing from memory - there is too much to remember - as every thing is new - but when one has lived with it a bit it will soak in - and as so far it is the Chinese things that appeal to me most - I ought to be able to do heaps when I get to Wei-hai-wei. Another nice thing I saw was on the way back when it was nearly dark - a lighted window with a little Chinese girl in a lacquer red garment sitting under it and above a great black and gold sign. Those two things have remained most vividly.

I forgot to tell you about our adventure. As we were going along in the rickshaws - my coolie suddenly precipitated me into the ditch and I was nearly overturned - the other four were all in the ditch too - one on top of the other! and where we had been on the road two motor cars had met in a violent collision - nobody was hurt - but one car was absolutely wrecked and the other was badly damaged. In this latter was a highly ornamental Chinese lady with a shrill voice which she used with great volubility - in fact she never ceased talking. Mr Cook wanting to show off his knowledge of Malay joined in - we were surrounded by native policemen - everybody argued and you never heard such a hub-bub - the Chinese lady easily getting first prize! Notebooks were produced and names and addresses taken and I was afraid we were going to be involved in the lawsuit!

Government House
10th May 1920 Singapore

Isn't this delightful - I've been whisked up here to stay until the ship leaves either on Wednesday or Thursday (today being Monday). I've got the most lovely cool room - and a real bed and a fat smiling Ayah and a bathroom all to myself and I'm thoroughly enjoying it all after my tramp steamer. (For which however I have a great affection - but not when she is in port - coaling and discharging cargo)

We got in at 7am and I got two letters from Ian, who has arranged for people to meet me at Shanghai and at Hong Kong - and he has also got rooms for the winter at Hong Kong at a boarding house, St George's, which Mrs Ede tells me is very nice and caters almost solely for soldiers' and sailors' wives. So Ian has been very clever and he is getting very excited - but not more so than me! I was envious of all the people who were getting excited meeting their husbands etc. this morning but my turn comes very soon now! After breakfast I got Arthur Mallett's note saying he was coming for me at 10 - so in a terrific scramble I packed my suitcase and changed - I'm wearing my white dress, the hat we got at Tyrell and Greens with the blue ribbon and I've brought my lace dress and my green evening dress (alas the silver is already tarnishing) and a white skirt and blouses.

At 10 Arthur Mallett appeared - such a nice friendly young man and we came along in a superb motor - a very nice elderly lady took me over and showed me my room and asked what I'd like to do. I said I wanted to write letters. This afternoon I'm to be taken sightseeing and then play tennis and tomorrow go to the races - so I'm going to have a lovely time. I'm feeling rather shy - especially as there is a Rajah and some other people staying. Will you thank Lady Grey very much - in fact I think I'll write to her myself. Just think of the difference of this to sweltering down in the ship for 3 days with all the people I had made friends with gone - and the ship coaling and the mosquitoes biting and all sorts of other which I was prepared for!

I started writing you a long letter about Penang - it is unfortunately on board - so I'll have to send it after this one.

As we didn't sail until 10pm on Saturday we again spent the day ashore. Mrs Stookes and I went out together in the morning and shopped - everything pretty expensive - some shops were Indian and some Chinese - you bargain in all of them - and as long as you look at their goods - they don't seem to mind whether you buy or not!

We rested on board from 11 until 3.30 then went and had tea at the hotel invited by Mr Stock and Mr Cook (it is now only a matter of days until Mr Stock proposes to the sister. Oh! I forgot - you won't understand this until you get my first letter!) We split up the party and roped in the ship's doctor and Captain Parker Smith and Mrs Stooke and I and we went for the most wonderful drive right round the island. It took about 3 hours and it was dark by the time we returned. First of all we went along the coast - beaches of white sand with palm trees growing down to the water's edge and reflected in it - at intervals little coves which looked perfect bathing places (alas though there are crocodiles and sharks; I saw two of the latter.) Just out at sea were little rocky islands covered with vegetation - a dream place. Once we came to a lagoon with a Malay village - the houses built on piles in the water - I wished I could have stopped and drawn it. The inhabitants sat at their front doors and fished!

Turning inland we went through Rubber plantations and then we began to climb. It was a most perilous road corkscrewing round and round with the sharpest hairpin bends. Most of the way was through jungle - palms and plants not one which I could name - some were bright coloured flowers and exotic looking ferns - but we saw very few birds. All the time there was the most delicious smell - like hyacinths and sweet briar. Eventually we got to the top of what was really a mountain and had the most magnificent view all round and on both sides. Then down again even more perilous than coming up - at the foot of the hill we crossed a swamp where innumerable frogs croaked. I thought I smelt something like bog myrtle. After the swamp a forest of palms with native villages, the little wooden houses with bamboo leaf roofs hidden away among the trees. Each village had a Chinese shop where the inhabitants seemed to collect. At intervals there were bonfires of coconut husks and as it got darker it was wonderfully mysterious and nice - through the window of the houses you could see the natives squatting round a solitary candle on the floor.

We stopped to see a Chinese temple built into the rock but it was too dark to go in.

Coming through the native quarter all lit up and with stalls with flare lights and all the natives, Malays, Indians and Chinese thronging round was like a thing out of a fairy story. Are you very envious of me seeing all this?

We left Penang at 10pm, I slept on deck - but between thunder and lightening and rain I got bored shifting from side to side of the ship - and so took my mattress below and bore the heat.

Yesterday was a placid day steaming slowly down the straits - most of the time in sight of land.

May 12
Government House
Singapore

I'm sitting all dressed up in my best clothes waiting for a garden party to begin - to which about 1000 people are coming - I have just been drilled in my part as one of the 'Houseparty' - but the part I am really looking forward to is accompanying Lady Guilluard's uncle - (a killing old gentleman, an MP for somewhere in Surrey) to eat ices!

I've washed my neck with great care(!) and pulled up my stockings - and tried to review myself in front of an imaginary you. I wish you could see my lace dress - it really is lovely - and so cool and comfortable and the very thing for this kind of show.

I do hope Ian will never be an admiral - at least I want him to be - but this sort of life wouldn't be my métier at all. I've enjoyed a day or so of it immensely - but I'm beginning to be very bored. One thing, having staying in Government House I shall no longer be petrified calling at other Government Houses. The Guilliuards have been most awfully kind and nice to me, and after the first I haven't felt a bit shy!

In the afternoon we went to the races. I felt as if I was Royalty, entering a red carpeted box in the middle of the grandstand to the strains of "God save the King".

It is the first race meeting I've ever been to - and I was rather disappointed. I did some very mild betting acting on Arthur Mallet's advice. I came out 3s to the bad - but had quite a lot of excitement.

The 'Tieresias' moves on again at 8am tomorrow morning. Arthur Mallet is taking me down at 7.15.

S.S. Tieresias
China Sea May 15th

It <u>has</u> been hot the last few days - hotter than anything we've had so far. The wind is with us - so there isn't a breath of air and it doesn't get any cooler at night - I simply sit still and drip and drip and it's no good changing clothes - because the effort this involves makes one pour instead of merely drip. At the moment I have to hold a piece of paper under my hand to prevent the letter getting soaked! 97 in the shade on the upper deck is what we've been having. I shall be very glad to get to cooler climes up north though until today I haven't minded it much - but just now I'm very limp. We get to Hong Kong tomorrow night and Shanghai a week today - so my travels are nearly over. The Captain says I can sleep on board until my ship goes to Wei-hai-wei when he will send me and my luggage direct to it in a launch which is very nice of him - and would be much the most convenient way - but of course Mr Stopford's friends may meet me - also perhaps Mr Lamond!

On Thursday Arthur Mallet escorted me back to this ship at 7.30am as she was supposed to sail at 8am. However when that hour arrived we heard she wasn't going until 12 so Mrs Stooke who came to wave goodbye to us - and Mr Stock and Mr Cook and I went ashore and ate ices.

I miss all my friends in this boat very much - you get to know people quickly leading this sort of life - and they were all so kind to me. The only nice people left now are Mr Stock and the Rotherhams - the latter asked me to sit at their table. Major Rotherham was in the 4th Hussars - and before the war he lived in Ireland and was M.F.H.

Mr Stock is a very nice young man - very serious minded and full of solid virtues and not a ray of a sense of humour - but most dependable and helpful. He has fallen very much in love with Mr Ede's nurse, rather a puss, I think - gentle and sweet and a bit of a dark horse - she is very coy and refuses to sit alone with him - so I am much in request as a third party and when sister isn't there confidences on the subject are poured out to my rather embarrassed ear. I think he intends to propose to her today before getting to Hong Kong - but I'm sure she won't take him and good thing too as she is older. The affair has been the great excitement of the ship and I've promised to let several people who got out at Singapore know what happens.

We saw a whale yesterday, a huge great thing that swam along beside the ship. I've also seen sharks and countless flying fishes.

May 16th

I slept underneath the southern cross last night - it was rather lovely - I brought my mattress up and put it on a long cane chair and lay watching the stars through the spaces between the awnings. Poor old Orion was lying right over on his side and the Plough was upside down and the Pole Star on the horizon nearly into the sea. Round the Southern Cross the stars are so thick that it looks as if the sky has been powdered - and the big stars are very bright and near. I love sleeping in the open - and about midnight a little breeze got up and it was beautifully cool. I woke up at about 6.30 to see the boatswain advancing with a hose and Miss Boys and I two islands in the middle of inches of water which was being sluiced over the deck. The boatswain remarked we looked so comfortable that he did not disturb us - one of the advantages of a ship like this over a properly regulated P and O!

Hurrah! It is so nice and cool today - we get to Hong Kong late tonight. The two days after Hong Kong I shall pack - I'm getting just sick with excitement - and the days seem to get longer and longer - I keep on going over in imagination the glorious moment when I first see Ian - and I know all the time the actuality will be far more glorious even than I can imagine. Mother, I realise more and more how lucky I am to have a husband like Ian - every time he becomes more of an excitement and a joy. I enclose a letter I had from him at Singapore.

Another thing in which I am very lucky is to have a Mother like you - it is <u>such</u> fun writing to you and to have the excitement of getting your letters to look forward to at Shanghai.

S.S. Tieresias
Hong Kong

We got here early yesterday morning and the mails came on at 5am. I had 3 very nice and excited letters from Ian. He said his friends the Moxons were unfortunately away from here just now - but they told him they would ask some other people to meet me - however nobody has appeared - which is rather sad, especially as everyone has left the ship (there are only 8 of us going on to Shanghai) so I have to go ashore alone. I was given a letter of introduction to Mrs Boritt (the wife of the 2nd in command of the Fleet) by Mrs Marshall at Government House. I telephoned to the dockyard and found Admiral Boritt had gone to Shanghai so that was no use - so I just set off and explored on my own. I think Hong Kong is the most enchanting place and I <u>am</u> glad I shall be coming back here to live and it will be the most glorious fun in the world to explore it all with Ian - even alone it was rather fun. The entrance to the harbour might almost be the West Highlands - great rocky mountains rising sheer out of the sea - and smoky islands and channels - then Hong Kong itself spread along the shore and climbing up the Peak - the houses getting more and more scattered. The harbour is full of every description of craft - liners, cargo boats, junks, sampans etc. The junks are lovely - built rather on the lines of an old Spanish galleon - with a great high poop. Whole families spend their lives in these little ships - there is one alongside us and I watched them this morning sitting under an awning eating rice with chopsticks out of such pretty shallow bowls.

The Chinese coolie is not as paintable as the Singalese or Malay - in fact he is very ugly and wears uninteresting blue clothes - his only redeemable feature is his straw hat. Some of the women though wear bright colours, and most of the babies - one family I saw the mother wore bright blue - carrying a baby in bright pink while two small things trotted beside her, one in primrose yellow, the other in apple green - with their smooth black heads and onyx eyes they were rather fascinating - but not as entrancing as the naked brown babies. The streets are wonderfully paintable - especially the narrow ones that run up the hill - everywhere the long, fluttering many hued signs and above that suspended across the street from window to window the brightly hued washing: and below street vendors of every sort - men sitting crosslegged selling mangoes - other men making shoes - and at one corner a flower market - all sorts of strange and wonderful flowers of the crudest most bizarre colours. I wished I could have lingered and taken it all in - but being alone I didn't like to - nor even go very far into the native quarter - but when I've got Ian we will explore every corner and when I've leisure I'll do lots of pictures. The surroundings of Hong Kong are much too grand to be paintable, like Scotland - not like Penang where every bit of the country with the palms and funny wooden houses was a picture - I wish I was staying there for a bit just in order to paint - but this will be a far nicer place to live in. The vegetation here isn't quite as wonderful as it was in the tropics - there are palms and coconuts - but only a few and they don't look very happy - but there are all sorts of wonderful flowering shrubs and wild flowers and the most gorgeous butterflies - you've probably seen them in cases - great huge blue ones as big as small birds - jade green and black ones - yellow ones - they look ripping darting about in the sun.

Yesterday after I'd wandered about the town a bit I took the Peak tramway - you would be terrified of it as it runs sheer up the mountain and is (apparently) only kept from hurtling backwards by a small wire rope! You see the rails in front of you rising like the wall of a house! The whole thing is rather like a scenic railway at the White City! I thoroughly enjoyed it. From the top (over 1000 feet up) you get what is supposed to be one of the most wonderful views in the world - you can see both sides and away into the mountainous interior of China. Hong Kong is like a map beneath your feet and the shipping like so many toys - I went and had a most excellent tea at the Park Hotel. You know how I was warned against the fearful expense of this place - well I had a delicious tea - buttered toast - Swiss roll and a delectable rice cake and the bill was only 30 cents (9d taking the dollar at 2/4 at which rate Ian gets his pay) - you certainly couldn't get that in England - and things in shop windows didn't seem very dear - anyway much cheaper than Colombo or Singapore. I believe if you know where to go among the native shops you get things very cheap - and when you live in a place the Chinese charge you according to your husband's position! Thus a Chinese tailor will make a coat and skirt for a commander's wife much cheaper than the identical thing for a Captain's wife - and the bigger the man's ship the more he is charged - so I think a lieut. in a submarine ought to get off rather well! That reminds me I saw an old friend yesterday - the "Titania". She and her 6 L-boats are alongside the jetty - little did I think last time I saw her at Blythe - that the next time would be Hong Kong!

I came down from the Peak and flattened my nose against shop windows for a bit. You would love the shops - such nice things - embroideries - mandarin coats - slippers - carved ivory - jade - crystal - silks and probably quite common but none the less most attractive china.

At Colombo and Singapore and the other places I had no desire to buy anything, the things struck me as tawdry - but here I really would like to be rich and send you and Ninny[1] rolls of silk and a mandarin coat to Muriel and things to everyone. But what you will think characteristic of me - I bought nothing but some postage stamps! As a matter of fact N. China is supposed to be best and if you poke around and get to know about things I may be able to acquire things even with a small amount of money at my disposal - beautiful mandarin coats can be got for £3. I know if you were here you'd find things - I think you really must come. One of the managers of the biggest firm out here, Butterfield and Swire, came on the ship from Singapore. He told me the dollar was almost certain in the near future to go down nearly to normal - though it probably won't touch its pre-war figure - just now it is 4/2 and in Jan. it was 6/-.

Ian writes that he thinks I will like Wei-hai-wei very much - there are beautiful beaches and bathing and lots of tennis - we shall be on the Island which has been taken over by the Navy almost entirely. Ian also says the hotel looks very nice - it is a series of bungalows and is run by an old Scotch couple. I am looking forward to arriving - I ought to a week tomorrow as the ship leaves Shanghai on Tuesday (we got in on Sunday).

At present we are anchored at Kowloon and at night the view of Hong Kong is marvellous (my stock of adjectives is running very dry!)

First of all you have the deep green water - then masses of bright winking lights, these get fewer and further between up the peak - but the whole of the mountain is hung with necklaces of lights rising out of them, the great black outline of the Peak itself against a clear sky and a couple of remote white stars.

Oh won't this place be fun when I've got Ian here!

This morning I wandered round Kowloon - it has a wide fine street with shady trees and houses with gardens where the

Europeans live - and rather a dirty Chinese quarter and a big barrack where an Indian regiment is quartered. Just now I'm going over to Hong Kong in the Ferry and I'm going to get on top of a train and go as far as it will take me and back again.

One gets most awfully pretty fillet lace here - or rather it is mostly made at the convent at Wei-hai-wei and so it is cheaper there. It would be awfully pretty for underclothes and if it is really cheap would you like me to send you some?

Goodbye - I wish you were here now.

S.S. Tieresias
China Sea May 21st

It was deliciously cool again and last night for the first time since the Mediterranean I had a blanket. Early this morning we got into fog which has made our going slow and the foghorn is making a horrible row. Still we shall get in sometime on Sunday and my boat goes on Tuesday at 3pm. It is rather lucky I've hit off the best boat on the run.

Today I'm going to be frightfully energetic - I'm going to wash my hair and I've got hold of an electric iron - so I'm going to wash and iron some things and begin packing. Since I've been on board I've made 3 pairs of gloves - two camisoles - I brocade bag and one blouse and done some mending and marking of clothes - I've also written a lot of letters and painted one portrait and read two books on China and knitted a small bit of sock.[a] More than half the time I've slept! In fact the last few days in order to make the time pass quicker I've gone to bed at 8.30 and slept until 7.30!

I'm getting frantically excited I scarcely know what to do - but it is a lovely feeling - it would be rather tragic if Ian were out at sea when I arrive - but let's hope he won't be - and anyway it would only be a day or so probably.

---

[a] Ruth was no knitter: I don't think this sock was ever finished.

The last day in Hong Kong I spent riding round on top of a tramway - a splendid way of seeing the native town - part of it was rather squalid and unattractive but the other end was very fascinating - and one place the tram runs along the waters edge where the junks are moored and where more than half the native population live - hundreds of people - men, women and children clad chiefly in immense straw hats were wading about in the mud - evidently looking for something - but what I don't know. The tram ride took over an hour then I went and had tea at the Hong Kong hotel and afterwards climbed up to the botanical gardens. They were very pretty - but the vegetation of course isn't a patch on the tropics. There was a fountain with water lilies and lotus and full of carp and lots of little Chinese children were playing round it and it was very attractive to look at. I think I shall love living in Hong Kong and I am longing to explore it with Ian.

We sailed at 10am yesterday - as we steamed out I saw several quaint little fishing villages round the other side of the island.

If you see Miss Dennison[a] tell her she taught me geography very well - I found I really had a very clear idea of what the places were we passed and the names of the capes etc. most of the passengers in this ship were very rocky about their whereabouts. I found my history pretty deficient. I think children ought to be taught Empire history - as well as English and foreign. For instance what do you know about Raffles? I'd never heard of the gentleman, but he is the persona grata of Singapore.

S.S. Tieresias
Shanghai May 23rd

I've had such a day today! and it began early too. I awoke about 6.30 and looked out of my porthole and saw we were gliding along the Yantze-Kiang between flat green banks - I lay and

---

[a] Ruth's governess - who taught me for a time in the late 1920's.

looked for a bit and then got up and dressed - fortunately, for when I was just finishing a message came that the tender was alongside and somebody shouting for me. I ran up and saw a smart lady with red hair who naturally I hailed as Mrs Macgregor - she replied she was Mrs Ebblewhite - which conveyed nothing - but she elucidated by explaining that she was Mrs Stopford's mother - she then explained in a distraught voice that the Macgregors were away - so Ian had asked her to meet me and to get me a room - and that she had spent all day trying to - but there wasn't a room to be had and she herself was sailing at noon for England and that she had spent a sleepless night not knowing what to do for me, but that there was just one last chance of a bed somewhere if I came with her at once. I soothed her by telling her that I could stay on board then I gave her breakfast and then went and interviewed the Captain. He really has been kind to me and I couldn't possibly have been better looked after - for instance we are anchored out in the river 3 miles from the town - a ferry runs from the wharf to the town - but to get to the wharf or back to the ship you have to take a sampan - well the Captain said it wasn't nice for a solitary female to have to depend on sampans - so he has given orders that I can order a launch whenever I want which makes me feel very grand! And he is taking me to the agents tomorrow to fix up my passage for Tuesday. In the meantime I live very comfortably here and so nice and cheap!

To return to Mrs Ebblewhite who was duly impressed by the private launch she and I went ashore in - she was a kindly female - <u>very</u> kind as she really had been terribly fussed about me. She hadn't been to Wei-hai-wei but Mrs Stopford is apparently sitting on the edge of her chair waiting for me and putting flowers in my room. (I think she is going to be a trial, between you and me - and there is only one other sailor's wife there, a Mrs Satow - but "such a nice lot of men" to quote Mrs Ebblewhite)

She took me with her to some rather awful people called Marshall who fed me on cake - I asked them if they knew the Dents and when they heard I actually was a Dent I went up 100% in their estimation! I can tell you Dent is a name to conjure with out here, even now. I was told it was the oldest English name in China and the best known and was shown where their place had been - a huge place right in the middle of the Bund.

Well Mrs Marshall said she'd ring up and find out if Vyvyan Dent was at home - so I thought that would be quite a good plan - I have nothing to do all afternoon - on asking for Mr Dent a voice at the other end asked "Old piece or young piece!" Old piece eventually came and I explained myself - he asked me to come to "Tiffen" and said he would come and fetch me. A short time after the door opened and an extraordinary figure came in - an oldish gentleman with long curly hair - long curly whiskers and an imperial - and an enormous wide-awake hat like Buffalo Bill. I was rather taken aback - but he had a delightful voice and friendly manners - so I bade goodbye to Mrs Marshall and Mrs Ebblewhite and set off with him. We walked along the Bund and I was shown what everything was. Then we boarded a train in the French Settlement and went along the Avenue Joffre until we reached his house which was out in the suburb. From the outside this house might have been a large Bournemouth villa with a garden with rambler roses and syringa and grass lawns. Another hairy and very foreign looking man appeared - the son Robert Dent - then a nice small boy aged 5, Louis the 3rd generation. He could only speak French having been brought up in Switzerland and only just brought out here. What they've done with Mrs Robert I don't know. I don't think she's dead - in fact as far as I can gather she's an invalid and has just been shed in Switzerland! I had an excellent lunch and we talked about the family - the old gentleman knew all about everyone - and located me directly I said that my father was Edgar Dent - "Oh" he said "You're one of the Black Heathens![2]"

After lunch a magnificent motor appeared, 85 horse power - and the "young piece" took me a long drive all round - it was very interesting - and more like England than anything I've seen since I left - at least it was a cool grey day (I wore a coat and skirt) and the gardens were full of English flowers. The country was dead flat like Belgium and everything bright - bright green. Every inch of ground is cultivated - it is supposed to be the most wonderful soil in the world. There were market gardens - bean fields - paddy fields and barley - no hedges in between - but lots of rather stunted, twisted trees and all the houses were low with fascinating curved roofs. Then we got into the town - a very fine large town - tremendously cosmopolitan. The European part might almost be London - huge shops and great stone buildings and congested traffic. The native part very picturesque - nicer really than Hong Kong. There is a great deal of bustle and activity and the natives are much better looking than in S. China - not so yellow - in fact they are brownish with nice pink cheeks and better features - and the higher class ones wear quite exciting clothes - bright colours and patterns.

I was taken back to tea and then driven down to catch the Ferry. It was a very funny menage - the three generations and not a woman in the whole house - and their appearance is quite unique - but they were awfully kind to me and I liked them both, they have told me to come and see them again - and have also given me an open sesame to people at Chefoo in case I should go there. I'm very glad I had the courage to go and look them up.

I forgot to tell you that during the afternoon we came to a basket fair - every sort and kind of basket being sold in the streets and crowds and crowds of natives. This fair has been held from time immemorial on one day in the year in a certain spot - and is still held there even though it is in the very middle of the European residential part.

Shanghai is one of the biggest ports in the world - and the river is full of every sort of shipping - American, Japanese and English warships, liners of every description and nationality - sampans painted green and red - and lovely junks with square sails. The junks from Ning Po you can distinguish because they are gaily painted and have on each bow an enormous eye - some of them have carving too. Aren't I lucky to be seeing all these places and things and I am enjoying it - but every minute I wish you were with me.

S.S. "Tungchow"
China Sea May 26th

I got your letter from the bank yesterday - and it was a great joy though it made me more homesick than anything. I felt I wanted to come straight back in the 'Tieresias' to you! Hearing about Cronkhill and what you were doing there seems like hearing of a previous existence - it all seems so long ago but then in the interval I've travelled about 11,000 miles - and tomorrow at noon I arrive - isn't that glorious and I am excited! I do hope Ian will be there. I think he ought to be - as they returned on the 21st from a week at Chefoo. I had two letters from Ian in Shanghai and a cheque for $100 on a Shanghai bank which was very thoughtful of him. Actually I had heaps of money but it would have been devastating changing it into dollars.

The last day or so I've felt rather like a lost cat in a house removal as I was about the only person left in the 'Tieresias' and they were very busy scraping and painting and cleaning her.

However I had my cabin and I fed with the ship's officers and everyone was very kind to me - and I really felt quite sorry to leave the old ship. At 10 o'clock yesterday I came up to this ship in the launch with my luggage - stopping at the customs en route where I didn't have any difficulty. I deposited my luggage here and then went ashore to get your letter - it had only arrived the day before by a French ship, the 'Porthos'. I then went to seek for lunch and in the French concession I found a patisserie where I had the most delicious chocolate and whipped cream and could easily have imagined myself in Belgium! (I found the old Chief Engineer on the 'Tieresias' knew our patisserie in Antwerp and we made the mouths of the others water with our recollections of the wonderful cakes and cream.)

On my way back to this ship I bought a hat in a Chinese shop. It is a lovely colour, jade green - just matches my jumper and double straw so is sun proof and very light. I shall make some flowers to go round it. The man wanted 3$ but I bargained and got it for 2.50 - I think I could have got it for $2 but hadn't the courage to go on! This ship is the height of luxury. I have a large single cabin to myself - with a real bed (not a bunk) and a sofa and a square window. There is a big saloon filled with flowering plants and the "Chow" (local name for food) is most excellent. My passage costs $45 - not really expensive at the rate Ian gets his pay 2/4 to the $. There is a Mrs Barker on board who is also bound for the Island Hotel Wei-hai-wei - her husband is a paymaster commander in the "Carlisle", she is 25 and seems quite nice. She has come out through America as she couldn't get a passage by Suez.

Chapter 2 Wei Hai Wei, 1920

The letters from Wei Hai Wei (and later Hong Kong) inevitably consist largely of accounts of the social life of the Naval Colony - dances, tennis, golf, bathing, picnics etc. - and this has been cut in favour of the more interesting descriptions of Ruth and Ian's explorations of the Chinese mainland.

It is notable that these young women in their 20's, living in close intimacy for months on end, continued to refer to each other as Mrs Satow, Miss Duff etc. - and their husbands of course also called each other by their surnamesWei-hai-wei

Here I am at last. I awoke on Thursday morning to find we were in sight of land - I dressed and had breakfast and then watched the island of Wei-hai-wei come nearer and nearer. We passed a submarine out at sea. I couldn't read its number and I was very afraid it might be Ian's But when we entered the channel between the island and the mainland, I saw the Ambrose with 5 boats alongside - then a launch put out and in it was Ian. It was the moment I'd looked forward to all this time and it was even more glorious than I thought it would be. Ian was looking very well - just as thin and not a bit changed except very brown which is most becoming. He is a loveable soul and I am so happy: if only I had you too.

We collected my luggage and got into the launch and proceeded to the island which is about 3 miles off the mainland. The hotel is quite close to the jetty - it is such a nice hotel - a series of long low bungalows in a garden and looking onto the channel and the mainland and you can see all the ships. We are very lucky and have one of the nicest front rooms - originally we were given a back room only looking onto the courtyard as Ian had written about rooms later than most people. However when he arrived the Scotch owner of the hotel said he must try and do something better for fellow countrymen so shifted us in here! We have a great big high bedroom - with two windows and several doors and just furnished with a bed, dressing table and cupboard also two chairs and a wooden table. The floor is unstained wood with no carpet and the walls are distempered cream colour - so it is very cool and clean. There is a sort of anteroom we use as a box-room and a big bathroom with a washstand in it which Ian uses as a dressing table. The bath I must tell you is a large china tub, exactly like the one we had in the garden that the Cootes lent us in fact I think it has the same pattern on it and is certainly the same size and colour! Then we have a big verandah which we use as a sitting room. You can have it quite open or else make it private by letting down bamboo curtains - it is furnished with a table and easy chairs - we have our tea there always, other meals we have in the big dining room - which has a very good floor and is used for dances. Each of us have a little round table to ourselves and submarines are put down one side of the room and cruisers down the other! The rest of the hotel is identically the same as our set of rooms - and just now it is a rookery of sailors and their wives - next month all the Shanghai people arrive - but the manager is very good and first of everything is given to the fleet. The garden is very gay with hollyhocks and correopsis and cornflowers and peonies and shaded with acacias which are in full flower and smell delicious. There are two hard tennis courts and they are making a third. I couldn't want to be in a more comfortable place - it isn't a bit like a hotel - but just like having a tiny bungalow to yourself - only with no trouble. The food is plain and unpretentious - but very good - and the Chinese of course are wonderful servants.

After lunch on Thursday Ian and I walked round the island and I don't think I ever ceased talking - I felt I had eight months to make up and he is such a delightful listener - and he also had quite a lot to say!

As to the island itself - in some ways it is very disappointing - it isn't China a bit - simply a naval camp. It is 3 miles from the mainland and so small that you can walk round it in an hour or so - it is very hilly but almost barren - as it hasn't rained here for three years. However they've managed to get a few fir trees to grow and heaps of acadias - and there is a sort of yellow coarse grass and quite a lot of flowers. The navy has pulled down all the Chinese houses and built up little stone ones all of a pattern and the ornate Chinese temple has been turned into the men's canteen! There is also a naval hospital here and a United Service Club and recreation ground and a little golf club with a very sporting little 9 hole course. A signal station - several obsolete forts (both Chinese and English) and the dockyard about make up the island. There is a main street (called the 'Hard') with a general store and one or two Chinese shops and a tailor called '"Jelly Belly" isn't it a gorgeous name! and a Japanese shoe shop where I got some very fine white canvas shoes for $3. The whole island is entirely run and administered by the Navy and the only Chinese on it are the coolies they employ. So you will see as far as picturesqueness goes it is rather dud. However it has it compensations: I've never seen any place so beautifully clean and swept and garnished - and no smells and no need to bother about the milk and water and you can even eat the strawberries (which you can't in other parts of China). When I first arrived too I thought the scenery very barren and disappointing after the wonderful tropical vegetation I'd just come from - and certainly the mainland is exactly like the country round the Red Sea! But you know I'm beginning to think it has a charm of its own though it is so completely different from my pre-conceived ideas. You get most lovely colour - an intense blue sky - dazzling white sands, green water and the reddish rocky, bare hills with blue shadows on them. In the evening gorgeous sunsets and still, starry nights - when the mountains are black and look just like the mountains of the moon.

A ferry runs between this and the mainland so many days a week. There is a big hotel and a lot of Shanghai people's bungalows there - and a bit inland there is an old Chinese walled town - very Chinese and rather squalid I believe but I'm longing to see it - I believe there are nice gateways. Further inland still there are quantities of mulberries on which they rear the silk worms for this of course is where all the Shangtung silk comes from.

The ships here at present are the "Carlisle" and "Cairo" (light cruisers), "Ambrose"[3] and 6 submarines and "Marazion" (destroyer) and various odd craft - oilers and so forth. The "Hawkins" (flagship) and "Alacrity" (yacht) arrive tomorrow - and later on the "Titania" and 6 L boats and the "Colombo" and some gun boats. The other sailor people in this hotel seem extraordinarily nice. It is rather funny at the end of the first day I told Ian the ones I thought I was going to like best and they were the ones he knew and liked best - and we both liked the same ones least - we generally do agree about people. The two couples I think are going to be nicest are Captain and Mrs Carrington - he is the captain of the "Carlisle" and was in the "Inflexible" with Ian - she is quite young and very sweet looking - then there is a delightful couple Mr and Mrs Satow - he is captain of "L4" and a most comic character - Ian likes him awfully - he is vague and casual with a great sense of humour and he is universally known as the "Bird", with badly fitting clothes. Mrs Satow is rather pretty and very friendly and they have a small girl. Then there are the Stopfords - Mr Stopford is rather good looking - but I gather Ian doesn't much care for him - Mrs Stopford is much nicer than her mother - she is really inoffensive and awfully kind.

Mr Dawson (captain of the Marezion) and Mrs Dawson and his sister Miss Dawson - Mrs Miller (wife of the Admiral's secretary) Mrs Henderson (wife of the flag captain and much older than the rest of us) and the Barkers make up the rest of the party at present

- but there are more coming. I find Ian is an enormous social success here and also looked upon as a first rate cricketer.

On Friday Ian left at 8 o'clock and spent the morning unpacking and getting straight - my things have really arrived in wonderfully good condition. Ninny deserves a gold medal for packing. My evening dresses are pretty crushed - but a tailor comes up and presses them so they ought to be alright. It is a funny climate here - quite cool - but a blazing hot sun and a cold wind - so it is difficult to know what to wear - next month it gets really hot - but it is always dry which is nice. In winter this place is ice-bound consequently the water is still too cool to bathe in - in spite of the hot sun - but when bathing does start you can stay in the sea nearly all day! There are lovely sandy beaches. After lunch I sat with Mrs Stopford and went down to the "Town" with her. Then we played tennis and at 6 o'clock Ian arrived back. Poor dear he can't play tennis just now - as he smashed the tip of his thumb with a cricket ball.

Yesterday he got ashore for lunch and then I went and watched him play cricket - the "Ambrose" v the island. Ian didn't distinguish himself very much - possibly owning to his thumb. The Satows had asked me to a picnic. It was great fun - a large party of us went to a little rocky bay where we had tea and then played games. I met Captain Talbot (the captain of the "Ambrose" who was very nice) and there were a lot of other sailors whose names I didn't catch.

Today Ian gets ashore again for lunch and we are going over to the mainland to explore and to call on the Commissioner and the Consul. Ian will generally get off on Saturday and Sunday afternoons and on other days at teatime or after, except every 6th day when he is "ON" and won't get ashore at all - but still I shall see a splendid lot of him - I think he is frightfully happy and I think this is going to be a delightful summer. It is rather fun living with a lot of people all leading the same life with the same interests as yourself in a climate that is perpetually a "fine" day with bathing and golf and tennis and dancing and above all with the person you like doing all these things best with. It rather goes against my conscience doing nothing but amuse myself - but I shall paint and get Ian's clothes into order (which I foresee is going to be a whole time job!)

We leave here early in Sept: and go to Hong Kong though we've none of us anywhere to go there - Ian has booked rooms but there is no certainty about their being kept for him, still we are all in the same boat and all more or less in the same way as regards finances. You see what the Admiralty does is this:- you get £350 a year at 10$ to the 2/- the old pre war rate) this you get whether you are a sub or an Admiral - the rest of your pay you get half at the 2/- rate and half at the current rate - this means that Ian whose pay is only just over £400 gets it nearly all at the 2/- rate - but a man getting £700 or £800 a year loses much more in proportion - which is very bad luck. Admiral Duff has been trying to get this altered - and he has managed something as up till he came all pay was given on a half and half basis. Our finances are quite sound just now. While we are here we can live on Ian's pay and for Hong Kong he has a reserve fund of £100 in English money and $400 and when that comes to an end I come home! It is really very clever of him to have saved so much because my passage was paid as well - and Mr Gieve (out of his gratuity). Hong Kong is expensive because it is full of profiteers and people who have made fortunes during the war. Here things are cheap - for instance the washing, which is most beautifully done is 4 cents a piece (whether a dress or a handkerchief).

We pay 8$ 16/- a day for the two of us here - which is really very cheap, you'd never get as good an hotel in England for that - but as a matter of fact Mr Clark who runs it lets N.O's have everything at half rate and doesn't make any profit off them - but sticks it on double to the rich Shanghai profiteers who come here later on - and who only get second best of everything. It gives us great satisfaction to think of all the profiteers having to pay for the luxuries we are enjoying - but as Ian says they ought to think themselves lucky to be allowed on the island at all as it belongs <u>to the Navy</u> - and it is popular because it is so healthy.

Ian got me in Hong Kong a fascinating pair of Chinese slippers - Kingfisher blue satin most beautifully embroidered in all colours - at Colombo he got two carved ivory gods - Shiva and Jumma - they are rather nice and he is very pleased with them - but I like the slippers best. He also got me a kingfisher brooch - a local product - the sort of thing granny would have loved but that you wouldn't.

Ian is very pleased with his gloves - they fit beautifully - you might send me a half skin sometime to make him another pair.

The Island Hotel
Wei-hai-wei June 2nd 1920

A mail came in yesterday - but no letter from you - but Ian got a "Punch" from you (much appreciated) and expect you posted it about the same time as the letter to me at Shanghai. Letters take a long time to get here and don't come very often, which is horrid and makes one feel very cut off.

On Sunday we went after lunch over to the Mainland - about ½ hours trip in a little steam launch. The Mainland is also very dried up and not much vegetation - though there are wonderfully kept market gardens. We walked along the road until we came to the walled city. This is an extraordinary place - proper Chinese - though not the China one imagines beforehand of palaces and jade and dragons and willow trees and colour - but a China of little low mud houses with curved roofs and doors covered with red "Joss papers" (to keep the devil away) dusty uneven and rather dirty roads filled with jolly children in blue patterned dresses - and cocks and hens picking about. At every street corner stalls of fruit etc. and through each door you could see the people plying their different trades - rope making - basket weaving and so on - all with the most primitive appliances. In the middle of the town is the temple with a stone screen in front of the door (to prevent the devil - who can't turn corners - from getting in). All round the town is a huge, thick, battlement wall, with a gate in it N.E.S and W - and at the highest point a watch tower. The predominating colours are yellow and blue - blue sea and sky - yellow earth and houses - yellow people in blue clothes. I was very fascinated by it all and there is heaps more to explore - we really had time to see very little - as our mission was paying calls and I had my best clothes on (the white skirt and coat). So we retraced our steps to the European part and went up to Government House and wrote our names. Lady Lockhart appeared while we were doing this - and asked us in to tea. She is so nice and so is Sir James - neither of them a bit official but very homely and kindly. We got onto the subject of Edinburgh - and I found Sir James was one of your father's students. He was awfully interested to find I was his granddaughter - and he told me he had always had an enormous admiration for your father. The Lockharts have a very pretty English garden - which however they say is a dreadful struggle to keep it going in this part of the world where it never rains. But still their roses were a sight - and they sent us home laden with them and our verandah is looking so nice now.

Yesterday Ian came ashore early to change for a cricket match. Ambrose v Carlisle - I watched it for a bit and Ian did me great credit - making top score of all - he is a very pretty batsman to watch and I'm told he is really very good - I was introduced to a lot of sailors who I chatted to while they waited their turn to bat - Mr Gregg and Mr Dolphin were both nice. I came back here when I got bored and had tea in the verandah - round the end of which two very shy men insinuated themselves - not a very dignified way of entering in to pay a call as you have to crawl round a pillar and do other gymnastics - the proper entrance being from the back. I gave them strawberries and they stayed a long time (being too shy to go) but they were very nice. One was Ian's sub. and the other a watchkeeping lieut. in the Ambrose. Thyme and Dicken by name. I've had a lot of callers and Mrs Barker and I are going to work off some return calls in the Island this afternoon. Yesterday evening I played tennis with the Stopfords and Barkers and played much better. After dinner Ian and I went a lovely walk in the moonlight. The harbour looks ripping at night with all the ships lit up and the occasional search-lights.

This morning I went up to the U.S club with Mrs Stopford and read the papers (pretty elderly ones - April 15th being the latest!) The club is the old Chinese Admiral's residence (this used to be a Chinese naval base before the Japanese-Chinese war). It is rather attractive and has a very pretty garden with flagged paths and Canterbury bells and quantities of nemophila - and a magnificent tree of wisteria in the middle of the courtyard - which however is just over.

Ian is out running torpedoes and diving today. I watched L7 steam out this morning - rather different from last time I saw her sail away - she will be back sometime tonight. One can see everything from this verandah - all the ships coming in and out and the people going past. This morning one of the ships had a route march and they swung along to a drum and fife band. I do like to see the sailors in their whites with straw hats.

The rest of this week we are going to be very gay. Tomorrow a garden party at Government House on the occasion of the King's birthday - Friday a sailing picnic given by the British Consul - Saturday a tennis tournament here - and Sunday I am lunching in the "Ambrose" with the captain (s). On Monday I hope to spend a long day over in the mainland with a sketch book. There is heaps to draw there - which is nice - as I was very disappointed in the

Island from that point of view. Still it is a delightful place to live in and Ian and I are enjoying it like anything. It is such fun exploring with him - in fact doing anything with him. In the mornings all the wives sit in each others verandahs and sew (I am getting Ian's disreputable wardrobe in order) and write letters etc. It isn't hot enough for bathing yet - though the sun is very powerful - it is pleasant waking up to a fine day every day! Though in spite of it I've had a very heavy cold in my head every since I arrived - which is most tiresome - though Ian says he still loves me even with a pink nose.

As Ninny says it is better to be born lucky than rich - Ian is one of those people.

Originally the terms of this hotel were 9$ a day for the two of us in a back room. On seeing Ian the owner gave us a front room and reduced it to 8$ a day - when the bill came in for this week we found he had further reduced it to 7$ a day - and we have one of the best rooms and a bathroom of our own and a verandah etc. It is really most wonderfully cheap because 7$ is really only 14/- and that includes light and attendance and bath and afternoon tea and everything - and Ian is always here to dinner - two days a week to lunch and often to tea - and everything is far better and nicer than any hotel I've ever stayed at before (much better for instance than the Grand Hotel at Lyndhurst.) One very nice thing is that the coffee after lunch and dinner is excellent and then all the jam and marmalade is home made and so are the cakes - and they grow all their own fruit and vegetables - so we have nice green peas and strawberries.

Old Mr Clark (the owner of the hotel and of everything else in this place) sends me presents of strawberries which I find in my room - and he is altogether frightfully kind to us - chiefly because we are Scotch.

We hear that all the boats are to be relieved by Sept. 1921 which means they will begin relieving anytime after Dec. this year - and

Ian thinks he may be possibly relieved among the early ones if he is due then for periscope school. Everyone is hoping to be sent back by liner - wouldn't that be fun - to come back with Ian and see all the exciting places together!

Did you know we hadn't any right to be in this island at all? But we just lie low and say nothing and nobody else seems to have remembered. This is the history of the place. It was strongly fortified by the Chinese (you can still see the remains of the forts) and was one of their principle naval bases. The Empress had a summer palace here - the remains of which is now the C in C's office. During the Japanese-Chinese war - the Japs had a great job taking this place - they eventually captured it and later on handed it over to us to hold <u>as long as the Russians held Port Arthur</u> - this fact is the one that has been forgotten. We started to fortify it and there are several of our forts about too - but we came to the conclusion it wasn't good enough - so the place is undefended and simply used as a health resort and summer base for the fleet.

The N. of China is far more Royalist than the S. in fact there is a war going on intermittently between the Royalists and the Republicans - but Ian says it is a very Gilbert and Sullivan sort of war and one hears little about it. The N. sticks much more to the old traditions, the men nearly all wear pig-tails and the women still have bound feet - and there is a deeply rooted belief in the devil. All the houses have roofs turned up at the ends because the devil likes sliding down the roofs but he gets frightfully angry if he falls off and gives bad joss to the house! Even the Church of England here has had to conform to this superstition and has turned up roof! Many of the houses have horrible little devils sitting on their chimneys!

The Island Hotel
Wei-hai-wei 6th June 1920

They certainly don't let you get bored with your husband in the Navy - we've just heard that the 'Ambrose' 'Marazion' and the 6 boats are leaving for Japan on Friday and will not return until the end of the month or beginning of July! Isn't it sad - and the saddest part is that everybody is to get 4 days leave in Japan. 4 perfectly good days of leave more or less wasted - as even if the wives could afford to go - by the time they got a ship at Shanghai or Chefoo - they might arrive too late. However it will be very exciting looking forward to their return and in the interval this is a delightful place to be in - with heaps to do and I shall be able to paint and my companions in my misfortune are very nice.

This morning we had a meeting on Mrs Dawson's verandah and decided to have a dance the night before the boats go to Japan. It is to be quite informal - the music being provided by a gramophone and the refreshments sandwiches. We drew up a list of guests. 16 men in all to be invited and Miss Duff[4]. After the meeting was satisfactorily concluded we all bathed - the first time for most of us. The water was pretty cold. This afternoon I'm hoping Ian will get ashore at 3 so that we can go over to the mainland as I want to do some sketches.

The Island Hotel
Wei-hai-wei 10th June 1920

No mails yet and if they don't come before tomorrow - I shan't get any for weeks - as they will go straight on to Kobe and have to come back again. It is a quaint life here - absolutely cut off from everything - one's horizon on one side the China Sea and on the other the rocky barren mountains of Shangtung and all ones life and interests contained in the little island and small strip of mainland between - and the said interests being solely and entirely connected with ships and the Navy - and everybody with the same interests so that it is rather being in a school or some sort of institution. As a background to it all is the funny picturesque Chinese life - that is going on exactly the same as it did 2000 years ago. Inside the walled city the English have no jurisdiction - and the people there have the same laws and customs - wear the same clothes, engage in the same primitive industries as they did when we in England were savages. Even their junks haven't altered in design since time immemorial. It all rather fascinates me - though this is a Cinderella China compared to the gorgeous China I had imagined.

Ian is feeling very pleased with himself - on Monday he sank the flagship! Four submarines were sent out to attack the 'Hawkins' and 'Carlisle' on their way out to firing practice - the object of the cruisers was to spot the submarines, L7 was the only boat to score a hit - and the Hawkins never saw her - didn't even see the torpedo until it hit the engine room - which if it had had a warhead on it would have blown them skyhigh!

On Tuesday I bathed in the morning with Mrs Stopford and Mrs Satow - it was very cold in the water though the sun was boiling hot. Ian got ashore for tea and we went and played golf. I've never played so well in my life - I got 7 really good, long clean drives out of 9 - and I feel I shall develop into an enthusiast if this continues - I beat Ian though of course he gave me two strokes - but several holes I won without them. It is a very sporting little links - full of pitfalls - but most exciting. The tees are hard baked mud with a coconut door mat let in to drive off. The 'greens' are also hard mud with a little magic circle of sand round the hole - on a windy day it is almost impossible to remain on the 'green' at all.

Yesterday I boarded the 'Foam' (the little ferry) at 3 and we picked Ian up from the 'Ambrose'. It was the day of the weekly sailing races and the harbour was full of whalers and cutters - I'm afraid the 'Ambrose' didn't distinguish herself.

We landed and went to do a commission for Mrs Stopford and then to Foo Sing the silk merchant to see if he had any mandarin coats. He had a lovely embroidered skirt - but I didn't like the coats. However he is getting some more later on. Then we proceeded to explore - it was very hot and dusty but most amusing - out in the fields harvesting has begun and it looks a lovely golden crop in spite of the drought - but all the streams are absolutely dried up. We entered the city by the N. gate and walked along the top of the wall. It is a wonderful thick wall - in perfect preservation though it was built about 1400 - it climbs up the hillside and on the top there is a watch tower from which you get a fine view all round. We returned through the centre of the town (the smells aren't much worse than Belgium) and out by the E. gate of which I did a hasty sketch which I'm going to work into a big pastel. At the gate we took rickshaws and proceeded to the hotel - we met old Mr Clark who asked us to tea - I've never met anyone so kind - and I respect him very much for one thing - he is a teetotaller himself and so won't allow any drink in either of his hotels - even though he loses tremendously on it.

Coming back in the 'Foam' it was so rough that I was nearly seasick!

They have begun sending people home from here already - so we may be coming almost anytime I suppose. I oughtn't to have any difficulty about getting a passage back - as the C in C has the first claim on 25% of all passages home.

Tomorrow night to console us for the absence of our husbands - we have all been asked to dine in the 'Carlisle' by the Captain and to go on to a seaman's dance which ought to be amusing!

One great thing I have discovered here is an excellent library at the United Service Recreation Club - and I am lucky that the other wives are so nice. I'll try and describe them to you - as we both agreed that Ian's letters were lacking in description of his friends.

Mrs Stopford is fair and plump - full of common sense and good nature - and not a bit like her letters which are the outcome I feel of being brought up by her mother Mrs Ebblewhite who was everything the letters led us to expect. Mrs Stopford usually wears rather dull gingham dresses and a panama hat.

Mrs Satow is small and with pretty fluffy fair hair and lovely eyes and rather pale and very sweet and gentle. She has a perfectly adorable baby of a year old - full of life and friendly to everybody with an enchanting head of curls. Neither Mrs Stopford or Mrs Satow are exactly stimulating - but very pleasant their chief interests in life - you might almost say their sole interest is their husbands. Mr Stopford is rather good-looking and rather entertaining - but I don't know a bit what he is really like. Mr Satow 'the Bird' is perfectly delightful - with a sad face and a great sense of the ludicrous and vaguer and more off the spot than anyone you've ever met - Ian says he is clever but never sticks to anything. The remaining submarine family are the Dawsons: Mr Dawson is very scotch and pawky and his sister Miss Dawson or rather her type I have met frequently at canteens in Edinburgh or at the Art School. Mrs Dawson is tall and dark and plain - but she is the only one who wears nice picturesque clothes. She borders on the second rate - but she is the only one who is always full of ideas and schemes and very clever with her fingers and full of vitality. I forgot to say that Mrs Stopford sings charmingly. These are the ones I have most to do with.

Island Hotel
14th June 1920 Wei-hai-wei

Isn't it too sad the mail came in just after the boats had left - so it has gone on to Kobe - and I shan't get any letters from you for weeks. I've only had one since I left home - and I do so want to hear from you. Oh mother I want to hear of you so - I <u>do</u> wish you were here - we should have such fun exploring the mainland together. I simply love poking about the Chinese farms etc. but nobody else cares about it except Ian. We he is here we have great fun - but it is rather lonely work alone - I was beginning some exciting paintings and was longing to get on with them - but ever since the boats left there has been a thick damp mist - not actual rain - so I've not been able to do anything - and it is dull but it looks as if it might clear soon.

I'm missing Ian dreadfully. I'm also very envious of Ian as I believe the Inland Sea is a wonderful place - and from Kobe there are expeditions to the most interesting places in Japan. We have all written letters to our husbands and put them in a huge envelope which we took to the Japanese shoe-maker and got him to address it in Japanese writing 'Man-of-War Ambrose'. It did look so decorative - and we hope it will hasten its arrival.

On Thursday Ian had a 'day on' so at 3.45 I went to the iron pier where a motor boat was waiting for me and went off to the 'Ambrose' and had tea on board with Ian. I love him extra much when he is in 'Whites'. I made him put on his cocked hat and epaulettes - but the effect was disappointing - very theatrical and it emphasises the size of his nose!

After tea I was taken over the boat - even more fearsome box of tricks than 'K7'[5] as all the same things are compressed into a smaller space - but Ian says they are splendid boats. He and his captain have each a minute cabin - the sub sleeps on the settee and the Engineer on the floor. Ian likes his captain Mr Peyton Ward very much - in fact I think he is his chief friend here - personally I find him a nice but rather dreary young man.

While Ian was attending to his battery I went and sat in his cabin in the Ambrose - Ian gave me various letters etc. to read - among others - one from a man asking him to write an account of the blowing up on the Invincible - as Ian was one of the few who actually saw the whole thing. The account was to be published in an official book that is being brought out upon the battle of Jutland. Ian said he would have liked to have done it - only as the account had to be sent in 6 weeks from the time the letter was written - it was of course impossible.

I get rather tired of meeting nobody but sailors and hearing nothing but 'shop' talked - or golf or tennis. I would like to meet someone who was interested in pictures or poetry or even Women's Institutes! It would be fun to have someone like Miss Brunton here to go painting with and who would appreciate the picturesqueness of the Chinese villages with their wonderful great gateways and temples and markets. I do love the 'foreign' feeling of it all and I like the Chinese so much - they are all so cheerful and smiling - and one great thing is that round here it is perfectly safe for females to wander about - even in the city. The thing you would enjoy would be poking about among the little shops - but that as you know isn't my line.

Island Hotel
17th June 1920 Luikung Tao Wei-hai-wei

Isn't it too tantalising - the 'Chungchow' has just come in with 19 bags of mails - I know there are letters from you there and I can't get at them and they will all go on to Kobe and have to come back again. The lot that was forwarded last week may be back by next week. There has been a wireless message to say the boats have arrived safely at Kobe - I shall be glad when we get the message to say that they have left - for I'm missing Ian horribly and feel very lonely without anyone belonging to me.

On Sunday night we had a downpour of rain and Monday morning the sun came out and everything looked clear and lovely and fresh - and now the heat has begun - though it isn't a bit too hot except just at midday when one rests.

We're having a frightfully gay time - tennis parties everyday - and dances and dinners etc. - the other ships are seizing the opportunity to hold their festivities while the Ambrose is away - as the submarine wives form half the population and they are supposed to dance so much with their husbands - that nobody else gets any dancing at all!

On Monday we had a very nice tennis party at the hotel - I played very well for me. Then the Dawsons, Mrs Stopford, Mrs Satow and I all went to dinner with the Admiral in the 'Alacrity'. I wore my wedding dress. The barge was sent for us and we got alongside the yacht the gangway was all lit up and the deck hung with flags. It was a delightful party - quite informal - we cut with cards as to who should take who into dinner! and the Admiral asked me to sit next to him. I liked him most awfully and I think Miss Duff is very nice too and she is certainly a splendid hostess - making everything 'go' and everyone <u>feel</u> at ease. The yacht is perfectly magnificent and it belonged to a Russian Princess and was abandoned at Devonport by her crew after the revolution - leaving all its contents including some perfectly beautiful Sevres dessert plates - apple green borders with beautifully painted women in the centres. I had Madame du Barri. The Admiral told me that the Admiralty is absolutely unaware of these and other treasures - so that he could perfectly easily pinch them! We had a magnificent dinner - asparagus soup - turkey and green peas, strawberry ice and a fruit I like awfully, Pomola - as well as other things which I have forgotten.

The Admiral told me that he had just received a letter from Sir Rudolph Bentinck in which he said 'in spite of the panicky Admiralty Order, I am glad to hear that some rash young women have risked going out' - I suppose this was a propos of me!

On Tuesday I went to a tennis party at the Engineer Commander of the Dockyard's - and yesterday we had another tennis party here. Today Mrs Satow, Mrs Stopford and I are dining in the ward room of the 'Alacrity' - my host is a Mr Lane - who was at Dartmouth with Ian - a pleasant youth but very plain. I expect we shall dance on the quarter deck afterwards. Tomorrow I am playing golf with Mrs Dawson and tennis party in the afternoon - and on Saturday the Captain of the Carlisle is having a dinner party before the dance. On Sunday I'm going on a sailing picnic in one of the 'Hawkins' boats - and sometime I want to go over to the mainland - but so far I haven't been able to fit it in. In the intervals I am doing a picture of Chinese children which necessitates much prowling about the island trying to find children. They are the nicest children - so comical looking with their flat round, brown faces - with either shaved head or long pigtails - slitty onyx eyes - and both sexes and all ages dressed alike in little shirts or jumpers and trousers - or in the hot weather just trousers and a quaint garment made of a square piece of embroidered material tied cornerwise round the neck and waist leaving the back perfectly bare!

They are such good mannered children - they never stare or make rude remarks like English - or specially Belgian children and they are always wreathed in smiles and they are extraordinarily clean looking.

I have just finished reading Maurice Hewletts 'Open Country' which I liked awfully - and now I have got a novel by Rose Macaulay called 'Views and Vagabonds'. The U.S.R.C has quite a good library of about 400 books - mostly novels from 4 to 10 years old and books upon China. One is allowed 3 at a time.

I wish you could see the hollyhocks here - they are so beautiful as to be almost theatrical - all single flowers of immense size and various colourings - from pale pink to deep maroon and they grow all over the place. There are a lot of flowering shrubs coming out - whose names I don't know - and one very pretty one with huge heart shaped leaves.

I think sailors of all degrees are most delightful people and very easy to get on with - and the wives here are a particularly nice lot - but what I rather miss it that there isn't a soul I've met so far who seems to have any desire or power to create - and I know that is the strongest instinct that I've got. Nothing gives me really so much pleasure as making things - from a hat trimming to a beehive or a picture. Ian hasn't really got a creative instinct[6] - which is as well seeing his profession gives little scope for it - but Ian appreciates the same things as I do and in the same way - which is a great thing.

June 18th

Great excitement - Ninny's letter which she addressed care of the Chartered Bank Shanghai turned up yesterday.

The dinner last night was great fun. We went in an open boat and had dinner on deck under the awning. Mrs Stopford, Mrs Satow, Mrs Bennett and myself were the guests. I sat between my host - known to his friends as the 'baby elephant' and a Mr Hirst - who I don't like and who doesn't like me and who I'm always being paired off with. There were about 6 other officers all in white mess jackets and all the deck was lit up with coloured electric lights and hung with flags. We had a very long - but most excellent dinner and at intervals we caught bursts of music from the band which was playing for the Admiral's dinner party down below. After dinner (we drank the King's health sitting - which is the Navy's privilege) we adjourned to the wardroom and played "Up Jenkins" and waxed very hilarious - then the dance music records arrived from the Carlisle and we went and danced on the quarter deck in a perfect gale of wind that had just got up. About 11.30 the Admiral's guests departed so he and Miss Duff came along and joined us - Miss Duff said they had had a very dull party and had felt envious hearing our sounds of revelry upstairs. At 12.30 the motor boat came alongside and our hosts escorted us home.

It is very hot today - I wish I could bathe. I've just had an itinerant silk merchant squatting on my verandah with his wares spread out - I thought how Granny would have enjoyed it - nearly every day men come round with packs on their backs - or rather suspended from a long bamboo pole - chiefly silk merchants - but as well men with silver goods and kingfisher jewellery and silk stockings - rather nice thick silk stockings for $2.50 a pair, any colour, and natural shantung colour is cheaper. This morning I bought a 7 yard length of very pretty pale pink thick silk for $6.50, the whole piece 30ins wide - I thought it would be nice for blouses. Do you think it would be a good plan to bring back a 20 yard roll of white silk - it is very soft thick silk like Japanese only softer and thicker and not so evenly woven - I can get 20yds for $25 or I might get it at a little less - with the $ at 3/3 is that cheaper than you can get it in England? Shantung silk natural colour I can get a 20yd roll for $15 in the blouse thickness - skirt thickness about $20 - or $1.20 a yard - lovely colours - blue - mauve - pink and grey but I'm afraid they would fade. You might let me know how these prices compare with England.

I really must stop this letter now - as the mail is just going.

Island Hotel
22nd June 1920 Wei hai wei

It still seems a long way off before Ian comes back - it does seem such a waste to be in this lovely place without either him or you to enjoy it with.

Sunday evening it cleared up in the evening so Mrs Stopford and the Dawsons and I went for a walk round the island. Mrs Dawson told me about the awful time they had at Harwich during the war - to begin with - out of every 3 submarines that went out - only 2 came back - later on the average dropped to losing one boat every 6 months. If a boat was overdue more than a few hours there was practically no hope and as each wife knew exactly when the boats were expected back the strain must have been appalling. She went on to Blyth afterwards and had to take the news that one of the G boats was lost to one of the wives. It does make one thankful it is all over - because at the time I know I didn't realise what the danger was.

On the end of the island we stopped for a bit to watch the wonderful sunset - the Shantung Promontory standing out purple against the yellow sky - and the jagged rocks which are supposed to be the relic of a bridge the Emperor Yu tried to build with the aid of Ocean spirits and the mountain spirits to the islands of P'eng-lai where the herb of immortality grew.

In the afternoon I went over to the Mainland and returned a call on a certain Mrs Southcote - an American from Virginia - rather nice - and with a bungalow with some attractive things in it. She gave me an excellent tea - and afterwards I walked to the city - about 1½ miles - and every step of the way interesting - what rather marred my pleasure was that a small boy dogged my footsteps the whole time and never took his eyes off me - and when I got to the gateway and began to draw - a large crowd of Chinese collected and I got so self-conscious (not to mention nearly sick with the smells) that I had to give it up and I will have to wait until Ian gets back - as I don't mind so much when he is there - though he does rather! Everything is so new that one can do so little from memory - I'm just beginning to be able to memorise the people and their clothes and give them different expressions - without departing from the Chinese type. Yesterday out of all the thousand things I have seen - the only things I had really stamped on my memory were a beautiful Chinese lady with a pink and white enamelled complexion - sleek black head with flowers in it - mauve silk coat and pink trousers - also a solemn baby in a red coat - with a tuft of hair left on top of his shaved head - at a street corner an old man with a snow white beard and pigtail and huge horn spectacles making shoes - and glimpses through various open doors, of an inner door with latticed windows - filled with oiled paper instead of glass and with strips of red joss paper pasted on - and through this the corner of a courtyard with plants and pots all round. At every turn there is a picture - if only I had the courage to sit and do it - but even if I try my pencil is paralysed - and it does infuriate me! I suppose the only thing is to go on trying to memorise.

In the evening we held a meeting in Mrs Henderson's room about getting up a tennis tournament and a small dance - as a return for the hospitality we have received from the ships. The dance is to be on July 1st and I am inviting Mr Lane as my guest - the tournament is on the 3rd and 4th.

I bought 50 cents worth of china yesterday - just the common stuff the coolies use - a chow bowl - two tea bowls and a peanut bowl. It is very rough and unevenly painted - but such an attractive shape and rather nice colour. One bowl is green - the other orange - the chow bowl ducks egg colour with paintings on it.

Island Hotel
20th June 1920 Luikungtao Wei hai wei

Great joy, a mail has arrived today and I got your 2nd letter forwarded on from Shanghai - and the various enclosures. I loved getting your letter and hearing all the news.

I think you should get Mrs Keswick to bring you out in her yacht! You would be able to get accommodation at the Peak Hotel alright. I believe it is quite good - it is 8$ a day "tout compris" and much less (6$ I think) if you sign on to stay for a period of months - to this you must add 60 cents return train ticket each time you go down to Hong Kong - and I think the tram would terrify you! We my have to fall back on the Peak Hotel if St Georges can't take us - but they have promised to - so I hope its alright as it is much more convenient for the dockyard and cheaper, 9$ a day for both of us. Ian has got his name down for a flat - one of Jardines - but there are only 4 flats and we have all got our names down! There is also a remote possibility of a flat in Kowloon. I doubt if we could afford it - as out here you can't keep less than 3 servants - cook - No 1 boy and coolie - even in a tiny flat - of course they aren't as expensive as in England and feed themselves. If we did secure one I'd cable to you to try and come - but I'm afraid there really isn't any prospect - at any rate until we are on the spot.

I'm awfully glad Mrs Keswick will give me introductions to people in Hong Kong - it will make all the difference in a place like that. I gather the Fleet hasn't been received with open arms there - and they feel rather hurt as at Shanghai and all the other places people were very kind and hospitable to them - threw open their club - gave dances and so whereas at Hong Kong they have a very poor time. The Admiral is most indignant about it. By the way though he thinks he will be able to have one of the much sought after Jardine flats - but it shows you how difficult accommodation is if even the C in C can't get what he wants.

Island Hotel
June 26th 1920 Luikung Tao Wei hai wei

This is a hot Sunday afternoon - I am sitting on my verandah writing - and everyone else I think is sleeping! In these parts people always do between lunch and tea - I don't as I sleep at least 10 hours at night so I always either read or write or sew or paint. My bamboo curtains are only half down so I can see out - first of all a bed of hollyhocks - very nearly over - then a pergola, then a strip of deep blue sea - occupied by the "Alacrity" and I just see the bow of the "Hawkins" and motor boats and sampans are buzzing to and for. Beyond that is a nice little fresh breeze that rustles the acacias, and the grasshoppers are making a tremendous row. This morning I went to church (Communion Sunday) the congregation consisted of myself - a marine and a converted Chinese! Then I came home and had a lovely bathe - and after lunch I sat with Mrs Stopford who is in bed with a chill - then I painted and now I'm hoping that tea will shortly appear and then I shall go for a long walk with Mrs Satow.

On Thursday the Clarks (proprietors of the Hotel) look us all in the steam launch for a picnic to Sun Island - a little island between this and the mainland on which there is an old Chinese fort. In the Chino-Japanese war - this fort held out longer than any other - it was commanded by a Scotchman! It was a very pleasant picnic and we all overate ourselves on the most wonderful iced cakes.

Next week is full of dissipation - Tuesday dance in "Alacrity" - Wednesday dine with Admiral - Thursday dance here - Saturday dance at Southcotts - also tennis tournament. I'm thoroughly enjoying having a "good time" and all the dances etc are such fun - as they are very unpretentious. It is hard work on one's evening clothes but the great thing is nobody has more than about 3 evening dresses - and we are all - submarines at any rate - in an equal condition of poverty. In fact we are all contemplating returning home together in the same ship 2nd class - if we can't go with our husbands. It would be quite fun if we all went together - and absolutely imperative if it is true that all passages have been put up 50%.

There is a joyful rumour that the boats <u>may</u> return of the 5th - anyway the 7th or 8th is assured so more than half the time is over thank goodness. Everything will be ten times more fun when Ian is here and we are going to have all sorts of festivities for the submarines. The "Titania" comes tomorrow and two sloops arrived today - so when the "Colombo" and "Curlew" arrive we shall have a huge fleet here. A few Shanghai taipangs have arrived too. (A Taipang is a word meaning a man who has made a fortune.)

In spite of having a very good time and everyone being awfully kind - I've felt horribly lonely sometimes without you or Ian. The more men I meet the more glad I am that I married Ian!

The Island Hotel
29th June 1920 Liukung Tao
Wei hai wei

No letter from you yet - though I got one from Ian this morning from Kobe - they don't seem to be having much of a time there - I <u>shall</u> be glad when next week comes and he is back again.

Yesterday I went over to the mainland and took sandwiches with me. I couldn't get anyone to come with me they all said it was too hot - and I must say when I got there at 1 o'clock I wished I hadn't come. The sun was blazing down and the baked earth seemed to throw the heat back against one's face and I couldn't find any shade under which to sit and eat my sandwiches - which meantime had got all dry - after wandering about a bit I found a dried up watercourse in the middle of a bean field where there was a little shade so I sat down.

After that I nearly chucked my hand in and went back by the 2.30 ferry - however I'm glad to say I didn't but set off towards the city and climbed the hill at the back - where you get a magnificent view and there was quite a nice breeze. I'd never been the other side of the hill - and I found all sorts of interesting things - first a small boy hoeing who had the most enormous straw hat I've ever seen - much bigger than himself - like an umbrella! Then I met an old man weaving silk by the roadside - on a loom rather like Ban Hill's - he was working all by himself and very leisurely - and it was rather comic to see the long warps (or woof - I never know which it is) just pegged out on the road! No motors are allowed here which is perhaps as well.

Wei-hai-wei City is built on a very simple plan like this: a high thick wall all round, gateways at each point of the compass - and each gateway different and all very massive and decorative, a joss house in the middle and endless little streets of low houses interspersed with market gardens - at one point the wall climbs right up the hill and down again with the watch tower on the top.

On the N. side of the City runs a shady road and a stagnant stream beside it where willows and bamboo grass grow and there I saw all the Chinese women washing their clothes - rubbing them between stones and beating them with sticks. I entered the city by the N. gate walked to the joss house and turned at right angles - then I produced my sketch book and began to draw the W. gate - the inevitable crowd collected - but the Chinese child takes a much more intelligent interest than the nasty Belgian child - also he doesn't crowd up close and never spits - but he does smell - I bore it until I had got what I wanted - then I went out by the W. gate and along by the sea to Port Edward. I must have tramped miles - but I collected heaps of material for pictures.

One rather nice thing I saw was a group of Chinamen sitting under a tree eating with chopsticks out of bowls - one was smoking a funny shaped pipe and another was asleep. The shadow of the tree was very deep against the dazzling whiteness of the sunny road - and beyond was a line of deepest blue sea.

At Port Edward I bought a very ormolu bathing cap and then went on and had tea with Mrs Clark at the hotel. I drank a whole teapot full I was so thirsty! I got back at 6.30 and just before dinner Miss Dawson and I had a lovely bathe - and afterwards I sat on Mrs Satow's verandah - and we watched some Chinamen letting off fireworks - horrible things - all noise and smell!

I enjoyed my day - but I'm afraid it's getting too hot now for those sort of expeditions. Today is grilling - I spent most of the morning in the sea. A merchant came round this morning and I bought a lot of fascinating Chinese ribbons for hair ribbons.

July 1st

The "Alacrity" dance was great fun - and had no disastrous ending like the "Carlisle" as it was a beautiful moonlight night and very nice and cool dancing on the deck. I dance the whole time - I met a very nice man Chapple by name who was a snottie in the "Inflexible" with Ian.

Yesterday I had tea with the Hendersons and dined in the "Alacrity" - rather a dull party - and I got paired off with the Admiral the whole time after dinner - it was uphill work - as our conversation link was dear Mr Duff who the Admiral thinks a sad failure and is rather ashamed of. I have now been asked to spend from Friday till Tuesday in the "Alacrity" - which will be rather fun I think - though of course she will just be stationary here - but I feel it is a great honour as I am the first of the wives to be invited. I should like to get to know Miss Duff better - I am sure she is nice.

I'm sure our finances won't last long in Hong Kong! Here we do everything just comfortably - Ian gets 9$ a day - we pay 7$ for everything in the hotel - and Ian's expenses on board are about $1 a day and washing $1.50 a week - that leaves us a margin of about 5$ a week and really nothing to spend it on - golf, tennis, newspapers and library all free - so there is only ferry fares - postage and entertaining - the latter is just having people to tea and tennis which costs 50 cents each - and to hotel dances which we all share and run very simply - so that last time Ian's and my share was only 85 cents. Hong Kong of course everything is on a different scale I'm afraid.

Island Hotel
5th July 1920 Wei hai wei

Ian returned yesterday - four days before we expected them - wasn't that gorgeous! You should have seen us last night - I unpacking my box (having just returned from the "Alacrity"). Ian unpacking his and eagerly showing me the things he had brought me - I tearing open your letters - both of us talking at the same time - Ian at intervals plaintively murmuring that we should get no dinner unless we hurried - I was in a wild state of excitement! Ian is just nicer and nicer every time and he does purr so when he is pleased! He brought me back a lavender coloured soft silk kimona with pink embroidered roses - it is really a very pretty one and very much Ian's taste! He also brought me a cotton kimono as a bathing wrap shaded blue with wisteria and a little china powder box in damascene ware and some pictures and a bathing cap! They had rather a poor time - fog all the way there and back and they had many narrow squeaks of colliding with each other - when they got to Japan it rained most of the time - but Ian had two happy days with another man playing golf at a place up in the mountains called Rodeasau where the scenery was lovely - but otherwise he was very disappointed in Japan. Oh I am so glad to get him back and we are going to have great fun now and with luck they won't be away again until the end of August.

I loved getting your letter and all the Burley news and hearing about the W.I. and your visit to London and the people you had seen. I'm so glad too that you had got my Port Said and Suez letters and now I feel we are really in touch again.

Now I must tell you of my visit to the "Alacrity" which I enjoyed tremendously - of course it was cut short by the return of the boats - but I'd been asked by both the Admiral and Miss Duff to go again next time the submarines go away and to go in the Alacrity if she ever goes with them. Wouldn't that be fun!

I went on board at 7 o'clock - and was greeted by the news that the boats would return on Sunday. Miss Duff, the Admiral and I dined alone - I was rather terrified of the latter to begin with but I discovered that if you "answered back" he became more than urbane - except at breakfast time when the best plan is to say nothing at all! He is pretty brutal to poor Miss Duff and abuses her in public which is rather a shame and she takes it so well. We went to bed at 10.30 - but Miss Duff sat on the end of my bed until after midnight talking about out many mutual friends.

I now know what it is like to feel like an American millionaire - having slept in one of the "Alacrity's" cabins, not that you'd know it was a cabin except for the portholes - the room being as big as my bedroom at home - and with chests of drawers, cupboards, armchairs etc and a gloriously comfortable bed - one belonging to the Russian Princess I feel - as it had cane work and carving on it.

I do wish we could go to Pekin - as it is apparently the only place you can still pick up really gorgeous things and bargains - but alas it would cost us $100 there and back as well as hotels so I fear it is impossible - it is as far nearly as if you wanted to go to Rome for a few days though out here of course distance means so little. Of course we shall go to Canton and you can get things there. Miss Duff also had a white jade bottle - she couldn't run to green jade. I must say this is a place where I should like to be really rich in order to bring things home - still one gets on very happily being poor. I think actually living out here is much cheaper than in England but you <u>have</u> to live at a much higher standard - a small instance being you can't play golf here without a caddie - Ian and I never have caddies in England. But given a sufficient income to enable you to live at the required standard - you get a lot for your money. The difficulty with the impoverished is that you can't economise on the things you want to (travelling 3rd class and that type of thing - you have to go 1st) which means you have less for the things you want to do. At home with £600 a year you can live on £500 and have £100 to do what you like with - here you've got to spend your £600 which enables you to live as if you had £1000 - but nothing to play with!

I danced with the usual people and we had a magnificent supper and everything was very well done. Great excitement at one function - when a ship came in and dropped anchor in Half Moon bay and six little lights obviously submarines sailed on into the harbour - we thought it was the "Ambrose" and were very agitated that our husbands would hurry ashore and find the hotel deserted. However it was only the 'Titania' - the 'Ambrose' came in at 11 on Sunday morning - I'd gone with the Duffs to church in the 'Hawkins' - but from where I sat I got a fine view of the boats coming in and anchoring - which you can imagine was distracting!

Island Hotel
6th July 1920 Wei hai wei

We are very relieved - having heard from the proprietor of St. Georges, Hong Kong that we can have rooms in Sept. - I believe it is a nice place and ideal situation half up the Peak - so below the fog line - and only 10 minutes from the N. Dockyard, also it is cheaper than we thought - as he says his charge is from 7$ for the two of us per day and we thought it was from 9$. When we get to Hong Kong the boats are to refit so lots of leave - after that there are rumours of a Southern cruise - if the whole fleet goes Miss Duff has offered to take me into the 'Alacrity' - (I hope she really meant it - as that would be simply glorious!) but I'm afraid the submarines generally cruise independently. Still if the boats spend a month or so at Singapore - I have several invitations to stay there. In meantime of course it is just a "buzz" and as the Prince of Wales is coming to Hong Kong in the winter - it will probably alter all programmes.

Some people MacMicheal by name - Shanghai Taipangs on the mainland were giving a dance - and Mr Henderson asked to bring us. Miss Duff asked us to dine in the 'Alacrity' before it - just the Duffs, Bennetts and ourselves. Very characteristic incident of Ian - the dance rig people wear here now that it is hot - is white waistcoat - black tie and white jacket - most of the N.O.'s haven't got the latter so wear mess jackets - with plain buttons - Ian hadn't them so arrived on board the 'Alacrity' without the buttons at all and so had to disappear hastily in the Captain's cabin - the captain having offered to lend him some.

Directly after dinner we got into the barge and had about 20 minutes run to Narcissus Bay - there the water got too shallow - so we embarked in a sampan - presently that ran aground though there was still a long stretch of shallow water in front of us. However a rickshaw came alongside led by a man with a lanthorn and one by one we were conveyed to dry land - rather a unique way to go to a dance!

From the sampan it looked extraordinary picturesque.

(At this juncture from my verandah I've just seen the American Admiral's yacht come in - the 'Hawkins' band playing enthusiastically - if tactlessly 'Rule Britannia' - Britannia rules the waves!)

To continue about the views from the sampan - a steep flight of steps led up from the water - with Chinese lanthorns hung at every step and at the top the bungalow blazing with light and all reflected in the black water (very like the picture by Rackham of the twelve dancing princesses in 'Grimm') In the foreground the rickshaw lurching through the water - pushed by a wild looking Chinaman with a pigtail wound round his head and another man leading with a bobbing lanthorn.

There weren't many people - I danced chiefly with Ian - never - never have I eaten such delicious ice creams! We came home in the barge.

Yesterday I played golf with Mrs Bennett - we had a very good game and I won by two up and one to play. It was very hot - so we came home and had a gorgeous bathe. Ian got home to tea and I played golf with him afterwards. I really am improving - Ian gave me a stroke a hole and I played from the ladies tees. We were all square at the 9th tee and then Ian got bunkered and I won the hole - it was great fun - and I am getting very keen. After dinner we went for a long walk.

The inevitable has happened in a small community like this - Mrs Flag Captain (Mrs Henderson) has had a terrible row with Mrs Flag Commander (Mrs Bennett). Miss Duff supports the latter - and the atmosphere is rather electric!

Island Hotel
12th July 1920   Wei hai wei

Ian and I are becoming terribly social butterflies - we've started an engagement book and it seems full up for a long time ahead. My chief ambitions at the moment seem to be to become really good at tennis and moderately good at golf. The latter fluctuates - but at the former game I'm beginning to be able to play quite hard. Ian is very thrilled and pleased and I am on his account - because he is so keen and now we can really have good matches together - which we couldn't before.

I've been painting all morning and just finished a decorative piece of a Chinese family - I did it purely as an exercise in decoration in the arrangement of figures - one is very successful - the others aren't.

Ian went to dinner at the Club. He is President of the 2nd Captain's Union (otherwise known as the Soviet Club!) and the Ambrose 2nd Captains were dining their opposite numbers in the Titania - and playing them at bowls afterwards. Mr Satow was also dining out so Mrs Satow and I joined forces.

Ian returned in a very convivial mood and full of spice - may he attend many dinners as I hadn't been so entertained for a long time. We talked until 1am and I heard all the Fleet gossip - though I could have wished Ian was less discreet!

Island Hotel
8th July 1920 Wei hai wei

We hear that over on the mainland the Chinese wearied in praying for rain that never came - so they finally took their gods out and beat them! This has proved much more efficacious and the night before last the rain descended in torrents - turning the tennis courts into mud pies. However it has been very good for the crops and will put an end to the various epidemics which have been going about - everything is looking very fresh too and much greener. It rather looks like more rain which will do in the Flagship's dance tonight.

I think the gods in revenge for their beating will probably overdo the rain!

Two such nice fat mails this week and lovely long letters from you. I do enjoy them so - though at the same time it makes me feel very homesick!

Thank you so much for the 'Punches', a never failing joy and they add greatly to my popularity too! I loved getting 'Colour' do send me anything like that and reviews of exhibitions etc. - also would you send me Saturday Westminster - and 'Books of today' and 'Times Literary Supplement' if ever you get hold of one of them. One never hears or sees any new pictures or books out here - books on China and elderly novels being the literary resources of the place (I'm reading just now 'A Houseboat on the Yangtze' and Locke's 'Stella Maris') Tell me if you come across any new poems. Miss Duff is the only person here who cares one rap about those kind of books - and there isn't anyone who is the faintest bit interested in pictures - or painting - though there are several exceptionally musical people - but that doesn't do me much good.

I like your story of the two old ladies in the 'bus - I can cap it with a vulgarer one! A grocer instructed his new assistant that should they not happen to have in stock what a customer wanted - he was always to suggest a substitute. Shortly after a female came in and demanded lavatory paper - remembering his instructions the assistant replied "I'm sorry Madam - we have no lavatory paper at present - but I can supply you with emery paper - fly paper or confetti!

Isn't it a pity Ian's captain (for whom he has an enormous regard and affection) is a woman hater - where the unfortunateness comes in is that he has been left £60,000 on condition that he marries - until he does he can't touch a penny and he says he's hanged if he'll marry! This all happened on the way out here - the discreet Ian of course never breathed about it but its leaked out through some other channel and everyone is excited about it. It certainly is romantic but rather trying for the young man!

Island Hotel
18th July 1920 Linkungtao

It's rather like wartime again up here - the 'Hawkins', 'Carlisle' and 'Cairo' have gone and all the others are standing by - the submarines won't be taken - but the crews are to be sent up in the 'Titania' as landing parties if necessary. The officers haven't been told off yet - and Ian is hoping he will be one to go - naturally I hope not - but I suppose we shall know this afternoon and I hope there will be some further news. Pekin is cut off - and the railway has apparently been attacked - but we've had so little news - and really scarcely know who is fighting who. The ships of course are simply being sent to protect British interests and guard telegraph and railway.

By the time you get this letter it will be all over and forgotten I expect and very likely you won't even have heard about it in the English papers.

Friday was a very strenuous day altogether. I went over to the mainland in the ferry and picked Ian up from the Ambrose en route. Then we worked off a call and had tea at the Southcotts and went for a long walk. It was a nice day for walking as it was cloudy and consequently not too hot. All the crops were looking much happier after the rain.

The Indian corn is ripe and there were all sorts of weird plants which we had never seen before. The Chinaman certainly knows how to grow vegetables - every plant looks as if it was tended individually even when they are grown in large fields - and you never see a weed - and every inch of ground -even in crevices between rocks - grows something. There are no hedges at all and not many trees except weeping willows and plane trees and generally they grow round the grave yards - though graves in China of course are ubiquitous. Outside the city we passed a temple - and as usual in front of it was the village theatre - a platform with a highly ornamental roof - several small Chinese boys were giving a very dramatic representation with sticks as swords - children are exactly the same all the world over! Further on we passed a cottage with the door open and through it we could see the family spinning silk. We came back by the 6.30 ferry - arriving at 7 and as we were dining at the club at 7.30 you can imagine we had a bit of a scramble dressing. Ian was resplendent in gold laced trousers - wellingtons and miniatures (medals) (borrowed) and looked rather nice - but thereby hangs a sad tale - for when we got to the club we found everybody else (except Mr Stopford who had also come from the hotel) in plain trousers - the 'rig' of the day' which had been mess dress being changed at the last minute to 'mess undress' - Ian suggests the change was caused by the Admiral finding his own trousers were tarnished! However Ian and Mr Stopford signalled to their servants to bring their plain trousers to the club - and we proceeded to get on with dinner which we had out in the verandah there were a lot of other parties and all the tables were decorated so it looked very gay. Our hosts were Mr Beech, Mr Hutchinson and Mr Miller (all Ambrose). The trousers not having appeared the rest of us went on to the 'Hawkins' leaving poor Ian at the Club.

The 'Hawkins' is a magnificent ship and she was beautifully decorated and lit up and the huge quarter-deck was exactly like a ballroom. About the end of the 3rd dance the officer of the Watch summoned me and in a stage whisper announced 'the trousers have arrived, but where is your husband?' The two were eventually brought together - but by that time everyone's programme was full up - so Ian got no dancing except the ones I had saved for him.

Halfway through the 'Marazion' and the 'Bluebell' were told to go to sea immediately - so their officers disappeared - and we also heard the 'Hawkins' was to sail at dawn - and the rest of the dance on had a nasty 'ball before Waterloo' feeling - especially as the dancing ended early we saw the decorations being hurriedly stripped down and the guns uncovered.

Saturday it rained and rained and rained and we were all rather sitting on the edges of our chairs waiting for news. I did some painting and we all tried to cheer Mrs Dawson up - her husband is in command of the 'Marazion' which is the only ship with a shallow enough draught to cross the sandbar at Tiensin - so he will have to land all the troops. Ian had a 'day on' I went and had tea with him in the 'Ambrose'. She is lying a long way out and it was rather a rough journey out for the picket boat.

Monday

Still no news and the excitement is rather petering out - though everybody is still 'standing by'. Ian went off at 6 this morning as the boats are going out to practise gunnery. Yesterday it rained in a way I have never seen before - it came down solidly with no space between the drops exactly as if someone had turned on a tap - everything was blotted out - and one got soaked going to the dining room which is merely crossing a gravel path. All the horrors I had been warned of took place. Everything leather went mouldy and all ones clothes felt damp and the cupboards and beds smelt musty - and it was altogether pretty nasty and of course no fires or anything and all the rain blew in through the verandah.

Before it had really set in wet Mrs Stopford and I set off for church - a Chinese conjurer was there - a wonderful old man - but you wouldn't have enjoyed the performance - as his star turn was producing piebald mice from unexpected places. Ian came back for lunch and one of his dull and worthy friends came to tea and stayed a long time. After dinner the Satows, Dawsons, ourselves and Mr Blood from the 'Titania' joined forces and played childish games - 'Up Jenkins', Charades and Dumb Crambo and so on. It was really great fun. Tomorrow "weather and war permitting" we are dining with Mr Carrie in the 'Titania' and seeing their cinematograph. Ian and I were having a tennis party yesterday but of course the rain did it in - but we are going to try again on Thursday.

Island Hotel
23rd July 1920 Wei hai wei

A mail came in yesterday and I got your letter of June 10th - it didn't take so long really did it? I expect it came via America. The Fleet mails all come via Hong Kong and so really only arrive about one a fortnight and generally take longer on the way.

I have very little to tell you except the usual pleasant round. It's getting horribly on my conscience, but really there is no escape from it. It is such a very unnormal position really - a handful of Europeans - all of the same class and with the same interests planted on a mile square island 3 miles off one of the barrenest parts of the coast of China and cut off from the rest of the world entirely except for a weekly mail - add to this a hot climate and a Chinese population who wait on you hand and foot at every juncture and the result is not stimulating to the brain.

Ian as a matter of fact has quite a lot of work as it is during these months that gun practise attacks and other exercises are put in - so he can enjoy himself without any qualms - and in spite of the said qualms I do too - thoroughly!

I painted a picture which was a complete failure and made me cross for days - however I've begun a new one which I think is going to be nice so that has consoled me.

On Monday we were asked to the Alacrity to see a cinematograph show that was being given for the men. Tuesday Ian and I played golf and I beat him 2 up and one to play - we were both playing well. At 7.30 we went off in a boat to the Titania where we were dining with a delightful man by the name of Carrie who was in Ian's term. It was rather an amusing dinner party - it was given in a very small cabin - so the table took up all the room and Ian, Mrs Satow and our host were wedged between the washstand and the wardrobe and the marine couldn't possibly get in the wait so food was handed through the door - and a very good dinner it was too. Mr Powell did most of the talking - being a great raconteur and very funny. Ian had known him at Blyth. After dinner we sat on deck and watched the Titania picture show.

The war has ended in an anti climax and all the ships have returned - they stood by for two days ready to land parties while the staff went and interviewed the Chinese general who was more than friendly and as there was no anti-foreign feeling at all and we hope the Chinese were impressed by the ships and landing parties - there was nothing more to do but come home! The Colombo is still away down in Shanghai - in order to make a wireless connection as the Shanghai Telegraph Communication has been cut off.

Island Hotel
26th July 1920 Wei hai wei

I've never seen two such beautiful days as yesterday and the day before. On Saturday we woke up to see a sparkling sun and the cicadas buzzing and chirruping among the acacias. Our bed is drawn up to the big verandah window and the trees are just outside. Ian got ashore at 12.30 and we went and bathed. Bathing really is a joy now - the water is quite warm and in intervals one suns oneself on the hot hot sands. I swam out to the raft by myself and we all sunned ourselves there - then swam back and lay in the shallow water and felt very pleasantly cool. In the afternoon it was very very hot - so we lazed on the verandah and stuck photographs into a superb book we got a Chinaman to make for us. We spent the whole afternoon, the other day ordering it, because the Chinaman had very little English - so everything had to be explained by pantomime and drawings - but in the end he made us exactly what we wanted and so cheap. After tea we played tennis with the Stopfords and a Mrs Mackenzie and I played vilely. Then we went and dressed for the Hawkins dance.

Before dressing we went and sat on the sea wall and watched the sunset. A flat calm sea and smoke from the ships funnels going straight up - an orange sky - and the mainland mountains every shade of purple - while the sea had wonderful pink and mauve and green colours and one little wreath of mist drifted along - I can't tell you how lovely it was.

The dance began at 9 o'clock and we went along in the barge. I wore my wedding dress. It was a delightful dance though pretty hot. It was beautifully got up - the whole quarter-deck was hung with coloured Chinese lanthorns and in the bows it was all red lanthorns and a wonderful pond and fountain had been rigged up. The pond was full of live fishes and octopus - unfortunately some of them got electrocuted! Ian got a lot of dancing in spite of the shortage of females - I danced with him and his nice friend Mr Carrie and with other Ambrose and Titania people, who I like much better than the Carlisle men who have been very spoilt. At midnight we had supper on the upper deck - Ian and Mr Carrie and I supped together, then Captain Woodhouse collected a bathing party and we went back to the hotel and changed into bathing clothes and went down to the beach. The moon had set so it was pitch black - until one got into the water which whenever you touched it broke into phosphorescence - you looked down and saw your beautiful silver legs and feet in the water - while your hands splashed silver stars - and it was gloriously cool after the heat of dancing. We only stayed in a few minutes and then went straight to bed.

I'm reading rather a fascinating book 'Peking' by Juliet Bredon - it does make me long to go there - but even if we could afford it (which we can't) things are too unsettled up there and it is the wrong time of year - but it is the place where you can see the real Imperial China and all the wonderful Chinese art. I believe it is full of old curiosity shops where you can get lacquer and embroideries and china and jade and would be a very happy hunting ground for you - but nowadays the Japanese get all the really good things and bargains are hard to come by. Mr Dolphin was telling me of some bowls he saw - yellow china with orange dragons - sounds rather nice doesn't it - he thinks they will become very valuable as they were made for the old dowager Empress - at present you can get a bowl for $6.

The Island Hotel
30th July 1920 Wei hai wei

We really are having heat now. Every day is hotter than the last - and the local prophets say it will continue until August 8th - and then begin cooling - by the time it is cool we shall be catching the heat again at Hong Kong - but I must say I like it and Ian and I both flourish in it - I've never seen him look fitter. Most people have been sick - and the Admiral has been very bad and in hospital. I think one reason I have escaped is that I never touch meat. One gets quantities of chicken and eggs (eggs are 10 cents a dozen). The Millers are frightfully fussy - they never eat salad or ice cream - went through the strawberry season without eating one and in spite of it they always get any illness going and generally worse than other people!

From breakfast until teatime one sits and drips - and a blazing sun shines out of a blazing blue sky on to a blazing yellow earth - at 12 am we all bathe - and that is really lovely as the water is cool but very pleasant. I can easily swim out to the raft now - and we sit and sun ourselves there and splash in and out and return to tiffin at 1.30. Most people sleep in the afternoon - but Miss Dawson generally sits on my verandah and I sew or draw and talk. Ian returns at 4 and we have tea - it is still hot but quite possible to take exercise - and we bathe again before dinner and sometimes just before going to bed. It was heavenly the other night as it was full moon and we went to bed feeling so nice and fresh.

Today I am having a tennis party - ourselves, the Satows, a Mr Gregg (captain of L3), all quite good so it ought to be fun. Tomorrow Ian is playing cricket and I am playing tennis with the Carringtons and we are going to a dinner party on the Hawkins. Sunday we are lunching with Captain James in the 'Curlew'.

On Monday Ian and I went for a delightful picnic by ourselves. We took a thermos and food and tramped along one of the mainland roads until we came to a shady bank under a hedge - and not in a grave yard (generally the only shade is among the tombstones!) We had a view over the bean and maize fields to the hills and a glimpse of the Chefoo main road - down which came at intervals mule litters and rattley old droskies and other traffic. We came to the conclusion that if we suddenly woke up there and didn't know where we were - we'd never think it was China - it was more like one's idea of Southern Spain or Portugal. Then we tramped round - took photographs and I did some quick sketches. I've found a perfect thing for a woodblock - a joss house painted red with a curly roof - in front a well with an arched bridge over it - funny trees with huge heart shaped leaves and extraordinary stone animals. I began drawing it until the crowd of dirty children got too offensive - and were going to go back - probably on Sunday. I'm rather depressed about my painting - the last one I did was terribly laboured - and the one I did that I really like the sky which was meant to be bright blue has faded to an ugly grey which is most trying.

So far I've painted chiefly because I felt I ought to - not because I was inspired - but I really do feel inspired about this joss house - I wish it wasn't such a long journey to get to it.

I've finished making myself an evening dress out of that faded blue crepe de chine which I had bleached white. I've put a georgette frill round the neck and a sash of blue and yellow Chinese ribbon and I think it is quite nice and very cool.

My clothes are really being very successful and they've practically re-covered from the damp. I'm saving my white coat and skirt and yellow silk dress for Hong Kong as one doesn't wear good clothes in the day time here.

My evening dresses are doing well too - but two and three dances and dinners a week is a great strain and I think I'll have to ask you to send me out a black evening dress - get Miss Rogers to make it. I think a very plain satin bodice with net sleeves (very short) and a skirt of net flounces and a bunch of very gay coloured futuristic flowers at the waist (I believe the best place and cheapest is the Bon Marché in Paris for flowers - you could chose from a catalogue). Net stands the climate beautifully. The most becoming kind of skirt for me is one with big frills one on top of the other (like my lace dress) and above all the very simplest plainest body with a low round neck. Silver on black looks nice - it is a pure toss up - some people have silver dresses that haven't tarnished and some have. My green and silver went directly in one place - but has never got any worse.

I've been very busy putting Ian's wardrobe in order and keeping my own in repair.

I always think of Granny and how she would have loved the travelling merchants who come round nearly every day here and spread out silk and ribbons and lace and silver ware on the verandahs and let you look and finger and don't mind a bit if you buy or not - and if you do buy go in for protracted and amicable bargaining.

Yesterday an old Chinese from Chefoo came with lace - and I bought enough for a slip to wear under jumpers.

Yesterday Ian went out to sea for gun-firing - they are very anxious to come out top in it - as that would make 'L7' top in everything - she has already best record for attacking and torpedo - as well as at football - so I hope she will get the gunnery too - Ian thinks they ought to.

Rumours of a mail on Monday - Hurrah.

The Island Hotel
2nd August 1920 Wei hai wei

The great heat still continues and makes me feel terribly lethargic - for the last week it has been round about 90 in the shade and so sticky.

I'm afraid it is pretty definite now that the boats leave on the 17th of August. A direct steamer for Hong Kong leaves here on the 28th arriving Hong Kong on Sept. 3rd and Mrs Satow, Mrs Stopford and I will all probably go by it - we have written to fix up rooms at St Georges and hope it will be all right. I'm sure Hong Kong will be great fun but I have enjoyed this so - Ian thinks they will call in at Shanghai on the way down and I've told him to go and look up the eccentric Dents. I think they will rather appeal to Ian - or any way their motor cars will!

The Island Hotel
5th August 1920 Wei hai wei

Tuesday was very hectic - we started at 9.15 by going off to the 'Alacrity' (that is to say Mrs Satow and myself). At 9.30 the 'Alacrity' weighed anchor and we sailed round the Fleet - each ship coming to attention as she passed - we sailed well outside into the China Sea to the submarines exercising ground where the gunnery competition was in progress which the Admiral wanted to watch. It was really most interesting and entertaining - we were alongside the umpires boat quite close to the target. At a given signal the submarine submerged - steamed full speed under water to a certain bearing and then abruptly appeared fired ten rounds and then closed down. Unfortunately by the time we got there 'L7' had finished and was just going home - she won the competition - only taking 2 mins 22 secs to emerge - fire ten rounds and close down - also her shooting was all round best - though she didn't get a bullseye - 'L15' (Mr Stopford) was the only one who did - everybody else's shooting was fairly wild and they all took 3 mins or over. The target was too small really - it was only the size of the smallest kind of sailing boat with one sail and the range was 1500 yds.

We watched three boats perform in the intervals lying on deck chairs on the bridge - a very pleasant way of spending the morning - then we had lunch - the party consisting of the Admiral, Miss Duff, the Flag Lieut., secretary, Mrs Satow and myself - also Mr and Mrs John Johnstone - he is manager of Jardine Mathieson - and she comes from Dumfries so perhaps you know her - also a Mr Beth in Jardines (a brother of Ian Hay's). We had a most sumptuous lunch beginning with iced grapefruit and cherries.

After lunch the 'Alacrity' did turning trials and we all sat on deck and talked. I got passed off as usual with the old Admiral which always rather paralyses me - however he was really very interesting telling me about his experiences with Lord Fisher and Winston Churchill. He is very nice in that way - that he takes as much trouble to entertain and be agreeable to the junior N.O.'s wives as he does to a Governor's wife - while Miss Duff much prefers them. We got ashore again at 4.30 and then Ian and I went and played golf - had a lovely bathe at 7 o'clock and then dressed and went off to the 'Titania' where we were dining with a very nice Mr Coltart (captain of L20), there was just the three of us in a rather hot small cabin - after dinner we went to an Entertainment given by the men - they were really wonderfully good - a sort of 'Follies' only called the 'Pharies' one man - an E.R.T. was dressed as a girl and an extraordinarily pretty girl too - he was in Mr Coltarts boat - and as we were sitting in the front row - he was giving Mr Coltart the 'glad eye' the whole time! When we got back we had a gorgeous moonlight bathe - and so to bed.

Tomorrow will be the 2nd anniversary of our wedding day - doesn't that seem a long time - though actually we haven't spent more than half of it together. I am quite certain that Ian and I are far more in love with each other than we were two years ago - or even a year ago - as I think it goes on getting more so every day. It is an excitement every day when Ian comes home and it is the greatest joy just to be together and to do everything together. The more I see of other men the more I think I am lucky to have married Ian - he has the most loveable nature I have ever met - you never come across anything that isn't sweet and unworldly and he has the sunniest, happiest temper imaginable and conscientious which is the most admirable as it is an acquired virtue - very much so. It is very good for me to live with such an unfussy person who takes life so very easily as it comes along - and though we are so different really in nature - we do understand each other very well - I am most frightfully happy - perfectly happy if I had you too.

Island Hotel
9th August 1920 Wei hai wei

I don't think there is anything particular to chronicle this mail - just the usual succession of cloudless hot days and still warm nights - bathing and golf and tennis - painting and letter writing and Ian's society.

You always say you like living in a Community - well I've come to the conclusion I do too - it amuses me very much the various small interests and jests - the friendships and quarrels and reconciliations (in the two latter the submarine wives don't take much part - being peaceable dispositions). We are all very friendly - sit on each others verandahs - borrow each others books, look at each others clothes - play tennis together and bathe in large parties at all hours of the day and night. In the dining room we each have our little table - but conversation is pretty general and we often join forces.

I love this place too - the gorgeous sunsets and the wonderful colour of the sea and the joy of bathing in it whether at midday or midnight. All the English flowers are over except the giant sunflowers - but there are lots of strange plants come out whose names I don't know - some of them with sweet heavy scents. Yes it is a place that grows on one - but I often and often miss and long for the subtle loveliness of England. "The scent of hawthorn in the sun and bracken in the wet". I think I'm rather writing "hot air" so I had better stop. You must be in Scotland now - and I hope enjoying yourself very much.

The Island Hotel
13th August 1920 Wei hai wei

I'm afraid my letters get duller and duller the almost inevitable result of living on a bare little island in midocean, not that it is so bare now as all sorts of attractive shrubs and plants are in flower - one especially is quite beautiful - called crepe myrtle - it is bright pink and flowers in masses either in standard trees or in bushes. There are heaps of hydrangeas and lotus lilies and a weed with an enchanting smell like jasmine.

There are a marvellous collection of insects too - beautiful moths and butterflies - beetles and grasshoppers and praying mantis - and mosquitoes! Every night we search round inside the net and slay two or three and then tuck ourselves in thinking we are secure. Not a bit of it - in the morning several bloated forms are always found on the roof!

The Island Hotel
14th August 1920 9pm Wei hai wei

I've just been down to see Ian off in a sampan. He is off to sea tonight on a mission rather wrapped in mystery - but he expects to be back by Monday and I thought I'd sit down and write to you now as we've had rather an amusing day and it is best to write while it is all fresh. Being Saturday Ian got ashore at 12.30 and we went and bathed. Then soon after 'tiffin' we took a sampan and sailed over to the mainland - an ideal day - sunny and radiant - but with a nice little breeze. It took us about ¾ of an hour to sail over - we had tea with us in a thermos and a bag of eatables and apples and we bought chocolate on the way. Then we secured a droski - an awful old shandrydan drawn by a mule and driven by a gentleman with a straw hat which he had the greatest difficulty in keeping on!

So we set off along the bumpy road to the first Lagoon. The road wound along through yellow countryside between fields of every kind of strange looking crops - peanuts - black beans and others whose names I don't know - as well as familiar Indian corn and cucumber. Yellow stone farmhouses with thatched roofs and gateways at frequent intervals - and crowds of yellow naked children - shady mounds which always betoken the family burial ground - weeping willows which indicate a long ago dried up stream - and at the back of all the great bare blue mountains like the mountains of the moon. Occasionally we rattled through a village with the inevitable temple with the inevitable red poles in front of it! - at one place by the roadside was an old man weaving - we took his photograph and tried to converse with him by signs - he was a cheery old gentleman.

After three miles of this absorbingly interesting rattle through a strange land we came over the top of a hill and below us lay a wide marsh ending in a deep blue bay with miles of hard white sands. The marsh was covered with women and children grubbing up herbs into baskets and their interest in us did in our bathing - as we felt they might pinch our clothes while we were in the sea! However we told our Jehu to mau-mau' (this is the only Chinese I know! It means wait!) and we plodded over the marsh which was covered with pinks and a pretty aromatic blue flower and yellow lilies and bamboo grass which pricked. When we came to a large mimosa tree we sank into its shade and proceeded to eat a large tea. A couple of Chinese children watched us from a little distance off - to attract our attention they wove garlands of flowers and waved them at us and we became very friendly and took their photographs - finally we gave them lumps of sugar and became embarrassingly popular. Except for them it was very peaceful - the wide sweet scented marsh the hills and the lap of the sea - very primitive looking it all was too - just what I imagine the moon would be like if one suddenly found oneself on it - the mimosa trees giving the only exotic note. Ian and I basked in the sun like lizards. I do love going on expeditions alone with him - he is an ideal companion - you are another and I would love to do these expeditions with you.

Thoughts of the ferry sent us back to our droski and we proceeded to bump back again - and an even nicer drive as the sun was behind us and the level light very attractive as it always is. And now I will tell you the really thrilling part of the afternoon - we came in for a Chinese theatrical entertainment - a real genuine one - such as I suppose was acted in exactly the same way 1000 years ago and was very like one's idea of Medieval English Miracle plays. As we were driving out to the lagoon we passed a temple from which hung red banners - then we heard gongs beating a saw a large crowd - so we stopped hopped out and pushed out way in - and there on a raised open air stage with a matting awning overhead and three sides open the play was going on. At the back of the stage was a room with two curtained doorways the exits and the entrance. The setting round was attractive - green weeping willows and blue sky: at the back was the temple (the village theatre always faces the temple). On the steps and on the ground sat the audience - some hundreds I suppose - interested but not applauding. A wonderfully clean crowd (for Chinese) and not too offensive to the sense of smell. The ladies were all dressed in their best - rouged cheeks and magenta lips and brilliant artificial flowers in their sleek black heads and gay embroidered shoes on their poor deformed feet. The men sat and fanned themselves - the children played private games of their own. There were several hawkers of water melons and other delicacies and in one corner some quiet gambling was going on. Meanwhile the play went solidly on - it does I believe for days on end. We watched for some time - simply thrilled - but couldn't make much head or tail of it. The principal figures were two gorgeously dressed monstrosities in wonderful rainbow coloured robes with towering head-dresses and absurd false beards. One had his face painted in vivid terra cotta - the other was camouflaged in black and white stripes - they were truly hideous. First one and then the other sang in a shrill falsetto voice - posturing and bowing the while and accompanied by gongs and cymbals - to our ears very inharmonious but most pleasing apparently to the Chinese. There was a chorus of men armed with swords and dressed in red jackets who stamped round in a manner very reminiscent of the Burley school children in "Emperor's Honour". A bored gentleman in plain clothes - evidently the property man who remained on the stage the whole time occasionally brought forward a table to which the devils(?) and the chorus made profound obeisance. We did wish we knew what it was all about. On the way home we stopped again and found the play still going strong. Our two friends of the red and striped faces had been superseded by two more of even more terrifying aspect who were doing a sort of devil dance. The property man then appeared with a stick from which was suspended a crude drawing of a gateway in a wall - one devil and his retinue retired behind it - the other and his followers settled down to have a carouse - the falsetto singing and the jazz band still going on.

We weren't much wiser as to the story - but I believe it has all some sort of semi-religious meaning - or more perhaps mythological. I could have watched for ages - but unfortunately we had to catch the ferry. Ian took several photographs which I hope will be good. He proved a great counter attraction to the play as half the audience gathered round him thrilled by the camera.

I forgot to say that out at the lagoon by the seashore we found a lovely little shrine - rather like a large dog kennel with a devil screen in front and the red poles. Inside the dog kennel were two effigies - with covered faces - some charms and a tray of burnt joss sticks. These shrines I believe are Taoist - a religion with certain features in common with the Ancient Greek nature worship.

We were lucky to see a proper Chinese theatre weren't we? We were the only Europeans there. Altogether it was a topping day and Ian simply loved it too. I wish we could have had more expeditions - but getting over to the mainland is such a business and Ian seldom gets off for long enough - but today we were really lucky. We were a little early for the ferry so we went into the 'Robber King's' and bought some silk handkerchiefs and some Chinese ribbon which I am sending to Iris and Muriel.[7]

The day nearly ended disastrously as there was a heavy swell coming in from outside and the little ferry boat pitched and rolled for ½ an hour and I felt so sick! However a bathe restored me and now I am quite all right.

Yesterday was a nice day too - but quite a different sort. We went and played tennis at Government House - rather poor tennis and lots of garden party - but ice cream which is always a compensation! In the evening we dined at the Club with Mr Stewart the Flag Lieutenant - a very nice young man with a rather tired manner - not at all one's idea of the typical suave Flag lieut. but very nice and natural and with a great sense of humour. We were his only guests and had a small table out on the verandah wedged between two large parties. The Admiral's band performed and we had a very good dinner(more ice cream). Afterwards we danced - Mr Coltart joined us - he really is nearly mad and priceless as Mr Barry. Mr Carrie was there too but retired to a quiet corner with Ian - poor youth he had been suffering with hiccoughs for 48 hours - I overheard Ian tell him that I would sympathise - being a sufferer myself from that complaint! Miss Duff was dining again with Mr Dolphin - there must be something in it I think - they look so happy together.

Tomorrow is going to be a dud day - with Ian away - and a Sunday too which is such a swindle as he generally gets off for lunch on that day.

The Island Hotel
20th August 1920 Wei hai wei

There was a mail in yesterday - but I didn't get anything which was very sad - perhaps you've begun writing care of Ian again when of course the letters would come in the Admiralty bag which always seems to take longer. Rather a tragedy is I've told everyone to write c/o S/M L7 and now a new order has come out that any letters addressed to submarines are to go to the Titania - the Titania will be up here and we shall be in Hong Kong - so it will take a bout a month longer to get them.

Ian went off this morning carrying all the things he had forgotten to pack - a pair of wellington boots - a huge Chinese umbrella - a solar topee a coat and a few other trifles of this sort! 'L7' sails this afternoon and is going with the Ambrose direct to Hong Kong -

and arrives there about the same day that as I leave here. I've got my passage all right in the 'Kinchow' but we haven't heard yet whether the rooms at Hong Kong are all right or not. However it is too late to cancel the passage now - so Ian will just have to find some sort of roof to cover me! but it is rather going off into the blue! Mrs Stopford and Mrs Satow are in the same condition - the former rather worse as they've taken no steps of any kind - the Satows like us have a promise - as yet unconfirmed. It is funny here how one looks upon a six day journey of over 1200 miles as no more than from London to Edinburgh! I hope we shall put in at one of the ports going down - Amoy or Swatow.

We are dreadfully sorry to be leaving this place as we have been so happy here and it is such absolute country - while Hong Kong is very much a town - still now that Ian is gone I am anxious to be moving too.

I am making myself a new bathing dress (very necessary) it's going to be a very superior one - the best black silk - and so you know what it is really made of? Three sailor's neckties which Ian got me from the ship. They are the most beautiful thick silk and a yard square and not expensive at 6/- each.

Island Hotel
23rd August 1920 Wei hai wei

I got a letter from you yesterday.

Saturday I went over to the mainland on a solitary expedition not very successful as I collected my rabble of Chinese children before I'd even opened my sketchbook - however just as I was hurrying along to catch the ferry - in a secluded spot I saw a perfect idea for a wood block - so back I go to draw it on Wednesday - it was a funny old well with children watching an old Chinaman drawing water and little thin willow trees at the back. The figures would be in the shade, the background bright sunlight. It was very hot tramping around, and I didn't see anything exciting until on the way home when we passed two beautiful junks from the south that had been driven into the harbour by a storm. I think they must have been from Ning Po as they were so beautifully painted - red and green and blue and in shape so like pictures of Spanish galleons - huge high poops and funny old lanthorns in the bow:- on the bows too they each had a great rolling eye painted - to show them where to go!

In the evening Captain Lambert had a 'grass widows' party in his cabin - Mrs Stopford, Mrs Satow, Mrs Carrington and me and three other 'Cairo' officers. Captain Lambert is charming - an ugly little man but Ian says an absolutely ideal captain - the commander Captain Johnston is equally delightful - an excellent mimic and very humorous and interested in things Chinese - instead of turning up his nose at them like most of the English out here do. So it was a nice dinner party and followed by a dance which I enjoyed very much though I missed Ian. An Italian sloop is in here just now down from Tiensin. I was introduced to one officer who danced very well but though he spoke English, conversation was uphill work and rather on the lines of "Do you like China" "Yes, I like China very much". The Italian captain was very good looking and his English was more ambitious if less correct. The Italian sailors wander round the island with their arms round each other's necks singing in operatic voices!

Yesterday I went to church and painted in the afternoon - it was a hot and rather sleepy day and after dinner went off to 'Alacrity' to see the cinema - an extraordinarily good show. This morning Mrs Satow came along early and woke me up to come and bathe with her and it was really perfectly delicious - the sun wasn't up and the water was all grey and pearly and it was so fresh though the water was warm. This afternoon I am playing a single at golf with Mr Coltart - which I feel is rather dashing - still his handicap is 18. Tomorrow Mrs Satow has a tennis party which I attend and

Wednesday I am going to the mainland to draw - pay farewell visits and finally tea with the Southcotts and golf afterwards. Thursday Miss Duff has asked me to lunch with her in 'Alacrity' and have 'a good gossip' and Friday I'm dining at the Club with a 'Titania' party and Saturday dining in the 'Alacrity'. Sunday I think must be devoted to packing and Monday we leave. I really enjoy this social whirl very much - and anyway it's the sort of life all English people out in the East lead. But it becomes very demoralising and I'm glad I shan't have too much of it. What I really enjoy most is going off exploring with Ian and I wish there was more scope for it. I'd love to go camping with him into the interior - that sort of thing. In Japan it is possible to go walking tours because the native inns are clean - but in China they are incredibly filthy. Residents out here ignore the native life as much as possible and it brands you as an eccentric tourist if you talk about it or take interest in it. It's a pity.

The Island Hotel
5th August 1920   Wei hai wei

This is the last letter you will get from Wei hai wei - as we leave before the next mail. It is sad the Ambrose had to go down so early as it is simply lovely here just now - clear and cool and delicious like a perfect Sept. at home - the grapes are all ripe and the morning glories are a joy climbing over every bank - also the snipe are in so Ian would have had shooting.

Hong Kong I'm told will be beastly for the next five weeks - but I am so longing to be with Ian again. This has been a delightful summer - an endless succession of 'blue days' spent in lazy enjoyment of the sun and warmth and the joy of bathing three or four times a day - seeing a lot of Ian and meeting many delightful people. As a background to it all the quaint primitive not to say squalid Chinese life and the amusing feeling of 'being abroad'. For a long time it gave me a childish pleasure to put stamps on my letters with 'China' written on them! and to handle the different coinage - some of the huge silver dollars are most attractive with dragons on them and the mystic words 'four mace and seven candarini' two words which fascinate Ian! I've not yet mastered the intricacies of the coinage though - if you take a silver dollar to the Post Office they give you 115 cents for it - but if you buy two 4 cents stamps and pay for them with a 20 cent piece you only get 10 cents change!

The only achievements of the summer are that I can now swim - (slowly but quite steadily) and I'm about 100% better at golf and tennis - the former I am awfully pleased as Ian is so keen and I can now really give him a game with a stroke. We've written one quite Chinese fairy story - and I've begun illustrating it - the first picture is nice - otherwise my painting has been dreadfully disappointing - I've done one big pastel (quite nice - but it was third try - the first two were failures) one water colour which would have been nice if all the blue hadn't faded a dirty grey - and two other water colours both failures and a little decorative picture quite nice. I've got material for a woodblock and the fairy story will keep me busy but I wish I was more inspired. I've made myself two dresses and a bathing dress is in the process of being made and I've read various books on China and improved a lot at dancing. Ian I think has been blissfully happy - he adores a leisurely life.

Yesterday I went over to the mainland at 12.30 and had a last look at all the places I liked - the temple and the gateways and the wall and then went for a walk along the Lagoon road. Walking in China is rather like walking in a vast kitchen garden - every inch of ground is cultivated in endless squares of different crops with no hedges between. The Chinaman is a wonderful gardener and every plant looks as if it received individual attention. On each side of the valley high bare mountains rise. In the fields you see the coolies working with implements such as Adam might have used and with their funny cone like straw hats. In the little yellow villages there are swarms of naked brown children and in front of every cottage are strung heads of Indian corn turning a vivid orange. At one of the temples a service was going on - not very impressive - much beating of gongs and incense burning and a bearded priest doing a sort of dance. Then I went to say goodbye to Lady Lockhart and the Clarkes and then picked up Mr Nicoll (a lieut. in the sloop 'Bluebell') and we joined Mrs Spence and her party and had a picnic tea and then played golf.

Aren't the Admiralty wonderful - having been bribing N.O.'s to leave the service and doing all they could to get rid of them - they are now forbidding any officers in certain branches (submarines for one) to leave at all!

The Island Hotel
29th August 1920 Wei hai wei

You see after all I'm still here - but I think we really go tomorrow at 9pm. The boat is two days late - but thank heavens we didn't start yesterday as there was a typhoon - a howling gale - driving rain and a rough sea - but today it is lovely again - so the sea ought to have calmed down by tomorrow. Even with the prospect of seasickness in front of me I can't help having an excited feeling about starting off on a journey again, it is a never failing joy and I even enjoy the packing! Still I expect six days in a small boat will be more than enough! I'm very glad Mrs Stopford and Mrs Satow are coming too - the more I think of it the more amazed am I that I ever had the courage to set off here alone - though it turned out to be such an easy journey. I'm just longing to see Ian again - I really believe it gets more thrilling to meet him after every time we've been separated. I hope he will have got somewhere for me to live! I hear Mrs Ackworth is going home as soon as she can as they can neither get anywhere to live or afford it - sounds cheerful for us doesn't it? But then of course she has three children and a nurse which complicates things. At the moment she is housed in the Bishop's Palace!

Clothes are a worry out here - one always has to be on at them - airing them and so on and they go so quickly - silk stockings go into countless holes and all my evening dresses have 'gone 'together. The sapphire blue is in rags - but the foundation is good so I will re-cover it in Hong Kong. The silk dress Granny gave me (the dark one) the top has gone - but I think I can remodel it by taking a bit out of the skirt. Everybody else's clothes are in the same plight which is a consolation!

The new bathing dress made out of sailors handkerchiefs is going to be a wild success - most 'Chic'. Little short black silk trousers joined onto a fairly roomy black silk tunic and all bound with black. Mrs Dawson has made one too and yesterday we ran to and fro to each others verandahs clad only in pinned together silk and did gymnastics to see if we had allowed sufficient room.

On Friday we had a very amusing dinner party at the Club - our hosts were Mr Coltart, Mr Jackson and Mr Richardson of the 'Titania' - the females Mrs Satow, a Mrs Mackenzie (from Hankow) and myself. Mr Coltart would make any party a success being of the Mr Barry type - a thorough rattle with a great zest for any form of amusement - rather a knut but at the same time an extraordinarily nice simple soul. He goes every day and makes sand castles with the hotel children on the beach and gives wonderful children's parties in his submarine. There were a lot of people dining at the Club and the whole length of the verandah was occupied. It was a lovely moonlight night and the Club garden with its funny shaped exotic looking trees (I've never discovered their name) and Chinese buildings looked awfully picturesque. I wonder if the ghost of poor Admiral Ting ever walks there.

After dinner we danced - the great excitement was that a very famous American moving picture actress had come over from the mainland where she was staying - she certainly was very good looking.

At about midnight the party broke up as our hosts had chartered a junk and were going twelve miles down the coast to shoot - they took us home and then started from the hotel pier letting off fire crackers as they left!

S.S. Huchow
Swatow S.China

As a pleasure trip I cannot recommend five days off the coast of China at the height of the typhoon season in a small tramp steamer carrying a cargo of saltfish and live fowls in the company of a jokey missionary, a Chinese crew who dope the first mate - a few rats, cockroaches and innumerable flies - add to this we met and dodged three typhoons (but came in for all the aftermath of fearful rough seas) and terrific steamy heat. Who would be a sailor's wife!

To begin at the beginning - last week was a week of alarums and excursions. We were told our ship was to leave at 9pm on Monday - so Monday afternoon I spent hectically packing - in the middle a Commander Jackson from the "Titania" wandered in and asked if he could help me - I prayed he would go - but instead he sat down to chat - in despair I threw coats and etc at him and asked him to do my wraps - he proved most helpful and I sent him out to buy me some labels from the Mission Press and he returned with a dozen beautifully printed labels which gives my baggage a great air of distinction. Whilst still in the throes of packing Miss Duff blew in and sat down and talked for hours and I thought I'd never be finished - or get all my possessions in to my boxes.

However by 8pm everything was packed and ready and locked and we had a farewell dinner with the Hendersons and then sat and awaited our summons. Nothing happened - so at 11.30 we went to bed expecting to be fished out any moment - but no news came until teatime on Tuesday, when a cable announced the boat wouldn't arrive until Thursday - which was rather a blow. We cabled to our husbands and began to partially unpack and having no faith in the ship's ever coming accepted invitations to dinner in the "Titania" on Thursday and to the club on Friday. The Huchow really did appear though on Thursday night - the first we heard of it was at 4 o'clock when we were told to be ready to go over in the ferry in half an hour. I hurled my baggage together again and we set off in a tropical downpour of rain. You never saw a more pathetic trio crouching under inadequate umbrellas and getting soaked - our luggage getting soaked too as <u>nothing</u> keeps out Wei hai rain when it does rain! We were incarcerated in bedrooms at the Mainland Hotel and given dinner while our clothes were dried. A nice way to start off on a week's journey - but it had its comic side too. A Mr Nicoll from the "Bluebell" came to say goodbye to us also the chatty Mrs Spence and being once more clothed in seemly garments we went down and danced! At 11pm we re-embarked in the ferry and went out to the "Huchow" - coming on board we were greeted by the smell of fish which has never since left us. Kind Mrs Clark sent us each a hamper of apples and homemade marmalade. My cabin companion is a soldier's wife a Mrs Davis and our cabin is quite nice and large only unbearably smelly and hot. Friday morning we awoke to heavy seas and found ourselves in the tail of the first typhoon and rushing out to Japan to avoid it - from that moment until Tuesday morning I was prostrate - and during those four days I ate nothing but fruit - never can I bear the sight of grapes again! Mrs Satow and Mrs Stopford were equally bad and for those days and nights we just lay on camp beds on deck in untidy heaps. Whenever we ventured downstairs we were sick and dressing and undressing was impossible. The first day I sick seven times and after that it was much worse because I still felt sick but couldn't be! The only happy person was the baby. I was very sorry for poor Mrs Satow having to look after her as her Amah completely collapsed and lay with a piteous face moaning "No chow today - no chow yesterday - me belong velly bad" and then later informed us "tum tum velly sore-sore"

Oh it was a dreadful journey - it rained most of the time and the sea heaved and the ship smelt and a large rat came and looked at me and the missionary made feeble jokes and talked incessantly (except one day when he was mercifully sick!) and each day seemed as long as a week and the nights even worse - two nights we slept on deck as everything had to be battened down below and the heat would have been impossible. On Tuesday we felt better and early on Wednesday morning we came in here. You enter the harbour through a winding channel between islands covered with huge boulders and we saw any amount of tiny sampans like planks with men standing on them fishing with cormorants (they train the birds to catch the fish).

Satow is a Chinese port - one of the Treaty Ports but there are very few Europeans - and those few live mostly on one of the islands. The Chinese town itself is horribly squalid and unattractive - we went ashore in a body and wandered down narrow streets which were shut in with straw awnings overhead and so very dark - all the shops were open fronted and filled with appalling trash from Birmingham - the people have all shaved heads and are either thin skeletons or else fat and greasy - the children are dirty and yellow and not at all like the delightful Shantung babies - the S. Chinese altogether aren't a patch on the N. Chinese who are really a fine looking race. The chief manufacture of this place is pewter - it is very cheap - but I thought rather nasty - you can also get wonderfully cheap hand embroidery - and a whole bedspread in linen or grass cloth - embroidered beautifully and with fillet lace let in for from 10 to 18$ and teacloths etc. for 3 and 4$ - but so far I've seen none of the lovely coloured old embroideries or lacquer or things one expects to find in China. We went to the English

Club and read American papers - I must say the American posters and advertisements and covers and colour illustrations are awfully good - some frightfully well drawn.

We had tea in the "Hollyhock" (a sloop) they gave us a superb tea in the Captain's cabin - it was the first meal we had enjoyed for nearly a week then we went ashore to the club to play tennis. The tennis court was an asphalt one in the middle of a dripping bamboo grove - the court was like a lake and the balls splashed as they bounced so you can imagine it was rather a ragtime game.

This morning Mrs Stopford and I went ashore together to explore but the smells and the squalor and the beggars so disgusted us that we came back to the ship quickly - especially as we couldn't explore far as Swatow isn't a safe place - foreigners being unpopular and it also being the battleground of the N and S armies and the place overrun with comic opera looking soldiers. This afternoon we sail for Hong Kong arriving about midday tomorrow. Hurrah! Won't it be lovely to see Ian again - I haven't even heard of him for three weeks - and I'm simply longing to be with him again. The next excitement will be to see if he had got anywhere for me to live and where and if our income will be adequate (which I doubt). So I expect my next letter will be announcing the date of my arrival home.

I'll post this letter directly I get to Hong Kong and then write and tell you all about what happens to me there. I'm hoping I shall perhaps find a mail from you.

P.S. I forgot to explain about the first mate and the Chinese crew that I spoke about on the first page. The said first mate was taken frightfully ill - fainting and fever etc. No one knew what it was - when we got here the doctor said he must have been give dope in his food by one of the crew who had a grudge against him. He's recovering now - but it has rather a pirate story sort of touch hasn't it.

Chapter Three Hong Kong 1920

Some letters are missing after Dec. 24th, including the departure of Ruth and Ian for home in the 'BREMEN'. In contrast to the numerous letters sent home on the outward voyage, only one was posted on the homeward voyage at Port Said - since the writer would reach home as quickly as any letters.

Among the missing letters is the confirmation of the 'exciting news' of Dec. 14th. In the letter from Port Said the expected baby is referred to as 'Paul', but in fact Paul turned out to be Eleanor (not I hope too great a disappointment).

St Georges House, Kennedy Rd
12th September Hong Kong

Here I am in Hong Kong and a weeks journey nearer to you which is rather a nice feeling and also means letters won't take so long. I found a lovely pile waiting for me here and many thanks for the hair ribbons - such pretty ones - and as all my own were rotting they were very much appreciated. Well I'd better begin at the beginning and tell you of our arrival. I wrote you rather a hectic letter from Swatow - it was written under difficulties - sitting on deck with much stir and conversation going on around. We were rather depressed as we tried to cable to the Ambrose announcing the time of arrival - but found the line had broken down - so there was no way of getting into communication and we knew they must be expecting us for days - as Amah remarked "Masters all sit makee look sea - missies no come!" We were further delayed by the fact that the cargo wasn't unloaded until after dark so we couldn't sail till daylight as it is a difficult channel. We had rather a dreadful night - as first of all my cabin companion suddenly fainted and it took about half an hour to bring her round (she apparently faints frequently as she has some heart complaint -

but it was rather terrifying) - then in the middle of the night an old lady (one of the eight passengers) nearly choked and we had to send over quickly for the doctor from the "Hollyhock"

We actually got away by 8am and had the one nice day of the whole trip. We were in sight of the coast all the time and kept passing through fleets of picturesque fishing junks with sails of tawny coloured matting. The coast was mountainous and edged with lovely yellow sands - water was very green and the sky was covered with beautiful clouds. We got into Hong Kong at 7am in pouring rain - and we were just sending off a message to the Ambrose when the dockyard motorboat appeared - at first we could only see Mr Stopford - so Mrs Satow and I were filled with disappointment as we knew some boats were away at Mins Bay - however I suddenly saw Ian huddled under a Chinese umbrella - and Mr Satow was there too. It was lovely to see Ian again and to pour forth the woes about my journey and get him to see to the luggage etc. Of course the first question we all asked was "where are we going to live?" Mr Satow had got a two roomed flat at Kowloon - but they couldn't move in for ten days so were going to Kowloon Hotel. Mr Stopford we feel relied on kind friends inviting them to stay - and so when nothing turned up was rather had - so they've had to go to the Peak Hotel which we all hear is very bad and very expensive. Ian I think has been quite clever - as this is really awfully nice and absolutely ideal as regards situation. It is at the first station up the Peak tramway - so well above the town and very airy and yet not in the fogs. We overlook the Naval dockyard - so it is only a 10 minute walk for Ian - and we are right on the tram which will be most convenient for dining out etc. on the Peak. The town itself is only 5 mins walk away and about 10 mins or less to the Kowloon Ferry. We've got one of the nicest rooms on the second floor with a very fine view over the harbour on one side and the side of the Peak on the other. The room itself is big and like all rooms out here sparsely furnished just bed -

cupboard - dressing table and chair. On one side it has two big windows opening onto a balcony - and on another side two more windows onto a covered in verandah which is our sitting room and is furnished with two armchairs - a table and a nice big writing table. We have also our own bathroom - where the washing stand lives and a rail for hanging clothes on a proper long bath (not a Soochow tub like the one we had in the garden!) I had hoped the sanitary arrangements would have been less primitive here - but apparently there is no drainage anywhere in the East. Anyway we've got electric light. It all looks very clean and the boys are attentive and the food good (except very dull teas - but that's the same in every hotel except the Island Hotel where we used to have strawberry jam and scones and iced cake - and are consequently spoilt!) The only snag really is the other people look rather awful - American missionaries and tourists etc. but after all you don't mix with them and besides I think more naval people are trying to get rooms here - the Greggs for one - which would be nice. We pay eight dollars a day for two of us - which is as cheap as anything to be had in Hong Kong - at least anything nice - we could have had a back room without a verandah for 7$ but Ian thought it wasn't good enough and we can just manage all right paying 8$ leaving us a small margin for clubs and expeditions etc. (the margin is the reserve fund of 300$ which Ian saved and which we spreading over the next seven months - and we've still got a further reserve of English money (about £200) which we don't want to use as with the present exchange it would be so much better to have in England. So I really think we are very lucky after all the tales we had heard concerning the difficulties of accommodation etc. It was a great pull coming down early as later on there really won't be any rooms to be had and you can't look ahead.

We came up here in chairs - a horrible mode of conveyance - which nearly brought on seasickness again! You sit in a sort of sedan chair with a canopy over it and the coolies lift the supports on to their shoulders and you go jolty-jolt up the steep hill at an angle of 45°. Ian had the whole day off - so we unpacked and talked and made plans and read letters and ate chocolate biscuits which he had brought me as a present - shifted furniture round and were pleased to be together as if we'd been separated for months! Meantime the rain was coming down in torrents - like water out of a tap - after tea it stopped for a little so we wandered down and looked at Uncle John Dent's fountain - which he presented to the city - rather a dreadful piece of masonry with steps and four stodgy lions. We flattened our noses against the enchanting Chinese shops and I yearned to be a millionaire - but not as much as you would have! Heavenly embroideries - crepe de chines of every colour - strings of jade - ivory - china - mandarin coats etc. etc. but all in grand shops - but I believe you can get the same things in Canton pawn shops and Captain Johnstone is going to take me to a low haunt called Cat Street where treasures are to be found. We returned by the Bund and I was very fascinated by all the life around.

Today Ian has a "day on" alas, and the night as well, but I'm going to tea in the Ambrose. It is still deluging - which is most annoying - as the rainy season ought to have been over last month. Our pillows smell vile - which really is a trial - musty feathers have such a nasty smell and there is nothing to do about it. All our clothes will grow mushrooms too and all the georgette things will rot. The tin lined boxes are a blessing. However the rain can't last much longer and the next four months I believe the weather is heavenly. It isn't so very hot just now - only sticky. I've been "settling in" all morning and I've really got our little verandah to look awfully nice with our Chinese bowls and Japanese prints and my chintz work bag and books etc. It is quite good fun and Ian always applauds my efforts enthusiastically! Which is encouraging.

I'm sure I shall be awfully happy though it won't be as free and easy as dear Wei hai wei - but it is very beautiful and I love the semi tropicalness of it and there will be heaps to explore - and there are a lot of nice people to get to know and I imagine one will have more than enough of social gaieties. We have joined the naval battery club, a great institution - they run a launch to Repulse Bay (round the other side of the island) every afternoon, and you bathe there and have a picnic and play water polo etc and come back in the evening. I expect we shall go whenever Ian can get off early enough. We have also joined the U.S.R.C which has tennis courts and dances. On Tuesday the Acworths have asked us to a bathing picnic. I'm longing to meet her - every single person says the same, how charming she is. He is not so popular - as he is a great cadger. I suppose we shall have to go and write our names at Government House and the Commodore's soon and Ian is going to take me to see various people who were kind to him last winter. Apparently "L7" is to be in dock for about six months re-fitting - but not a leisurely re-fit like at Camell Lairds as here the crew have to do most of the work so Ian will be very busy - but the great thing is he will be stationary, and so Singapore is off indefinitely.

I shall have to be busy now re-modelling my clothes. I'm really getting rather good at it. The blue dress I made out of the old skirt and jumper is quite a success - while the bathing dress made from sailors handkerchiefs is a wild success - and Ian is very impressed. It is very decent but at the same time most chic and awfully comfortable to swim in and the silk doesn't cling in the water and dries in two minutes. I'm longing for the parcel to turn up so as to make the hat and dress etc.

I have just returned from the Dockyard and tea with Ian in the Ambrose. It's a small dockyard - just a basin and one big dry dock. The "Tamar" lives there - a regular Noah's Ark of a ship - it is the Depot. The rain had stopped when I returned and I saw the top of the Peak which had actually emerged - but now the rain is at it again harder than ever. The coolies here wear the most extraordinary rain coats made of bamboo leaves, so you see trotting along a sort of bundle of dead yellow leaves crowned with an enormous hat and a pair of bare legs below (note the development of the calf - due to the constant hill climbing).

These sort of things never fail to enchant me. I think Hong Kong is going to be very fascinating - but it isn't really China - but it is interesting as being a miniature British Colony. Shanghai is a wonderful cosmopolitan city and Swatow is the horrible result of Chinese semi-Europeanised Republicanism (what a sentence). Wei hai wei island is an example of Naval administration - the mainland is primitive peasant China - almost unspoilt and therefore very pleasant - but for the remains of Imperial gorgeous China - I fancy from what I've read and heard Pekin is the only place where you get it. For the real real East and the tropics I haven't seen a place to hold a candle to Penang and I long to see more of it - Colombo too - only that's more sophisticated and you don't get the Chinese element which seems somehow more picturesque in the F.M.S[a] than it is in China itself.

I've just had dinner - tomato soup - roast chicken and ham and a delicious salad made of pineapple, banana and pomola with mayonnaise sauce - ice cream and sponge fingers and coffee - very good don't you think?

St Georges, Kennedy Road
17th September 1920 Hong Kong

A mail yesterday with two letters from you and various papers. I'm glad my letters are turning up regularly - I always write twice a week. It is funny - my past letters about Wei hai wei must have read as if I was disappointed in the place - and yet it did grow on me so - so that in the end I thought it an enchanting place. I'm glad you got 'The Lion and Dragon' it is rather fascinating isn't it? and gives you the best possible idea of the place. I was interested in the 'Studio' with the account of the 'Edinburgh Group' - so kind of Cloggie to send it. I love hearing about Ormsby and N. Berwick etc. and wish I was with you - but almost more do I wish you were here.

I'm awfully smitten with Hong Kong and as usual we have fallen on our feet - because these are really delightful rooms - and a very nice manageress. She confided to me that she thought my husband was quite charming and he had been so nice when he came to look at the rooms 'Not demanding this and that and then making a fuss over the price like some gentlemen do' and so she added 'I thought I'd just do my best for him' and she certainly has. You see St Georges is four different houses and the rooms in this house are the cheapest because you have to go to one of the other buildings for your meals - a walk of about 100 yards - not much of a snag

---

[a] Federated Malay States - now Malaysia.

really. Well in this building there are five rooms and three bathrooms and each room is 180$ a month - so the manageress gave us the big room and the bathroom all to ourselves and ours is the only room with a closed in verandah - while the Fleet Surgeon in the 'Carlisle' who came about rooms at the same time as Ian and made a fuss about things - has been given the smaller room and has to share a bathroom - and Mr Hastie Smith (the Engineer Lieut. in the 'Alacrity' and my special bête noir) apparently wrote a high handed letter which the proprietor took exception to so he's been told they haven't any rooms at all. Really Ian's gift of winning the hearts of landladies is very useful and he does it so unconsciously! The hotel keepers here are absolutely unscrupulous - to tourists and Americans they charge exorbitant sums - (hence the tale of the high prices here) but on the whole they are very good to service people and if they like you especially so. For instance the manageress here pointed out to me that it was stupid Ian paying a fixed rate of 2$ a day - it would be so much cheaper if he just signed for his meals and then - she added it would be clear gain whenever you were asked out! She also asked me to choose new matting for our verandah and has produced a big table for me to paint or dressmake on - so we are awfully comfortable - and the food is very good, everything very clean. The only thing that is very bad is the laundry - but later I hope to shares in a wash Amah with someone - Mrs Stopford if she comes here - or perhaps Mrs Gregg who arrives next month.

One thing that is attractive in all the houses round here is that all the flat roofs and the edges of verandahs are covered with glazed green pots with lovely plants in them. I don't know the name of one - but they are awfully gay. Along the tramway line there are bushes of poinsettias and heavenly blue flower, one of the few blue flowers I've seen which is a true blue and not mauve. On Monday the rain stopped and it has been lovely weather ever since - but hot, hot. It is a terribly relaxing place and one gets very footsore walking on unaccustomed pavements. Ian and I are generally so exhausted that we go to bed soon after dinner.

On Monday morning Mrs Stopford and Mrs Barker came to see me and we all went shopping together - in the evening Ian and I explored together in the main streets where I was seeking a tube of Cerulean blue (which I can't get here - you might send me one ½ tube Windsor and Newtons). We drifted into a wonderful shop 'Wing's On' a sort of Chinese Harrods.

Tuesday morning I went up in the Peak Tram (how you would hate it!) to the Hotel and picked up Mrs Stopford and together we went to see Mrs Davis who lives in the top house but one on the Peak. At 2 o'clock we all foregathered at the jetty where we started for a bathing picnic in a launch. I met the Acworths for the first time. She is very sweet and gentle and I feel, a little overpowered by her husband who is a man of appalling energy and full of bounce, and chivvies and hurries his wife around. Don't you think it was noble of her - she came out here with three children 2nd class in an Italian ship, with no other English passengers - and she was hung up for a month at Port Said where she lived at the Y.W.C.A.

Friday afternoon

To continue about the picnic. Our destination was a place called Island Bay and it took about 1½ hours to get there as the launch was slow. It was hot and sleepy sitting on the little deck - the party consisted of the Acworths, Satows, Stopfords, Barkers, some stray men, ourselves and Lady Stubbs the governor's wife - so nice and friendly. When we got near the bay we went down to the saloon and undressed and then swam ashore, it was an ideal place - a little cove of sparkling white sand surrounded by rocks and hills - at one side a stream ran into the sea - a stream like you would find in the West Highlands - with pools and rocks and waterfalls - but the water was warm - so Ian and I paddled up it - swimming the deep pools and sitting under the waterfalls and scrambling over the sun baked rocks. The stream was bordered by thickets of bamboo and tree pines with lovely orange pineapples on them - and banana trees (which are the ones I like best of all) and all sorts of funny little flowers and overhead the blue sky - and the sea was equally blue and dotted with little islands and yellow sailed junks. We all met for tea - provided by the 'Tamar' who have a special and most delectable brand of iced lemon cake. After tea we explored and found a little Chinese village - very dirty. Up one of the hills were a group of Chinamen - who suddenly became very excited and one blew on a conch shell - a most barbaric noise. Whereupon the entire population of the village came rushing out with fishing nets and tumbled into junks and sampans - the watchers on the hill having sighted a shoal of fish.

We got home about 8pm. The harbour looked too lovely at night - and I'm going to try and do a woodblock of it. The black mass of the Peak against a deep green sky - the blazing lights from the Chinese restaurants and stores getting thinner as they go upwards until they just end in loops of lights that mark the different roads. It was extra beautiful the other night by reason of a somewhat theatrical sickle moon.

Wednesday Ian and I worked off writing our names at Government House and the Commodore's and then explored the slums - which I adore and Ian really enjoys though he rather holds his nose in the air. The side streets which climb up the mountain side are rather attractive all hung with signs - one street we walked though was devoted entirely to the manufacture of paper goods - every little open shop was filled with kites and lanthorns etc. Some of the lanthorns were made like orange fish - rather nice. The people are dull - all dressed in brown or white or shiny black - not the cheerful patterns and colours of the north - they are also yellow and less good looking and none of them have pigtails.

The only picturesque thing there is their huge hats. We were pretty weary and footsore when we got home.

Yesterday Ian was inoculated and so couldn't do anything very active. We went to the Hong Kong Hotel and ate ices and watched the rank and fashion. You never saw such a collection of 'funnies'. American Jews, Chinese taipangs, half castes, French Naval officers, Bengali merchants, besides the celebrities of Hong Kong society. It was most entertaining to watch and such good ices! Then we walked along the docks: more than half the native population live there in little junks and sampans - families of twelve in one small boat!

St Georges, Kennedy Road
20th September 1920 Hong Kong

A mail yesterday with a letter from you and a Saturday Westminster - my opinion of Ian's intellect always goes up when I find he understands their competitions, which is more than I ever do - he was sadly disappointed to find he couldn't enter for the poem entitled 'The Quillet' the closing date being about a month ago! I like reading the reviews of books - you never see a new book out here - but I'm reading a very attractive novel just now called 'Thorley Weir' by E.F.Benson. Miss Duff lent it to me.

What joy and excitement coming home will be - I hope I shan't be sadly wearisome and a talk a lot beginning sentences 'when I was in China'.

I think I ended my last letter just before we set off for Government House - or rather the summer place Mountain Lodge. We went up in the train and then it was quite a climb beyond that as the house is on the very tip top of the Peak with a wonderful view. We had several sets of tennis - but I found the grass courts very slow after the hard ones at Wei hai wei. Lady Stubbs is very charming.

On Sunday we went in the 'Tamar's' launch round to Repulse Bay - which takes about 1¼ hours but quite an amusing journey -

first of all through the harbour and then through the countless little islands and past Aberdeen, a funny little fishing village with a harbour crowded with every sort of junk including some comic armed junks - the armament being extraordinary old cannons - like the ones in Nelson's 'Victory' or even older - while the 'armour' is bits of old boiler plating nailed casually on. Repulse Bay itself wasn't attractive - it has a lovely beach but covered with an absolute town of mat sheds and very crowded - and at the back there is a new hotel which has just been opened and is thronged with Yankees. We undressed in the naval mat shed and had a lovely bathe in the clear warm water - then we went up to the hotel for tea where we met the Stopfords. It was rather amusing watching the 'Funnies' and funny they were too. I felt rather as if I was in a cinema film sitting on the white meretricious verandah surrounded by flashy Americans and looking out onto semi-tropical scenery. We were rooked off 2$ for tea, an awful swindle as in Hong Kong it is 60 cents! It was dark when we got back and I always love seeing the harbour lit up - we came past the Chinese restaurants which are one blaze of light. Then we did a swift change and hurried along to the Bishop's House to dine with the Acworths.

On Monday we went for a lovely walk up the Peak - but very tiring as the roads are all asphalt - but they go along under groves of palms and bamboos and flowering shrubs and all the time you get the magnificent view over the harbour. Yesterday Ian played Rugger of all games in this climate (84° in the shade). But a French battleship came in and challenged them and Ian is one of the few in Ambrose who play.

So we went out to Happy Valley in rickshaws and I sat and watched with Mr Dolphin and Mr Gregg. It was a ragtime game - but Ian scored a 'try' and the Frenchmen were defeated.

Happy Valley is a priceless place - it is a racecourse with a golf course round the edge and tennis, cricket and football grounds in the middle - frightfully dangerous - as the golfers drive straight through the cricket matches! Ian refuses to play golf there! Ian came home for dinner - but had to go back on board for the night as he was charging his battery and his sub is in hospital.

In the mornings I often go out and prowl round - and the streets never cease to fascinate me - the huge Sikh policemen with coloured turbans - the coolies and coolie women (it is difficult to tell t'other from which as they wear the same clothes and do the same work). They carry the babies strapped on to their backs. Then you see fat old Chinamen carried in chairs fanning themselves and the shops are a constant amusement - Indian shops and Jap shops and Chinese shops and stalls and pedlars. Hundreds of 'poky' shops in side streets - but I think most of them sell rubbish to catch the tourist. One thing I have seen though is lovely mandarin petticoats like the Manchu ladies wear. They fit awfully well and with a plain black charmeuse top would make a most fascinating sort of every-evening dress I think. They are very cheap too - from any peddler on in any of the silk stores you can get them for from five to twelve dollars - a really nice one for 30/- even at present exchange. They are all ones that have been worn - but are cleaned and in good condition and on beautiful silk and the embroidery is very lovely - even though it isn't valuable. The skirts are made with a straight panel back and front and kilted at the sides and with strips of black down from top to hem - the embroidery is all at the foot and the top is gathered into a coarse linen waistband. They 'hang' very well and are just the right length. You can get any colour - lovely kingfisher blue, apple green, deep pink, pinky mauve, rather a mustard yellow, scarlet etc. If you hear anyone who would like one do let me know. It seems such a waste not to get things while one is out here - and I can't afford to get more than one for myself - and if possible one for Muriel - but I should love to buy others for the fun of buying them and sell them when I get home at cost price.

St Georges
2nd October 1920 Hong Kong

I got a letter from you addressed here on Thursday. It came as a great joy for though I knew the mail was in (they always fire a gun as the mail ship comes in to the harbour) but as Ian had a day on I thought I wouldn't get anything till the following day. I had spent the day with the Acworths and was going sadly into a solitary dinner - so you can imagine how thrilled I was to find a fat letter from you waiting for me.

A great excitement - the parcel has turned up at last - and many thanks for getting the things. Ian's socks are superb - a perfect fit and so 'sumpshous' looking. He is very pleased with them.

I've already made a really lovely hat - I began it the day the parcel arrived. Ian and I spent the whole of Wednesday evening making the wire shape - Ian displaying surprisingly nimble fingers - Friday I worked at it all day and had it finished just before Ian got back at 4 o'clock and wore it when we went down to have tea with Mr Stock at the Hong Kong Hotel. It is a great success - rather like the one we got at Humphries - only really I think prettier. It is short at the back and widest at the sides with a gathered little brim and a little straight edge which hangs down - and I've threaded some oxidized silver thread through - the crown is draped satin (kind Mamma to give me her best petticoat!) and a very gay little bunch of flowers with bright green leaves - some of the flowers I had - and some I made. It was fun doing it and I've enough stuff over to make another.

All the things arrived in wonderfully good condition except the yellow rose which was quite squashed like a Chinese duck. Thank you awfully for getting them all.

On Wednesday Mr Satow (the 'Bird') worked a most successful surprise. Mrs Satow was coming over from Kowloon to do shopping and was coming to see me at about 11 am - not having seen these rooms yet. Well at about 10.30 Mr Satow rang me up from the dockyard and told me to lure his wife into the Hong Kong Hotel at 12 - but not to let her suspect he would be there,

Accordingly after Mrs Satow had been here for some time I said casually I'd accompany her down to the ferry and we'd look in at the H.K.Hotel to see if we could find some address she wanted - so quite unsuspectingly she walked in - and now my part of the surprise comes in for not only was the Bird sitting in the lounge but Ian too! And it was a surprise for Ian as well because Mr Satow had just said casually to him - 'Come and have a cocktail with me' and didn't know it was a pre-arranged foregathering - so it all came off beautifully. They had also collected a rather nice Captain Oliver (husband of the famous Mrs Oliver) and we sat and watched the gay world and ate ices and the men had eggy cocktails. At 12.30 like Cinderellas Ian and Mr Satow sped back to the Yard and Mrs Satow and I went off in the opposite direction. It <u>was</u> fun seeing Ian in working hours unexpectedly - and he did look so nice in a starchily clean suit of whites and his most becoming service topee (his plain clothes topee is anything but becoming being just like an inverted soup plate!)

Thursday I lunched with the Acworths and we went a picnic with the children to Stonecutters Island - going in the R.A.S.C launch and picking up a very pleasant Major and Mrs Greenaway. We had a lovely bathe and a huge tea and got back at about 6.30.

Today we are going for a picnic to Stonecutters again - I feel rather guilty as the organ from the cathedral is plainly audible - but it really is much too hot for Church at midday. I went last Sunday to the Early Service. The cathedral is of the strictly conventional pattern and might be in any midland town except for the waving punkahs. Yesterday morning I went to the Club - really it is a Womens' Institute - started for nurses and governesses and so on - but now embraces a much wider circle. It has quite a good library, also a big cool room where you can read all the English and some

American magazines. I was very happy with a whole bunch of 'Studios'. They also have classes there and Mrs Acworth and I are contemplating joining French and cooking classes - we feel life isn't long enough for 'colloquial Chinese'.

The other evening Ian and I wandered round trying to find Cat Street - this is the place in the Chinese Quarter where all the stolen goods are sold (a sort of Caledonian market). We couldn't find it - and we rather think now it only exists (the booth part of it) just before Chinese New Year when wonderful bargains are to be had. It was dark when we came home and so lovely - there was a sort of deep blue mist overhead - and below the narrow sign hung streets and stalls lit up by lanthorns. The people are sadly dull here - all exactly alike dressed in black - blue or white and no nice pigtailed mandarins or painted lovely ladies like you see in Singapore or occasionally at Wei Hai. But the streets are endlessly fascinating and so are the flowers and shrubs and butterflies and palms.

We haven't met many people yet - various taipangs have called and we have duly shot our cards into their little letter boxes - but so far haven't met but I believe when the 'season' begins they bid you to dinner and dances and other festivities. Ian and I are always really happiest on our own and with the other ship's people. Ian is awfully sweet the way he is perfectly happy spending a whole afternoon smoking his pipe while I paint or sew and with a heart entirely at leisure from itself not only to soothe and sympathise, but also to do dull things like lettering on posters or attach hat wires or anything - and he is equally ready for any expedition or ploy or prowl in Chinese back streets. I don't expect I shall have as much of him later on when the Rugger, Hockey and Cricket begin in earnest - as he is in the first team of all of them - but it amuses me watching. Also we shall have a lot of tennis directly we're made members of the club which ought to be soon as our names have been proposed and seconded.

We had a great 'flap' a few days ago about a typhoon. The warning signals were hoisted and all the junks hurried along to a safe anchorage. The submarines were anchored off - and everyone stood by. Ian hoped it would come as he wants to see one - but everyone else was relieved when it turned off in another direction.

St Georges Hotel
7th October 1920 Hong Kong

We had a perfectly glorious day on Sunday. It was one of those clear radiant days when 'the hills shouted for joy' and the sea and sky were both deep blue and only just the tiniest little cool breeze.

Directly after lunch we went off in one of the duty boats to Stonecutters Island which took about 30 minutes - we landed on the South pier and proceeded to walk over the hill to the Naval wireless station on the other side - first of all we took the wrong path which only led us to a battery - but it was such a lovely path that we didn't mind the detour - we soon got onto the right road and you can't think how attractive it was - running partly under scrubby pine trees with the gorgeous hot smell of pineneedles - and past all sorts of beautiful shrubs and flowers - at one place there was a smell just like a greenhouse - which we found came from a little purple climber that was covering all the bushes - a little further on a large bright blue bird with a red head flew out and everywhere there were marvellous butterflies as big as small birds and every colour of the rainbow.

By this time we'd got up a fine heat - in fact we were as wet as if we'd been out in pouring rain - so we swiftly undressed in the wireless station and plunged into the sea - which was ecstasy! Near the shore the water was quite hot like a bath - but it got colder if you swam out a bit. We disported ourselves for an hour or so and then dressed and had tea among some extraordinary shaped rocks - which gives the island its name - and returned by the six o'clock boat - Sunday dinner with asparagus mayonnaise and ice cream made a very nice ending!

Monday we went to return a call on the Peak (so silly you just drop cards into a box and never see the people!) and walked down a Magazine Gap - a less arduous path than the one we did last time. Tuesday Ian played in a hockey match - Ambrose v. Wilts:Regt: I went over and had tea with the Satows and Mrs Satow and I went and watched - unfortunately it rained. The Ambrose was beaten by one goal - it must have been warm work playing with the temperature 80° in the shade!

Yesterday Ian had a 'day on' and it was a beastly muggy wet day - Mrs Acworth came to visit me early in the morning and asked me to tea - just as she left Mrs Stopford arrived and we went out shopping together. I had tea with the Acworths and we tried to draw one of the streets afterwards, but even with Captain Acworth to keep the crowd off we couldn't stand it for long. Then we went on the Cat Street - an extraordinary place right in the Chinese town - you can buy anything there from jade necklaces to second hand boots! Most of the shops are just stalls in the street - and it is a great place for buying watches or fountain pens or pen knives - as you get very good almost new ones (that have been stolen!) for very little. The actual Chinese things - embroideries - china etc. were very expensive - the time to buy being just before the Chinese New Year - when all the Chinamen have to settle their debts and so sell off all their stocks cheap. Its rather funny - a thing I haven't seen yet here is lacquer - apparently nearly all the lacquer comes from Japan. This will be the last chance of getting mandarin embroideries as since the Revolution they have been forbidden to be made - so they will become rarer and rarer.

It is still pouring with rain which will do in our picnic this afternoon but I hope we shall be able to go to the 'Tamar's' concert this evening - tomorrow is the 'Tamar's' dance.

Our little wash Amah is a great success - she washes beautifully and fetches things on Sunday evening and brings them back on Wednesday morning. It is a joy to have unlimited washing in this climate.

I've been trying to paint a picture of the little temple at Wei Hai treating it decoratively - but it hasn't been very successful - I've got stuck into such a groove - and though this part of the world ought to be so paintable and I see it all as I want to paint it and yet can't get it out - I get very depressed. The only thing which cheered me was the poster I did which really was a success.

The latest 'buzz' is that the boats are to be paid off in Jan: and that the crews are to be sent home in the 'Ambrose' who will bring out the reliefs - wives are to be given passages in the Ambrose. What fun! The only thing is the rumour has been traced to its source which is as follows:- A sick bay steward in the Ambrose heard from a sick bay steward in the 'Hawkins' who heard it from the Captain's steward that the 'Ambrose' was to be paid off in Jan. All the rest of the detail has been collected en route - Ian heard it in its present form from a Mr Leathes (No 1 of Ls) who heard it from someone else who heard it from the sick bay steward. So I don't put much faith in it!

St Georges
11th October 1920 Hong Kong

The next excitement is how to come home - we should try for Glen Line if we come together and I should anyway and you could meet me at Genoa! I don't want to come Blue Funnel as they whisk you home in 31 days - scarcely stopping anywhere - which is poor fun - P.O. is too expensive unless you go 2nd class which I'd only do I think if we made up a party.

If Ian is allowed to find his own way home there are endless possibilities from here to Calcutta by tramp steamer - stay with

Uncle Pugh and across India by rail (the insuperable snag of this plan is getting a passage from Bombay). Then we could go via Japan - Honolulu - San Francisco and New York (more expensive but being with Ian one could go partly second class) However with luggage and one thing and another we shall probably return unenterprisingly via Suez and do America next time. 'Once a China bird always a China bird'.

I'm suffering from a plague of ants - large horrible beasts that run over everything and this letter is constantly being interrupted by slaughterings - we also have cockers and mosquitoes - but nothing as bad as the Acworths - who caught forty-two fleas in two days in the Bishop's House (speaks ill for the late bishops!)

I had a lovely birthday - the weather was quite cleared up and it was a gorgeous day. Ian just had to go down to take Divisions - but got off at 11.30 and I met him at the Hong Kong Hotel where we ate ices to celebrate the occasion. After tiffin we went in one of the duty boats to our enchanted Island - getting there about 3.45. We wandered about and it was looking lovelier than ever - and the warm sweet smells more than compensated for the smell of mould which is one of the characteristics of this place! After we had explored for a bit and got up a really fine heat we undressed and plunged into the water and swam about and lay on the hot sands and thoroughly enjoyed ourselves. At 5.30 we went along to an old disused quarry and had tea - it was rather a fascinating place, all the trees covered with creepers and everywhere heavy hanging foliage through which you got glimpses of the sea and the mainland mountains beyond. Everything was quite still and made me think of the line.

'The stillness hangs so heavy
That you're half afraid to speak'

Stonecutters island is famous for its butterflies and I've never seen anything so lovely - one came and showed off in front of us -

a big black one with white markings and a canary coloured tail - but the big blue ones are the loveliest of all.

We got home about 7 - dressed and got into the Peak tram - I always rather heave a sigh of thankfulness when I get to the top and think 'Well we arrived safe this time anyway' (I feel you'd never go in the tram at all!) We dined with a Mr and Mrs Parr a kind middle aged couple - he is head of the P and O here and they have a lovely house on top of the Peak.

We had a proper Melly dinner and really enjoyed our evening very much and it was lovely walking down to the tram station - up on the mountain tops with the stars overhead and away far below the twinkling lights of the harbour. The said harbour is an endless source of joy to Ian and me and is one of the pleasures of going to Stonecutters - because you go right through it. It is great fun recognising the different ships. P and O's, N.Y.K's, Blue Funnel, 'Messagerie' - then the Pacific boats 'Empress' 'Admiral' 'Doolar' and all the other lines and I'm becoming quite a connoisseur under Ian's tuition! Then of course there are always hundreds of junks and sampans - and then Japanese warships - and American and French. One noticeable thing about the harbour is that there are no seagulls - because no seagull can pick up a living in China - as the Chinese throw nothing away - and half the sampans live solely on the refuse from the liners that come in - they even dredge round ships for lumps of coal. The same principle is carried out in this hotel - if we have asparagus for dinner one night - next night asparagus soup - which we feel is made from the end one leaves - a nasty thought - but as Ian philosophically remarks 'Its very good all the same!'

On Saturday we played tennis at the club all afternoon and had very good games. Friday was wet and we went down to the Chinese town to see if there were any celebrations on it being Confucius's birthday - but except for the decorated streets there didn't seem much excitement and the decorations were tawdry beyond words. In the evening we went to a delightful dance in the 'Tamar'. I wore my green dress for which I had made some new and rather attractive flowers - and now that I've removed the worst bits it doesn't look tarnished by nightlight. Dances out here are very spoiling - your programme is filled directly you arrive and you more or less can pick and choose your partners. Ian and I danced about half together and the rest with other people from the Ambrose and L2 and 'Carlisle'. I was introduced to some of the soldiers but too late. It was entirely a service dance so I didn't see many of the Hong Kong celebrities except Mrs Oliver who is very striking looking and had on a lovely dress of black tulle and silver tissue but what Ian called 'alarmingly low' - you would have looked the other way I think! - for I've never seen anything so scanty before.

The rest of the females were more than respectable - in fact mostly dowdy and all sorts of funny old ladies in white net dresses were merrily footing it. The 'Tamar' has a beautiful teak deck and the sides are all open so a breeze came in devastating to the coiffure but very pleasant as dancing was hot work. I hope Ian will be Commodore one day as the 'Tamar' would be a splendid place to live in!

On Thursday we went to a Ship's Company concert in the 'Tamar' - a wonderfully good one. We sat next to the Acworths and a charming Captain and Mrs Grey (gunner) I took a great fancy to her, but unfortunately they are just going home.

We went to look at my poster which is framed in black and hung up at the Peak tram station - it really looks rather nice.

Ian is going to give me a mandarin skirt for my birthday - we've seen a lovely jade green brocade one - but we think we'll wait until we've been to Canton as everyone says they are better there - so in the meantime he gave me chocolates and silk stockings.

In the Admiralty Weekly Orders they gave notice of what clasps are to be issued for the general service medal - Ian we think will have nine! One for each year in the North Sea (4) one year in the Mediterranean (1) one for Jutland - one for Falklands Islands one for Dardanelles and one for serving in submarines - this last Ian thinks is the one most worth having.[8] Ian also expects shortly to get his prize money - about £50 - quite nice.

Ian is playing Rugger today - poor dear though the temperature has dropped to just below 80.

St Georges
15th October 1920   Hong Kong

Wednesday was a lovely day and at 2.30 Ian and I, the Acworths, Stopfords, Mrs and Miss Gurner, Mr O'Callaghan and Mr Greig all went off in the 'Dayspring' (a launch belonging to the Missions to Seamen) to Island Bay. Getting ashore there was most thrilling - as there was quite a surf and we landed in a tiny dinghy. The first trip it capsized altogether - and Mr Greig lost his topee - we all got pretty wet before we'd finished. I'm rather putting the cart before the horse - because the first time we landed we swam ashore and spent the afternoon exploring up the stream - you can imagine how nice it was paddling through the shallows swimming the pools and sitting under waterfalls or sunning on the rocks. Sometimes the tree ferns and banana trees met over one head and made lovely green tunnels and the water was so warm. Ian and I took photographs of each other with suitable tropical background. I hope they'll come out well and I'll send them to you. Then we swam back to the launch and dressed and going ashore for tea was when we got wet. We ate a colossal tea of Macoa bun and the 'Tamar's' celebrated lemon cake and then re-embarked getting even wetter than coming. Miss Gurner and I went off together and a huge wave completely swamped us - so that for the journey back I had to sit in a petticoat and Ian's sweater and Miss Gurner was lightly clad in some bath towels and her Mother's coat. Still it was a most delightful picnic and a lovely trip home with a sunset and Venus looking about the size of a large lamp. We arrived home about 8pm.

In the afternoon Ian and I and an unattractive youth called Hargreaves (new spare third hand) went over to play tennis with the Satows at Kowloon and had splendid games - Ian and I against Mrs Satow and Mr Hargreaves - the first set we played out and it ended by their defeating us by twelve games to our ten - the second set we soundly defeated them - the evening we spent looking up quotations having borrowed the 'Birds' Oxford book of English Verse. Ian read aloud to me - and for once we managed to stick to the older poets and not hurry back to Kipling and Masefield and the Moderns - but we came to the conclusion we do like them best - there was nothing that gave us the same pleasure as 'Tewksbury Road' or 'Cargoes' or lines like

    'Can you e'er forget
    The scent of hawthorn in the sun
    or bracken in the wet'

or   'To meet gold dust sunset

Down the owl light in the lane' (do you know where that comes from?) Also I bet you don't know where that quotation comes from

    'Youth at the prow and pleasure at the helm'

We came upon it quite by chance and were amazed to find it where it was.

Don't you think this is rather a nice epitaph - I can't remember whether it was on Hawkins or Drake -

    'The waters were his winding sheet
    The sun became his tomb
    But for his fame, the ocean wide
    Was not sufficient room'

Ian shares your affection for Grey's Elegy and knows most of it by heart - but I've never been able to overcome an early prejudice against it.

Two most tragic and upsetting things have happened in the 'Ambrose'. First Mr MacArthur (captain of L1) was sent to hospital about three weeks ago and they found that he was very bad with consumption[9] - so bad that he's been invalided right out of the Navy and sent home - the very day he left (Monday) Ian's captain Mr Peyton Ward was sent to hospital and they find he's consumptive too - but with him they hope they've caught it in time - his lungs aren't badly affected and he may be able to remain in the Service - but of course is finished for submarines which is very sad as he was frightfully keen and one of the best captains we've got (L7 was top in everything this summer). Ian is very sad about it as he as he and Mr Peyton Ward were great friends - I liked what I saw of him which wasn't much as he was a woman hater. It makes one wonder rather if submarines isn't a very unhealthy life - but Ian says it is only so in wartime - in peace time you live in them so little. Mr MacArthur and Mr Peyton Ward had been in submarines most of the war.

It has really begun to get cooler which is a relief - last night for the first time we slept with a coverlet. For two nights we were sadly afflicted by an invasion of millions of bamboo bugs - little green insects who came in such swarms that we had to take refuge by sitting under the mosquito net - but the dry weather seems to have killed them all.

St Georges
19th October 1920 Hong Kong

Wasn't it annoying - the mail we expected on Saturday never turned up - as it had been put into the wrong ship and gone to Manila; and won't be here until Wednesday. Papers turned up all right and parcels and I got the 'Rescue' for which thank you very, very much. Ian and I have both begun reading it and we both like it awfully and I think the cover design is rather clever don't you? I've never read any of Conrad's and I expect I shall like his books all the more for having seen the sorts of places he writes about. New books are a great joy here and are lent all round.

On Friday Ian played Rugger and I went and sat with the Acworths and watched. It was a most thrilling game though the 'Ambrose' was just beaten. The papers next day gave a long account of it and in all of them Ian was singled out as one of the most promising of the 'Ambrose' team - on the strength of which he nearly decided to go into training.

On Saturday we played tennis all afternoon. We are going in together for the mixed doubles of a tournament so we are practising as much as we can. After dinner some people the Hunts who live here (he is P.M.O of the 'Carlisle') asked us to motor out to Repulse Bay with them to a dance. It was a lovely run in an open car of about 10 to 15 miles - first of all along the upper road above the town which used to be the residential part before the Peak houses were built - but it is inhabited now by rich Chinese and several streets are entirely Portuguese - leaving the town behind we turned off inland along a road bordered by tropical trees - it is a fine road - wide and beautiful surface and we travelled at an absolutely hair raising speed - the last part being down a steep hill round corkscrew corners which took us into Aberdeen and in sight of the sea again - the moon was just setting and the islands were silhouetted black against the sky and reflected inkily in the still water dotted with junk lights - the rest of our journey lay along the coast and presently we came in sight of the brilliantly lit Repulse Bay Hotel which looked just like a pantomime castle. Inside it was just like a cinema film - people still dining at little tables round the sides of the room and in the middle other people danced to the strains of a jazz band. At intervals the floor was cleared and Russian dancers came in and performed - but the thing that amused me most was the people. I've never seen such 'funnies' mostly American[10] - a big Empress boat had come in in the morning so the place is extra full of them. We didn't know any people there so I danced alternately with Ian and Dr Hunt - he is quite a nice man - she is a Swede and ought to be interesting - as she was out in Serbia during the war and also in Russia - but actually she is rather a bore. Another lovely drive home arriving about 1am.

Sunday I went to church at the Cathedral. An American was preaching - the most awful bosh and platitudes you've ever heard.

In the afternoon we went our usual Sunday expedition to Stonecutters. It is beginning to get colder bathing now - but it is still ever so much hotter than anything you can imagine in England. We ate our tea perched up on a rock from where we got a magnificent view - Ian had managed to acquire one of 'Tamar's' lemon cakes.

Today Ian has been 'day on' - which though only one in six seem to come round frightfully quickly - at present he is doing duty captain instead of poor Mr Peyton Ward. I went out to East Point to play tennis at the Bell-Irvings. I went in a rickshaw along the 'Praya' (harbour front) past all the Japanese shops. I called en route at the dockyard to collect my tennis racquet which the ships carpenter was repairing and had a few words with Ian. The Bell-Irvings have a lovely house and garden - one of the oldest in the Colony. Mrs Bell-Irving was charming - like all the people in Jardine Mathesons they come from Dumfrieshire.[11] Do you know them I wonder?

Such a pleasant surprise - Ian discovered in his cabin the other day a cache of 80$ the existence of which he had completely forgotten - though he said he remembered a couple of months ago feeling unexpectedly short of money but as we managed to get on without it - it now seems almost like a present! I've never seen anyone so untroubled about money as Ian - and our finances seem to be of the widow's cruse variety - in fact we should be doing quite well out here - if it wasn't for this beastly 50% business for the next two months which at present exchange means we shall lose about 60 or 70$ a month and have to draw on some of what Ian saved before I came out - otherwise we can just live on Ian's pay - irrespective of clothes and travelling.

St Georges
2nd October 1920 Hong Kong

Wednesday we played tennis and when it was too dark to play anymore we went down to the town and try and get Xmas presents, it is so difficult to get Chinesey things that aren't brash and yet aren't expensive. I got Sybil Petre an ivory cigarette holder which I'm sure she'll like - and for Mrs Macnair and Janet we got rather attractive cups for soup - you know a big cup with two handles with a lid and a saucer - in a rather attractive sort of china - very fine - and a lovely clear yellow with the dragon pattern - they pack it beautifully and I'm going to ask poor Mr Norman to take it back! There were coffee cups in the same china which were rather nice and cost $4.50 a half dozen - and nice bowls - I thought of sending you one - but thought 'd better wait and see if I couldn't get something old in Canton and in the meantime I'm sending you two pictures. One of them is going into the Art Club Exhibition on Monday for the open subject - the set subject was a poster and so for the last few mornings I've been busy painting one - and I think it is quite good. It is 'Blue Funnel Line' to Hong Kong and has a lurid representation of Hong Kong harbour at sundown - with all the lights on the peak and the 'Tiresias' in the foreground - done in water colour on dark brown paper. This gives a rather dead effect and would be much better in pastel - but

I felt I couldn't cope with carrying a pastel to the other end of the Peak where the Exhibition is to be held. I did enjoy doing it.

St Georges
20th October 1920 Hong Kong

Dearest Aunt Carlo[13],

I've been meaning to write to you for such a long time. Mother very often sends me on your letters - so I feel quite up in all your movements - but I expect by the time you get this letter you will be thinking of going abroad again. I wonder where you will go this year and if you have let 3 Rosebery Crescent? Do write to me sometime and tell me what you are doing. Mail day is the great excitement here and I love hearing about everyone at home - but after reading letters from mother, Mrs Macnair and Aunt Eppie yesterday - I felt how lucky I was to be here! With no coal strikes or even any need of coal as it is simply gorgeous weather. All the steaming heat is over and now we are having days of brilliant sunshine - hot and dry and cool nights. It is rather nice at the middle end of Oct. still to be wearing ones thinnest clothes and going bathing picnics - There is no servant difficulty either - the Chinese 'boys' are perfectly splendid - and I feel it is very spoiling being waited on hand and foot. Another sailor's wife and I share a wash Amah - she comes every Sunday evening and collects our things and brings them back on Wednesday morning most beautifully done and we pay her 1$ a week (which even at the present high exchange is only 4/-) and for that we have absolutely unlimited washing. Doesn't that make you envious? We like this hotel very much and it is quite close to the Naval Dockyard and from our windows we have a view over the harbour - which is the loveliest I've ever seen. A Captain and Mrs Acworth live here too and I have made great friends with her. She is very keen on painting and on making things so we have lots in common.

People here are awfully kind to us and we are having lots of tennis and dancing and other festivities and the place itself is a great joy. You've never seen such beautiful flowers and butterflies and we go picnics to all sorts of enchanting places. I also love prowling about the native part of the city - Ian kindly accompanies me, though I think the smells take away from his appreciation of the picturesqueness! I think perhaps I loved Wei Hai Wei more as it was so primitive and unspoilt - but the feeling of the tropics is attractive here - though it isn't a bit one's idea of the East. The glimpses I had on the way out of Port Said and Colombo and Penang were much more what I had imagined the East to be like and I long to see more of them. We are hoping that Ian and I will be able to return home together - and there are rumours that the submarines are to be paid off after the New Year - but nothing official.

Ian's submarine is in dock just now - which keeps them mercifully stationary for the next few months - his captain is being invalided home - so in the meantime he is in command. Tomorrow, Trafalgar Day - the Wardroom is giving a dinner and dance which ought to be great fun.

Did Mother tell you that Admiral Duff had told me he had had a letter from Sir Rudolf Bentwick who had said he was glad to hear some rash young women were coming out here in spite of the Admiralty Order! Admiral Duff himself had nothing to do with the said order as he is all for wives coming out here - he himself in his young days having been the first lieutenant to bring a wife to this station. I like him very much though he is supposed to be rather alarming especially at breakfast time! Miss Duff is a dear and we have great gossips about Edinburgh.

St Georges
28th October 1920 Hong Kong

This week has been rather a dull one - as Ian has had to play Rugger, Hockey, Cricket and tennis for the ship - it is rather difficult really as he doesn't always want to play - but there are so few officers who are any good (he and Mr Peyton Ward were the only ones who were all round pretty good - and now of course Mr Peyton Ward has gone), that if he refuses to play it is rather letting the ship down - so in any important matches he has to take part. However Rugger will be stopping soon as the ground gets too hard and he isn't in so much demand for hockey as more people play. On Monday he played Rugger against the Army - it was rather sad as he wanted to some to the Art Club Exhibition which took place up at the Peak - the subject was a poster. I sent in one and Mrs Acworth sent two - both very good - there was one other quite good poster and one brilliant one by a Mrs Humphries, wife of a soldier - she is as good as a professional and streets ahead of anyone else. The rest of the posters were very bad and so were most of the open subjects. Mrs Acworth had rather a nice one of Malta (she says Malta is far more paintable than this) and there is a Colonel Loring who paints ships well. After eating a large tea and looking at the pictures and desultory conversation we all voted and the votes were counted. Mrs Humphries got the most and I was second with one vote less.

On Wednesday we played tennis and after dinner we thought we'd go for a long walk as it was a full moon and looking quite beautiful - we didn't know that a total eclipse of the moon was due and got a great shock when we looked up and saw a piece had gone from the moon! It was very interesting to watch - but by the time we got home it was quite dark and all that was left of the moon was a brown smoky looking thing like a dim Chinese lanthorn.

St Georges
1ˢᵗ November 1920 Hong Kong

Yesterday was a grey day - rather thundery - however we determined not to be done out of our Sunday expedition to 'Stonecutters'. We landed at the south jetty and proceeded to walk over the hill. The island was just as attractive on a grey day as on a sunny one. Everything was looking very green and fresh and smelling sweet after the rain and all sorts of new wild flowering shrubs had come out - a very pretty drooping pink one - while the ground was covered with a little white Michealmas daisy (the kind that grows in the garden at home and you get rather bored with!) and a lovely delicate blue flower rather like a campanula.

Half way over the hill the inevitable rain came on - but we luckily found an observation point - which being made of concrete and underground was bone dry - so we sat there and ate marmalade sandwiches and chocolate cake and in about 19 minutes the rain had stopped and we continued on our way down to the wireless station. There we undressed and had a swift and glorious bathe - the water is getting colder - but it is still very lovely. Mr Hunt and Mr Thyne (Ian's sub:) were there and we all came back in the boat together with Mr Hunt's two month old terrier pup 'Joss'. It was a sad evening but very beautiful - absolutely still and no colour at all - everything a pearly grey. Today however all the clouds have gone and it looks settled fine again.

I have made my fancy dress for the 12ᵗʰ and for the sum of $1. I am going as a Quartier Latin Art Student - clad in my blue smock and black tam-o-shanter (both of which I had) and my hair done to look as if it were bobbed. An enormous black silk bow tie and in a Japanese shop I found some rather nice blue and black check material like they make kimonos of - and from this I manufactured baggy trousers - and with black stockings and shoes it is really quite a becoming rig. Ian's costume I've still to tackle.

(Two Chinamen are having a quarrel outside my window and you've never heard such a row in your life!)

I'm beginning rather to make Ian's life a burden to him by fussing about my plans. His very characteristic advice is to leave them alone and hope something will turn up to settle things. In the meantime I've got a room at Wei Hai Wei for the summer and a passage home by Blue Funnel - and one or other I shall have to give up in March.

St Georges House
5th November 1920 Hong Kong

Isn't this thrilling! We're coming home. You'll probably have had my cable already and I shan't be much after this letter! My first thought when I heard the news was how glorious it would be to see you - for I'd been wanting you so badly the last week or so and I'm awfully glad for Ian's sake - for it is a big step up. The appointments arrived by mail yesterday and Ian was appointed to periscope school - which means Portland for an indefinite time (from 6 weeks to 6 months according to how appointments to boats fall vacant) the command of a submarine - almost certainly an H boat based either at Portsmouth or New Zealand! (Let's hope not the latter yet!) and with any luck he ought to have at least two years' command before he does his sea time.[14] It also means of course another £1.1 a week pay and he will love having a boat of his own. I'm altogether rather proud of him as yesterday he also heard he has jumped up five months in seniority (the maximum possible).

In the meantime of course we are dreadfully sad at leaving China for we've had an absolutely glorious time and it has been well, <u>well</u> worth my coming out for it and I wouldn't have missed it for anything. I'm feeling exactly like I shall feel on the Day of Judgement - all the things we have put off doing here because there seemed such a lot of time - we've now got to cram into the next few weeks! Sad to think we shan't see Pekin or Shanghai again or dear Wei Hai Wei but we hope to get up to Canton - and anyway we're pretty sure to come out here again one day.

The next burning excitement is if we can get a passage together - but in the meantime we can't take any steps - until Ian knows his plans.

Ian's relief is at present in the 'Titania' up North - and we don't think will come down until the ship does on the 10th of Dec. - and then Ian has to turn over to him - also the Captain of the 'Ambrose' won't let Ian go while he is just now - so things are very vague - but I feel any moment we may have to pack up and come away at a day's notice. Isn't it a life!

St Georges
13th November 1920   Hong Kong

Still no more news - and in the meantime we are making the most of our time here. I haven't been to bed until 2am for the last three nights and we have a fortnight's solid gaiety ahead of us and I shall also have to be busy as I've been put on the hanging committee of the annual Art Exhibition in the City hall and have to do a poster for it as well. I hope we shall be here for it - it is on the 12th and 13th of next month and I am to hang the decorative pictures. I'm going to exhibit some of my old ones and hope to sell them!

Yesterday I worked hard at the Fancy dresses and in the afternoon played tennis - we began dressing at 6.30 - and I was frightfully bucked with Ian's appearance - his dress having cost 5 cents! He looked awfully fine. He was meant to be Starky (one of the pirates in 'Peter Pan'). He wore a red rugger vest embroidered with a skull and cross bones - white duck trousers tucked into his wellington boots and kept up with a black silk handkerchief in which was stuck a pistol and a dagger and on the trousers I had sewn huge coloured patches. A bandana handkerchief round his neck and a red one round his head - brass earrings and a black mask. I was a French art student in blue smock - black tie - tam o'shanter and seemingly bobbed hair - Ian said it was very becoming - but I wouldn't really go by him. Just as we finished dressing the boy came to say Ian was wanted at the telephone - on seeing our get ups he gave one gasp and then retreated in a spasm of hysterical laughter. We dined with the Commodore in the 'Tamar' where there was a party of about a dozen. I sat between the 'Curse of Scotland' and a brigand - in private life a Commander in the 'Curlew' and the Commodore's secretary. Mrs Bowden-Smith was a Turkish lady and Mrs Carrington the Ace of Clubs, both very home made looking. Mr Hunt was there too as a pierrot. When we got to the Peak Club there was a huge crowd - but you can't think how jolly it looked - all the walls hung with orange lanthorns and the stage at the back full of bamboo trees and lit with blue lights making a most decorative background to the gay dresses - of which there were every sort and kind from the most elaborate ones down to the most home made. Mrs Acworth was quite charming as a Ranee and Captain Acworth rather a comic as a Rajah - Mrs Stopford was a black pierrette - the most popular costume seemed to be a Spanish one. We danced until 1am and thoroughly enjoyed it - but I'm feeling sleepy today!

   Miss Duff has asked us to join their party for the St Andrews Ball and we have got to go and practise reels - Miss Duff is organising a Naval Reel. I'm certain there is a romance going on between her and Mr Dolphin - I am always meeting them going off sailing or walking or something together. Quite suitable too - for though he is slightly younger I think - he is a widower - and he is a very delightful person. It would be a bit of a come down though wouldn't it having been as good as Lady Admiral to be Mrs Lieut.:!

St Georges House
20th November 1920 Hong Kong

I've been laid up all this week with Dengi Fever - a most unpleasant but very common complaint out here. It started on Monday evening with violent aching all over and on Tuesday I felt miserable altogether and went to bed and had a temperature of 102 - the same on Wednesday and I stayed in bed all day also on Thursday. Yesterday I got up - but stuck to this room and today I've been out - but feeling very weak and wobbly and my temperature hasn't quite gone down to normal - but I'm feeling perfectly well - and very disgusted at missing everything - a tennis tournament this afternoon and a dance last night and one in the American Flagship some nights before.

Ian has been so good and sweet and the very best of sick nurses - he spent his time rushing up the hill from the dockyard at odd times to see how I was getting on and to administer quinine and take my temperature. He rang up the Naval Hospital to find out the name of a doctor - and the doctor at the Hospital Dr Saunders said he would come himself if necessary - but that there was nothing to be done except take quinine. Mrs Acworth was laid low with this same complaint about a fortnight ago - so has been able to tell us all about it. She has been so kind coming and sitting with me and I went out with her this morning. I'm hoping I shall be quite all right tomorrow - it seems such awful waste of time of one's last few weeks here.

I managed to get my poster for the Art Exhibition finished with Ian's assistance - it was a trifle bilious looking!

St Georges
24th November 1920 Hong Kong

My last letter was rather depressed I think - as I wrote it when just beginning to recover from Dengi - a most trying complaint - I became very cross and fractious - and the more uncontrollable and surly I got the more sweet and loving Ian became. He really was a saint all that week - running backwards and forwards from the dockyard and looking after me so well - and now I am absolutely recovered.

Mr Dixon has returned - but Ian has still to wait for his proper relief to turn up and everything points to our returning in the Bremen - which arrives here on Boxing Day and sails early in January. I hope we shall go in her as I know a lot of nice people travelling in her and she is a fine ship (of Hun origin) in fact we hear she has 300 1st class passengers. The burning question is do I get free passage or not? Nobody knows - but there is more hope of working it from this end and I have various friends at court. Wouldn't it be delightful - like a present of about £70! I believe the Bremen is going via India which would be amusing.

I'm getting a little tired of the exclusively social life one leads here though it amuses me too - but it isn't China a bit - and I like Wei Hai Wei much better.

St Georges
29th November 1920 Hong Kong

For the first time today I am wearing a tweed skirt and jumper - hitherto I've worn nothing but cottons - but today is grey and inclined to rain.

You've never seen anything as pretty as the valley below us looks - it is almost theatrical. The banks are covered with a wonderful scarlet flower - which I've only seen before in Church decorations - it makes a great vivid splash of colour then there is a shrub with a reddish purple flower and ramping all over it the beautiful morning glories which are intense gentian blue in the morning but fade to lilac by midday - then there is a low growing yellow flower and masses of pink oleanders (I *think* they are oleanders) and all along our wall in green pots red dahlias and yellow and white chrysanthemums - the whole effect a little like the cover of a Suttons seed catalogue - but very fine.

On Wednesday Ian had a strenuous day - he played in a cricket match commencing at 11.30, Navy v R.A.M.C. Ian went in first and made sixty odd runs - pretty decent. I sat with Mrs Gregg and watched for a bit. Then I went to play tennis with Mrs Bell-Irving and Ian came directly the cricket was over.

Mrs Bell-Irving is the person you'd like best here - she is delightful and he is nice too and we had a very pleasant party with bad tennis and a super tea in a very English looking garden. Then we hurried home and dressed and dined in the 'Alacrity' - the old Admiral very genial. After dinner we practised reels. The Naval eightsome consisted of Miss Duff and Ian, Mr Stopford and me - Mr Kelgour and Mrs Stopford - Mr Dolphin and Mrs Bowden-Smith (the Commodores wife) of this party only Miss Duff and I know anything at all about it! However I'm drilling Ian in private and he is getting quite good.

Miss Duff gave a priceless description of herself and the Admiral and six sofa cushions practising the Lancers to the strains of a gramophone. While in the middle of solemnly 'visiting' two cushions - some callers were ushered in!

Yesterday Ian had a whole day off - so we had a 'long lie' and then went to Church at the Cathedral. After an early lunch we went over to Kowloon and took rickshaws out to the old city. Pretty squalid thank you and smelly and nothing much to see - not nearly such a good city as Wei Hai Wei. We penetrated into a temple where a 'joss' was being propitiated but we proved a distinct counter attraction! Then we tramped along the Yaumati road which led principally through Chinese cemeteries or through lovely but smelly gardens and the hills all round were very barren looking. We had tea by the wayside and got back to Kowloon about six and took the ferry over.

St Georges
4th December 1920   Hong Kong

We've had a delightful week except for rotten weather - wet and warm and sticky. I've been to my first two really pukka 'Balls' (as distinguished from dances).

On Tuesday we had Mrs James and the Acworths to tennis. The former is so nice - rather like a nice school girl - but I think I like Miss Duff best. Then the Acworths and Greigs and ourselves all dined together and went on to the City Hall for the St Andrews Ball. It was huge fun - but a terrific squash - absolutely everyone in Hong Kong from the Governor and Taipangs down to shop people all in two rooms! The said rooms were decorated in futuristic stripes of black and orange and white with black thistles. The Naval reel was a great success though mess dress with the little short jacket was the worst - imaginable costume to dance in! Ian looked like a conscientious little boy at a dancing class - very mindful of his toes! Miss Duff was his partner. Then we all hurried into supper where one of the party had secured a box. (Supper was given in the theatre adjoining the City Hall) all the big wigs supped on the stage and a haggis was brought in with appropriate ceremonies and everything was more Scotch than the Scotch. Mr John Johnson was chieftain and the old Admiral was in great form. After a superb supper we began dancing again and stayed until 2.30 when we left though it wasn't quite the end.

Thursday was an 'off' day and wet - in the evening Ian and I explored - I love the Chinese streets in the evening when they are all lit up and all the stalls and signs etc. We discovered a Chinese fur shop with grey squirrel coats make like all Chinese garments. If cheap it would be rather a good thing for a coat lining. There was one little coat made of such wee skins - that we think it must have been mice! Ian also gave me his belated birthday present - as we found a really lovely mandarin petticoat - Primrose coloured brocaded silk crepe - with black satin stripes and lovely blue embroidery with the famous Peking stitch which always shows it is a good one - and also in very good repair. Ian frightfully bucked with it. The man wanted $12 but we beat him down to $9.50 and I think well worth it.

Yesterday we all went on to the ball at Government House - which I enjoyed more than any dance I had been to - so did Ian. Nearly all the ships are down here now so I saw many Wei Hai friends and also know a lot of nice soldiers now - so the only sad part was there wasn't nearly enough dances to go round. It did look so pretty - a fine room with a lovely floor and decorated with white chrysanthemums and crimson poinsettias - and nearly all the men either in scarlet coats or in naval full dress with gold braid trousers - and lots of lovely dresses and the Wiltshire Band - and the big stone terrace with a lovely outlook over the twinkling lights of the harbour to sit out on - in fact a No 1 dance. We got home at 1.30 having a stayed until the very, very end. In the big intervals of these dissipation I have been getting pictures ready for the show - I'm sending eight - three old (the woodblock - a Belgian one and the 'Gooseherd' an improved copy) and five new Chinese ones - which I rather hope won't sell but I can't resist trying - I am charging from 10 to 20 dollars each. It is going to be a very swish show - with the Governor's wife opening it and 50 cents charged for admission and about three hundred pictures are expected. I am on the <u>very</u> select hanging committee - consisting of the only two people in Hong Kong who can paint (they are both very good) a Mrs Bowen who can't paint for toffee and the

Colonel of the Gunners (who thinks he can paint) and the secretary. I attended a meeting on Monday but like all committee meetings nothing was done.

St Georges House
8th December 1920 Hong Kong

It is now quite definite that we both come home in the Admiralty transport 'Bremen' supposed to sail from here on January 10th but expected to be delayed a few days. We don't know which route she is going back, but probably via Suez - nor how long she will take. The last Admiralty Transport from here the 'Professor' took nearly three months - but questions were asked in Parliament - so this one ought to be speedier. I think Ian is cabling Mrs Macnair today and the next cable will be to you announcing our date of arrival and probably sent from Port Said. The P and O are agents so any information about our movements you can get from them - and you will also see it in the shipping news in the 'Times'.

As to my passage I've got a free one given by the Commodore - but with the proviso that should the Admiralty not approve we refund the money.

The Admiralty's actual reply to the Commodore was 'Passages to be allotted in the following order, 1st service passages, 2nd Paying passages, 3rd indulgence' which meant the Indulgence people might not get a passage at all - so the Commodore has kindly reserved one for me with the proviso above stated. So if the ship has any empty berths we are quite safe for a free passage - the only case in which we might have to pay up is if my berth could have been sold to a full paying passenger. But there are 280 1st class passages and a very short time in which to dispose of them - so it ought to be all right - in which case I shall have been frightfully lucky!

We had an absolutely <u>gorgeous</u> day yesterday, kind little Captain McCowan of the 'Alacrity' - asked if we would like a drive in his car - so at 11 am we met him at Kowloon and packed into his large two-seater and went off to Fanling by the New Road about thirty miles into the New Territory. Such an amusing drive: first of all along the coast - scenery that might have been the W. Coast of Scotland, mountains and channels and islands and little sandy bays and funny small fishing villages where there are wonderful arrangements of nets out in the water. There we turned inland onto a wide plain surrounded by hills and with purple vistas of mountains beyond going on for ever and ever. Every inch of the plain itself was cultivated chiefly with paddy which grows in a sort of swamp. Our wide straight road was bordered with eucalyptus trees with occasional groves of bamboo and a few fine old gnarled trees near the villages. The villages were almost all walled - half a dozen squalid cottages with an immense thick wall round them with watch towers. I rather longed to get out and explore. The road was covered with blue clad coolies trotting along with baskets - directly they heard the car their universal impulse was to dash across the road in front of it - like chickens, and we had some narrow shaves and as near as nothing ran over a 'wonk' dog. It was a very beautiful day - England when everything is diamond clear and sharp - the only snag was a high and very cold wind that blew me about and made my nose rose pink and my hair wispy which was rather trying. But when we got to Fanling it was wonderfully sheltered and so nice and hot in the sun. No wonder Ian raved about Fanling - an enchanting place - a little valley between great hills and opening onto the big plain. Such a good links - of the Newcastle[15] calibre. Ian and I lunched at the Club House and then played eighteen holes. I played vilely - so disappointing after the way I had improved at Wei Hai - but I bucked up towards the end and anyway it was so delicious to be out in the country in the wonderful air and new and beautiful scenery. Ian was very 'on' his game. Then we had tea and went home by train - as Captain Cowan was staying out for a few days.

The train journey of about an hour was very amusing: at one place we passed a real old Chinese bridge with three arches and steps - and a very exciting looking walled village called 'Sha-tui' to which we are going to make an expedition.

Monday we went for a long walk - penetrating into Kennedy Town - the real Chinese part - and we gazed at the wonderfully lit up Chinese restaurants - we long to feed there but you can't unless accompanied by a Chinaman. It is amusing the way each street is devoted to one trade - but we made one very bad shot and got into the streets where all the dried fish shops are collected together - the smell was sufficient to lift one off the earth - we held our noses and fled!

We have six dances in ten days ahead of us - all rather nice ones - but how I hope my black dress comes in time!

St Georges
14th December 1920 Hong Kong

We had a great day on Sunday - although not at all a sabbatarian one. We went out to Fanling by the 12 train - a huge party of us. Ian and Mrs Peyton-Ward were playing Mrs Dicken and Mr Bouchir - and nice Mr Coltart and I were playing Mrs Bennet and Mr Hirst. We had lunch out there first and then played eighteen holes. It was a still, grey day and very pretty - though not as lovely as last time we went. We heard all sorts of exciting rumours of wild beasts on the course - a herd of wild pigs - some wolves and a female python - but I'm glad to say we didn't see any of them. It was difficult even to imagine them - for except for the clumps of bamboo and the paddy fields one might easily have been in Scotland. We had a most exciting game - all square at the turn and then they beat us by two and one. We all played pretty wildly but it was tremendous fun. It was too dark to look out of the window on the return journey so we all played 'Up Jenkins'.

Dec 15th

Hurrah! I've sold three pictures at the Exhibition yesterday and got an order for another which means I am the rich possessor of 44$ - and of course I might sell another day. I'm afraid the ones I sold are the two best Hong Kong ones and the best Wei Hai one - but still I've got the original rough sketches - so can do them again. On Monday I spent all morning at the City Hall hanging pictures - most amusing - but very hard work as there were only six people on the job and nearly three hundred pictures. I did the Decorative Section - in which I had entered all my own - as well there were six huge pictures by a Mrs MacPherson very well done but I thought too Burne-Jonesy - two excellent posters by a Mrs Humphries and three awful ones by a man I don't know. Some really beautiful book plates and illuminations which I liked best of any and two little pastel sketches by a Russian.

It was an extraordinarily good collection altogether really - some complete duds of course but on the whole I've seen many worse exhibitions in London. Mrs Macpherson had some fine oils and big water colours - much better than Miss Emily Patterson - a Swedish lady had a couple of large rather crude paintings of Pekin - very modern and full of vitality - a Russian girl had first rate portraits and water colour sketches and the French Consul had some brilliant wax models of Chinese types as well as good water colours. A nice Mrs Humphries had a lot of wonderfully done black and white drawings and Mrs Acworth seven quite charming sketches of Malta - full of imagination and romance and such clear clean colour - she says Malta is so paintable. The sketches she has done out here I don't like half as much - as a matter of fact she has only done two - as she says it is far too green to paint. Mrs Acworth got one of the extra prizes in the water colour section. The was only one 'Decorative' prize won by Mrs Macpherson.

Wednesday Mrs Acworth and I met our respective husbands at the City Hall and spent all afternoon looking at the pictures (Ian chiefly rooted in front of mine - and Captain Acworth in front of Mrs Acworth's!) I arrived rather early and saw very few pictures had been sold - so imagine my joy when I reached mine (at the far end of the room) to find three sold! Mrs Acworth said she'd much rather have cash than the glory of a prize - however I hear one of hers sold this morning - and this evening the Exhibition closes and it will be exciting to see if any more have gone when we go to collect them. I enclose a newspaper cutting - I wish I had got the other newspaper - it was far more amusing as it properly went for people - instead of doling out indiscriminate praise - one gentleman was told he was guilty of every fault in the artistic calendar! Others that their pictures disfigured the walls! Mrs Acworth got a very good critique - I was humped with Mrs Humphries and Mr Cole as 'attractive and well worth a visit.'

It has turned out quite cold and the Chinese have burst forth into strange padded garments and they all wear about six coats one on top of the other! But still it is difficult to realise that it is Christmas Day next week - when one looks out onto green trees and flowers.

Au revoir - a few weeks after you get this we shall be together again. I'm <u>hoping</u> to have something exciting to tell you - but it's early days yet. Can you guess?

St Georges
20th December 1920 Hong Kong

The black dress has arrived in the very nick of time and is the greatest success - it came most beautifully packed and took no harm on the journey and is a perfect fit and I think very becoming and will be awfully useful.

I shall wear it for the first time at the Staff Dance at Headquarters House on Wednesday and it will also appear at the 'Wiltshires' dance - the Admiral's dance and the Submarine Ball.

I think it is still a little early to tempt Providence by telling you my exciting news but I am full of hope.

On the way to Fanling we noticed a curious sort of fortress at Sha-tui so on Sunday we determined to go a picnic to it - we looked up trains and found one at 2.15 - however just before it started we fortunately discovered it was an express to Canton - the slow train having stopped running in September! We then had reckless thoughts of taking a motor - but when we discovered it was only nine miles we settled to walk. The first mile or so we did in rickshaws until we got beyond the houses of Kowloon and when the road began to go uphill we started to walk. Up and up we went along a road bordered with aromatic smelling pine trees and bamboos and getting fine glimpses across the harbour. I suppose we climbed for about 2½ miles then we crossed the Pass and down the other side to Mix's Bay. Halfway down we chose a sunny spot and sat and ate a large tea and then hurried on as our train home left at 5.40 and we wanted very much to explore the fortress. Down on the level valley we walked among paddy fields and market gardens little villages and bamboo groves and I wished we could linger - but the fortress was in sight - so we crossed a bridge and over more fields until we reached it. Such a strange place - a huge wall with a tower at each corner in an excellent state of preservation - a little doorway in the middle with a formidable looking iron gate - we penetrated inside into a courtyard filled with children and chickens and shallow baskets of millet and a woman grinding millet in a primitive wooden mill. Everything was so clean and <u>unsmelly</u> that I thought it must be a mission settlement - but a very flourishing Joss House in the middle did in this theory. We poked about accompanied by a retinue of children and found some funny paintings and various amusing things and we really felt we were in China - much too soon we had to go back and catch the train. We took some photographs on Mr Dickens' camera - but I'm afraid the light wasn't god enough. Altogether it was great fun - such a lovely day - warm and sunny and I know when I get back these picnics and expeditions will stand out above everything else - that lovely one we did to the first lagoon at Wei Hai - and Stonecutters and yesterday.

I didn't sell any more pictures but got another order and copying my beastly picture twice over has kept me busy the last few days - such dull work - but I consoled myself by thinking of the 20$ with which I hope to get a present for you.

If I had done a woodblock of my 'Hong Kong' picture I could have sold it six or eight times over - but I couldn't have printed out here not having room or facilities.

St Georges
24th December 1920 Hong Kong

Imagine a glorious end of September day in England and you'll see how difficult it is for me to realise that it is Xmas Eve. One has become so accustomed to the association of snow and holly and cold with Xmas time that one forgets the real Christmas was in a hot country. We are going to have such a nice day tomorrow. We will both go to church early and then I've been invited on board the 'Ambrose' in the forenoon and we will go round and see the decorated mess decks etc. Then we are going to the Acworths to help decorate their tree and they are having a lot of people to tea - and we are finishing up the dining with the Carringtons.

I wonder what you are doing for Xmas? I do wish you were here too - next Christmas I hope we shall all be together and I'm hoping perhaps Paul too! I shall not be able to tell you about this for absolute certain until I see you (which is much more satisfactory than writing) so in the meantime it is a secret. I daren't count on it - or think about it too much for fear of being disappointed.

It is a heavenly day. Ian and I and Mr Hunt and someone else are going out to Fanling by the 1.8 train to play golf and it ought to be simply beautiful out there. This morning I am going with Captain Johnstone (Cairo) to Cat St.

Captain Johnstone is in hospital just now - but allowed out and he is the only person here except myself who loves exploring the Chinese quarter - so we ought to have great fun. He draws well and is clever at 'Picking up' things (like you) so I am taking him to get his opinion of a little China box I rather covet - Ian and I found it in a case full of old watches and bits of iron and chop sticks and other oddments. It is rather a heavenly blue with a gold pattern - however I didn't want to give more than $1 and the old man wanted 2$ so today we may come to a compromise.

The 'Bremen' is due in on Wednesday and is supposed to sail again on the 15th but here movements seem erratic. We don't even know her port in England - Plymouth, Portsmouth or London. Ian has never been told: he will probably have to report at Fort Blockhouse - not the Admiralty - in which case we shall get out at Portsmouth (if she stops there) or Plymouth and I will come straight to Burley.

I'll cable the port of landing to you at Port Said. Our packing is very complicated as Ian doesn't know where to address his things to - also he doesn't know whether he will be on duty on the way home and require uniform or not! I do hope we shall get a cabin together.

<u>Dec 26th</u>

Friday was a delightful day - I went out with Captain Johnstone in the morning - such an intelligent person to go with and most amusing. He knows a lot about the Chinese and all the quaint places in China town and the meaning of most of the funny things one sees. He showed me one shop that sold nothing but shark fins - and another with Chinese pillows which are made of porcelain. In Cat St I found a nice little present for you over which we had great bargaining.

Then I joined Ian at the ferry and we went out by train to Fanling. We played 18 holes on the long links and though I was playing pretty vilely it was so gorgeous to be out in such lovely country on a warm delicious day that I thoroughly enjoyed it. We finished up by having boiled eggs for tea in the Club House.

We had a delightful Christmas Day. It was very sunny and warm and I wore my white coat and skirt. Church occupied the morning and at lunch time I got a letter from you - a short one that you didn't expect me to get.

Directly after lunch we went up to help the Acworths decorate their Xmas tree - which is always great fun. The room was hung with red Chinese lanthorns and the tree in the middle - no holly of course but a big bough of mistletoe - at teatime Captain Somerville, Captain Turner, Mr Coltart and one or two other 'Titania' people arrived and we all had a large tea and crackers and played games with the children. Then the James came up (rather attractive children) and the Christmas tree was lighted.

We dined with the Carringtons - themselves and Miss Eyres and five or six people from the 'Carlisle'. After the orthodox dinner we played games 'Up Jenkins' and 'Gyab' etc. On the way there in rickshaws we were bombarded by Chinese crackers - most terrifying.

'S.S.Bremen'
31st January 1921   Arabian Sea

It was lovely getting a fat bunch of letters from you at Colombo - and I am hoping you will get this if I post it at Port Said about four or five days before I arrive myself. At the moment we are due at Plymouth at noon on Monday Feb 21st and I don't really think it is worth your coming to meet the ship as we shall either come straight to Burley or just spend one night in Plymouth. Ian will have to go and report at Blockhouse (Portsmouth) and if he gets leave we will return at once to Burley where we would like to stay a fortnight before going to Voelas[16] - and I expect Mrs Macnair will ask you too. You will have to fix up plans with her. If Ian doesn't get his leave until after the course he will have to go straight from Portsmouth to Portland and I will come to Burley.

We are having a very good trip so far - only one rough day - but Paul is making me very sick which is rather spoiling things - still it will be worth it.

It is great joy having a cabin with Ian - even though it is a very tiny one - like one of the ones in an Irish Channel boat. We sit at the Captain's table between the Acworths and Miss Eyres - the food is most awfully good - if only I wasn't sick after almost every meal!

We stayed 24 hours in Singapore where it simply poured with rain. Mrs Charlwood (Miss Dunkley my ex cabin companion) met us and motored us out to their bungalow for tea and we all went to a dinner party at the Bribosias - who Ian thoroughly appreciated. It was amusing meeting 'Tieresias' friends again and I enjoyed showing Ian off! Mrs Charlwood is going to have a baby in March. She told me she was frightfully sick for the first few months but since then had felt very fit - so I'm hoping to have got over it by the time I get home.

We had two and a half days at Colombo and heavenly weather - we motored with a party up to Kandi (72 miles) an absolutely gorgeous run - through forests of palms and across swamps - through native villages and finally away up into the hills. Kandi itself was a beautiful place and I wished I had more time there. We ran over a huge snake at one place and at another we saw elephants carrying loads - a fascinating sight - but they were so like pantomime animals!

The second day we stopped and then we went out to a place called Mt Lavinia where we had a superb bathe and watched the catamarans coming in. Altogether we had a perfectly lovely time and it made all the difference having Ian to do things with I also felt much better on dry land - though I disgraced myself for ever by being sick in Colombo harbour coming off the ship in a row boat!

Now we have three rather dull weeks ahead of us broken only by a few hours at Port Said and possibly at Gib - but every day is bringing me nearer to you - and you can't think how I am longing to get home now and how excited I feel. Won't we have a lot talk about and to plan?

I think you would really hate a sea voyage. One's cabin gets awfully squalid filled with half dirty crumpled clothes and no means of having washing done except by the sailors who don't make much of a job of it - so I shall arrive with all my clothes in the last stages.

There are about 1000 sailors in this ship and they have all managed to acquire livestock en route - monkeys - cockatoos - parrots and canaries - so if they don't all die in the cold the landing ought to be an amusing sight.

I'm just longing to see England again and revel in reading poems like Kipling's 'Sussex'. I can't tell you how glad I am to have seen the East and what a gorgeous time I've had - but I think it makes one appreciate home all the more and I'm not a bit sad to say goodbye to it - though I'm sure Ian and I will both yearn for the sun and heat - we did love that and seldom or never found it too hot.

Chapter Four - Voyage To China 1927

In 1927 Ian was again in China, as Captain of the submarine L27 which he had taken out from Portsmouth to Hong Kong against a background of 'Troubles' in the Far East. He had shipped in L27 the stripped-down components of a three-wheeler Bleriot Whippet car known as 'Bobjohn', and having reassembled it with a homemade body in Hong Kong he obtained a licence to take it to Wei Hai Wei where it was the first car to be seen on the mainland (and as far as I know the only car to be transported in a pre-nuclear submarine).

In January 1927 Ruth set out to join him, starting by train across France and joining the 'City of Calcutta' at Marseilles. I was left (aged 5) with my grandmother, and Ruth's old nanny (Ninny), who having brought up Ruth from a baby was to look after her three children and to be a prop of the Macnair family till she retired in 195-. Ruth, now a seasoned traveller of 28, was chaperoning the 20 year old bride of the first lieutenant of L27. (Note that in contrast to 1920 she soon became known as 'Betty'.) Thanks to introductions from friends and relations particularly Aunt Carlo the two girls were royally entertained at their various ports of call, including a stay at Government House at Singapore and hospitality from the U.S Navy at Manila. Ruth discreetly refrained from telling her mother about her problems in delivering Betty to her husband; she later told me that Betty nearly absconded after a shipboard romance.

S.S.Calcutta
Monday 10th January 1927

Here am I emerged from my usual couch of sea sickness - though this time I think it was really liver chill. It got fairly rough soon after leaving Marseilles and very bad in the night - but I slept and was all right - but yesterday as it was calming down I was very sick and returned to bed and slept for over 24 hours and am now recovered though weak - how I detest the sea - especially when it is too windy to sit on deck. But this is a most airy and comfortable ship - not much to look at outside - in fact very shabby - but inside quite the nicest I've been in. My cabin is nearly as big as the little spare room and has two portholes and a wardrobe and a sofa and I have all my luggage in with me. There are very few passengers. Besides Mrs B and myself there are two very nice looking Australians (sisters aged about 30) they have written a novel which was rather a success and it has been dramatised and is appearing in London next year. They are now writing another. I sit next to one of them and they are both bridge players. There are two other Australian sisters, elderly and rather like Aunt Alice to look at, who run a huge farm to which they are returning after a year's holiday in Europe - another elderly spinster bound for Shanghai and the pretty blue-eyed daughter of an American missionary. That is all the females. The American missionary with a white beard looking like a patriarch and half a dozen young men (planters etc.) completes the 1st class saloon. It is rather pleasant as there is no competition for baths etc. and as the Australians and one or two of the men are nice it is all the company one requires - not that I've seen much of anybody so far except the stewardess - a nice scotch 'buddy'. Mrs Brown is rather a little pet and so pretty - but I can't quite make her out - she prattles about 'lucky numbers' and her Borzoi dog etc. but the books she has brought with her are Conrad and Henry James and the 'Oxford Book of

English prose' and the 'Spirit of Man' and Shakespeare - in fact John Buchan's latest is the only frivolous one in the collection. Her people looked so nice - I wish you'd seen them at Victoria. Her parents quite youngish and very upset at parting with her - she has one brother at Oxford 'Ben'. They filled her cabin with flowers and huge boxes of chocolates etc. and she very kindly put violets in my cabin and when I was feeling ill - longed to come and minister to me with eau de Cologne! I hope I wasn't snubbing! I imagine Brown is the usual impecunious sailor but that her people are well off. Her grandmother gave her a diamond bracelet as a parting present and another relative all her hats from Woolands.

We are just passing Stromboli which is smoking but not very active and this afternoon we go down the Straits of Messina. How nice to see land quite close! We passed Corsica and Sardinia yesterday but I was too ill to take mush interest! It is quite warm but too much wind to be pleasant on deck.

I enjoyed the first part of my journey - the channel was like the proverbial mill pond and I had lunch at Calais. Until dark I looked out of the window - one goes through part of the war zone and though there is little to see the country still has a blasted appearance. My stable companions were a kind, elderly couple of what Muriel calls the A.B.C. variety (ancient British cats!) They were bound for Mentone! The woman was rather nice and just typical of the type pensions abound in! The gentleman wore an Inverness cape and was very chatty. A grim looking Frenchman got in at Paris and it transpired he was going to the middle of the Sahara - the old gentleman bombarded him with futile questions to which the Frenchman replied in curt monosyllables - finally I nearly giggled aloud when the old boy asked "Are there many rabbits in the desert?" and the Frenchman gave a snort and disappeared - never to return! I had an excellent dinner and talked to my vis-à-vis - a nice woman who was going to Tiensin but by another boat - she seemed to think China would be quite all right. I slept dreamlessly in my 'couchette' and awoke about 7 in time to see all the delightful country down the Rhone. Have you ever been to Avignon and Arles and Orange? They looked fascinating in the early morning sunshine. How I'd like to do a motor tour down there and the roads looked good. We got to Marseilles at 9.30 and I rescued my luggage from the Douane. I was rather harrowed to find both locks on my box were burst and it was wide open - but nothing is missing and I had it corded up. Then boarded a rickety motor bus and came down to the docks and the ship sailed almost at once - so there was only just time to scribble a letter to you and some postcards which Mrs Brown's mother promised to post. I found a dear letter from Ian full of excitement and joy at the thought of my coming and saying not one word about Chinese troubles. I ought to hear from Ian at every port which is nice to look forward to. We apparently stay two days at Bombay - one or two at Colombo and Port Swetenham and three or four at Singapore and one at Manila. So we shall se quite a lot of the world and I'm glad I've come this way - I think Mrs Brown thinks it rather dull!

I'll go on with this letter the next few days and post it at Port Said.

<u>Thursday</u>

I must have picked up a germ in the train - anyway it developed an absolutely poisonous cold which laid me low all Tuesday. However it is on the mend now. Yesterday it was lovely and we lay on the deck in the sun all day - we get to Port Said this evening and go through the canal at night which is rather a pity.

It is simply everything having a large cabin to oneself and they look after one very well - the food is bad - but one gets oranges - grapefruit and the beef tea at 11 and the buns for tea are good so one won't starve. Yesterday evening we danced on deck - there are two terrible young men who are such good dancers that I suspect them having been professional partners at a Palais de dance! They are trying to teach us the Charleston! I also played bridge and I've nearly made up that mauve voile dress Aunt Carlo gave me. I've finished 'The Brimming Cup' which I liked and now I'm reading the Forsyth Saga; the library on board is pretty dud.

I feel as if I'd been at sea for months and I can't believe it is less than a week since I said goodbye to you. I think the parting with you was even worse than the parting with Eleanor - because you minded and fortunately she didn't. Still I don't expect it will be so very long before I'm home again - at least not judging from what I've heard about the expense of Hong Kong!

I'm getting very attached to 'Betty' - she has been very spoilt - and yet isn't spoilt. The other people on board are really pretty deadly - there is a young Russian who was in Deniken's White Army and a funny old boy who is in the pearl fishing business and is very interesting talking about it. Quite a nice young Indian policeman - the two elderly Australians are sporting old birds - they came to England and bought a Morris Cowley, learnt to drive and set off for John O'Groats and then down to Land's End - camping out most of the time. The old captain is very nice to Mrs B and myself - we sit next to him and he looks upon us as his special charge.

S.S. City of Calcutta
16th January 1927 Red Sea

I got three letters and some books from Ian at Port Said. The last letter was dated Dec. 21st and contained no word of Chinese troubles. They seem to be doing their ordinary programme of exercises etc. and he is very busy with Bobjohn and playing lots of games and he doesn't think rooms are at all expensive in Hong Kong as he saw some very nice ones at £25 a month inclusive and lots of others that were cheaper. He was awfully pleased with the cake you sent him - he says judging by its excellence he expects it was made by Ninny and it was beautifully packed.

We got to Port Said at 7pm. Mrs Brown and I went ashore with the Captain and another man - we got a free trip in the agent's motor launch to the shore and then went to the Consul's with the Captain who had to report there - then we looked at the shops and ended up at the big hotel where we had a very good dinner and we were back on board again by 10 and sailed shortly after. It was dull arriving at night as Port Said is nothing without the sun and the fortune tellers and the rest of the forty thieves. I got up early to see the sun rise over the desert. It gets up so quickly that it is like the electric light being turned on. The canal is always very interesting - but there was such a cold wind that one couldn't sit and watch the banks slide by - but had to walk up and down - we saw a large herd of camels. Suez was reached at lunch time and for the rest of the day we saw land on both sides. A lovely sunset - like the ones you get in the West Highlands sometimes - the sharp pointed mountains plum coloured and pink against a gorgeous sky and huge stars and a moon. Everyone is in whites today - but the wind is still pretty chilly - though the sun is hot - I haven't cast many 'clouts' yet.

This is a very dull ship - there are too few passengers to get up games etc. and I find the people who play bridge play all day (starting after breakfast) and as I don't want to do that - the result is one doesn't play at all - Betty Brown is very bad - in fact hardly knows one suit from the other! She and I play 'tig' round the deck to get exercise and dance to the gramophone and the rest of the time we sit on deck and sew and read and sleep a good deal. However I'm glad I came this way as it is a very comfortable ship - one can get washing done on board and there is a lovely table where one can go and iron ones dresses with an electric iron - my cabin is delightfully airy and they give one constant clean towels and bedclothes - I think it will be the greatest fun seeing Bombay

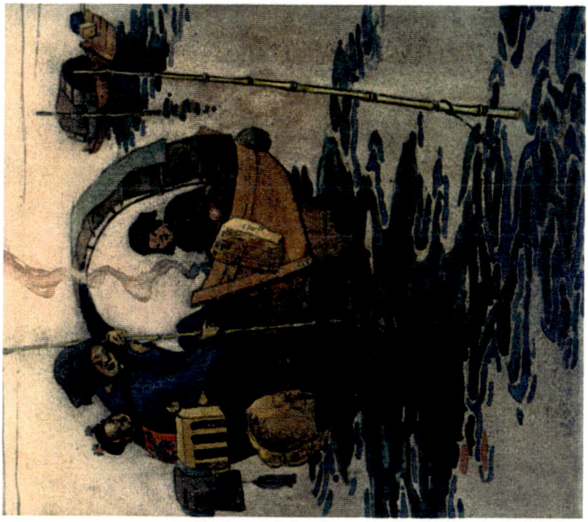

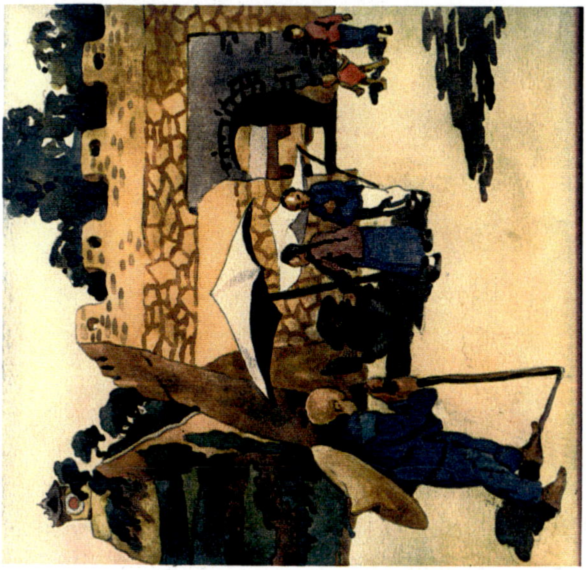

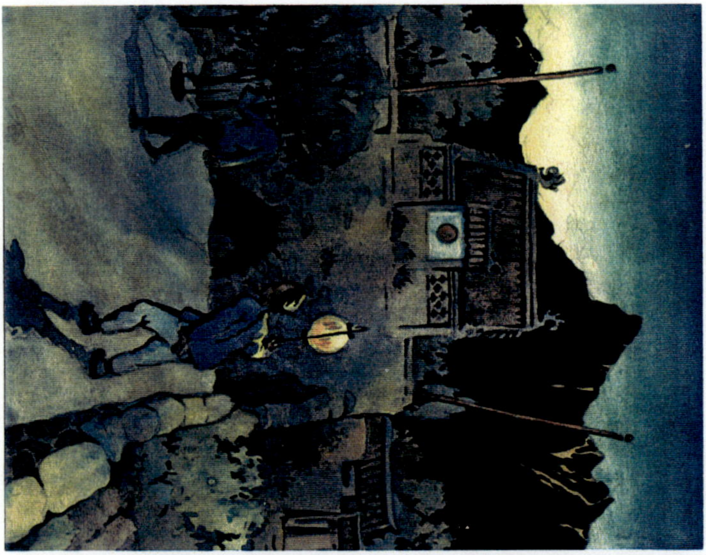

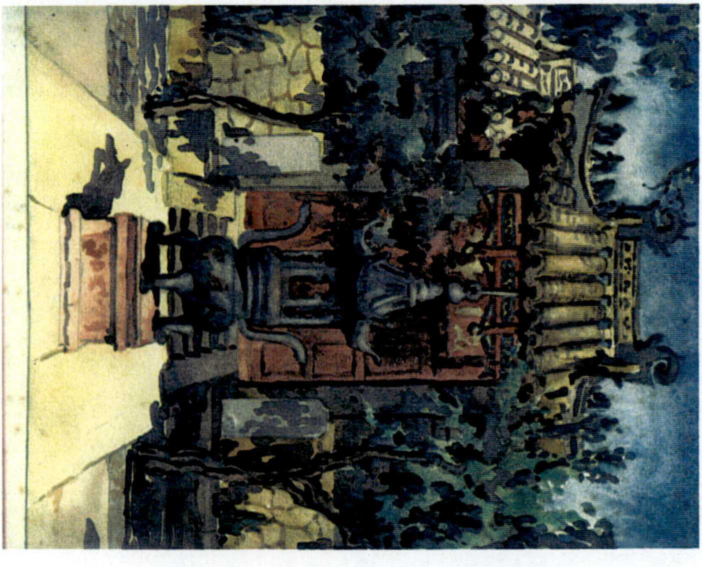

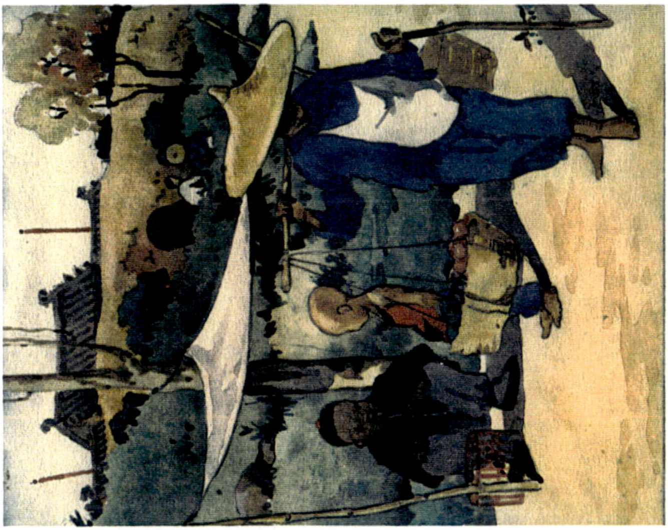

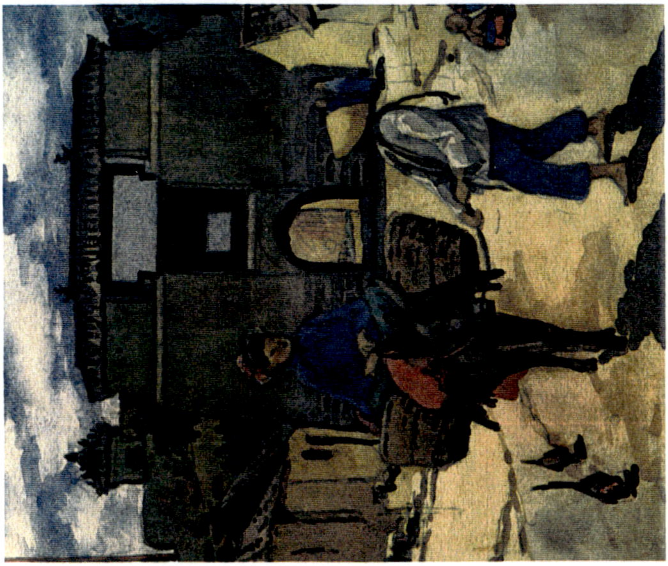

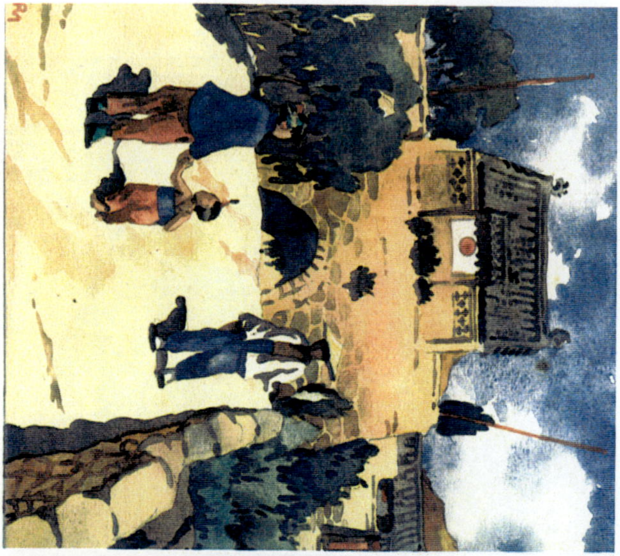

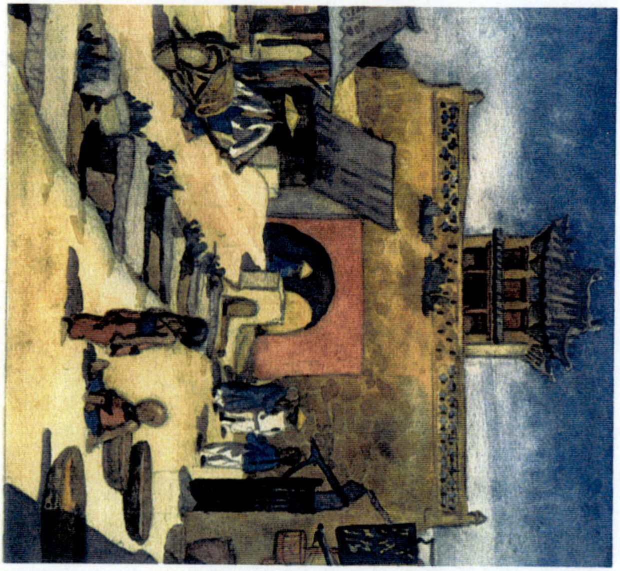

and these other places. I'm getting very fond of Betty Brown - she is like a nice little kitten - and she is 20 - her name was Worthington and her father was a surgeon but retired many years ago. I imagine it is her mother who is very rich. I rather wonder how she will like the life of a sailor's wife - as so far I imagine she has never travelled except under ideal conditions and always stayed at hotels like the Berkley in London etc. All her trousseau came from Paris except a few things from Reville and shops like that - but she is wonderfully unspoilt and very sweet natured and natural - and very much in love with Brown. I gather the one fly in the ointment is the name which is rather an affliction to her!

Jan. 20th

It is beginning to get pleasantly warm - but not a bit too hot - there is quite a lot of breeze all the time. We've seen no land since Suez except for Perin Island - a most desolate looking spot without a scrap of vegetation but where half a dozen English people live (it is a coaling depot). Yesterday we saw a dhow under full sail and some flying fishes otherwise it has been a week of nothing but blue sea and blue sky. It is such a funny feeling where time and space cease to count. It is like being suspended in space and I feel equally remote from you and Ian, and one leads curiously intimate life with people who under any other circumstances one would never chose and who one will probably never think of again. I like the elderly Australians so much - (they know the Greatorex's). These two sisters and two other unmarried sisters run a farm of 3000 acres entirely themselves - their only labour being one man and his wife - they do all the rounding up of the stock etc. themselves as well as the dairy work and garden and market etc. These two are about 50 I should think and very skittishly dressed and full of interest in all sorts of things. I rather like the authoresses though they are a thought second rate and affected! The man in the pearl fishing trade is a genial old buffer and I like the young Russian and he is a beautiful dancer.

On Sunday we had church conducted by the Presbyterian American missionary who gave a devastatingly long sermon (it was rough and I wasn't feeling too well!) - his daughter is rather nice. The 2nd class is full of missionaries - and of every denomination - from French nuns to American Methodists - but no C. of E. The Americans look too awful for words. I can't feel they can do anything but harm - but the nuns look charming - such serene faces.

We are still getting wireless news every day from England - China still seems pretty disturbed and there is apparently going to be a huge fleet out there - I hope we shall be welcome!

We get to Bombay on Monday and I am very thrilled to see a new place - I hope Barbara Bowen will ask me to a meal and let me take Betty Brown - we don't want to get ashore with the other awful young man - but it is difficult going ashore in the evening at a strange place without men unless you have somewhere to go. At Colombo and Singapore we shall be all right - I suffered from this in the 'Tieresias'. It always seems to be the people you don't like who ask you first to go ashore with them - and if you refuse there is unpleasantness as there already has been because Betty and I went ashore with the Captain at Port Said - as we thought he was the safest escort! I'm rather thankful I've not got Helen Hog to look after. Betty Brown is altogether too attractive to go for a long sea voyage alone and I think she is very glad to have me. I wonder very much how she will get on as a sailor's wife - her people say she must have an Amah in China to 'maid' her and she has always had everything she wants and everything of the highest standard (she paid £10 for her trunk etc.) but she told me that Ronald hasn't one penny except his pay and his people (who she doesn't care for) don't allow him anything - so I feel there may be difficulties. Her father (after he ceased to be a surgeon) was Managing Director of the Dunlop Co, but retired from that some time ago. Her greatest friend is the daughter of Sir Woodman

Burbridge (Harrods) but I've been able to find no 'links' with her in the way of mutual friends. I feel she comes from a 'Different world!'

You can't say I'm like Ian and never mention people in my letters! I only hope you'll be interested in them.

I'm now playing almost too much bridge - what I win after tea I always lose after dinner so I'm almost square.

The food is improving - or perhaps it is just I feel more like eating it! and I really think this is a very good line. All the white crew are Scotch - the carpenter who came to repair the locks of my trunk might have been Blair's twin brother!

I think so much of you and my beloved Eleanor and I long to hear about you both but it is very nice to think of you together.

23rd January

We've just passed the P and O mail boat so I'm afraid this letter won't leave Bombay for another week, though we get in at about 10 o'clock tomorrow morning. We shall have two whole days there which is nice.

It isn't a bit hot - I still sleep with a blanket but the sun is very delicious - it is the season of the N.W. Monsoon so that is why there is a good deal of wind and quite cool. It got a bit rough yesterday but I managed to attend every meal!

Life has got into a regular routine now - I get up and bath about 8 - and then run round the deck until breakfast time - then write or do odd jobs in my cabin (washing or repacking etc.) - then sit on deck and sew and talk - after lunch sit and read or sew (most people go to sleep - but I sleep 11 hours at night I think that is sufficient!) Tea is at 4 and then I play deck tennis or take some form of exercise and then play bridge till it is time to dress for dinner. Then more bridge and if it is not too windy dancing to the gramophone and bed about 9.30! I occasionally play bridge at times other than those stated! We have taught the young Russian to play - and he is now one of the best players - there is a Hindu doctor who is also very good - the other men are average and the authoresses are good - Betty Brown and the Australian farmer lady are quite the worst - the missionaries of course don't perform. I've become quite 'matey' with one of them - the pretty daughter of the American Presbyterian minister. She is a very nice girl and takes a most frivolous interest in clothes - she is so kind to her dreary old father - I think she is sure to acquire a good kind husband!

Last night just before I went to bed - I climbed up into the bows of the ship and watched the full moon get up. It was quite lovely as we were sailing straight towards it down a silver pathway. You looked down and saw the sharp bow cutting through the water. It gave a wonderful feeling of speed - and space with nothing but water and sky around you and the huge moon and stars and the wind blowing through your hair.

I ought to hear from Ian at Bombay - but not from you until Colombo. Do you know the feeling when you've been away for the day that when you get home you will find something has happened - the house burnt down or something like that - well think how intensified that feeling is when you've been cut off for ten days - and even from wireless news now so for all I know we may have gone to war with China by this time!

I don't seem to read much - I'm still at the Forsyte Saga though I've also read Hilaire Belloc 'The Emerald' which didn't amuse me frightfully - and Saki's 'Toys of Peace' which did.

The saloon is being rigged for church - so I suppose I'd better pack up - especially as there is really nothing more to say - except that I love you very much and I hope it won't be too long before I see you and the beloved again. My heart sinks at another six weeks voyage - I think I'll come back by the Trans Siberian railway or by next year there may be an air service.

S.S. City of Calcutta
at Sea
20th January 1927

Darling Eleanor

I do wish you were with me. You would like running about the ship and seeing the flying fishes and the black sailors.

I will draw you a picture of the one who hands the food round. He is rather like a black jumbo.

It is so nice and hot now.

THIS IS THE BLACK STEWARD.

THESE ARE FLYING FISH
↓

THIS IS A SHIP
↑

S.S Calcutta
25th January 1927 Bombay

I feel rather sorry for you - as I'm afraid you must be fussing about the news, which I must say is pretty bad. Personally I can't help feeling very glad in spite of everything that I am on my way - because otherwise I should be fussing dreadfully at being so far away from Ian - whereas now I think I'm bound to see him at any rate even if we are shipped home! But it is all rather horrid. We didn't get any letters here - there is no direct mail from here to Hong Kong (it has to be transhipped twice) so either they didn't think it was worthwhile to write here or else letters will come after we've gone - but anyway we get to Colombo on Saturday and there should be a good mail there and I hope one from you.

We had a very festive day yesterday (though feeling far from cheerful at heart!) Also I started badly by being sick after breakfast - it having turned very rough just before we got in here. We went ashore after lunch. I'd forgotten Barbara Bowen's address - so one of the officers belonging to the company said he'd enquire for me and eventually ran Capt. McEwen to earth who said Barbara was ill in bed - but if she was better she'd come and look me up today or at any rate he would. Betty Brown and I went and had our hair cut and then to an Italian tea shop for tea - then a Mr Jack (belonging to the Ellerman Co:) took us for a drive up Malebar Hill and all round. Bombay is a fine city - but not awfully interesting - the people are very picturesque - with turbans of the gayest and most attractive colours - pink and yellow and orange, and the women have coloured saris and silver rings on their bare toes and in their noses!

The pearl fisher Mr Murphy who is leaving the ship here to pursue his pearl activities in the Bay of Cutch gave farewell dinner party at the Taj Mahal Hotel - Betty and I were bidden and the two elderly Australian ladies and the captain and three other men. We had a most excellent dinner and then went on to a sort of fair and subsequently for a motor drive returning to the ship at 12.30!

At 1am Betty appeared in my cabin with her boy carrying all her bedding and she spent the night on the sofa as she was nervous of all the black men prowling round her cabin! We got up at 7 o'clock and went to the fruit market. It was very picturesque, the natives all in white clothes squatting beside their baskets of fruit as gaily coloured as their turbans and the women in draperies (saris) - I think I got some notes for a picture - but I couldn't actually do any sketches as we were pestered as it was by natives wanting us to buy cheap things etc. That is the worst of these places. We went on to the silk market and Betty bought some rather nice Benares silver tissue and then we returned to the ship for breakfast!

27th January - At Sea

Barbara McEwen asked me to lunch - I rang her up and did my best to get her to ask Betty too - but she didn't rise - so Betty went off with one of the nicer young men from the ship - they dropped me in their taxi at Barbara's home - a very nice one up on the hill. There were several other Anglo-Indian females at lunch (a very good one) and I felt rather out of it as they were all dicussing local politics and people and amusements - but Barbara was very nice and she sent me back to the ship in her car. I changed and went off with a party to play tennis at the Gymkana Club. Betty was to have come too - but owing to some hitch up failed to appear - so I was the only female. However they none of them played well (in fact I think I was really the best!) I was very glad to get some exercise and we played till dark when we went and had tea at the Club. Mr Jack took Betty and me out to dinner and we went to the Taj Mahal where there was a dance - collecting Mr Murphy and his young partner en route. However when we got there it was very late and hot and crowded - so we decided to get back to the ship and so to bed.

Yesterday morning we did some shopping but had to be back on board by 11 to be medically examined. In the corner of the saloon was a native woman in a yellow sari we thought she was a fortune teller! But she turned out to be the lady doctor! she felt my pulse rather perfunctorily and that was all.

We have acquired a lot of new passengers mostly stout American globe trotters - one rather nice American girl with a determined 'Momma' with a 'grip'! Also a very nice ex Naval Officer who I played deck tennis with - travelling with a boy who was at Uppingham with Betty's brother and he knows all the family.

In Bombay we were berthed beside the transports - which are nearly ready to sail for China. The Ellerman agent - an awfully nice man who was in the Navy - said he was standing by to be recalled and simply longing to go! The Captain doesn't think the lady missionary will be able to go to Shanghai - but he thinks we shall get to Hong Kong alright. If it is to be a huge base - I expect we shall be turned on to work at a canteen - rather a different time in China to what I expected! But the great thing is I shall be near Ian and ought to see something of him. I see they are sending nurses out to Hong Kong from Malta - so that shows they must think it is safe for women so you musn't fuss. From what I heard in Bombay they didn't seem to think there would be anything more serious than rioting and strikes and our extensive preparations will be the effective stop to that. I also heard that the Singapore Base was a great deal further on and more ready for this emergency than people at home have any idea of! But perhaps I oughtn't to write about these sorts of things.

I'm enjoying this part of the voyage - it is flat calm and enchantingly hot and I feel a different person - and everyone says I look it too. The heat instead of making me pale and languid like it does most people makes me pink cheeked and energetic - and I feel really warm through for the first time since I left China last! We get to Colombo on Saturday afternoon and stay till Monday. I hope Betty Brown's friends are going to be more hospitable to me than mine were to her in Bombay - though it will make me feel rather guilty! However I'm hoping the Guillards will ask us both at Singapore as we are to be there several days.

<u>29th January</u>

We are just halfway through our jounrey and I am really enjoying it now and getting quite attached to the ship. The first ten days were detestable - chiefly because I felt so miserable at leaving you and Eleanor.

I'm very lucky as my cabin is in the centre of the coolest side of the ship and has two port holes so it is always cool and airy - not to say chilly and draughty - rather an achievement in the tropics! I still sleep with a blanket. Yesterday was perfectly gorgeous, hot but a little breeze and we were just in sight of the coast of India. I sewed most of the day (Baby's green linen frock) and after tea played some very strenuous deck tennis which is a really good fast game - the lady missionary and I took on two of the ship's officers and made quite a good struggle. I looked out clean clothes of Colombo and did some ironing - it was like the Black Hole down in the laundry. After dinner we danced on deck. We are very sorry most of the new passengers are leaving at Colombo.

The Americans are rather amusing - there is one quite nice family called Taft (relatives of the ex President of that ilk) but most of them are rather terrible. One is a Mr Mossop whose husband is a Crown Advocate at Shanghai and Wei Hai Wei. They are just returning to Shanghai and seem very calm about it - she says she has lived there seventeen years and is quite used to strikes and riots etc. They say that Hong Kong is particularly quiet just now and they think the submarines are almost certain to go to Wei Hai Wei this summer as we have taken it back again! (as far as I can make out it was never really given up - but it is now run by the Foreign Office instead of the Colonial Office.)

Peak View
30th January 1927 Colombo

We are having a lovely time here. We actually arrived at noon - but had to wait outside the harbour to let the four cruisers in (the ones on their way from Malta to China). At 2 o'clock we got our mail - none from home but four letters from Ian - such nice ones and as excited as I am! Again no word of war or rumours of war. He has been playing hockey against the K.O.S.B's and against the two cruisers that came out from here - he has also got Bobjohn running and altogether seems very pleased with life and he says people tell the most awful lies about the expense of living in Hong

Kong. He has made extensive enquiries and we can live in great comfort for less than £30 a month (exclusive of mess bills and amusements and laundry but including everyting else.) He has also got a room at Wei Hai Wei but unforetunately Mr Clark is at home this year.

The ship is anchored out in the harbour - but as soon as we got ashore a chaffeur came up to us and sid he'd been sent to fetch us - so away we were whisked in a superb car up to this lovely bungalow in the Cinnamon Gardens. Our host is a very nice middle aged Mr Cary - and Mrs Cary is most awfully kind. After tea we went back to collect our luggage and we did some shopping. (I got a family of elephants for Eleanor which I will post from Singapore) Mr Cary rang up a young man Tony Riley (a friend of the Macnairs) and he came with us to collect the gear. She found out I knew Peggy Paton - so rang her and asked her to dinner - I was so glad to see her again and I'm going to tea with her today.

Betty and I are sharing a beautifully cool bedroom with a bathroom and a verandah looking out onto a green open space surounded by palms and tropical plants. We had tea and toast at 6.30 am and then Mr Cary motored us to Mt Lavinia to bathe. Everything looked beautiful in the early morning light and the water was quite warm and there were fishing boats and natives fishing from the rocks and palm trees and morning glories and the whole place was a sort of fairy land. We got back at 9 o'clock and went straight onto the church and now (12.30) we've just finished 'Tiffen' (a sort of mixture of breakfast and lunch) and are by way of having a siesta - I go out again to Peggy's at 3.45 and she is taking me a drive. We were to have gone back to the ship after dinner - but we hear there is a strike of dockyard hands - so we shan't go before tomorrow night and perhaps not for five days! So aren't we lucky to be with these kind people, and Colombo is an enchanting place - so green and clean and prosperous looking -

ever so much nicer than Bombay. I do wish you were here - I'm sure you'd love it though you might find it a bit too hot.
    Kiss my darling Eleanor for me.

S.S. City of Calcutta
2nd February 1927 At Sea

    I hope you ever get my letters - I give them in to the purser's office and I hope they post them!
    There was a strike in Colombo - so instead of leaving on Sunday, we only left this morning (Wednesday). However we enjoyed ourselves tremendously and I can't tell you how kind the Carys were to us. On Sunday I went to tea with Peggy Noel Paton at the Y.W.C.A - it is a very nice place with a guest house - most useful for the lone females travelling - as for one thing the hotels at these ports are always so fearfully expensive. After tea we took rickshaws and went for a 'hurl'[17] and then walked along the Galle Face and talked. On Monday we again rose at 6.30 and Mr Cary took us for a lovely motor drive into the country - we went through palm groves and across swamps and paddy fields and through little villages of leaf thatched houses and it all looked so lovely and fresh in the early sunlight. Colombo is very attractive because it is so green and beautifully clean and open spaces with trees and flowers everywhere. At night there are myriads of fireflies that hover round the trees and make them look almost like xmas trees! We ended up at Mt Lavinia and had a gorgeous bathe and so back to breakfast. After that we went to the Museum - rather a good one with a fine collection of old Dutch colonial furniture made out of the local woods. We went to the Garden Club at teatime and two young men came to dinner and we all went on to the Motor Show and dance.
    In the afternoon Mr Boyd and another youth came and played tennis with us and we returned to the ship about 10.30 pm. It was

awfully rough. First we went to an Australian ship and nearly smashed up its gangway by crashing it and the man who was getting on it half fell into the water - had to be pulled out - when we got to this ship we had to circle round several times before we got near the gangway and we smashed a bit off the side of the boat. The only way to get on was to wait until a wave lifted the launch to the level of the gangway and then jump and hope the Bo'sun would catch you. We all got on board without any casualties, but we were very relieved when we did arrive safe!

It was very interesting staying in a private bungalow in the East and seeing how people live. The Cary's had a lovely 'compound' (garden) with a tennis court surrounded by coconut palms. They have nine servants including a little brown boy who doesn't look much older and bigger than Eleanor - he helps wait at table and had gold earrings! Mr Cary has retired from whatever his business was - and now runs the Diocese - and is on every Board and Committee.

Sunday 6th February

The day we left Colombo there was nothing to report except two whales which passed us quite close and a delightfully playful school of porpoises - who did back somersaults and other stunts for our benefit.

Thursday was a perfectly miserable day. Very hot and sticky and the rain came down so hard that we had to put lights on and blow the fog horn which is the most melancholy noise on earth - it also thundered and lightened and was a bit rough and one couldn't go on deck so I spent most of the day in my bunk. However it's the first rain we've had since leaving home.

Yesterday on the other hand was lovely - flat calm and sunshine and a little breeze - we passed quite close to a gorgeous island - very hilly and covered with vegetation and covered with the brightest green grass and yellow sands and you could see the smoke going up from the native villages. On the other bow was

Sumatra with huge, mysterious mountains with clouds sitting on the top - looking like 'Faery lands forlorn'. There was a fine sunset which I unfortunately missed most of, as I was sweating down in the 'blackhole' ironing some dresses ready for Singapore - I slept out yesterday, rather an over rated amusement as you can't retire until 10.30 and have to get up at 6.30 and the 'boy' is very disapproving about moving your bedding - and in these climes you have to be prepared to take up your bed and <u>run</u> at any moment on account of thunderstorms which are sudden and violent. But to set against this it is rather heavenly to be with a warm breeze playing over you and look up and see the stars and hear the splash of the water and to awake at 5 and lie and watch the dawn - but it isn't conducive to rest - whether like Masefield "I couldn't sleep for thinking of the stars" - or whether the hatchway is a very iron bed - I don't know.

Government House
8th February 1927 Singapore

Here I am again - isn't it luck the Guillards should still be here - though as a matter of fact Lady G is away up country but H.E. is being very kind and hospitable and there is a charming naval A.D.C. who is looking after us. About 5 o'clock yesterday evening I got a marconigram saying 'H.E. the Governor of Singapore hopes that you and Mrs Brown will come and stay at Government House and will meet you on arrival'. Ensued a scene of frantic packing and titivating which was quite unnecessary as though we got in soon after 6 o'clock nobody knew we had arrived - so we weren't fetched until about 10 o'clock when the A.D.C in a Rolls Royce accompanied by a lorry for our luggage (the three suitcases and one hat box looked a bit lost on it!) arrived - Really rather a good time as we went straight to bed. I've got a room like a railway station - with so many and so complicated lights that it took me ¼ an hour running round snapping them all off before I climbed into my oasis of a bed under its Mosquito net in the middle of the room. I've also got a vast marble bathroom - so when I've nothing else to do I just go and have a bath! It is really rather fun - one feels like Royalty - and though the life would bore me after a bit it is amusing seeing what it feels like. We really are seeing the world 'de luxe' - what with our lovely visit at Colombo and then here and Ian writes the U.S. submarine flotilla are going to welcome us at Manila! It is also very cheap as one has no expenses except tips. The only thing I have against it is one seems so little of the place or people - but anyway we couldn't go exploring alone in the bazaars - when we tried in Bombay we had to abandon it as we were so pestered. I was very glad they were so late fetching us as I had a gorgeous mail that kept me occupied for over an hour. I got one from you - and from Ninny, a darling one from Eleanor and five from Ian - and all such nice satisfactory letters with no fussing news.

Ian's letters as usual made no mention of international crises or anything like that but were records of golf - hockey and tennis matches - Bobjohn's progress (he is nearly complete) and successful exercises in L27.

It is so funny travelling by oneself and meeting people who know none of your people or surroundings - I don't feel myself - but quite a different person and as if I didn't belong to you or Ian or Eleanor but as if I was a stranger - a touring female called Ruth Macnair! Still I must say I'm enjoying myself, especially when I get away from that foul 'City of Calcutta'!

Yesterday was a glorious day, not too hot, and we drifted down the straits on a glassy sea in sight of land all the way - We passed the old city of Malacca (which we could see quite distinctly through glasses - and Mount Ophir where King Soloman got his jewels or is reputed to have) and countless little green tropical islands - each more fascinating than the last. How I longed to land

and explore on of them. It was rather disappointing not calling at Port Swetenham - but I believe we didn't really miss much - and anyway we would only have been there a few hours. We passed the 'Tieresias' so close I could have thrown a stone at her! I felt quite sentimental about her! and she looked a much smarter boat than the old 'City'. All the nice people on board left here - I found I had got on to kissing terms with the nice elderly Miss Langhams!

This morning we had breakfast at 9 with the A.D.C. and the Secretary - then we were sent off in the Rolls to the town - I had to go to the Bank to change money and Betty went to the ship to collect her riding habit. The A.D.C. had meanwhile made an appointment for us with a french hairdresser and we were both cut and shampooed - rather waste of time I thought but I suppose we were a bit shaggy and it has been very well done - but terribly expensive. I nearly died when the bill was presented 12/6 each. I supposed because we arrived in a Rolls attended by a dusky gentleman in a red and gold sash and turban!

Government House
10th February 1927 Singapore

This nearly as good a place for writing letters as Preston! One has a large writing table with an unlimited supply of stationary on one's verandah (also stamps if you like!) and as I hate sleeping in the afternoon I've got through a lot of letters.

On Tuesday a Chinese professor came to tea - and two men to play tennis with us - we had some excellent games - but you have to stop at 6.15 as it gets dark. We then adjouned to what is known as the 'Servant's Hall' or really the A.D.C's and Secretaries' sitting room - it has a back door and there apparently every day about 6.30 all the young things in Singapore foregather and eat chip potatoes and drink squashes or 'stingahs'! This meeting is known as 'the children's hour' and the A.D.C's are supposed to be off duty but the telephone went almost continuously and how they dealt with it amidst the babble of conversation I can't imagine.

That night there was a large dinner party in honour of a bride who was married yesterday. I sat on the Governor's left - he is awfully nice and easy to get on with - after dinner we all drove down to the Europe Hotel and danced - amonst other people I danced with the Naval Intelligence Officer who said to me 'I lost my heart to your husband who is one of the most charming fellows I have ever met.' 'L27' seems to have made herself popular where ever she went and I've heard lots of nice things about Ian. Mr Brown wrote to his wife and said 'L27' was the happiest submarine in the flotilla. He also said he hoped when he was a Captain of a boat he would be as nice as Ian is to his subordinates and get things to run as smoothly - at the same time without ever fussing or getting 'peeved'. It is nice hearing these sort of things.

Wednesday morning I was awakened at 7 am and brought a dish of fruit to eat (pomola, passion fruit, bananas etc.) - wouldn't you like that? Betty Brown went out for ½ hours ride - I couldn't not having any kit. We breakfasted again with the A.D.C's and once more the Rolls Royce was put at our disposal. We went the most lovely drive - about 25 miles - through jungle and rubber plantations and past Malay villages built on piles with palm thatched roofs and Chinese villages all gay with red joss papers for Chinese New Year - and across swamps of mangrove and palm.

There was a short shower of rain and the jungle smelt perfectly lovely afterwards - like a greenhouse. We passed the Naval Base - but there isn't much to see there yet!

At lunch time H.E. suggested taking us bathing so after an early tea we drove out to the swimming club five miles away where we swam about in a shark proof enclosure. The water was quite warm but very refreshing. I do wish Eleanor had been there - she would have loved it.

This afternoon we returned to the ship as H.E. is going up to Kuala Lumpar and Government House is to be shut up. It was great luck just hitting off this time - as they only returned here the day before we arrived! Our ship is by way of sailing at midnight or very early tomorrow morning. How we shall dislike the ship again after our spacious days here!

I really think I had quite suitable clothes and they all emerged wonderfully unscathed from my box. I wore the green dress the first night and the black one last night. The white silk dress I got in Edinburgh for tennis and the blue Walpole dress yesterday afternoon and the flowered voile in the morning.

S.S. City of Calcutta
13th February 1927 At Sea

Your second letter just caught me at Singapore.

We stayed nearly a week at Singapore - we should have left on Thursday night - which we thought very tactful as the Governor was going up country that evening. However on Thursday morning the agents rang up to say we weren't to leave until Friday night or Saturday. So we were in the amusing position of being left the sole occupants of Government House after tea time! However Mr Baker (the Naval A.D.C.) has turned us over to his confrere the extra A.D.C. who wasn't going up country and he did his duty nobly. First of all he took us out to bathe and then to dinner at the Europe Hotel where another man Mr Murphy joined us and we danced there - then went on to another place where there was a better band and danced again. Various kind people had offered us their cars - so Friday morning we went off in one of them taking the poor missionary lady with us. We went a perfectly lovely drive - first along the coast through groves of palm and past the Malay fishing villages - then inland across swamp and through jungle and finally over a hill from the top of which we got a beautiful view.

Oh! I forgot to tell you we saw a very swagger Chinese funeral just outside Singapore. First came small boys carrying banners and lanthorns - then a band clad entirely in the brightest green - even their hats - then the hearse (red and gold with bits of looking glass let in) followed by the professional weepers clad in sacks! I got a photograph of it which I hope will be good.

We were very sorry to leave Government House and I fear I will not stay there again as the Guilliards are just leaving. They are so kind and nice - the A.D.C told me they were very keen on the Navy and much preferred giving impecunious N.O's and their wives a good time to entertaining wandering M.P's or American millionaires!

It is of course just like staying in a super hotel - as you only see your host at lunch and dinner and the rest of the time you come and go as you like and have a car at your disposal and someone even to do your telephoning for you and if you express a wish to play tennis two young men seemed to be always on tap! It is a very fine house - the outside a little reminiscent of one of the Wembley buildings. Inside there are huge reception rooms with polished floors and glass chandeliers and very little furniture. There is a vast red carpeted staircase with plants on both sides all the way up. The Governor always walks into a room first - do you think he'll remember to let ladies go first after he retires - or after seven years will the habit have grown too strong!

It is quite rough today - but so far I'm feeling perfectly well and have eaten a large breakfast. I suppose it will now get colder every day - At Hong Kong they are having the coldest weather in the memory of man - so I shall have to do some extensive unpacking and repacking.

I am not a lover of the sea - in fact the days at sea I've really enjoyed were those down the coast of India and the Straits of

Malacca when we were in sight of land the whole time! I've done a lot of sewing and reading - and even more sleeping - I suppose it is lack of exercise which makes one so terribly torpid! I can't think how poor Ian survived this journey boxed up in 'L27'!

S.S. City of Calcutta
Manila

Never again will I abuse the Americans after the wonderful hospitality and friendliness I've found here - Starting by the Captain of the 16th U.S. submarine flotilla and three of the flotilla wives getting up at 6.30 and coming to meet us and hanging about until we were allowed ashore at 11 on Thursday and ending a short time ago by half the flotilla and their wives coming to give us a 'send off' - giving us each about eight bouquets of roses not to mention boxes of 'candy'!! I've never met such easy friendly people - we were on nickname terms with them all in about one afternoon and they all tried to out do each other in making us feel happy and pleased with ourselves. The moving spirit was the Captain, Symington by name though known to everyone - even the subs as 'Tommy' (how different from the 'Sir' of the British Navy!) He was about the only bachelor in the flotilla - all the others were young and married and full of spirits. The three who met us were Mrs Hass, Mrs Conor and Mrs Jones. They all looked about the same age - but we afterwards discovered that Mrs Jones was a sub's wife whereas Mrs Connors had a daughter of 15! There were considerable delays and hitches up about our landing - as the Medical authorities said that as we'd come from Colombo where there were cases of Plague we must be fumigated which meant every soul leaving the ship for 10 hours - however we were told we could come back again to sleep at 9 o'clock that night - so we just packed a little bag with evening dresses and shoes etc. and drove off in 'Tommy's' car to the Army and Navy Club. There we had lunch (a most exciting lunch of American dishes and mangos etc.) and then we drove out some miles along the coast to the polo club. Oh - first Mrs Jones took us to her 'Apartment' for a rest and a wash. It was much the same sort of furnished flat and I and other N.O's wives inhabit at Plymouth and Weymouth - the American submarine wives seem to lead very much the same sort of lives as we do and it is quite refreshing to meet American's who aren't rich!

We watched some excellent polo and met dozens more submarine officers and their female belongings - a particularly nice girl called Kitty - whose surname I've forgotten. At 6 o'clock we all had tea on the lawn which slopes down to the sea. There was a marvellous sunset and then the full moon got up and the whole thing was most romantic looking with the garden hung with the Chinese lanthorns and all the palms and tropical flowers - one very sweet smelling one called 'Donna di noce' (lady of the night). Then we went back with Mrs Hass to her 'Apartment' and dressed and then met the 'Bunch' as they call themselves at the Club where we had dinner out in the garden. The table was all decorated with pink lotus lilies - it was by no means a 'dry dinner' - in fact champagne flowed and they drank our healths and to 'L27' and made us pretty speeches until we blushed - one was that the American submarine service prided themselves on getting the nicest girls - and so apparently did their brothers in the British submarine service! After dinner we danced - and played absurd games - one being that each lady took off a shoe and threw it into the middle of the room and all the men raced for them and whoever got your shoe was your partner for that dance! Up till this time Betty and I had behaved like perfect ladies - and I think the American girls were trying to shock us by their informality - however in the end the tables were turned - they suggested playing 'follow my leader' and Betty was leader - she first of all crawled under a table then played Lake Ontario over some furniture - then wrapped herself in a tablecloth with a palm frond in her hair a la Red Indian and finally turned a neat somersault over the verandah bar (like you did once on Thorney Hill Road) From this moment they took us to their bosoms and I heard one exclaim "Say - these were the girls we were so scared of meeting this morning!" It all sounds rather foolish not to say rowdy - but they were so light hearted and spontaneous and like schoolboys and girls that it was really tremendous fun. We went on and danced at the Manila Hotel and finally at 2am the conducted us back to the ship which we found absolutely deserted with a large notice 'Danger Keep Out'. The second mate appeared and told us arrangements had been made for us to sleep at an hotel but we weren't allowed on board even to get a toothbrush - so what was left of the night we spent rather uncomfortably sleeping in our petticoats in a single bed - I got up at 7 and walked down to the ship - meeting the Captain on the way - he and I were the first to board her and found the deck strewn with dead rats and cockroaches - I asked if anyone had remembered to save the ships cat - and was relieved to hear she had been taken off with the crew - but had seized the rather inopportune moment to have an 'acouchment'! I washed and dressed in my cabin and then returned to the hotel where we breakfasted at the Company's expense. At 10.30 the 'gurls' (three of them in 'Tommy's' car!) came and took us round the town and to the shops. I lost my head completely and bought three hats and a dress! I feel very extravagant - but I may never come here again and I felt it was too good an opportunity to lose. You see this is the place where all the good straws (Bangkok etc.) are made and exported to Paris and New York and London - we went to the actual factory - and there was the most bewildering collection of all the latest shapes in every colour and size and so cheap. My three hats trimmed came to under £2.10, the price of one of them would have been in London - I really did need one or two as Mrs Jackson's was the only new one I got and it isn't awfully satisfactory. Anyway I got a best hat in the shape of a large <u>red</u> crinoline - very smart with a folded crown and curving brim trimmed with grosgrain ribbon - quite unlike anything I've ever had before - but Ian has always wanted me to have a red hat - it was about 23/- and looks so nice with my brown lace frock. Then I got a beige coloured bankok bound and trimmed with ribbon and quite a new shape - very useful as it is the sort of hat that goes with everything and has nothing to spoil - that was 16/- (in London it would have been £2.20) and a little yellow straw hat for tennis 8/-. So now I'm well set up - but heaven knows where I shall pack them! The dress is white voile beautifully smocked and hand embroidered in a sort of Russian design in red and blue and yellow - it was 28/-. They are made by the Filipino women and all the Americans here were wearing them and they look charming and wash well and will be very useful. Betty got one too - embroidered with flowers - also a hat. The usual hats people get here are dreadful things in coarse straw or with shaggy brims (I've got two dolls' ones for Eleanor) The ordinary tourist would never discover the factory as it is right in the old Spanish town (it was nearly as exciting as our visit to the Como silk factory). Also in the tourist shops the dresses were £3.10 - but we were taken to a little Spanish shop which again we could never have found alone. We lunch with 'Kitty' - she and the other two were so kind and interested in our purchases and full of helpful advice - I've learnt some most useful tips from them - one - how to keep my stockings straight and neat without suspenders and how to make a 'brassiere' without shoulder straps! American girls are all extraordinarily neat and well groomed (though they use too much make up). The men on the other hand are not nearly as well groomed looking as Englishmen. Again we dined with 'Tommy' and another man and as the evening wore on the others joined us and we all went to the Carnival - not amusing in itself - but interesting as we saw all the Filipino women in their national dress

- long skirts and small waists and bodices of transparent muslin with stiff sleeves and ruffs (the fashion I imagine in Spain at the time - the Spaniards discovered the Philippines about 1570). The men wear sometimes jackets of flowered muslin! and huge sombrero hats. In fact they are a mixture of Spaniards, Chinese and Negro!

This morning Betty and I arose very early and went and explored the old walled city - 'Intermuros'. It is exactly like a Spanish town and there is a fine cathedral - we also wandered into the charming cloisters of an Augustine monastery. There was a garden and a stone fountain in the middle and we were just enjoying looking at it when a horrified monk appeared and we were evicted!

A large party of us went down to the Polo club where there is a lovely swimming bath in the open air. Alas! I had to look on and not bathe. We lunched with about half a dozen of the 'Bunch' at the club and then they came down to the ship to see us off - the ship was due to sail at 5 o'clock - but it is now 10 and she is still here! Every soul we'd met in Manila came to say goodbye all bearing bouquets and sweets etc. and we felt very sad and as if we were parting from old friends.

It really has been rather a wonderful trip out - full of variety. First of all Bombay - seen entirely from the tourist point of view - then Colombo staying with the Carys in their comfortable, English, respectable atmosphere. Then Singapore with the pomp and grandeur of Government House (followed by two rather hectic days on our own) and finally this time here with twenty young people so like ourselves in some ways and yet so different. Everywhere we were strangers and yet everywhere we've met with the most amazing kindness and feel we have made real friends. It has been fun having Betty as a companion and being able to discuss it all with her afterwards. I wouldn't have missed this trip for anything - though the sea bits have been a bit dreary - but anyway it has been good weather. We have only two days now until Hong Kong and I shall be very busy packing. It has been frightfully hot here and I've dirtied all my washing dresses except the blue one which I'm saving to wear to land in - though it may be too cold and I shall have to dig out a coat and skirt. I had a letter from Ian yesterday saying that Bobjohn was all ready to meet me and has now got one of the new fashionable fabric bodies but as he couldn't get in it yellow - Bobjohn is now an unripe banana! He says they are spending the week exercising at Mirs Bay but will be back all right to meet us next week. He says Chinese New Year passed off very quietly in Hong Kong - but today the news from Shanghai doesn't look too good. There is a buzz that the submarines may be kept down in Hong Kong and that they will go to Wei Hai Wei later if at all. (needless to say this wasn't in Ian's letter - but in Mr Brown's.)

'Gee Whiz' (as my American friends would say!) It is hot - believe me! I feel I have acquired an American accent and a whole new vocabulary!

One of the kind things 'Tommy' did was to send a radio to an American gunboat at Hong Kong telling them to signal to 'L27' to say we had arrived here safely and sending our love!

Chapter Five - **Hong Kong 1927**

Lauriston, Bowen Rd.
23rd February 1927 Hong Kong

I had two lovely letters from you on my arrival here and the thrilling news from Basil Blackwell![18] We are both frightfully bucked and can hardly believe it! I long to know which story or stories he is keeping.

Personally I think I hope its 'The six green parrots' and 'How the cat's paw got into the wind'. Do write and tell me anything you hear - also how much pay we are going to get! I can hardly wait for Xmas now and I'm rather sad not to have the fun of seeing proof etc. - but the business side of it you will manage much better than us - and I feel you and Mrs Macnair and Aunty will boom the sales of No 5 Joy Street! The permission from the Admiralty in this case will be purely formal - but we might have to send a copy of the story or stories - or anyway their names. Make a note we particularly want 'Ian Macnair' <u>not</u> 'J.H. Macnair' as there is a man who writes the most awful tosh in magazines called 'J.H. Macnair'.

We feel terribly overcome at being included in the same volume as Walter de la Mare etc. It really is a good publication though I didn't think their colour reproduction good. I wonder if this proves a success they might re-consider 'Wong Wing Wu'? Anyhow it is all very pleasant - but I'm afraid you and Aunty won't let us be lazy now and take eight years over our next effort!

Well we arrived here at daylight yesterday morning and it all looked very familiar - Mr Brown was on the jetty and Ian came in Ambrose's motorboat in which I crossed over to the other side. He was as nice as ever and looking very pleased with life. At Murray Pier who should be sitting waiting but little Bobjohn! Looking pretty disreputable but going like anything - it was his first run and he fairly romped up the hill here and it is a hill like the side of a house. By working like a black Ian has just got it going in time to meet me - though the body is as yet far from complete and it all needs a clean - but he is going to be the greatest use and amusement here. Ian has constructed a marvellous body out of rubberoid roofing covered with green American cloth (which he bought at a bargain sale!) He has really made a car with his own hands. Everyone here is thrilled with it and we created quite a sensation yesterday when we drove round the town after tea!

I wasn't sorry to say goodbye to the 'City of Calcutta' and thankful to be at my journey's end. This is a most awfully nice place - very clean and first rate food and an ideal position - in walking distance of the town but well above it - looking over the botanical gardens and with a nice garden of its own. The other people look dull and inoffensive and there is one other very nice naval couple called Nichol (he is in the 'Hermes'). The only snag is we have a large and rather gloomy room with a bathroom - but not an enclosed verandah. The room is so big that it is curtained in half - one bit furnished as a bedroom and the other as a sitting room - the latter has comfortable chairs and a writing table etc. but I don't feel you could make it look cheerful or pretty - but I hope to get one of the nicer rooms with an enclosed verandah as soon as one becomes vacant.

Everything here seems normal and peaceful - but there is a slight feeling of living on a volcano and of course the submarines might be sent to Shanghai at any moment - though it isn't likely. Anyway Ian's battery has to come out soon and that will ensure three weeks here.

The 1st Battle Cruiser Squadron from Malta arrived the other day breathing blood and thunder and going ashore armed to the teeth and were rather dumped to find everything so calm and all the proper China 'birds' inclined to laugh at them! The Hermes is here and her aeroplanes play about every day. 'L27' is out at sea today,

I am glad to say that Captain (s) wrote to authorities giving Ian much credit for bringing L27 out here so successfully - so it ought to be a good mark for him when it comes to promotion.

Ian's Xmas present to me was some Foochow lacquer. The things in the shops here are most devastatingly tempting - prices have gone up very little and the dollar is now only 2/- instead of 4/8 as it was when we were last here.

The china shop is one of the most fascinating - but so are the jade and amber and ivory and silk and blackwood shops as well as the things like drawn thread work and Canton shawls etc. I wish I had a lot of money to spend!

I'd forgotten how attractive the streets here are with their coloured signs etc. - but one misses the vegetation and colour and sun of Colombo and Singapore. It is beastly cold here - I am in tweeds and had a hot water bottle last night and we cower over a fire in the evening. Yesterday was sunny but today is grey and horrid with swirling mists. It is amusing seeing all the changes here. Many more European shops and big buildings - several considerable landslides and one road that used to be on the water front is now well inland owing to reclamation. The junks and sampans don't change nor do the jolly little children or the coolies with their big hats and bamboo cloaks.

I joined the Women's Club again - it is wonderfully cheap, $2.50 (5/-) for three months, which gives you the run of the lovely club house where you can get meals and entertain and there is a reading room with every magazine from the 'Tatler' to the 'Guardian'! (and includes 'Colour' - the 'Studio' - all the Fashion papers and the Times Literary Supplement.) They also have lectures etc. and an extensive library. I also belong to the U.S.R.C and the Golf Club without paying any subscription, Ian being a member.

Lauriston, 1 Bowen Rd
27th February 1927 Hong Kong

We are beginning to get settled down at last. I've unpacked and had all my clothes washed and ironed (There is an Amah who does this in the house) We have also paid all our official calls and we're getting to know quite a lot of people. On Thursday we took Bobjohn right to the top of the Peak - 1,500 feet slap up from the sea - so it was rather an achievement - though it is a beautiful road. We didn't see much when we got there as there was a dense fog - but coasting down the hill home was lovely. Bobjohn is really going better than ever before and he is going to be the greatest joy - also an economy as no one walks here and rickshaws and chairs etc. mount up so - Ian goes down in him every morning and I walk down in the afternoon and get a lift home. (Uncle John Dent's fountain is our rendezvous!) We've still got a lot of work to do on the body and I'm going to make blue linen covers for the seat. Yesterday we drove out along the coast to a fishing village Aberdeen where there are lovely junks - it will be a wonderful place for sketching and I could never go there last time because you can only reach it by road. We went on to Repulse Bay - where there is a bathing beach and a de luxe hotel - we called in and saw Agnes Thompson (Wilson that was) her husband is in command of the destroyers and is just going up to Shanghai - so Agnes is going to Japan. Funny how people who you fly screaming from at home you welcome out here!

We returned over the Gap and by Wantchai (a native quarter - very smelly but awfully picturesque with all the shops lit up.)

Life is very funny out here just now - everything going on as usual - dances and races and games - and yet the place is a vast armed camp - soldiers arriving every day - ships in the harbour ready to dash off at a moment's notice - aeroplanes swooping about all day and no one knowing what tomorrow will bring forth.

The Chinese here seem as friendly as ever - but I don't think I shall go down Cat Street alone this time!

The housing problem is rather acute as so many hotels etc. have been commandeered by the military - we were really lucky to get in here. It is the ideal situation and such pretty surroundings - looking over the harbour and surrounded by bamboos and palms and fir trees and a garden (like most Chinese gardens all grown in pots arranged into flower beds and not direct into the earth) It is all beautifully clean and nice 'boys' and the food is excellent - quite plain but everything very good and wholesome and unlike a hotel. The only snags are that it is about the most expensive place (though cheap compared to the same accommodation you would get in England.) Prices have really gone up very little - washing is still 5 cents a piece (just over 1d) and yesterday for 30 cents (8d) I bought a huge bunch of lovely roses and sweet peas.

Flower Street is enchanting just now - you can get any English flower you want - roses or violets - delphiniums - dahlias - freesias and chrysanthemums - all the seasons mixed up.

The shops are terribly tempting. I never looked at them last time with the dollar at 4/8 - but now it is 2/- things are so cheap. You can get rather fascinating towels and tray cloths and things worked in coloured cross stitch and beautiful tea cloths - fillet lace and hand embroidery done on Irish linen which is specially imported (all this work is done in Swatow convents) Then there are carved jade and crystal and old china and modern china and very nice modern lacquer etc.

Lauriston
3rd March 1927 Hong Kong

I can't tell you how nasty the weather is - like Edinburgh in May! Alternate days of bleak east wind or grey, damp, mist - I've only seen the sun once since I arrived and the top of the Peak has emerged today for the first time! One hates it after gorgeous sun and heat we had on the way out - and I am back into all my winter clothes and we cower over a fire! Not one's idea of the tropics!

I am being very lucky in the way of seeing a lot of Ian. L27 has just gone into dock for three weeks to have its battery taken out and the density altered for the coming hot weather - so whatever happens we are bound to have this month together, he gets away most days at 4 o'clock and sometimes earlier and doesn't go down until 8.30 in the morning and only keeps one day on in six.

This week has been the famous Hong Kong Race week. We went on Monday afternoon and on Tuesday we went in the morning and lunched in the Navy box. It was very amusing as we saw heaps of people we knew - it would have been nicer if it had been warm and sunny. The K.O.S.B band played. We weren't very successful at picking winners, but only lost $12.

Another evening Ian and I drove round to Deepwater Bay and played golf there and we are going again today. It is a lovely drive along the coast the road edged with pine trees and palms and bamboo and views of the surrounding islands - and you go thorough Aberdeen (a fishing village) where there are fine junks and a temple and I mean to go and sketch there as soon as the weather gets at all decent. The roads on the island are excellent and Bobjohn is going like a bird.

After having lunched at the Hotel at Kowloon I am thankful Ian settled to come here even though it is 50$ a month more expensive. Kowloon is incredibly dreary - all railway lines and cranes and half finished buildings and surrounded by barren hills -

the Hotel was very bleak and horrid food and dirty looking boys - so I don't want to go there even with an inducement of a geyser and a 'flush'. In this establishment our bath is a Soochow tub (just like the one the Cootes lent you for the garden) and the hot water comes up in wooden pails - but it is really very adequate and we have a fixed basin with cold water.

At the races Ian introduced me to a very nice man in the local police - he and a Mr Bethiel in the Ambrose have started a pack of hounds called 'The Taipo and Shamshin Stag and Boar Hounds'! It is a very exclusive pack and I am highly honoured that I've been asked to their next Meet. It ought to be great fun. The policeman knows all about the head men of the villages on the Mainland and he gets them to come with dogs and beaters - you them set off on foot armed with rifles and shot guns and where the undergrowth is too thick you throw in Chinese crackers to evict the game! The Chinese are awfully keen on it and you end up having tea with one of the head men of the village. So far they've killed a stag or a boar every time - but it is a highly unconventional affair and it is much despised by the Fanling Foxhounds which are a completely orthodox and European pack!

Lauriston, 1 Bowen Rd
7th March 1927 Hong Kong

Ian spent the day working on Bobjohn as he was officially 'day on'. Yesterday we went for a drive in Bobjohn right round the Island - about 25 miles. It wasn't a very nice day - a strong wind and monsoon - which like an easterly blight takes the colour out of everything - but still it is a lovely run and bits of it might be the West Coast of Scotland. Late in the evening we went for a prowl round the back streets. In the dusk they look fearfully picturesque - especially the smaller ones which are lighted not with electric light but with great lanthorns with red signs on them. You peer into the little shops and see people gathered round a table eating with chopsticks out of bowls. Then you turn into a brightly lighted street full of red and black and gold signs and nothing but silk shops - every window full of the loveliest brocades. At the street corner you see a professional letter writer painting his characters with a brush and every sort and kind of itinerant vendor. By daylight the dirt and squalor rather take away from the attractiveness of these localities - but at night they are most theatrical and amusing. We returned with a large jar of ginger - Ian is to eat the ginger and I'm to have the charming blue and white pot as a flower vase!

We had a pleasant dinner party with Roddy[19] in the Tamar - he is such a dear and the other Miles were nice. She is a very energetic lady and runs everything here - Girl Guides - tennis tournaments etc etc. - I am to start work on Saturday on her shift at the canteen - a big new Y.M.C.A is opening this week for all the extra ships and troops.

On Wednesday Tim Taylor has asked us to dinner and dance at the Repulse Bay Hotel. That is the great feature of Hong Kong just now. If you can imagine a little bay like one at Arisaig with white sands and islands all round and quite deserted - and there they have built an hotel like a thing in an American film surrounded by exotic gardens and fountains and where you get food and band and dancing similar to the Savoy in London. It sounds most incongruous but it is really rather attractive and on a moonlight night is a most fascinating expedition.

Everything is peaceful at present - but League of Nations or not - if we hadn't had a large disciplined force to send out - and sent it we did - there is no question that the most awful disasters would have happened out here. As it was it only just arrived in time and things were very anxious at Shanghai - and still are - but the presence of an overwhelming and highly disciplined force will do more than anything else to <u>prevent</u> any bloodshed. So you can tell that to any pacifists you may meet.

Don't you think enclosed replies of Ian's are rather neat? The first was sent as a real Naval signal and refers to the fact that Ian refused to paint L27 until the weather improved (Ian is S.S.O Ambrose). Mr Hutchinson's comments on Bobjohn's new green body are hardly high class verse!

From: Chaps. H.M.S Titania
To: S.S.O. H.M.S Ambrose
Feb 28th

(to the tune of 'My little grey home in the West')
"There's a submarine lying at West
Wall, who's certainly not at her best:
All covered with rust
And sugar and dust,
A pretty grim sight it's confessed.
Tho' its only a tumble down nest
The crew have all had a nice rest
So please put on more paint
And we'll cease our complaint
For we really think grey boats are best!"

Reply:
From: S.S.O. H.M.S Ambrose
To: Chaps. H.M.S Titania
March 1st 1927

Alas, for those who today prepare
And for tomorrow give us no thought or care;
When thriftless days have vanished, who can tell
What stringencies will catch them unaware?
Like he who pours good liquor down the drain
Is he who paints his vessel in the rain
and he who splashes paint on in the damp

May never have the cash to try again."

From: Lieut. Cmdr. Hutchinson R.N. H.M.S/m L19
"Bananas are yellow
They must not be green
Oh! How could a fellow
Ever be seen
With a flying banana
Green!!

Reply
"I hold that bananas - like people and tripe
Are much better green than a bit over ripe.
And when your banana's a thought over mellow
And turning to brown from that fair cream-yellow
Then Oh! What a very superior kind
Must be the banana that changes its rind
And growing a new one of verdant complexion
Begins life again at the age of perfection!

Lauriston, 1 Bowen Rd
12th March 1927 Hong Kong

It is getting warmer and we occasionally see the sun - Thursday was a lovely day and we went out to Fanling Bay by the 10.30 train. It takes nearly an hour to get there - but every bit of the journey is interesting. You first go through a tunnel and come out on to Miss Bay and run along the coast - very like parts of Scotland - then you stop at a Chinese station (a very fancy building with dragons etc. on the roof!) called Taipo Market - after that you go inland across paddy fields and past farms and one place where there is a hump backed bridge. You see the inhabitants ploughing with water buffalo and the odd looking local pigs running about everywhere.

At Fanling itself they have got a large camp where a lot of the troops which have been sent out from England have gone to - a very pleasant place too.

I'm just going off to the town now to buy some flowers. You get the most lovely branches of flowering cherry and japonica etc. and glorious roses for about 6d a huge bunch. Yesterday in the town I saw a wonderful wedding procession - an amazing mixture of grandeur and squalor - picturesqueness and tawdriness. In front there were a dozen little ragamuffin boys in gorgeous crimson and gold jackets (under which hung their own little ragged trousers), they carried huge red lanthorns: the band followed clad in pink brocade - some with huge white hats trimmed with tinsel and flowers and some in old Homburg felts and some with one on top of the other! The bridesmaids in every colour brocade and beautifully painted faces were carried in triumphal chairs - so was the wedding feast! There were also some weird creatures with remarkable head dresses mounted on ponies. Accompanied by a salvo of crackers the bride appeared - or rather her cage as she is invisible - the cage is made of looking glass and kingfishers feathers and woollen pom-poms and tinsel and flowers and is carried by coolies dressed in pink - it creaks and rattles and jingles and the poor little bride is hermetically shut up in it - so that sometimes if they have far to go is unconscious by the time they arrive and half suffocated!

Lauriston, 1 Bowen Rd
15th March 1927

The weather is foul at present - if it isn't rain or fog it is bitter cold. The only expedition was Sunday - which was very warm and though it started foggy it cleared at lunch time. We had meant to go over to the Mainland and do a 60 mile round and take lunch, but as most of the way was through mountains we were afraid of the fog and so waited until after lunch and then went exploring the other side of the island - a most successful expedition. We 'wandered' Bobjohn on the high road and struck off down a most seductive little track between pine trees and flowering shrubs and tree ferns - the whole place smelt like a greenhouse. Then we emerged on to a boulder strewn hillside with red leaved bushes (very like the scenery in my Ah Chong picture[21]) and there we ate our tea. The track ended at a very nice little fishing village - wonderfully clean for China and with quite a good temple set in a grove of trees and guarded by two huge stone dogs of the Pekinese variety. The roof was green tiles and a little stone bridge led to it. I did a sketch of it. Further on we came to a dear little secluded bay with white sand and clear green water which will come in very useful for bathing later on. We returned by a new and lovely coast road and didn't get back until after dark. Ian enjoys these sorts of expeditions as much as I do and with Bobjohn to take us over the dull bits there are limitless places to explore.

Lauriston
16th March 1927 Hong Kong

Tomorrow's Ian's day on - if fine I'm going to pay 10 cents and sit on the ferry boat all afternoon and go backwards and forwards across the harbour drawing junks - it is much the best plan as you see them under sail and I want to do a woodblock print of one.

Lauriston
22nd March 1927 Hong Kong

I was so glad to get your letter yesterday as I hadn't heard for over a fortnight when I got one via Siberia - it seems a most reliable route and will take just half the time when we are in Wei hai - but I should write occasionally via Suez letters to 'L27' as the naval mails always arrive first and they sometimes get an extra one.

On Sunday we had a delightful day - we took Bobjohn over to the Mainland and drove 60 miles through the New Territory - I should think one of the most beautiful drives in the world. It was very exciting setting off into China in Bobjohn! It was an ideal day - all morning sunny and hot and in the afternoon clouding over to a still greyness - but very clear and fresh. Until you get clear of Kowloon it is hideous - but once into the mountains and on to the coast road it is too beautiful for words - Blue islands and deeper blue channels between little bays of white sand and shrub covered hillside.

After about 10 miles you turn inland across a densely populated and cultivated plain. Dozens of little walled villages each with its grove of trees and all round paddy fields and market gardens - with no hedges or fences, only divided from each other by raised paths. It was all very neutral in colour with a curious flat effect - the only colour being the blue clothes of the peasants and their huge yellow and orange hats and an occasional emerald green tree. At one place we abandoned Bobjohn (rather with misgiving as the back was full of coats and food and spare tyres etc. but not a thing was touched and we were away over an hour). We followed along a little path which led us to a three storey pagoda in excellent repair (I did a little sketch) and further on to the walled and moated village - we explored another village which contained some fine Chinese houses and a temple and the inhabitants were most friendly and nice - at another place further on I got a drawing of a humped back bridge. We stopped at Fanling and had tea at the golf club and after that the scenery changes and one gets up into the mountains which are covered with trees and shrubs and then one drops down into the very fertile Sha-Tiu valley where all the Imperial rice used to be grown. It was just beginning to come up in some fields and is an extraordinary vivid yellow green - the Chinese plough their fields with a most primitive looking plough drawn by water buffalo - horrid beasts like grey India rubber oxen and very fierce. We got home just after dark and I'm just longing to do the expedition again and get some more sketches - the snag is it cost 8/- to get Bobjohn over and back - so it isn't worth going unless one has the whole day.

Saturday was fine - though cold - in the morning I went to see Captain Raikes being rowed over from 'Titania' to the P and O in a fourteen oared cutter manned by the Captains and 1st Lieuts of the submarines - they gave him a fine send off with crackers and syrens. Everyone is sorry he has gone - his new job is appointments officer at Fort Blockhouse which may be very useful to us as Ian will be able to find out from him later what his next job is to be.

In the afternoon we had a tennis party. The captain of the Ambrose (Poland) came and his wife who has only just arrived - she is charming and is a great friend of Phil Acworth's - she has also left her children in England. It was very cold but otherwise successful.

After dinner as it was a gorgeous full moon we drove over the mountains to Repulse Bay and danced there coming back at midnight by the coast road - a very nice expedition.

I've quite blossomed out as a golfer! I played with a lady the other day and beat her eight up! And Ian only gives me a stroke a hole on the long links and we have very good games. It is funny how one suddenly gets the knack of a thing and Ian is so bucked.

It's been wonderful luck hitting off Ian's three weeks in dock and his proper refit is due in September and will probably last until December after which I hope to return home! Owing to this refit Ian probably won't go to Japan even if the others go - but I believe it is possible to get to Pekin now - Mrs Carson went the other day with another female and said it was quite wonderful and lovely things to be picked up dirt cheap. I should love to see something of Imperial and Mandarin China - as of course here one sees only coolie and peasant China - though that is interesting as the life and houses and clothes and agriculture of that class have scarcely changed in the last 1000 years. We are reading an absorbingly interesting book called 'China and the West' by Soothill. Do get it. It is very clearly written and shows how the peasant situation is only the logical outcome of the past and is in a way a repetition of what has gone before. It also speaks of a Mr Lancelot Dent, a merchant in Canton who behaved very courageously during the troublesome time before we acquired Hong Kong. Was he Uncle John's father? Or who was he? I wonder so much if any letters are still extant written from Hong Kong during its early days? I know you haven't any but I wonder if Aunt Mab has - I remember Uncle Herbert giving me envelopes with old H.K. stamps - I would love to know something about life out here in pioneer days. It seems so incredible that 100 years ago this was a barren, pirate infested rock. What would the early traders think if they saw it now - a huge and very fine city and all beautifully planted with trees and flowering shrubs and all accomplished in the span of a man's life. I'm trying to get a book on Marco Polo's travels - at the moment Ian and I are both frightfully thrilled with the whole subject - I wish I had a 'race memory' which could show me what life was like here when my ancestors first came. Your theory about Dent money having been made into opium is at any rate partially correct - as all the original merchants traded in it - even after it became illegal - though the Chinese did the actual smuggling. But when a certain point was reached the English merchants all agreed to give up the opium they had in their ships (to the value of a couple of million pounds sterling) but Chinese wanted to have Mr Dent as a hostage (whether because he was the leading merchant or whether he was more heavily involved in the opium! It doesn't say) Anyway he was prepared to go though he risked death and torture but the other merchants wouldn't consent and so the question arose for the first time of extra-territoriality - which is now such a burning question. After this lot of opium had been destroyed the English merchants seem to have behaved honourably about not importing any more themselves - though other nations continued to and the Chinese Imperial Authorities held the British responsible - they being the principal merchants - a very difficult situation.

Lauriston, 1 Bowen Road
29th March 1927 Hong Kong

The Spring cruise is indefinitely postponed owing to the rather hectic situation that has arisen - so I'm glad I didn't take a passage and we've been able to keep this room on. But the air is full of wars and rumours of wars and every time the telephone bell goes I expect to hear that Ian is off. He nearly went yesterday being emergency submarine at a couple of hours notice but L1 and L5 went instead under sealed orders. The Ambrose and Titania are off to evacuate missionaries - but in the meantime six submarines are to be kept to defend this place and L27 is one of them - much to my joy. They are living in the submarines now and drawing 'hard lying' which is something! I'm awfully glad I'm here - as if I were at home I should be fussing dreadfully - but here one knows more what is going on - also even if they are sent away they are bound to come back for docking etc. so one will see them from time to time. It is interesting to be in the midst of things and this place is as safe as England really and wonderfully unmoved by everything and not even full of refugees. The great thing is of course if Japan and America stand in with us which they now show signs of doing. Wasn't it a mercy the troops and ships arrived here just in time. If a Labour government had been in power and not sent troops the Shanghai concessions would now have been overrun by the defeated Northern troops and the Europeans looted and burnt and massacred - as this has happened in the Chinese city and would have been worse in the settlements - and no League of Nations or peaceful persuasion can deal with undisciplined rabble. One of the Southern generals[22] is supposed to be a good man and if he can maintain his power there may be some hope. He is not under the Red influence and he is a very able military commander and seems to have control over his troops. There is not much use writing about the situation as by the time you get this letter it will all have changed.

On Saturday I was on at the Canteen from 6 till 10.20 working the tea urn - it was quite hard work - but de luxe compared to the Overseas Club as there were 'boys' to do all the washing up and other dirty work. I think the Y.M.C.A is a most excellent institute.

On Sunday afternoon Ian and I went for a delightful picnic - always our favourite amusement - this particular picnic was rather blighted by the fact that we forgot the tea! But we had the eatables and a bottle of milk. It was a clear day with a good deal of cold wind - we abandoned Bobjohn at the police station and set off to look for a village which existed for years without anyone being aware of its existence as it is hard to find. It used to be inhabited by pirates. We started off along a barren and boulder strewn promontory with sea on both sides - where there didn't look as if would be cover for a wigwam let alone a village - but after scrambling up hill for some time we suddenly came out on a fascinating plateau of short grass and flowering shrubs and the track we were following plunged down into a little wood entirely composed of a tree covered with insignificant green flowers which smelt like gardenias - rather nice. We wound through the wood and sure enough at the end we came out into a little village surrounded by small fields with bamboo hedges quite hidden in a hollow. Since piracy on the island has ceased to be the recognised profession the village has fallen on evil days - the chief pirate's house is falling down and the place was chiefly inhabited by chow dogs. In the evening Maurice came to dinner - we asked him at 8 and of course not knowing the way here he allowed lots of time and arrived at twenty to while I was dressing! Such are the disadvantages of a bed sitting room! However there is a curtain right across the room so I dressed behind it (Ian was in possession of the bathroom) while poor Maurice had to sit and converse with an unseen host or hostess. (At least I hope unseen) The Nichols joined with us and we played childish games.

Yesterday the 'Resolute' (the last of the tourist ships) was in and the silk shops were thronged - when I asked the price of the washing crepe - the wily salesman showed me the ticket marked $4 a yard and then bent over and whispered 'You resident - I do it for you $2.80' and I'll probably get it in the end for $2.50 - only not if there are Americans in the shop!

Do my letters amuse you - the mixture of dances and frivolities and alarms and excursions going on all around - well that is just what life is like and one enjoys everything and takes no thought for the morrow. Anyway I'm not sorry the Southern Cruise is off as I doubt whether the family purse would have survived the strain and yet I couldn't bear to have been left here with all the other wives going south.

I feel I've been very lucky to have been seeing so much of Ian. So what ever happens it has been well worth coming - he is a darling - I go on loving him more and more and nothing ever disturbs his serenity - which is most soothing to my not always needless wild alarms - He is not really socially inclined but he is always prepared to enjoy a dance or other festivity and he is very popular among his contemporaries. Until I arrived he never went out at all (being too busy with Bobjohn).

Lauriston
1st April 1927 Hong Kong

Alas! Ian has been whisked away - we'd been rather expecting it for the last week and on Wednesday evening he had orders to sail on Thursday. I don't think his destination is a secret - but perhaps it is safer to say it is a place I have been to and didn't think much of!

The idea is they may have to evacuate it and the two submarines are to cover and defend the ship taking refugees. The Ambrose has gone further up the coast on the same mission. I'm not really anxious as under the circumstances a submarine is quite the safest thing to be in - though pretty uncomfortable as I gather they won't get ashore much and of course haven't a depot ship - but the idea is that it won't be for long - as either the evacuation will take place very hurriedly or not at all - or if it settles down into 'standing by' two other boats will relieve them from here at the end of ten days or a fortnight - so really it isn't as bad as the Southern Cruise - from the point of view of separation.

Things seem suddenly to have taken a more serious turn and one doesn't know what will happen next. I am not at all lonely or dull - as an unattached female here is of great social value - so the difficulty is not to get too many engagements - the trouble is I feel it is such a waste of time as if I can't be with Ian I'd like to be with you and Eleanor - also without Ian I can't explore the country or back streets etc. - so one is simply reduced to playing golf and tennis and dancing - which however is great fun in its own way.

Tomorrow Tim Taylor is taking me out to dinner and to 'H.M.S Pinafore' and on Monday I am going to a dance given in Helen

Hog's honour and on Wednesday is her wedding. I hope it will be a fine day so I can wear the dress we got in S. Moulton Street and the red crinoline hat I got in Manila. I've also got engagements with other grass widows (Mesdames Brown, Poland, North and Lushington). Ian has promised to write a story and send it to me to illustrate - poor dear he won't have much to divert him where he is just now - so he ought to get some writing done.

It is horrid this uncomfortable atmosphere - especially as one likes the Chinese so much and - left to themselves they like us - the population of Hong Kong is going up by leaps and bounds on account of Chinese coming to live here as they prefer British rule - and all the War Lords bank their money here and in Shanghai under our protection!

It is these dreadful Bolsheviks who really are at the root of all the trouble - or rather the anti foreign part of it. There is also a definitely national spirit growing amongst the Chinese - but this is a most excellent thing and one we are more than prepared to encourage - it is all very difficult and I pity the people who have to direct our policy. Take the 'Bias Bay' incident for example - I don't know what version you've had of it in the English press - but these are the facts. Bias Bay is a few miles from here - but on Chinese soil not in the British governed New Territory. It is known to be headquarters of a gang of pirates who for months past have been boarding British ships and robbing the passengers - mostly Chinese - the worst case being the 'Seary Bee' which was entirely filled with rich Chinese returning home for Chinese New Year from Singapore. The pirates came on board as passengers - and then when out at sea captured the English officers - robbed all Chinese passengers and made off in junks - the officers being released when it was all over. Our repeated requests to Canton to do something about it met with no response - or rather the Cantonese Government kept saying they would do something but never did. The pirates grew bolder and things were getting to such a pass that the other day we sent a primitive naval expedition round Bias Bay who burnt all the villages to the ground and the junks - but destroyed no other property and there was no loss of life - the people were given warning to clear out and it was explained to them why it was being done. Now your labour or socialist man would say we had no right to use force on a foreign government's property - but on the other hand Chinese passengers travelling in British ships expect to be safe guarded and if the Chinese authorities can't and won't interfere - I think we are justified in taking the law into our own hands and smoking out the pirates' lair as this was the only remedy as it is impossible to send armed escorts with every ship. I rather doubt if this was perhaps a tactful moment to do it - but we had borne it for many months and it was becoming insupportable.

Lauriston
6th April 1927 Hong Kong

The last few days have been rather depressing - what with Ian away and not very good news in the papers and <u>foul</u> weather, one day hot and the next bitter cold and always rain and fog or wind. I caught a bad chill on Monday and had to go to bed instead of to the Philip's dance. But I'm quite all right now. I see in the paper that the one place in China that is peaceful at the moment is where Ian has gone! The cruiser up there has just been relieved - so I expect L27 will be relieved next week too. I do hope so as it seems so pointless being here without Ian - also without him I can't explore or sketch (not that the weather would have permitted either) and altogether it would be terribly mouldy if it weren't that there were such nice people here - and every day someone rings you up and asks you to play bridge or golf or something.

I'm driving Bobjohn with great success as he is going better than he has ever done in his life - but my runs are restricted to Repulse Bay and Deepwater Bay as I promised Ian I wouldn't go to the Mainland or through the town. However I feel very grand offering people lifts out to the golf course!

I went a 'bust' yesterday and bought some silk for a dress (5/- a yard double width) I enclose a pattern - also enough white crepe de chine for a petticoat for 4/6 and a lovely fillet lace six inches wide hand made for 2/3 a yard to make 'bust bodices' and a most amusing cross stitch table cover.

Ian promised to write a story while he was at Swatow - I hope he has as I long to get started on some more illustrations.

I've made Bobjohn some superb covers - with a white monogram a la taipan!

He looks so smart and I'm sure Ian will be very bucked. Bobjohn is both the joke and the admiration of the Colony! I'm generally introduced as the owner of the car that was brought out in a submarine - and I can get through any dinner party with the dullest partner with that as a subject to start on!

I'm longing for some more news of you and my beloved - I feel I really ought to hurry up and start a baby if possible - before I am 'evacuated' from China, which I suppose will happen if there is any trouble here.

Oh bother! All my envelopes have stuck together and all my shoes have grown green mushrooms - what a loathsome climate - but I don't care about anything because Ian is returning on Saturday!

Lauriston
8th April 1927 Hong Kong

Talk about Plymouth or Skye or even Ireland being rainy - all these put together are not as bad as Hong Kong at this time of year. It has rained for a week day and night practically without ceasing - sometimes a downpour and at the best a scotch mist - as for clothes I've worn nothing except my old Aquascutum and felt hat - it has also been very cold and dark and pretty melancholy and I've got a sniffley cold and cough as the result.

Tomorrow Ian returns at midday so I am rejoicing - I wonder what the next move will be? We hear thousands of tons of coal have been ordered to be sent to Wei hai - so that looks as if we might be going there after all - one thing is there is no difficulty about rooms as the Island Hotel has to give preference to the Navy as it is on Admiralty property.

Lauriston
12th April 1927 Hong Kong

Ian employed his time at Swatow most profitably by a quite charming story called 'Ginger'[23] - one of the very nicest and full of the incidents we've seen on our various expeditions and so will be delightful to illustrate. I find it very difficult to settle down to making pictures as all the time I feel I ought to be out wandering about collecting 'copy' as the pictures themselves can be done any time. I'm doing a sketch of a little boy of three the son of the Engineer Captain of the Fleet who is living here. He is a dear little boy and nice looking and stands as good as gold and I think it is going to be rather a success. I could make money out here doing children only I should be far too paralysed by shyness!

After a week of continuous rain and fog it cleared up yesterday and one fine day here makes up for the many bad ones. The great clouds of mist rolled off the hills and left a landscape of sparkling freshness and vivid young green and hundreds of the most gorgeous butterflies flew out - some as large as birds and every colour - yellow and black - and orange and peacock - and everything smelt warm and sweet and most like a greenhouse and all the junks spread their matting sails to dry and everything was flooded with sunshine - today is foggy again on the heights but fine below and pretty hot and sticky.

It was funny to think that six weeks ago I didn't know a soul here - and yet at the dance last night I found I knew about half the people - and how quickly one gets interested in and absorbed into a new milieu.

Lauriston, Bowen Road
17th April 1927 Hong Kong

Yesterday I went to church in the morning and in the afternoon we took tea and went for an exploring expedition up into the hills. We discovered a dear little valley filled with most wonderful sorts of lily flowers - most exotic - also wicked looking spotted arums with black tongues - another hillside was a blaze of red azaleas - so though it was a grey and ugly day we enjoyed our expedition.

In the evening we went to dine up the Peak - this is always an undertaking as first you have to walk to the station then take a train to the top and finally go off into space in a rickshaw! There was a dense fog at the top and the rickshaw coolies in their palm leaf coats were most sinister and macabre figures.

Tomorrow we are going out sailing as Mr Ede has a little yacht, the 'Plover'. I hope I <u>shan't</u> be seasick! What is even more fun is they are getting up a hacking party and are going to lend Ian and me ponies and we are going over the hills by coolie paths to the Country Club at Sheko. I haven't any suitable clothes - but the tailor will make me a pair of khaki breeches for a few shillings.

The Ambrose is still away - but things are looking rather better on the whole I think. I am lucky to have Ian back and I feel quite ashamed to meet poor 'Ambrose' wives. Bobjohn let me down badly the other day. Ian had a 'day on' so I asked Mrs North (the Ambrose doctor's wife) to come for a drive round the island - which she'd never done. It was a lovely day and we started off gaily - but just beyond the University (about three miles out) the magneto chain dropped off - and so we had to return ignominiously in a 'bus - go and dig Ian out and collect the wretched machine from the ditch where I had abandoned it! Of course it only took him five minutes to put it right - but too late for our trip and I felt very ashamed!

I've finished the little Bartlett boy's portrait - quite a success and begun to do the illustrations for 'Ginger'.

I'm trying to get Ian's summer wardrobe into order. He acquired several pairs of khaki shorts from the soldiers at Aden - but they must have been meant for the guards - as Ian is pretty long in the leg - but they come well below his knees and looked very dowdy! But it is a difficult job shortening them.

Lauriston
22nd April 1927   Hong Kong

Ian was whisked off again upon Easter Sunday as a few hours notice. This time up to Amoy. However once more Roddy is relieving him and they are due back on Sunday or Monday complete with Ambrose - then they take in fuel and provisions and off again to Wei hai wei. This is a very pleasant surprise as we had all given up any hope of getting there this summer and I had begun negotiations here to move into a very charming service flat next month.

However in the meantime that is 'off' and we go to the simple - you might even say primitive - life of Wei hai. It will be fairly cold when we first arrive and to begin with at any rate there will be nobody there except the submarines and Petersfield. The submarine wives are myself - Betty Brown, Mrs Poland (captain's wife, quite charming) Mrs North (Dr's wife) and Mrs Lushington if she is out of hospital. One of the sloop wives is coming too, a Mrs Anderson Morsland who was an actress before she married. The Peterfield females consist of nice Lady Tyrwhitt and the girls and that's all - and there we shall be on a little island one mile long by half a mile broad and some miles from the Mainland and quite cut off from the rest of the world except when the Shanghai steamer comes in once a week with mails and newspapers. If the weather is up to standard and Ian is there I shall love it - except for the feeling of being frightfully cut off from you and Eleanor - though not really more than here once the letters start coming direct - in fact via Siberia it only takes three weeks to Shanghai and on if it catches the connection.

I wish I thought we could get a passage up in Ambrose - as otherwise I see nothing for it but my old friend the 'Hiuchow' who probably smellier and more rat infested than ever! However it ought to be calm weather at this time of year - and I feel as long as I'm not sick I can put up with almost anything else even pirates! I also hear that there are Bandits at Wei hei - not on the island of course - but I feel sketching expeditions on the mainland won't be encouraged.

What a pack up I shall have - as already we seem to have acquired a vast amount of things - mostly rubbish - one encumbrance is an entire suite of doll's furniture (two armchairs, a sofa and a table) most beautifully made - that Geoffrey's mother gave me to send to Eleanor (as a sort of thank you for the picture I did of Geoffrey which is now framed and looks very nice) also two fragile Chinese dolls and some other trifles. I had hoped to send them back via Captain Homan for Eleanor's birthday - but now of course we shan't be here when he arrives.

Lauriston
30th April 1927 Hong Kong

What a comic incongruous party we shall be in the 'Huichow'. Betty Brown for whom I really have an affection though she is incredibly silly sometimes and annoying (Yes your guess about Mr Murphy was more than correct. What a time I had over that affair but mercifully it has all worked out all right. I can tell you a very entertaining story about it when I return!) Then Mrs North - older and plain and was a hospital nurse and is wrapped up in her baby - there is something nice and rather pathetic about her. Then Mrs Poland - very charming and beautifully dressed and smart and social - and finally Mrs Lushington who ought to be so nice - she is very nice looking (fair hair and blue eyes and fresh colour) aged about 30 - very clever - her first husband was a brother of the man who wrote 'Lady into fox'[24] - but as a matter of fact I find her rather tiresome - she has a gushing manner (which always puts me off) and is pretty 'D - d superior'. Now can you imagine a party with fewer points of contact (we may have an addition a Mrs Morshead who was the leading lady at the Plymouth Repertory Theatre) It is almost like our desert island game - and there we start off together in this little coasting steamer and travel for six days and then arrive on an island one mile long and half a mile broad where we are shut up together for the rest of the summer. It ought to be priceless. The great thing is that they are all nice in their own way and I don't think any of them are quarrelsome - and Mrs Poland may turned out to be very nice indeed on closer acquaintance and is the only one I suspect of having a shadow of a sense of humour.

The whole American submarine flotilla are in for a few days and so I'm seeing my kind Manila friends again - our tennis party was for their benefit.

In the evening we went for a dance at the Commodores. Twenty-five of the Yanks had been dining in the 'Titania' first - not wisely either and the trouble of prohibition is that when they get a chance of a drink it goes to their unaccustomed heads. I'm glad to say my special friends behaved like perfect gentlemen - but one or two of the others had to be tactfully removed by a special party told off from the 'Titania' for the purpose - and I danced with a man who informed me that I was the most 'wunnerful gurrl' he had ever met! I told this to Ian who was frightfully amused!

Today I am lunching with a Gunner's wife over at Kowloon and then riding with Mrs Nichol on army horses. In our jodhpur breeches and khaki shirts and felt hats we look like cowgirls off the films! I'm hoping to get riding up at Wei hei too with any luck.

I'm going to ask Maurice to lunch and come for an expedition on Sunday - alas! Our dear Bobjohn has gone north in the Ambrose - I miss him sadly. On Sunday we went out a picnic to Skeko and for a lovely walk and to a delightful Chinese theatrical performance - much more amusing and attractive than the Russian Ballet! It took place in a huge bamboo and mat shed at one of the fishing villages. We were the only Europeans present and my nearest neighbour was a Chinese baby who couldn't have been more than a few days old. I've never seen anything so tiny.

We ought to get a good pay day this month as Ian has been drawing 'hard lying money' $1.50 per day and also pilotage into Swatow. However as he has lost most of his clothes and possessions while severed from the Ambrose - perhaps we won't really score very much! Would you be an angel and do a detestable job for us, and that is post out to us that roll of Donegal tweed Mrs Macnair once gave Ian and which is in the camphor wood chest in the box cupboard. He has gone through the knees and elbows of his 'plus fours' suiting and it is difficult to get tweed out here - but a Chinese tailor makes up your own material excellently for a few shillings so this is the opportunity to get that not very nice but hard wearing stuff made up and it would see Ian through the next cold winter. The postage oughtn't to be very much as it won't require a box or anything - just brown paper and a label. 'H.M.S/m L27 China Station (C/OG.P.O.)

I'm reading 'Java Head' which is interesting and re-reading 'Potterism'.

Lauriston, 1 Bowen Road
7th May 1927 Hong Kong

I've heard that Ian has arrived at Wei-hei-wei - the sickening thing is that our ship - the wretched old 'Huichow' has postponed its sailing for the third time! and doesn't now go until Thursday - nearly a fortnight wasted - Ian sitting quietly at Wei hei and me kicking my heels here however there is nothing to be done about it.

One night I dined with Mrs Lambert and played bridge. At dinner I sat next the District Officer who said to me "I hear you and your husband were at the Chinese theatre in Aberdeen" - I asked him how he knew as we were the only Europeans there and he said he'd heard from a Chinese who had told him where we lived and everything. Rather amazing that they should take such an interest in one as Aberdeen is a little fishing village miles away. The D.O. said if I was interested in Chinese things he would take me to a Chinese dinner - so I'm going on Monday which will be great fun. He is such a nice man and very interesting as of course he talks Chinese.

Lauriston
11th May 1927 Hong Kong

I'm still here as for the forth time the 'Huichow' has postponed sailing and now goes on Friday the 13th (so we think we are sure to be pirated!) It is sickening wasting all this time - but we are so thankful to be going to Wei hei at all - for a few days it seemed quite likely that we shouldn't be allowed there - but a reassuring cable arrived yesterday and now I gather it is looked upon as the safest place in China - and anyway we should be all right on the island surrounded by the Ambrose and eight submarines and one or two light cruisers - but I daresay sketching expeditions to the mainland won't be encouraged. It is frightfully interesting seeing the English papers - one gets no news out here except 'buzzes' and the ships are suddenly shot off we know there is trouble and occasionally one hears things privately. Of course at Wei hei we shall get no news at all until the four week old papers arrive from England! On the whole though there seems to be much less tension in the air and one hopes things are calming down and that it is not the calm before the storm!

I've just come in from a delightful day out in a launch visiting some of the Islands with the local district officer Mr Wynne Jones - a very nice Mrs Sayer was there too and another female and a 'makee learn' D.O. We left at 11 o'clock and first went to a large and more or less uninhabited island. We bathed and landed on a sandy beach and the D.O went to interview the head man of the tiny village, a presumably satisfactory visit as he returned with a basket of eggs - a friendly gift. Then we went to Cheng Chow where all the refugee missionaries have gone. There is a rather fine temple, but the flies were so awful that we fled back to the launch. We got back at 5.30 having had a picnic lunch and tea on the launch. I was very interested to see these outlying islands - most of them larger than Hong Kong itself. On Monday Mr Wynne Jones took Mrs Nichol and myself and a Mr Wood to a Chinese restaurant. We sat on stools round a round table and ate with chopsticks out of little bowls. All the food was piled in the middle of the table - and excellent it was. We started with the sharks fin soup which looked horrid all gluey - but tasted delicious - then fried prawns in batter - and fish with a marvellous sauce. The best thing of all was varnished duck skin so crisp it melted in your mouth and was eaten with a funny sort of bread - then rice with shrimps and nuts - and finally to end up with 'gold and silver' eggs (pigeons eggs in soup) very difficult to compete with chopsticks! You drank tea all the time out of a bowl and at intervals towels wrung out in hot scented water were brought for one to wipe one's face and hands.

It was a most amusing dinner and going with the D.O. who speaks Chinese one knew one was getting the proper things. We ended the evening by going to the very European cinema.

The Chinese are quaint people. I saw two dear old gentlemen today walking along hand in hand! And everyone sees them solemnly taking their birds out in cages for a walk!

I've just made such a nice corn coloured silk dress with smocking - it's a comfort silk is cheap here (and washing) as one requires two clean dresses a day and underwear. That pretty printed crepe de chine I got last summer at Harvey Nichols has 'run' badly in the wash and the silk dress I got in Paris has split - otherwise my clothes are doing well.

S.S. 'Huichow'
16th May 1927 At Sea

The Captain said he will post this at Tientsin and from there it is only twelve days to London so you ought to get this letter in just over a fortnight - that makes you seem much nearer. While I am at Wei hei I shall send all my letters via Siberia as - at present at any rate - it seems quite safe - you better write that way too. We go to Wei hei on Wednesday forenoon and we are all getting very thrilled. This has been a very different trip to my last one in this ship!

For one thing there is a new and very efficient captain and everything is beautifully clean and spick and span and food excellent - and though it is cold and wet it is quite smooth (touching wood!) and I haven't missed a meal.

One can't take exercise as there isn't enough deck space and I put in a good deal of time sleeping! We all help Mrs North with her dear little one year old baby - I generally have here while Mrs North is bathing and dressing - she is such a friendly little thing. The Amah refused to come to Wei hei, so they will have to find another up there. We play a good deal of Bridge - the Captain and Mrs Poland are very good - but our choice of a fourth are all equally bad. Extraordinary how intelligent people can be so abysmally stupid at Bridge! Mrs Lushington who has a degree in Social Philosophy cannot grasp a 'finesse!'

I try to sew but it is difficult because every spot is draughty and blows your things about, we spend a good deal of time in desultory chat - but so far we are a very harmonious party.

On Friday morning I packed hectically and we came on board at 3.30 and sailed almost at once. It was the first really overpoweringly hot day and I nearly melted away trying to stuff my swollen possessions into my shrunken trunks! I left 'Lauriston' with mutual expressions of goodwill on all sides. I may go back there in the autumn if I can get one of the corner rooms and if I can't get a service flat. I was really sorry to be going away from Hong Kong (apart from the Ambrose and submarines not being there!) though really life at Wei hei is more in my line - but people have been so nice and kind - it is funny to think that three months ago I hadn't even heard of people with whom I am now really friends - one is thrown so very much in contact and ones lives here on such similar lines that you become friends quicker than at home. However several of them expect to come up to Wei hei later on.

This is a dull voyage as one is out of sight of land and we haven't even seen a junk - and the sea always looks the same all over the world!

We are off Shanghai just now, but are not calling there.

What a funny life this is and what pity I dislike the sea so as I am on it so much!

I do miss you and Eleanor so dreadfully.

Chapter Six

The Island Hotel
21st May 1927 Wei hei wei

Here we are back again in this enchanting place - which hasn't altered one little bit since we were here last and is as nice as ever and the people just as smiling and friendly. If only you and Eleanor were here I should be completely happy - and I'm sure it is a place you would both like. The air is dazzlingly clear and the sea so blue and everywhere there is a scent of honey with a tang of salt and the whole island is so beautifully clean and tidy like a well kept garden.

We arrived at 10am on Wednesday and as we passed the Ambrose a boat full of husbands came to meet us and another boat for our luggage. It was a lovely sunny day - but still pretty chilly. The hotel opened upon our arrival and we have got the room the Stopfords had last time - right in the middle with a nice big verandah. It is all very primitive - lamps and candles and one's bath water arrives in a kerosene tin!

The bedroom is quite big with a wood floor and had exactly six pieces of furniture in it! 1 bed, 1 wardrobe, 1 dressing table, 2 chairs and a wee table. By working my old connection with the establishment I succeeded in raising a chest of drawers and a rather battered wooden table for a writing table and I have made orange shantung silk window curtains and a curtain behind which Ian can hang his clothes - a blue shantung cover for the writing table and a jade green one on the verandah - Ian has brought the pictures from his cabin (Japanese prints) and with our blue ginger jar and a green bowl of wallflowers and Scissory's bookcase and your wastepaper basket we have now got it really very nice and comfortable. And the walls have just been re-distempered a pretty butter colour - I'm going to get a nice embroidered bedspread and then we shall be complete. The verandah has two wicker chairs and a table and I brought up a vast wicker chair from Hong Kong and Ian's 'boy' Ah Chong is going to get us some pots of flowers. It is rather fun trying to make it all nice and one feels it is worthwhile as we hope to be here at least four months. Also the bare bones of the place are so clean and nice and the view so lovely that it is easy to add the odds and ends. The food is very good and some of the 'boys' are old friends.

Mrs Poland and I are sharing an Amah - we each give her 12$ a month and she does all our washing and our husbands' washing and mending and also irons our dresses and is on tap daily to do odd jobs etc. So it think it is really a good scheme - though perhaps an extravagance as sending washing out is only 6$ a hundred pieces - but it will be nice to have all one's clothes overhauled and put in order, also Ian's - and will give me more time for painting. I've spent the last two mornings up at the Club doing a picture in pastel of the wonderful wisteria tree which is in full bloom. The Club was the Chinese Admiral's House and is very picturesque. Poor Admiral Ting committed suicide when the Chinese fleet surrendered to the Japanese in 1998.

Ian is blissfully happy here as he gets every sort of game - one day he played hockey, tennis and golf one after the other! Today he played cricket and yesterday we had a family foursome against the Polands and just managed to beat them. It is a most amusing little golf links. Tomorrow Ian is taking a day off and he and I and Tim Taylor are going over to the Mainland in the 9.30 ferry and going for a long walk taking lunch with us. Tim Taylor speaks the local dialect and so can chat to the priests at the various temples etc which is interesting. Unfortunately since fixing this up the Commissioner Mr Johnson has asked us to go for a picnic with him and I should love to go as he is a most interesting man (He wrote the 'Lion and Dragon in Northern China' and he was the ex

Emperor's tutor) but we've no means of letting Tim Taylor know so I'm afraid we shall have to stick to the first ploy.

So far the 'Ambrose' is the only ship up here (except a sloop the 'Magnolia') so it is very quiet - but delightful having the whole place to oneself. All the alarms about bandits etc that we heard down in Hong Kong arose from a cable sent by the American Consul at Chefoo which by the misreading of one word - or rather the omission of it - completely altered the sense and gave rise to the whole panic (He said 'In the event of trouble send three cruisers' etc, or words to that effect and it arrived as 'In trouble send cruisers.') All in all it is more than peaceful - and as we don't even get a newspaper it is impossible to realise that the rest of China may be in chaos. (A propos of this - don't send all your letters via Siberia - as we hear that route may be disorganised at any minute.)

I can't believe it is eight years since I was here last - I feel just the same! How little one has to show for the said eight years (except Eleanor!)

Old Ah Chong and his Windy Weather

There lived an old Chinaman, many years ago -
Many more years than you or I shall know -
Who could never stay ashore when the wind began to blow.

He'd go beating out to see in the teeth of half a gale,
In his tubby old junk with its yellow, matting sail;
On each bow an eye, joss-papers round the rail;
Two bronze cannons behind a piece of plate;
A shiney brass capstan and highly scented freight;
A whole kitchen garden in pots along the poop;
A half score of women and children in group
Around a steaming rice dish and little bowls of tit-bits,

Picking with their chopsticks, turn by turn,
And a poultry farm of chickens in a big, round basket
Hanging, under two tall lanterns from the stern.

All day long, while the wind blew softly,
Dreaming he lay in the shade of the trees:
Days and days together, forgetting altogether
His junk lying laden with a favourable breeze.
While the sun warmed him and the gentle breezes charmed him
The woods held him captive, idly at ease.

But when the sun was hidden and the Storm Gods woke
And all around the mountains the thunder broke;
When the wind came tearing through the trees with a roar
And sudden, angry breakers came pounding up the shore;
Then he woke from his dreaming, cast his lethargy aside,
Turned his face towards the tempest, when his brothers turned to hide,
Climbed onboard and weighed the anchor -
The philosopher had died.

All down the coast it's a sign of dirty weather
When you see him beating out,
And traders and pirates and fishermen together
Will straightaway go about,
And seek the friendly lee
Of an island, but not he -
He goes to sea.

And still you can see him when the Monsoon's blowing
And you're feeling sort of thankful, with the shore lights showing -
A heavy squall of rain and the flood tide flowing -
Going beating out to sea in the teeth of half a gale,

In his tubby old junk with its yellow matting sail;
On each bow an eye, joss papers round the rail -
Till his lanterns fade away in the smother of the spray,
Where he's thrashing out to windward from the shelter of the bay.

Ian Macnair.

The Island Hotel
25th May 1927 Wei hei wei

On Sunday we went for a very long expedition - starting at 9.30. We walked to the 1st lagoon over the other side - it was very fascinating going through little villages where blindfolded donkeys were grinding corn with the most primitive grindstones - past snug little thatched farms and across streams where women in gay pink and red dresses were hopefully washing clothes in a pool of muddy water. All the people were wreathed in smiles and at one farm where a dog ran out at us the owner - a charming old gentleman with a white pigtail - came out and overwhelmed us with apologies - we went into a temple on a hillside and the old priest showed us round - it was a species of Buddhist temple and had a fine bronze bell. A bit further on we
heard sounds of music - rather like bagpipes - and we sat by the roadside and watched a funeral go by - all the mourners dressed in white. Then we had lunch and after lunch started to climb a range of mountains. It was pretty hard work - but well worth it for the view from the top was magnificent. We could see for miles all over the Shantung countryside to the bright blue sea on both sides and the lagoons with the salt pans. The hillside itself was covered with darling little irises and under the rocks grew white violets and Solomon's seal. We came back via the Walled City and we saw some very interesting stone tombs shaped like beeskeps which date from 1300A.D. By this time it was nearly five and we were pretty

exhausted and very thirsty - so we took a gharry and drove to the Claridges and touched them for tea.

On Monday Ian had a 'day on'. I took Miss Bardely (the nursing sister) over to the Mainland - not a too successful expedition as there was a thunder storm and we got very wet. On Tuesday Mr Claridge came to lunch and we played golf - Ian was playing cricket - he has raised an eleven in 'L27' and they are very keen. Yesterday we went over and walked round the walls of the city and ate our tea in the little watch tower at the top from which you get a wonderful view of the countryside - a Chinese poet is supposed to have exclaimed upon seeing it for the first time "This must indeed be fairyland!" The Walled City always fascinates me - it is so complete with its four gates and its watch towers and temples, and it is Chinese soil - as when Wei hei wei was ceded to the British the area inside the wall was not included as it would be a terrible disgrace to a Chinese to yield a walled city. This is about the last place in China where poor little girls have their feet bound and quite a lot of the men have 'queues' (pigtails). It is amazingly remote and unsophisticated and I imagine the country people are quite unaware that there is a war going on in the rest of China.

I wish you could see my room - it looks so nice now that I've got all the curtains up etc. and bowls of wallflowers and cornflowers. There is great rivalry as to who can get their room the nicest - the bare bones are the same for everyone - as all the rooms are exactly the same shape and size and with the standard six items of furniture! The first comers rather score as we pinch the few extras bits that are going. This place is a real democracy - as it matters not if you are a Captain or Sub Lieut. or if you have £500 or £5000 a year - you all get treated alike - same room - same food etc - and apart from bar club subscriptions and ferry to the Mainland there is nothing you can spend money on except the local silks and such like products or sweeties at the village shop - its rather a comfort after Hong Kong where temptation besets one at every turn! Also one all one's old clothes and sandshoes - one can get very nice stockings here - like Mrs Ree's only made of real silk - but only in white or shantung colour.

It is warmer today and no wind - we are playing tennis this afternoon and tomorrow we are going to a party at the Commissioner's and in the evening to dine at the Club - the first 'ladies night' of the season. I think there are only six ladies!

The Club has got an extraordinarily good and up to date library now - so we have really all the comforts of civilisation (except electric light and sanitation!)

The Island Hotel
29th May 1927 Liukungtao

There is very little to chronicle here. One wakes up every morning to find the sun streaming in and a sparkling blue sea. Ian goes off to the ship at 8 and returns about 4 - earlier at weekends and later sometimes on the two days a week that they go to sea. I sally forth sketching most mornings and in the afternoons play golf or tennis or go picnics. Our wildest dissipation is to dine and dance at the Club where you eat the same food and see the same people that you do in the hotel!

I wish I could give you an idea of the life - as it is so unique and so devoid of all modern things that one has come to take for granted - no trains or motors or telephones or newspapers - no daily posts (an irregular mail about once a week) no water laid on - a room like a summer house without carpets etc. and one walks through the garden to another place for one's meals. And it is all so frightfully nice - chiefly I think on account of the brilliant atmosphere - however hot it is the air is always shining clear and though the scenery in barren the colours are wonderful. The only hardship is the water. This used to come from the dockyard but now that the distilling plant has packed up we get it from the brackish well - and it is so hard no soap will lather in it - and for drinking it has to be so chlorinated that it nearly makes one sick even washing one's teeth in it.

The lovely wisterias are over - but the acacias are all out and the peonies, and all the roadsides are bordered with irises and every rubbish heap is covered with cornflowers. This island would please your tidy mind - there is scarcely a weed on it and all the road and paths are kept trim and rolled - the labour being supplied by convicts - most mild looking people who are chained together in couples - and you never catch more than one of the pair working - the other always looks on.

This morning we all went to Church on board the Ambrose. It looks nice to see the rows of blue jackets and the officers in their frock coats standing on the deck in the sunshine and it gives one a thrill when the chaplain reads "..............and a security for such as pass on the seas upon their lawful occasions..." and ending by singing "Oh Trinity of love and power" kneeling - before "God save the King."

Ian was 'day on' - so I went back and had tea in his cabin this afternoon I had meant to wash my hair there in the ship's distilled water - but the wind got up and it was so rough going over in the motor boat that I had to lie down on arrival to recover - isn't it awful to be such a bad sailor! Ian and Mr Taylor are busy composing a series of 'Submarine attacks according to the great Poets.' Mr Taylor did a very funny one a la Chinese lyric and Ian one based on 'La belle sans merci'.

We are still a very harmonious party - there has been only one new arrival - the wife of the 1st lieut. of the 'Foxglove' and late leading lady at the Plymouth Repertory Theatre, she and her spotty faced little girl are next to us. On the other side are the Browns - I am as fond of here as one is of a dear little black pussy but she's not an entertaining companion. Beyond is Mrs North, a Dutch woman with a long nose like a snipe - but very worthy. Mrs

Poland is charming - not original - in fact very conventional - but always sweet and very nice to look at and charming clothes and plays a good game of bridge and you feel has at home an attractive well run house and nice well brought up children. Captain Poland is awfully nice - the same type of man as Ian so I would naturally appreciate him! Mrs Lushington is a bouncy young woman with singularly unsuccessful clothes and an almost morbid passion for the works of Uncle John MacCunn! She was thrilled to hear he was my uncle!! In many ways she is the one I have most in common with and who I choose as a companion for explorations - I feel she rather despises my lack of intellect and education and I get a thought 'dry' feeling when she is playful and gushing - but on the whole I like her.

On reading this over it strikes me as being rather 'catty' - which I don't mean as really I'm very lucky to be cast on a desert island with such nice people and I like them all - I don't think there is a single unpleasant trait in any of them - I've only tried to describe their personalities so you can imagine them in the same way that I've tried to describe the dear island. I haven't attempted to describe the various men as there are so many of them - besides I know that like me, women interest you more. The only one who I seem to refer to a lot is Tim Taylor[25] as he is Ian's chief friend - he is also captain of a submarine, not married and rather taciturn and unsociable - very ugly and swarthy - looks like a Jew and is really a Cornish man and has a most unexpectedly whimsical turn of mind - likes poetry and is very clever at making things with his fingers.

I don't know how the war is getting on in China and can only say that everything is more than peaceful in this corner of it.

I'm engaged on some large pastels - they are very nearly nice - I wish I could manage water colour as well as I can pastel as it is such a much more attractive medium - but I cannot cope with it out of doors. Pastel on the other hand is delightful to work with but I don't really care for the result when done. I've been commissioned to do a picture of some part of the island for Captain Poland.

I'm really doing quite a lot of painting to salve my conscience to this otherwise completely lotus-eating existence - Mrs Lushington is writing an article on Chinese women. She apparently wrote a book on 'Fans' when she was in Japan and various articles on Japanese life.

The Club here has quite a good selection of books which is rather a joy - not of course very up to date. We see all the illustrated papers and Punch and Blackwood and the Times - only the latter so old that it is like yesterday's toast.

I've still got a cold - but otherwise I am very flourishing, so is Ian - even though we are among the rash people who eat strawberries - one would have to be very strong-minded to resist them at every meal and we always wash them.

The Island Hotel
4th June 1927 Wei hei wei

I always thought that climate or weather contributed more than most things to one's happiness - and here it is simply enchanting to awake day after day to either sunshine or a lovely still grey clearness. One reason for the marvellous atmosphere is I suppose that there is no large town within hundreds of miles and nothing to make smoke except the Ambrose! Ian says he can wear a stiff shirt for a week!

Yesterday we had a most strenuous day - we started at 11 o'clock and went to the Commissioner's to drink the King's health (it being his birthday). All the head men from the village had come and bowed to the King's portrait and drank ceremonial tea and one man brought a Chinese poem he had written in the King's honour. After that all the British community came - a pathetic little handful - and a certain number of us stayed on to lunch. I sat next to the Commissioner (on his left - so senior has Ian become!) He is a delightful man and most interesting - he is supposed to be the greatest living Chinese scholar - he can read all the old mandarin books and classics which is more than most Chinese can do and being attached to the Manchu court he knew every Chinaman of note. After the fall of the dynasty he became the poor little ex-emperor's tutor[a] and now of course he has got this comparatively unimportant job - but he is the ideal man for it as the Chinese love him and his sympathies are so very deeply with them. Apart from his being an interesting man he is a marvellous host and we had a superb 'tiffin' with strawberries and cream followed by an American tennis tournament in which the Macnair family did not distinguish themselves. At 7 o'clock we rushed back here and shifted and dined at the Club with a most hilarious party - our host being the Engineer Commander - Herbert by name - brother of A.P.H of 'Punch'. Then we danced and finished up with musical chairs!

On Tuesday Mrs Lushington and I went over to the Mainland to return the D.O's wife's call. She is a particularly pleasant woman - which is great luck as there are so few here, I mean people not pleasant ones only! Then Mrs L and I went on and prowled in the city and I nearly bought a mandarin dressing chest for 12$ (I may yet unless we go to Pekin where they can be had for 6$ - in Hong Kong they are 25 to 35$) We also saw a fine funeral procession with all the priests in blue mandarin robes - each with a silk umbrella held over his head.

In the procession were life sized paper horses (one bright pink!) Also a house completely furnished and a carriage. All these would later be burnt and so accompany the dead man to the spirit world. We wondered what the feelings of our relations in England would have been if they could have seen us in a vision - two unprotected

---

[a] Played by Peter O'Toole in the film 'The Last Emperor

English women in the midst of a large Chinese crowd under the walls of an old city! And what a nice, friendly polite crowd they were - I've never met nicer people than the inhabitants of Shantung!

This morning a large Blue Funnel boat came in - they only call here very occasionally. So Mrs Poland and I seized her husband's motor boat and rushed off the have our hair cut! (You can't get it done here - we have to do each others' with nail scissors) - so as the 'Sarpedon' had an excellent barber we both of us had species of Eton crop to last us for some time - I think it's rather becoming now that my permanent wave is almost exhausted! As we were leaving two men asked us for a lift ashore in the motor boat - they were journalists - one of the being Sir Percival Phillips of the Daily Express. They are en route for Tiensin - so that is I suppose the next trouble area - most annoying as I was hoping to get up to Pekin. On the same steamer were General Duncan and Viscount Gort - they landed here and were by way of in/cog. - I don't know what it means - probably that most of the Defence Force will be sent here for the summer and I can't imagine a better place for them - healthy and room for manoeuvres etc. You may set your mind at rest about it being safe anyway - as the C in C has now lifted the ban on the bungalows and Lady Tyrwhitt arrives next week and the Glencrosses came today.

The Island Hotel
8th June 1927 Wei hei wei

The other day a Jap came round with pearls to sell (we think that he is really a spy!) He had real pearls and sham ones and 'cultured' and you will be relieved to hear that these are not anything like real pearls - the front is just like a large and very good pearl and is gritty - but the back is quite smooth like a mother of pearl button and apparently they can't get the oyster to do any other way except by accident as in a 'real' pearl. Of course the cultured pearls look all right mounted as rings or earrings where the little smooth bit at the back is hidden - but it is hopeless for a necklace. The man had some rather attractive little Japanese prints at 4d each and I bought a dozen.

Wei hei wei is quite a hub of the universe just now what with generals and journalists.

The Island Hotel
10th June 1927 Wei hei wei

Darling Eleanor

This is a picture of mummy's bath water coming in in the morning!

Here is her bath! Would you like one like it?

I miss you so much and long to see you again and give you a real big hug and just smother you with kisses.

It is so lovely and hot here. Daddy is playing cricket today and we shall soon be bathing.

Love to you all and heaps to yourself.
    Your loving
       Mummy.

The Island Hotel
13th June 1927 Wei hei wei

The last letter I wrote to you was via Siberia - so I daresay you will never get it - but I don't think it contained anything interesting.

It is still lovely weather here - almost too hot to go out between 10.30 and 3.30 - though the last day or two there has been a fresh breeze. The hotel garden is so gay now and all English flowers - sweet Williams and Canterbury bells and peonies and an absolute riot of roses. We are also eating green peas and new potatoes and strawberries and on the Mainland the other day I heard a cuckoo - so it is quite easy to imagine you in England in June.

Ian has written a very good article on Bobjohn's adventure and we have sent it complete with photographs to the 'Light Car'. If it appears it will be under a nom de plume - so as to save getting permission from the powers that be - or under my initials I'm not quite sure which. I've been getting some lovely silk underclothes made here and very cheap. I wish there wasn't a silk tax - as otherwise I could send silk home but you can't pay the tax this end and if you sent it unpaid there might be complications with the customs at the other end.

Bobjonah at Wei-hai-wei

Bobjonah, otherwise known as the 'Flying banana', who started life as a chain driven Bleriot Whippet cycle-car, can claim the distinction of being the only car to have travelled to China in a submarine, and he now holds another record in being the only private car to run at Wei hei wei.

Up to last Summer no cars at all had been allowed in the place, but when the convalescent camp was started there for the troops at Shanghai these insisted on bringing a Ford ambulance and a couple of lorries with them, and this gave Bobjonah his opportunity,

He had been brought up to Wei hei wei at the beginning of the Summer for purely care and maintenance purposes and to prevent his turning into a mushroom bed in the damp heat of Hong Kong, without any expectation of being able to use him there. But on the strength of the rule having been waived in favour of the Army vehicles a licence was eventually granted to him to run for a fortnight, "for experimental purposes".

He was therefore taken from the shed where he had been stored on the island of Lieu-kung-tao and driven down to the stone pier below the Hotel at a time when the tide was just the right height to allow of driving him straight onto two planks placed across the top of a large motor boat. About half an hour later he was run off again at Port Edward pier, on the mainland and driven off into the interior.

That first journey, though filled with interest, was rather too hectic to be really enjoyable. By ill-fortune we had hit upon market day in the walled city of Wei hei wei, and at the time when we started out the entire population of the surrounding district was just going home, and the almost universal means of transport was the mule:- mules drawing carts or mules being ridden, mules in pairs with a litter slung between them, or mules loaded with packs being led singly or in strings of two or three; but always mules, an unbroken stream of them for about nine miles on a road just wide enough for two vehicles abreast and with occasional mules coming the other way to add to the complication. And quite definitely, the mules did not like us.

If a string of carts in close order was overtaken from behind, the rear animals had not much scope for giving trouble as they butted violently into the cart in front as soon as they started to try and bolt, but the leading animal was sometimes rather difficult, and if a cart was met with one could never be sure that at the last moment the animal would not swing right round across the road and go off in the opposite direction.

The drivers had no possible means of controlling them from the carts, as the only rein consisted of one piece of string attached to one side of the bridle and so, if they woke up in time, they would leap from the cart and make a frantic dash at the animal's head, sometimes trying to cover his eyes with a coat to hide from him the horrid spectacle. This procedure, not unnaturally, generally succeeded in reduced the mule to a state of panic. The temperature was about ninety in the shade; so it was a hot and trying journey, though not without its amusing incidents; but at last we got out into more open country without serious mishap and some little way further on came to the village of Liu-lin-tsiu. Everyone ran to their house doors to watch us go past and when we stopped at the far end of the village street a small crowd collected to examine us. They were not in the least afraid of the machine but on the other hand thought it most ridiculously funny and roared with laughter, and this in fact was the delightful attitude adopted by everyone we met. Even the men whose mules gave them a vast amount of trouble, instead of turning and reviling us, as they might well have done, seemed to treat the affair as a most excellent joke.

One day, later on, we overtook a venerable old gentleman in a covered cart with a square green wooden top to it and as we drew level the mule took fright and bolted, slipped its leading rein from the torpid driver, and went off down the road at full gallop, the top of the cart bumping and swaying most perilously from side to side and the driver, almost hidden in the dust, in hot and clamorous pursuit. Fortunately the cart stuck to the road and, as by a miracle, the top stuck to the cart, and the whole eventually drawing up was led off down a side road as we passed. Meeting the same equipage on our way back we stopped to let it be led past us and the old gentleman, wreathed in smiles and without a suggestion of reproach for the past, thanked us most courteously for doing so.

Neither the horses in the local shanderidans nor the little shaggy donkeys under their packs seemed to mind us in the least, but the mules, who unfortunately were in a great majority, never really took to us. One, in fact, attached to a cart that we had overtaken and passed, took such a dislike to us that, with ears back and yellow teeth bared, he came after us with obviously hostile intent: once again leaving his driver padding helplessly behind. The road was very rough at this point; so our speed was limited and for a time it was quite an exciting race, but in the end Bobjonah stuck it better than the cart and the mule was forced to give up the chase when both its wheels came off.

During our stop at the village we were examined minutely and the thing that seemed to intrigue them most was the knobs on the tread of the tyres. I suppose this was something whose strangeness they could really appreciate through its near relation to things they understood.

Our return through the village was like the progress of Royalty, with the whole population lining the street to watch us go by.

Some way on we stopped by the roadside to eat a picnic tea and here were treated to a most amusing spectacle. Five old men with neat black pigtails and straggly grey whiskers stopped on their way to stand staring at the car and then, very solemnly and all together, stooped down and peered hopefully along underneath. Presumably they were looking for the legs.

One day we went out to a village called Wen-chun-tung, about twelve miles into the territory, and wished to abandon the car there while we walked on to visit a remarkable sacred tree some way beyond the end of the road. Before starting we filled up with petrol at Port Edward, where the stuff is kept for the use of motor boats, and got the Chinaman in charge of the store to write out a chit to the policeman at Wen-chun-tung saying that we wished him to keep an eye on the car while we were away and that we would be back soon. On arrival we left the car at the end of the road and walked to the police station, where we found a policeman in khaki shorts and putties surmounted by a little black coat of flowered satin, and to him we showed this work of art. To our relief and surprise he seemed to understand it and immediately came down and took charge of the rapidly collecting crowd of sightseers, while we went off down the path to the sound of enthusiastic blowing of the horn. When we returned we found him proudly on guard with the villagers squatting at a respectful distance all round.

Thanking him as best we could with smiles and bows we started back, to the cheers of the populace, but our friend the policeman was not going to miss any of the show if he could help it and, mounting a bicycle, was evidently determined to keep up with as long as possible for he nearly ran into us from behind when we stopped round the next corner for a much needed iced drink from a thermos.

In these days of suggested rendition of the Wei hei wei territory to China, two stone tablets standing in the courtyard of a temple at a village near the border, are of more than ordinary interest. They record, in the picturesque language of classical allusion, the spontaneous appreciation of the justice and security which the village has enjoyed under British rule, while brigands and famine have ravaged the surrounding districts.

After our first experience we carefully avoided market days for our expeditions and of these there remain only the most enjoyable memories, both from the point of view of scenery and the delightful friendly behaviour of the population, not to mention the novelty of driving through a land where a car is still an unknown, though admittedly a comical, monster.

On the whole however we were able confidently to report, as the result of our "experiment", that the local conditions were definitely unsuitable for motor traffic.

B.G.B.B

The Island Hotel
18th June 1927 Wei hei wei

Darling Eleanor,
 Here is a little wei hai girl in her summer dress. When it gets really hot she sheds the trousers and only wears the funny red thing with the fancy pocket.

It ties at the back like this.

Daddy and I are just off for a picnic and to bathe. We wish that you were with us.

Heaps and heaps of love from us both.
    Your loving
        Mother

The Island Hotel
17th June 1927 Wei hei wei

You will think that the war plays little part in my letters - but really all we hear about it is from the English papers and occasional rumours. The latest is that Pekin has fallen - but I don't know if that is true and what significance it has. One meets a good many people here who have had to leave places up the river etc. and their accounts are most depressing, China seems to be going just the same way as Russia and all the nice Chinese going under - and however much in theory foreign intervention may be wrong - in practice you get a place like this where all the people are peaceful and prosperous and friendly and happy and all owing to the British Government as in the old days this part of the country was ravaged by brigands and pirates and wreckers. Shantung is still full of brigands but they hardly dare come over the frontier now - and that is sheer moral effect as the police force here is very small. The British have also encouraged the peanut industry and the local crops and crafts - so that now after a bad season - instead of starving they always have something to fall back upon. Talking about moral effect - Ian says the moral effect of submarines is excellent: when they went to Swatow the Chinese there didn't quite know what it was and a rumour went round that the whole submarine was filled with hundreds of armed men hidden away!

Life goes on here the same as before except that there are lots more people. The 'Despatch' and 'Carlisle' have also come up for two or three weeks - but I don't know anyone in either. The

Despatch is giving a concert in the Canteen tonight. Last night we went and danced at the Club and the night before we had a very successful dinner party for Mrs Macmicheal on board the Ambrose. Afterwards there was a cinema on deck. I wondered so much what all the sampan people thought of the motors and trains etc. shown on the screen - things that they have never seen in real life. Another night we walked to the end of the island - a lovely warm night with a full moon.

One morning Mrs Claridge and I went sketching and I lunched with her afterwards - yesterday I went over by myself and sat in the temple and tried to draw the details of the curvey roofs etc. It is a very well preserved temple with a dear old priest with a bun of hair on top of his head. At the back is a school and at intervals all the little boys rushed out to see how I was getting on - but most of the time I was left in peace. Ian is playing cricket today against the Light Cruisers and tomorrow we are playing tennis with the Tyrwhitts.

The hotel is full of children now and I just long for Eleanor.

The Island Hotel
26th June 1927 Wei hei wei

Thursday was the only wet day we've had and I went and read the papers at the Club and made a bedspread out of some very pretty gold coloured shantung silk. In the evening we went to the Ship's Company dance. It was most amusing - all the sailors looked so nice in clean white 'sailor suits' and most of them had drenched themselves in eau de cologne for the occasion! There were about 18 females including Lady Tyrwhitt and we were kept hard at work. As soon as a dance was over you were handed back to your chair and we sat in a line until the music struck up when all the sailors rushed over and bowed and carried you off. The various husbands sat and talked to each other in a corner of the room. The sailors dance most awfully well and everybody enjoyed it.

On Friday I went over to lunch with Mrs Lee on the Mainland. It was very rough and I got soaked, however I had brought a change of clothes. After lunch we went to the Commissioner's and played tennis and Mrs Lee returned on the Ferry with us, as she was dining at the Club. It was even rougher going back and the Ferry couldn't put into the pier and had to go alongside the St Preock (a tug) and as Mrs Lee was stepping from one to the other she fell in to the sea between and disappeared - it was just like a cinema but rather frightening as one was afraid the two boats would bump together and crush her. However the Captain of the Carlisle and two snotties who were in the Ferry jumped in after her and we all pulled and everyone was rescued and I brought poor Mrs Lee back to the hotel and gave her a hot bath and lent her clothes and Ian primed her with drink and she went off to the Club none the worse! We were dining with the Trywhitts and I was a bit late but Ian went on ahead and explained. The Trywhitt son and daughter and Ian and I went on afterwards and danced at the Club.

On Saturday I had a most wonderful day which alas! Ian couldn't share as he had to play cricket for the Ambrose against the cruisers. I started off at 10 with Lady T and the girls and a Mrs Southcott (who I knew last time I was out here) and the Glencrosses. We all went over to the mainland where three carriages were awaiting us (rather decrepit sort of Victorias) These we entered two by two. Lady T asked me to go with her and she was the most awfully amusing companion - I like her most awfully. We drove thirteen miles into the mountains to a place Wei-chen-tung where the Commissioner met us. There is a district officer's house there and he had provided a marvellous five course lunch (ice cream and all) After this repast most of the party went to sleep - but Captain Glencross and I walked out to a village two miles away where there is a sacred tree. This is called the maidenhair tree as it has leaves like a giant maidenhair fern - it is only found in Shantung and parts of Japan - though in prehistoric times it was common as it is often found in fossils. Now wherever it is found they build a temple and look upon it as sacred and it grows to a vast size. We went in to the Temple where there was a huge gold Buddha.

In the river bed at Wei-chen-tung there are hot springs and we saw all the inhabitants having their baths. The said inhabitants were frightfully interested in us and the women came and touched our clothes and even lifted Mrs Clencross's skirt to see what she wore underneath!

I don't suppose they had ever seen European women before and they thought us a priceless joke! We had a large tea at the R.O's house and then started our bumpy drive home - this time I travelled with Mrs Southcott and her dogs. The country was not really pretty - but *very* interesting as all the harvesting was going on, the women in their red and pink dresses and the men in bright blue with pointed straw hats made a very attractive picture among the corn - rather crude - but very gay. Then in the villages they were threshing (by the primitive method of walking on the corn and then tossing it in the air so that the chaff blew away). The whole countryside struck me as being very prosperous and contented and happy. We got home at 7.30 and then went on to the Carlisle's Concert.

On Sunday the Poland's had a sailing picnic - we started at noon in the whaler (a kind of boat) and sailed over to a little cove on the other side where we picnicked and bathed and explored and then had tea and sailed home with a nice breeze behind us - a very good day. The party consisted of the Polands, Lushingtons, Mr Purdon and ourselves.

Yesterday was a most disastrous day. It started by being perfectly heavenly and we thought we'd have a farewell picnic for Miss Barclay who is going back to Hong Kong. So she and I and

Mrs North and Mrs Poland set off armed with bathing things and a frying pan and eggs etc. to a place about five miles away on the Mainland called the first Lagoon. You drive most of the way through charming country -but the last mile you have to walk across sandhills. Then being low tide we scrambled out a long way over rocks and finally undressed and bathed - by this time it was nearly noon and blazing hot. Mrs Poland is a good swimmer and was some way out when she suddenly shouted 'My knee is out and I'm going to sink!' Mrs North and Miss Barclay couldn't swim a stroke and I'm not mush of a performer - however its wonderful what one can do if put to it! I swam out to her and she managed to keep herself afloat with her hands whilst I propelled her in. It appears that she has a cartilage in her knee that sometimes comes out when doing anything very strenuous, but had never come out swimming before. We couldn't put it back and she was absolutely helpless with that leg and we had to drag her and carry her (she is fortunately light) over all the rocks and then across the sand dunes. Finally I left them and ran on to the village and got a carriage and forced the driver (who spoke no English - but by a dramatic representation of Mrs Poland's condition I got him to understand!) to come across the soft sand and collect her. I shall never forget running that mile over soft sand under the blazing sun and not an inch of shade. The sand was so hot it burnt the soles of your feet. Mrs North was completely knocked up just walking! I don't think I feel heat as much as most people as after I got home and had a bathe and tea I was quite all right, though burnt the colour of a red Indian! I can't think how we ever got Mrs Poland back. I'm never going for another picnic without a man!

That was the end of our adventures but poor Miss Barclay had more to come. The Browns were giving her a farewell dinner on board. They started off for the Ambrose in the motor boat - the wind had got up and it was very rough - the boat broke down and they were thrown on the rocks where they were crashed about for half an hour until a rescue party appeared and they got ashore (Betty rather hysterical by this time.)

Ian was sailing at 3am and at 10 he and Mr Brown went off in a sampan and I was quite anxious about them as the weather was so bad. Just as I was going to bed there was a screeching on the door and Mrs Claridge appeared saying no sampan would take her back to the Mainland so could I put her up for the night - so I borrowed a camp bed and she spent a rather uneasy night with me as it thundered and lightened and blew great guns.

However today is lovely so the submarines ought to be all right - they don't return until tomorrow.

The Island Hotel
30th June 1927 Wei hei wei

We are rather thrilled as we hear the Ambrose and submarines are probably going for a cruise in September finishing up in Japan (where they will get four days leave) and so on to Hong Kong. At least this is the scheme submitted though not yet 'approved'. Mrs Poland wants me to come with her - first to Pekin and then on - probably via Dalmy to Japan and with any luck we should get a free passage back in an oiler from there to Hong Kong. We are also being given introductions to people in Tokyo and Kioto who will probably put us up, so it wouldn't be an awfully expensive trip and Mrs Poland would be a delightful companion. I would be grateful if you'd secure my bank book and let me know just how much money I really have - so as I know how much I can spend in Pekin and Japan - I want to get the Puss a jade and seed pearl necklace and a kimono and myself a fur coat not to mention embroideries and lacquer etc. as I hear it is a good time for buying just now. As to letters you'd better address them all from now onwards to H.M S/M L27 c/o G.P.O as then I shall get them in

Japan if we do go there. It would be a wonderful trip - and then Mrs Poland and I hope to go down after Xmas to Singapore etc. for the spring cruise and then on home together and I hope my other plan will work in tactfully with this and not commence either too early or too late! November has hitherto been the fatal month and would suit splendidly again!

Ian was out at sea all day yesterday and didn't return until midnight. Mrs Lushington and I went over in a sampan and worked off a lot of calls and ransacked the silk shops - I got enough white crepe de chine for a dress and trousers to match for just over a £1 and another lot for nightdress, petticoat and camisole for rather less. In the morning I played golf - doing the nine holes in 53 - I have to put in three cards for a handicap my best so far being 50. I went in to see the Trywhitts on the way back.

The evening before we had 'agreeable' bridge with Mrs Poland who is still laid up with her knee poor thing.

Today I meant to go over and finish my pastel of the temple - but the sun isn't out so that was no good - but I shall probably sketch this afternoon as Ian is playing cricket.

The Island Hotel
4th July 1927 Wei hei wei

On Sunday we went for a picnic with the Glencrosses and Claridges and a Mr Hackforth Jones and Mrs Fitzmaurice. It should have been a wonderful picnic but was rather spoilt by an absolute hurricane of wind. When we crossed over at 10.30 it was beginning to blow and by the time we had driven eight miles and reached our luncheon spot we didn't think it possible to compete with it in the open - so we rather unwisely took shelter in a temple. The Glencrosses brought their two 'boys' and we had a marvellous lunch of grapefruit and fish mayonnaise and cold chicken and chip potatoes and apple pie - but it was a case of holding it on to your plate and not minding the inch of dust that instantly settled on it. I trembled to think what germs we must have eaten! But so far no one seems the worse!

Fortified we proceeded to battle our way up the mountain side to the old Buddhist temple of Aishau which is built upon a pass and has the most heavenly views in both directions. When we arrived very hot and weary the dear old priest made us welcome and gave us green tea to drink - refreshing if rather nasty. This particular temple used to suffer from having its roof blown off at frequent intervals - so at last the elders consulted together and decided to make a tunnel underneath it as a passage for the wind - this they did - and politely begged the wind to use this route in future! We went through the tunnel and I did a pencil drawing of this entrance. We walked down to the carriages and after tea drove home and by this time the wind had subsided. It is the one drawback of this climate - otherwise it is perfect - lovely hot sun and cool nights and scarcely any rain and a clear atmosphere - but on three or four days a week you get this strong wind and all the doors slam and the lamps blow out and one loses one's temper!

I've been very extravagant buying lovely embroidered silk underclothes, but they are so cheap that it seems a pity not to get them while one can. If you'd send out a nightdress cut to the shape you like in fine tarantulle or linen I'd get it embroidered in a lovely grape design for 6/- and made up. You could send it by letter post and the embroidery would be a present from me so do send several. I'd get them done for you - only the cotton stuffs here are so coarse.

We are saving a little money here - the hotel is only £28 a month for both of us and no extras at all - washing is dirt cheap (I gave up the Amah when Mrs Poland left as I hadn't enough work for her) - one's entertaining is cheap too though one has to do rather a lot - but a tennis party of ten or twelve with two courts and ball boys and special cakes and sandwiches etc. only costs about 10/-. This week we are going shares with the Lushingtons and having a dinner party at the Club and dancing afterwards. Club subscriptions are very small (I'm thrown in free!) so except for buying silk and ferry fares to the mainland one can't spend much money.

Now that it is really hot in the mornings we have reduced our garments to the minimum. I wear a vest - drawers, a petticoat, cotton dress and sand shoes. After lunch we don stockings - Ian just wears a shirt and khaki shorts and a helmet and most of the children wear just one garment (a sort of romper) and the Chinese wear nothing at all!

It was interesting driving through the country on Sunday to see how primitive everything is here. The threshing floor of Biblical times and the flail and grindstone and no sort of machinery of any kind - and from the prosperous look of the countryside and the happy faces of the people - the fat children and the dear old men with white pigtails - it strikes one as a very good thing. (The old women don't look so happy - but that is not surprising if you think what torture their poor feet must be!)

The Island Hotel
9th July 1927 Wei hei wei

On Wednesday Ian and I went for a lovely picnic. We landed on the Mainland at about 4 o'clock and walked up a twisty path up the hillside and over the pass and down the other side. It was very hot and when we got to Waterwitch Bay we hurled ourselves into the sea and had a glorious bathe - then tea and we came back by a rather interesting village. The headman is a progressive Chinaman and he has planted orchards etc. and the whole place looks very prosperous and very picturesque as there are lots of twisted pine trees and craggy mountains behind.

Yesterday I went over by the 10 o'clock ferry and walked out to the walled city and did some sketching. It was an ideal day as it felt fresh after the rain - lately it has been too hot to walk about at midday - but yesterday though the sun was out it was delicious and I saw lots of amusing things. One old old gentleman with a snow white pigtail and a vast floppy straw hat walking along fanning himself - another man who's straw hat had lost its crown so his bushy black hair stuck up through the top like a pen wiper.

In the doorways were crowds of Chinese children - dressed in all shades of pink and red and their own little yellow skins - and one dear old gentleman hugging his little naked great grandson. They all smile and nod when one passes and are most interested in the sketches - but not really troublesome like they are in Hong Kong. If you wave your arm they all move a few yards away. They all smell terribly of garlic!

There are certain disadvantages in living on an island - for one thing you waste such a lot of time on the water going to and fro and it is a detestable trip - often rough and wet - and the ferry only goes at 10, 3.15 and 7.30 - and costs 80 cents a time (return). Then one is always borrowing clothes etc. from the Mainland people and they are constantly getting stranded on the island and wanting baths or beds or clothes. On Friday night it was so stormy after the dance that most of them stayed the night on the island and came down to the 10 o'clock ferry next morning looking rather sheepish still wearing their evening clothes - not having anything else to put on. However I'm glad we live on the Island - it is so clean and nice and the views of the mountains so lovely. Golf and dancing and library are all on the Island. The Mainland is best for picnics and sketching and seeing the Chinese life, bathing is equally good on both and tennis we play both sides.

The Island Hotel
16th July 1927 Wei hei wei

It has been rather a wet week - July is supposed to be the rainy season here - but after five weeks sunshine one resents rain - it is also very hot and one's things are inclined to mildew. Personally I always like a wet day to catch up with arrears of letters and mending and dressmaking - but leading the Communal life one doesn't get the time as you are roped in to make a fourth at Bridge or take part in a ping pong tournament or something. Thursday it cleared up and was a glorious day and Ian had to play cricket - but got back in time to play three sets of tennis. In the evening we had to attend the Chief Petty Officer's and Petty Officer's Ball. It was rather a trial of endurance as it was a very hot night and there were so few 'ladies' that we had to dance every dance and stay until the bitter end. I'm getting to know quite a number of the crew of 'L27' - they are mostly very nice. Captain Poland and Ian and the other officers sit in a gloomy row round the room like dowager chaperones of Victorian days and we are returned to them between each dance!

Yesterday was very hot and rather thundery. Ian and I took a gharry and drove out to the 1st lagoon where we bathed and had tea and walked home (about four miles) rather a nice walk across fields and through various little villages. We dined at the Club with Tim Taylor, the Polands were also his guests and the Claridges. We had dinner on the terrace and the band of the Middlesex played and we danced afterwards. Today we are bathing and golfing with the Polands and dining with the Glencrosses and going on to the Ambrose concert. Tomorrow Ian has a 'day on' and we are having a children's party over on L27. About eight little girls and boys aged between four and seven years old - four of whom I've got to look after as their parents can't come. I shall feel very sad Eleanor not being amongst the party. I hope it won't be very rough going off to the ship. I've got the cook here to make me a big iced cake as I'm told some of the small boys have amazing appetites.

The Glencrosses have commissioned me to paint the gateway and summer house of their bungalow - rather dreary subjects but 20$ is not to be lightly discarded so I'm going to have a try at it.

The local tailor has made me two such pretty dresses, a white crepe de chine with pleats which cost 30/- all told and a chiffon which I brought out and meant to do myself but he has done it much better for 12/-. I've made myself a yellow washing silk with smocking which is rather a success and cost 15/-. One needs such a lot of washing dresses now that it is hot and they only charge 1½d each for washing them.

'L27' gave everyone a fright the other day by disappearing for four hours. She was out attacking the Ambrose who however signalled her to come up - when she failed to appear they all got very anxious - but what had really happened was the 'L27' was lying in wait to attack and had got into a patch of 'dead' water where no underwater signalling penetrated and being a slight surface mist they hadn't seen the Morse signals. At 7 o'clock when the exercise was finished they came to the surface to everyone's intense relief. Of course I knew nothing about it - but the funny thing is just before 7 I began to feel awfully anxious for no reason - I suppose it was the general feeling in the atmosphere which one's mind picks up just like wireless.

Wei hai is very full now. The Argus with all her aeroplanes - the Hawkins with the C in C - the hospital ship Maine and the Carlisle and Despatch and the 'Titania' arrives next week. The hotel is also full of summer visitors mostly from Shanghai or else refugees from Hankow and Nanking. One interesting thing we heard from someone who has just come from Hankow is - that if we wait patiently the Chinese will give us back the concession. All trade there is at a standstill and the banks shut and the Chinese themselves ruined and the people starving, and they are already beginning to be anxious for us to start things going again.

The Island Hotel
19th July 1927 Wei hei wei

On Sunday we had our children's party - it grew and grew until the last moment and when the motorboat disgorged its contents Ian nearly had a fit! We first gave them a large tea, just managed to get them all into the guest room. Then we took them over three swaying planks and down into 'L27'. They were all thrilled especially with the periscopes and the voice pipes. Ian's third hand Mr Stirling Hamilton was a great help. There was one dear little girl Wendy Remmington just the same age as Eleanor - she insisted upon going up the Conning tower and everywhere - I was always losing her and got quite anxious as she had no parent or guardian with her. I was also responsible for a very active small boy of four - the other children came with their Mothers - one Mrs Compton a most exotic looking Italian lady popularly known as the Hong Kong 'vamp'. At 5.30 we had a motorboat back to the shore and altogether it was a most successful party. We were asked most amusing questions - one very small girl Pamela asked how the submarine was dried when it came up.

Yesterday Mrs Lushington and I had a lovely sail over to the Mainland in a sampan and then went and poked about the walled city and I picked up two carved soap-stone dogs for $1 each. They make delightful bookends. The Ambrose was coaling so Ian joined me at the Lees for lunch and we played tennis afterwards.

In the meantime our plans are working out so well that I feel there is bound to be a hitch - but the present idea is that the Ambrose and submarines leave here on September 27th and go to various places in Japan. Mrs Poland and I will meantime leave about the same time and go to Tiensin and Pekin and join the

Ambrose at Kobe where we have eleven days and hope to get four days leave and go to Kyoto - then we go for four or five days to Tokyo (a lovely train journey I'm told from Kyoto to Tokyo) and from there back to Hong Kong early in November. Then L27 goes into dock for her refit and stays there until the end of February (while we lead a peaceful and undisturbed life) and when they go on the spring cruise I hope to accompany them and come home from Singapore about April or May, but 'the best laid schemes of mice and men......!'

What incensing letters Blackwell writes - and he seems to have thoroughly divorced Ian's and my work which is sad, though I'm very glad that the lady in the chair[26] is going to be reproduced. We laughed until we nearly wept at the thought of Girl Guides[27] reciting Ian's poem! I wish Blackwell wouldn't shroud the question of payment in such discreet mystery! I wonder when No 5 Joy Street will appear and when we will get a copy? Blackwells ought to get Kelly and Walsh (the big Hong Kong and Shanghai booksellers) to lay in a stock as a good many people out here would buy it for our sake. Incidentally as Ian hasn't got official permission from the Admiralty his official status better not appear at all - just 'Ian Macnair' - The article we sent to the Light Car Ian made me sign - but that was perhaps not to draw their Lordships attention to the fact that a motor had been conveyed in his submarine! We have at last got permission to run Bobjohn here and are to be given a special licence marked 'For experimental purposes!' We take him across in a motor boat one day next week.

The Island Hotel
23rd July 1927 Wei hei wei

What heavenly weather we are having - and I don't feel it too hot except it rather prevents one going lunch picnics. We bathe two or three times a day and the water is enchanting - I can swim quite a long way now. Yesterday we had great fun - we went with Captain and Mrs Poland in his little motor boat over to the other side. We had a surf board and took it in turns to be towed on it by the motor boat[28] - most exciting - and at first rather difficult to keep ones balance but once one had got the knack it was very exhilarating.

Today we are playing in a tennis tournament Island v Mainland and tomorrow we are going a picnic with the Browns over to Mrs Macmicheal's bungalow - it is empty and she said we could use it to bathe from.

The Browns full of enterprise and undeterred by the coming infant are giving a fancy dress ball to celebrate their wedding day and her 21st birthday. I'm going to wear Janet's dress and Ian is going as Suzanne Langlen - I'm going to make him a little white cotton frock and a coloured bandeau - side curls borrowed from the concert party and white stockings and shoes - a nice cool costume anyway.

I enclose a chippy little article as a companion to 'Flower Street'. If you can get it typed and get the Daily Mail to take it it would be excellent - otherwise what about the 'Scotsman'? I'm doing a longer one about Wei hai which I'll send you anon.

Ask Ninny if she likes enclosed pattern for frocks for Eleanor. It is a stuff they make in Korea and is guaranteed unfadable and is supposed to last for ever and doesn't crush. You can get it in any colour (a very pretty yellow and a green) also in stripes checks etc. It is just over 30 ins wide and costs 70 cents a yard (about 1/9). How much would a frock and trousers require?

Did I ask you before - I can't remember - but will you get my bank book and let me know exactly what my balance is just now. This is important as I want to know exactly how much I can afford to spend in Pekin and Japan. I want to get a fur coat and some things like lacquer etc. with the £50 I took out of Debenhams. Ian has enough money saved here for my return journey and for my passages to Teinsin and Japan and of course if I get a cheap trip back to Hong Kong in an oiler we shall have that extra to spend. Ian of course gets conveyed free (in fact makes on it what with hard lying money and pilotage) and that we shall spend on our five days leave in Japan. We find we can live just comfortably on his pay out here and do the entertaining necessary - and his allowance (which we hope is being paid in at the rate of £25 a quarter!) is what we give you for Puss[29] plus some he had already had in the bank at home. Naval pay has gone down again this month - but on the other hand Ian gets a substantial rise in August. We hope to get into the Albany at Hong Kong in November which is as comfortable as Lauriston and half the price - in that case we should have quite a lot to come and go on. The tales of the expense out here are really very exaggerated - the only thing is one is always being tempted to buy because the silks etc. are so lovely and compared to home so cheap.

Flower Street

One of the first things seen after landing in Hong Kong, is a small steep street leading from the main thoroughfare up the hill. Officially called Wyndham Street, it is always known as Flower Street as one side is entirely occupied by the flower sellers stalls which form a bank of colour and dispel a sweet scent which even dominates the more characteristic Chinese smells!

There from early morning until late at night, Sunday and weekday, the rough plank tables are heaped with flowers. Roses, sweet peas, violets, freesias, larkspurs, dahlias and chrysanthemums - not each in their due season but at one and the same time - charming bouquets of mixed flowers like a Dutch painting, and great branches of flowering blossom. Above on the poles of the ragged awnings are hung wreaths which can be seen being made on the pavement at the opposite side.

As you ascend, flowers will be waved in your face and a chorus will great you "Missy! Missy! Look see here - velly cheap" You take no notice but choose what you require and then holding up the bunch ask "How much?"

Optimistically the vendor suggests a dollar (2/-) but you knowing this is all part of the game you counter with an offer of 30 cents. This is rejected with scorn so you lay down the flowers and proceed to another stall. A voice follows you "Missy 60 cents?" and casually you reply "40 cents" "Can do" and a hand is held out for the money and you receive a beautifully done up bouquet with a rattan loop to suspend from the finger.

A dozen deep cream rose buds - feathery sprays of larkspur and a stiff bunch of violets for 10d appears to be a bargain, but when you get them home and unwind the elaborate outer layers of damp fern you will find each separate violet is tied to a twig and some of the roses are cut off short at the head and speared onto a piece of bamboo, and after half an hours hard work you are surrounded by a heap of fern and bamboo and little bits of rattan and your sheaf of flowers has dwindled to a mere handful! But as your man gets to know you he will produce unprepared bunches, and nowhere in the world are there lovelier flowers than those grown in the Chinese market gardens round Canton and sold in Flower Street, Hong Kong.

Pedlars Pack

In Wei hei wei you do not go shopping - the shops come to you. Before you are up in the morning a patient row of pedlars have taken up their position in the garden and are squatting upon their bundles. As you emerge onto your verandah a figure in a long blue gown and straw hat rises and comes towards you murmuring ingratiatingly 'Missy wantchee buy? Have got velly good silks'. You shake your head but one of the other figures takes up the tale 'Missy look see - have got velly nice embroideries' while a third chimes in 'I belong silversmith'.

Sooner or later resistance is worn down and one of the importunate ones establishes himself upon your verandah and proceeds to undo the complicated knot of his bundle and lays before you a most tempting array of silks of all colours. Crepe de chines and satins imported from up the River - Canton crepes and the natural shantung silk which is a local product - and the coloured chefoo silks (these though crisp and attractive when new have an irritating habit of going limp in damp weather). From another bundle come silk underclothes and linen table cloths beautifully embroidered by the Chinese women - whilst the silversmith tempts you with brooches of kingfisher's feathers and silver and enamel goods made in the Chinese walled city on the Mainland.

These are the regular merchants and one soon gets to know them - on asking one his name the other day - he replied reproachfully 'You no savvy me? Your master (i.e. husband) savvy me well - he always calls me the Robber!' This with self conscious pride.

Then there is the immortal Wei hei wei tailor known to generations of the Navy as 'Jelly Belly'. The original stout gentleman is dead - but a descendant carries on the prosperous business under the sign 'Sin Jelly Belly and Co.'

Occasionally a newcomer appears and disappears - a man selling balls of fern - a Japanese with pearls both real and 'cultured' and two men from Nankin selling strange patterned brocades.

The question of payment is all too simple. After the price has been fixed through lengthy bargaining - you are not expected to produce the cash - merely to sign a 'chit'. It is no use to plead lack of money with any of the forty thieves - the villain will only smile at you and say 'Maskee - you buy - you tell me name of your master's ship - I go catchee money!!'

R Macnair.

The Island Hotel
25th July 1927 Wei hei wei

I do wish I had Eleanor here just now - she would love it. There are such a lot of children here now and mostly between four and seven years old - there are two dear little girls Wendy and Suzette just her age - they all play on the lovely sands and bathe and have the whole safe, clean island to go walks and picnics on and they are all as brown as berries and seem to flourish exceedingly. In Hong Kong where children are all white faced and spotty I was thankful I hadn't got her - but this place is really a paradise for children - I really think you had better let Beacon Corner and you and Ninny bring her out here next spring!

On Sunday we took the Browns for a nice quiet picnic - we sailed over in a sampan to Mrs Macmicheal's empty bungalow - there her gardener 'Wong' spotted us coming and put all the chairs etc. out on the verandah and even a bowl of roses on to the table! We bathed and fed and then Ian and I went off for a four mile walk while the Browns slept! We bathed again to get cool and sailed home through the most lovely sunset. Hardly had we got home than we set out again - this time with a large party in fourteen rickshaws.

I wore a cotton frock which I found was quite the wrong costume as most of the other females appeared in their husband's white 'shorts'!

We took baskets full of food and drink and one of the hotel 'boys' and we spread it all out on the sand and ate by the light of the stars and three storm lanthorns. It looked very picturesque - there wasn't a moon but the stars were gorgeous and it was enchantingly warm. About 10 o'clock we bathed in the warm black water which was all lit up with little balls of phosphorescence - so that it was like bathing among stars.

The Island Hotel
31st July 1927 Wei hei wei

All our beautiful plans for Japan are going rather awry - I felt that it had all fitted in too well to really come off - and now the C - in C says the Ambrose is to go down to Hong Kong with three boats in September. 'L27' is to be attached to the Titania for most of the Japanese cruise - returning independently to Hong Kong about October 20th from Kobe and not going to Yokohama.

I don't think I shall see Ian much in Japan except for his five days leave - but it is worth going just for that. Everyone says the nicest thing to do is a walking tour - taking a coolie as guide and to carry one's suitcase. You spend the night at Japanese Inns which are very clean and you really see the country and in October it is lovely weather and all the maples are turning red. The rest of the time Mrs Poland and I will throw in our lot together and a friend of Mrs Lushingtons - who is Principal of a Girls' University at Kyoto has offered to put us up. Kyoto is the old capital of Japan and there are beautiful temples and palaces and a red lacquer bridge etc. - so I feel a week's painting there would be very profitable!

I wish I'd been at home to deal with Basil Blackwell - as I could easily have done a black and white illustration for the Witch in the Woods also for the 'green parrots'[30] if I'd been on the spot. As it is it is all a little unsatisfactory though I shall be thrilled to see the said parrots in print (both story and picture!) I hope to get the picture back when they've finished with it.

A man from Pekin with a bundle came round the other day and spread out some lovely embroideries etc. I thought he was very expensive but in the end I made him an offer for two things which he rejected with scorn as it was sixteen to eight dollars instead of the thirty and sixteen that he was asking. However in the end he came back and let me have them at my price though I didn't really want them if I go to Pekin - but I'm quite pleased. One is a long strip of rose red brocade embroidered in various colours - it is a very decorative bit of colour and is old and would look nice on a sideboard or other long table. The other thing is a Manchu lady's coat and trousers - in a lovely coral pink brocade embroidered in dull blues - it is obviously an old costume which has been relined and done up. It will be a perfect fancy dress for the Puss later on and in the meantime the little coat looks charming on the top of a black dress.

Thank you *so* much for sending Ian's tweed. It arrived yesterday and Mr Jelly Belly will for a very small sum make it up as a suit for Ian to come home in - his present tweed having come through at the knees, elbows and seat! It wouldn't have been worth making up at home - but here where it can be done for 10/- or so it really is and it ought to be warm and hard wearing at any rate!

The Island Hotel
6th August 1927 Wei hei wei

Yesterday was the great day. We got our licence and took Bobjohn over to the Mainland. The trip across was most successful - Ian had it all organised and we seized the moment when the tide was exactly right and precariously balanced on two planks across the motor boat Bobjohn made his journey. The Lees have very kindly lent us a shed in their stables and everyone is much amused about it!

We started to go to a place Liu Lintzu about fourteen miles inland. The road is quite good if a bit bumpy and very attractively lined on each side with willow trees. Round Wei-hai no one took much interest in us - as they are accustomed to the soldier's lorry and ambulance - but as soon as we got inland we were as popular as travelling circus and all the inhabitants of the little villages we passed through lined the streets to watch us past. They all seemed fearfully amused! When we stopped a crowd collected to examine the strange thing and I hope that we have got some entertaining photographs! We passed a great many mules - both in carts and in "shensa's" a sort of litter hung on poles between two mules. Most of the animals took it all quite placidly - but occasionally one of them took fright an spun round in the road in front of us which made driving pretty difficult - however we got safely home and it was the most entertaining experience.

The Island Hotel
8th August 1927 Wei hei wei

Yesterday was the 9th anniversary of our wedding day! We had a really lovely time. We sailed over about noon and collected Bobjohn and drove to Narcissus Bay. A charming Mrs Fitzhugh has a bungalow there (she's a person who'd interest you as she runs an antique shop in Pekin). We parked Bobjohn in her garden and went and had a lovely bathe and a picnic lunch (cold chicken and potato salad and pears) then we drove fourteen miles out to 'Wen chuan tung' - no adventures but the last five miles an awful road. We had a chit in Chinese to give the policeman at Wen chuan tung and he looked after Bobjohn whilst I took Ian to see the sacred tree which I told you about before. When we got back a large crowd was squatting round at a respectful distance and the policeman clad in khaki shorts and a black brocade jacket mounting guard - he escorted us part of the way home on a bicycle the road being so bad that he had no difficulty in keeping up! All the villages turned out to see us pass but we were hotly pursued by a mule who galloped after us with open mouth! The country looked quite lovely - fields of Indian corn and the blue mountain beyond - the willow shaded the roads and the cosy little thatched farms and the smiling inhabitants clad in bright blues and pinks and reds with large straw hats and the fat naked yellow and brown babies which swarm everywhere.

The Island Hotel
12th August 1927 Wei hei wei

The Browns' dance was the greatest success - though as Lady Trywhitt remarked yesterday it turned into a 'Macnairs' Benefit' as Ian and I secured respectively the 1st prize for the best lady and man's costume - However it was by vote so it was fair do's. I really was pleased with the rig I made for Ian and he looked very like Mlle Lenglen[31] only with a nicer kind of face! I cut the feet off an old pair of my own stockings and he wore his own white socks rolled down in the approved fashion. My silk chemise and trousers and a white cotton frock with very full short skirt and embroidered in pink on the left chest. A bright pink bandeau with side curls attached - an arrow brooch in front and very chic garters - a dazzling complexion and four tennis racquets under his arm. He thoroughly entered into the part and asked people for dances in French. He is such a darling in that way, so unself-conscious and so enjoying things. Do you remember the charades at Burley?

I wore Janet's[32] very pretty early Victorian dress which I had washed and ironed all stiff. The local shoemaker made me some black satin sandals for 80 cents (1/6) and I fashioned a most fetching straw poke bonnet out of a Colombo hat trimmed with pink roses and green ribbons and with a ruche of lace that kind Betty wrenched off a petticoat! I got quite a lot of compliments!

There were heaps of good dresses nearly all made by the people themselves. In fact on Tuesday they held a Sewing Bee in the Ambrose! One man made a wonderful Roman dress - another twinked his jaeger pants orange as Elizabethan trunk hose! The funniest I thought was one of the Subs who came as a Governess and looked <u>exactly</u> like Susan Grant!

We had a dinner party beforehand - consisting of the two Millard girls and their Mama and Tim Taylor (who came in a wonderful dress as a submarine and could hardly sit down in it!) and Mr Tyyne and Mr Stirling Hamilton Ian's 3rd hand. The party was really for his benefit as the Browns introduced him the other day to the Millards and thought he had been very smitten by the youngest girl - so we decided to carry on the good work. They were both beaming and spent most of the evening sitting in the moonlit garden!

Betty looked charming in a wonderful Peacock dress - Mr Brown was a Rajah. Everything went with a great swing - the Titania's band was in great form and all the 100 odd people out to enjoy themselves.

The Island Hotel
13th August 1927 Wei hei wei

We had such a lovely day yesterday - we went over to the Mainland at four and collected Bobjohn and drove out along Chefoo Road as far as we could go. We didn't quite reach the frontier as the road became too bad but we went about twelve miles and such pretty country. The are gathering in the maize harvest now and we also went quite close to the lagoons where they collected salt. We ate our tea by the roadside and watched the crowd which collected round Bobjohn.

We returned at 6.30 and drove up in state to the Commissioner's front door - he was very amused! On Fridays he always has a tennis 'at home' so there were still quite a lot of people there and we were regaled with ices.

Then we went on and dined with the Lee's. After dinner we sat in the garden. It was full moon and enchantingly warm - then we wandered down to the pier and hearing gongs and cymbals we went into the temple - and there before a huge crowd a theatrical performance was taking place - we couldn't get near enough to see much but the whole temple looked fearfully picturesque with two large Chinese lanthorns at the door. This full moon is the Feast of Spirits and the Chinese set light to little lamps and float them out to sea to lead souls of the drowned to heaven - All the water was covered with these little bobbing lights and on the calm water and under the moon it was rather delicious. We sailed back and arrived at eleven. The day before a fine junk came in here - all painted green and white and red with red bow and goggling eyes - I wish one saw more of them.

I know we will have your sympathy when I tell you we have just lost a $100 note (£9) - isn't it too sickening especially here where one wants every penny to spend on things to bring home and for the trip to Japan. It can't have been stolen as Ian always carries it in his note case in his breast pocket and sleeps with it under his pillow. We know it was there in company of three 10$ notes a few days ago - and the only time he has opened his note case is unfortunately in the dark. We had landed from a sampan and Ian found he had no small change - so looked in his note case to see if he had a $1 note - we think he must have pulled out the $100 note at the same time and it just blew away - I feel I shall never get over it!

> The Island Hotel
> 17th August 1927 Wei hei wei

I had a visit from a charming young man, one of the third hands of the submarine by name Mr Lipscombe - it appears he is awfully keen on painting and does dry points on copper - so we had a long and heart to heart talk - he also takes in the 'Studio' which he is going to pass on to me.

We are still feeling rather shattered over the loss of our $100 note and I feel I daren't go near any of the silk merchants for some time to come. Another and even more irritating loss has occurred in the shape of the Glencrosses commissioning me to paint the Chinese gates and the summerhouse of their bungalow and having 20$ as the price. Feeling I'd like to earn £2 I undertook the job though I disliked it as the gates are entirely modern and uninteresting - I wasted an awful lot of time and trouble and many beautiful days when I might have been doing nicer subjects and when I finished them they said they were delighted and really did seem pleased - I thought I'd made a good job of the gates as possible though I wasn't at all pleased with the summer house. For some time they didn't pay me at all - and eventually sent me $10! I simply can't say anything especially as he is Captain (S) but it is pretty annoying!

The Island Hotel
20th August 1927 Wei hei wei

Yesterday I went over to the Mainland in the morning meaning to sketch and I had the luck to strike a festival. All the streets were hung with flags and all the children were dressed in their best clothes - pink coats and jackets and red trousers and the little girls had their hair tied up with bright pink (a very lucky colour) and with flowers stuck in and they were all sucking sugar canes - I went into the City and followed the sound of gongs and cymbals to the War God's temple and there on the stage in front a dramatic entertainment was in progress. I pushed my way through the most amiable (if garlic smelling) crowd and thought how funny it was to think of how dangerous people in England would think it for a lone Englishwoman to be in the midst of a crowd in a Chinese walled city and how very safe it actually is here. It is impossible to believe here that the Chinese could be anything but friendly - and yet a man has just arrived at the hotel from Nankin and he says there are only about two or three Englishmen left. At Ningpo no women are allowed though a few have begun to go back up the River. Pekin seems very quiet at present and I think we should get up there all right in September. I met Sir Miles Lampson[33] yesterday and he told me to be sure and bring riding kit, so I'm full of hope that Aunty's letter of introduction is going to bear fruit and that they may take us about in Pekin.

To return to my expedition yesterday - the next sight I saw was a funeral - the mourners literally clad in sackcloth and ashes and accompanied by the inevitable paper horse, then I went on to the big temple and there a really fine theatrical show was on. Just as good to watch as the Russian Ballet - there was one most exciting scene where a man with a face painted the colour of a pillar box and a black beard and gorgeous robes takes on single handed all the rest of the troupe and after brisk fighting slays them all and finishes up by slapping the soles of his own feet with triumph (this requires some agility!) The only female was a doleful lady in black with bright blue sleeves which covered her hands and touched the ground, she appeared to do little but weep. At intervals an army of men with banners and blue and rose coloured robes marched on and off and there was a man with a coal black face and another with sort of wings.

There is no scenery, just some rather fine orange and black curtains. All the property men stay on the stage - the orchestra is also on the stage and consists of a gong - cymbals and a sort of cornet - not at all musical to European ears. The plays go on all day for several days - never seem to get much 'forrader' - we have drifted in to this particular entertainment on three different days and the same characters seem always to be doing much the same things - striking attitudes and dancing and singing in a squeaky voice. The audience is as interesting to watch as the play. First you have the real enthusiasts in front intent on every word. Then all the women sitting together and not paying much attention and children running about everywhere. Dear old men sitting smoking and fanning themselves and one squatting beside a red birdcage. (All Chinese have pet birds and grasshoppers which they take for walks and seem very devoted to.)

The whole setting is so attractive - the paved temple courtyard - the curly roofs, the trees - the awnings of the fruit and sweetmeat sellers and the gay clothes of the children and the general air of simple enjoyment.

In the afternoon the Macnairs took on the Fitzmaurices at golf and beat them and in the evening we dined with Mr Thyne at the Club and danced till 1 o'clock by which time I was more than half asleep.

The day before we took Bobjohn out to Half Moon Bay and there we bathed and had tea and had a lovely time. We had a very sad breaking up of 'L27' party in the 'Ambrose' though the

Browns don't actually go until tomorrow. Betty has been lucky enough to get a troopship passage down to Shanghai. As far as I know at present we leave here on September 26th get to Tiensin on the 27th and Pekin next day - sail again from Tiensin on the 5th and reach Moji on the 8th and through the Inland Sea and on to Kobe on the 9th, the day the Titania and submarines arrive. Ian goes down to Hong Kong on the 21st and I follow as soon as he gets me accommodation. At present we are rather fussed as everywhere we have written to is full up and likely to be - and there are at least eight other wives coming out in September! The trouble about Hong Kong is that it is either very nasty or very expensive and you don't even get your own choice of which evil as you jolly well have to get in where you can. It is very agitating for people with children, a huge new hotel has been built to cope with the situation but has been commandeered by the military and even the Bishop's House which we'd thought of taking and running as an 'Ambrose annex' has been turned into an Officers Mess - our chief hope is that Dr Fitzmaurice will be kept up here all winter (there is talk of keeping the hospital going instead of closing down in the autumn as usual -) in which case they have given us first refusal of their room at the 'Albany' in Hong Kong which they have sublet until October. It is a lovely big room with a bathroom, dressing room and veranda and only 180$ a month including my food.

Did I tell you how I went to the Island Church on Sunday and there were only eight people there and no organist so Mrs Glencross and I had to sing the hymns in a sort of quavering duet, no one else having the courage - they were fortunately easy ones.

Tomorrow we are going a sailing picnic with the Polands.

P.S I've just had a charming letter from Lady Lampson (who left here today) asking me to stay with them in Peking and bring Mrs Poland too. Isn't that fun. Tell Aunty - I feel it was owing to her letter.

The Island Hotel
25th August 1927 Wei hei wei

Today is about the only really pouring wet day that we have had. Rain was terribly wanted and we hope has come in time to save the pea nut harvest. I'm rather sorry as I was to have gone a picnic with the Commissioner and he was lending me a pony ride.

On Sunday we went a lovely picnic with the Polands and Captain Herbert - we went in a sailing boat - but there was so little breeze that we were towed most of the way by the captain's motor boat.

We went to a fascinating little beach 'Joss House' Bay and there we lit a fire and fried sausages and potatoes for lunch - a proper Naval picnic! I went off and explored in the afternoon while the others slept! and found masses of lovely wild flowers - irises and campanulas etc. and came to a village with a sacred maidenhair tree hung with red rags and joss papers. Then we bathed and had a large tea and were towed home through the most lovely sunset - the water all gold and flame.

On Tuesday the submarines had their great shoot - they are all submerged and at the given signal they all crash up to the surface and fire at a target, points being given for speed and accuracy. We haven't heard the result yet but L27 is one of the possible winners - it takes a lot of working out by various umpires.

Yesterday we lunched with the Commissioner - there was no one else there which was nice as he is so fearfully interesting when you get him alone and talking about China - I spent the afternoon sketching while Ian took the Commissioner out in Bobjohn who behaved beautifully. It was a most successful trip - they went right to the frontier - the last part of the way being across a salt marsh with no road! (but fortunately dry at this season!) They collected the usual large and admiring crowd and one old Chinaman offered to buy Bobjohn for $200 whereupon another promptly bid $300! and they got quite excited about it. The Commissioner took Ian to a temple and showed him where the villagers had put up a tablet to commemorate their appreciation of British Rule. They did it quite of their own free will and not to curry favour as no one knew about it until the Commissioner happened to go to the temple one day and saw the new tablet with his own name and that of his predecessors (in Chinese of course) and the quotation 'The people all love those who sit under the sweet pear tree' - he being a great Chinese at once understood the allusion which refers to a famous Duke Sha - a mandarin who was famous for his love of justice and fair dealing and who used to travel about the country personally enquiring into the welfare of his people and settling their disputes and he always sat under the sweet pear tree to do this. It is really rather a charming compliment. Certainly this place is the best possible testimony to British Rule - it is self supporting and all the people are contented and happy while just over the border of our territory the country is ravaged by bandits and half the population starving. The bandits never dare come over the frontier - though we have no means of preventing them - it is entirely because of that much abused attribute Prestige. The population here is entirely one of peasant proprietors - each man owns his little bit of ground and his snug stone thatched roof cottage - each village is more or less one family. Of course the population is too large which keeps them very poor - but one is immensely struck by the fact of how cheerful they all are - always smiling and friendly.

I hear that my designs for the 'Ambrose' concert party costumes executed by Mr Jelly Belly are very successful. I'm longing to see them at the performance on Saturday. In the evenings we are very occupied making Ian's fancy dress for the Ambrose dance. We are going as a sort of modern Dick Whittington and his cat - Ian the latter role as an Amoy cat (like Wong li fu's blue lion) We constructed a magnificent head mounted on a solar topee and he is going to wear a blue boiler suit covered with the necessary markings - white socks, shoes and gloves and a tail! I'm going to be a Boy Scout (don't have ten fits - it's really quite becoming!) in a pair of Ian's khaki shorts that shrank in the wash, a tussore silk shirt - that very gay pink handkerchief and all the necessary badges etc. and a scout hat. It ought to be rather fun as everyone is supposed to make their own dress and preferably be comic. Lady Trywhitt is awfully pleased because she has thought of a dress in which no one will recognise here!

You must think my letters are nothing but a frivolous record of picnics and dances. Life here is of course just a prolonged summer holiday. I think that is the reason Mrs Lushington went home - her conscience smote her so at leading such a useless life! I'm afraid I am enjoying it thoroughly - but I do try to do some drawing or painting every day. I've done one water colour that I'm quite pleased with - the result of many hot expeditions to the Mainland.

The Island Hotel
29th August 1927 Wei hei wei

I enclose the poem Ian has written to fit the lady in the Palanquin. I am awfully pleased with it as it seems to so exactly go with the picture and I think it has more real poetry in it that anything he has written. I feel if I had met it in an anthology I should have been attracted by it. Will you do what you think best about sending it with the picture to Basil Blackwell for the next No. of Joy Street.

We did our last expedition in Bobjohn yesterday as tomorrow he has to come back to the island to be embarked in the Ambrose for Hong Kong. We started at four and drove out to a lovely valley about ten miles away and there had a picnic tea and climbed a hill from the top of which we had a marvellous view - there was a lovely sunset on the way home and it made a very gay picture with the threshing floors covered with orange maize and yellow millet and the women in their pink and red and blue clothes - the green willow trees and the mysterious blue mountains behind and the painted sky. We had to sampan back against the wind so didn't arrive until 8.30.

Saturday was one of the loveliest days we have had. It wasn't too hot and wonderful clouds. We sailed over at 2 o'clock and went to the Commissioner's where a huge cavalcade was assembled. Ian took some children in Bobjohn - and there were about four gharry loads of more children and various grown ups and one gharry full of food and the Chinese cook and his family! - and Colonel Stewart of the Middlesex Regt. on his charger and I mounted on the Commissioner's Mongol pony - we ambled out through the pleasant countryside to the 1st Lagoon and the moment we got on the sands the pony set off full gallop and we raced up and down: as he had a mouth like iron I couldn't stop him but as I managed to stay on I thoroughly enjoyed it. The whole lot of us bathed in the enchanting warm lagoon water - Meanwhile the cook and his small boys lit a fire and we had a huge tea and wonderful chocolates from a German shop in Tiensin. Then all the children played pirate ships in a derelict junk and the rest of us walked over to a little temple dedicated to the Dragon King. It is the most heavenly place - absolutely lonely - just the stretches of white sand and blue water and hills behind which were a marvellous grape colour.

I came home in a gharry, lent my riding breeches to Mary Lampson as she wanted to ride the pony home (it succeeded in throwing her too!) Mary is only 12 but as big as me. The youngest Lampson Margaret is a pet and reminded me very much of Eleanor. It was nearly dark driving home and the children sang all the way! Mr Johnston sent us home in his launch the 'Gallia' but we didn't arrive till 8.30 and had rather a scramble dressing and dining before the Ambrose concert at 9. It went with great swing and I was very pleased with the dresses I designed and the leading lady wore my old black and silver evening dress which looked so good that I wished I hadn't parted with it!

The Commissioner was very impressed with Bobjohn and I think thoroughly enjoyed his trip. No - he isn't really a performing Buddhist - though he has great sympathy with it. For eight years he lived the life of a hermit in the mountains contemplating nature and reading and writing and only seeing Chinese - now in his old age he has become a most genial and sociable person and enjoys nothing so much as these vast picnics and is an excellent host. He himself only has one meal a day and drinks nothing, but provides a regular feast always for his guests.

The Island Hotel
8th September 1927 Wei hei wei

It is heavenly weather now - not too hot - I am sitting on the verandah with no coat on - there is a lovely moon shining on the water and the Mainland hills look like black cardboard. I can see the lights of the 'Curlew' and 'Carlisle' (one is playing a band) and the little lights of the sampans go to and for like fireflies. I shall be sorry to leave this place, apart from missing you and Eleanor I can't conceive a happier summer - perpetual sunshine - lovely surroundings - no worries - one can even live comfortably on one's income (without effort!) Any amount of bathing or exercise so that one feels very fit - plenty of pleasant company - a charming room and living on an island full of flowers and sweet smelling and clean and safe and yet with real Chins to explore ½ an hour across the water. It has been rather a time of lotus eating and my results in the way of painting haven't justified the time I have spent on them. However the chief thing about the summer is that I've never seen so much of Ian before and he has been so happy. I also think I've collected a lot of material for future illustrations.

I think I've improved at golf and tennis (certainly the latter) and swim a little (though not much) better - the only other permanent gain I think of is that I've acquired enough beautiful silk underwear to last me the rest of my life!! not to mention some silk dresses.

I feel now it is quite time to settle down to the real business of life and I hope to cable you at any moment. I shall be really disappointed if nothing happens - I was quite bucked when I had a sick attack last week - but so had Ian and most of the people in the hotel so I don't attach much importance to it now.

Mrs Poland and I set off on our adventures on either the 20th or 23rd arriving in Pekin two days later. I hope these dates suit the Lampsons but I haven't heard from her yet - we leave Pekin on the 5th and get to Kobe on the 9th where I hope Ian will meet us. Our plans in Japan are vague and will crystallise when we get there - if possible I shall return to Hong Kong in a ship which calls at Shanghai as I have so many acquaintances there now who I could go and see, and it would give Ian time to get me a dwelling place in Hong Kong. I arrive there the first week in November in a probably bankrupt condition! I am getting a little nervous that this trip may work out more expensive that we anticipate - Japan especially is appallingly expensive - however I feel I should be an idiot to miss such a chance of going there and besides I've nowhere to go in Hong Kong and this hotel will be shutting up so I couldn't stay here. We have about £100 saved in the bank here which makes one feel rich but there is always the devastating thought of my passage home which may now be any time from December onwards! I don't feel I can twice have the luck to get a troopship home.

Chapter Seven **Pekin and Japan, 1927**

T.S.S. 'Hector'
21st September 1927 Blue Funnel Line

Little did I think when I awoke this morning that this is where I should be in twelve hours time!

It was a heavenly morning and I started gaily off in the 9.30 ferry to collect our tickets etc. from the Mainland for the 'Tingchow' sailing for Tiensin tomorrow. To my horror when I got to the agents they said there was no hope of a passage as the ship was full up and the next one too probably and we should be lucky if we got away by the end of the month - this was shattering as we booked six weeks ago and all along were told there would be difficulty about passages. The end of the month was no use as we had to be in Japan by October 9th in order to meet Ian and also the Lampsons had asked us for this month and Ian was leaving on Monday and Captain Poland already gone. We were filled with impotent fury and nearly burst into tears. We were lunching with the Lees (the District Officer) and they had some nice people called Turner staying with them - Mr Turner being high up in the Legation. They were frightfully sympathetic and finally had an inspiration and said why don't you go in the 'Hector' (a large Blue Funnel bound for Shanghai which was in the harbour) and get off at Tsingtao (the old German Kiaochan - and go by train from there to Pekin! At first this sounded quite mad but in the end we came to the conclusion it was our only hope of seeing Pekin - besides of "two courses always choose the most entertaining." So we rang up the agents - found we could get a passage - then accompanied by the Lees we caught the 2.45 ferry to the Island (Mr Lee came in order to convince Ian that it was really quite safe and reasonable) Meanwhile Mr Turner cabled to the Consul at Tsingtao to meet us and to various other consuls on our route so we shall be looked after and treated like royalty!

Incidentally I had a tennis party this afternoon! But we sent the Lees to cope with it. It was 3.15 by the time we got back to the Island and the Hector sailed at 5! Ian was none too enthusiastic - but was finally convinced by Mr Lee and then went off to signal for a boat from Titania to take us and our luggage off at 4.30 - so I had just over an hour to pack and settle everything. (So far the only thing I've discovered I've forgotten is a hot water bottle!) I've left a good deal for poor Ian to clear up and cope with and most of my baggage is going with him - I have only got hand gepack. So before we had time to turn round we found ourselves sailing off in the wrong direction! We get to Tsingtao tomorrow morning and are met and probably spend the day there - then go by a night train to a place with an unpronounceable name twelve hours inland - there we change into the Blue Express. We are met by the Consul at this place and may spend a day there - then we have another twelve hours onto Pekin - rather a lark! The only thing I resent is that it is going to cost exactly double - however I hope to get some back by writing an article for Blackwood - as it really will be an experience worth describing. Mrs Poland is very sporting and we are going to thoroughly enjoy ourselves.

This is a lovely ship and we have a cabin with a wardrobe and chest of drawers etc. Sir Sydney Barton (the Consul General) is on board and he assured Ian that it is safe and the trains are as good as the Riviera Expresses and all foreign run. Anyway I prefer train to sea travel and we shall really see something of the interior of China though my Geography is so vague I don't quite know how we go.

I hated leaving Ian and I feel we rather bounced him into consenting by sending off the cables before he knew anything about it!

British Consulate-General
22nd September 1927 Tsinan

Here we are two hundred miles inland in China and on the second stage of our journey. We had a very comfortable night in the 'Hector' and arrived at Tsingtao at about 8am. There we were met by the Consul's car and a man who took charge of our baggage - and we drove to the Consul's (Mr King's) house. Mrs King was very kind to us and there was a nice grown up daughter. The house was an ex-German house and full of gables and alcoves and semi gothic decoration - but very comfortable. We had lunch and them went to the beach and bathed and then they took us for a lovely motor drive - unfortunately in a shut car which I never enjoy so much. Tsingtao is just like a continental town with its little red roofed houses set among trees and further out still it might be a suburb of Bournemouth. It is all beautifully tidy and well kept and the only incongruous note is the rickshaws and any Chinese walking about. Behind the town are lovely wooded hills - but more reminiscent of the country round Ascot than one's idea of China.

After an excellent tea we played bridge until dinner time and at 9.30 our train departed. The Kings came to see us off and put us into the only 1st class carriage - in it was a Chinese official in grey gown and black brocade jacket - two Germans (one female), two Japanese men and a nice old Scotch missionary lady Mrs Forsythe aged nearer 80 than 70. There was an armed guard on the train, quite smart looking Shantung soldiers with white gloves and a sword. They clanked up and down the corridor all night - but I'm told if we'd been held up by bandits they would all have disappeared! However we had the most peaceful and comfortable journey - I had a beautifully clean bunk with little curtains all round and sheets and pillow and I could lie and look out of the window. One couldn't undress owing to the other people in the carriage - but one could regulate ones own supply of fresh air which was a great thing. I slept like a top until 5.30 when I awoke to watch the sunrise. We went through very pretty country - hills and walled towns and temples on the top of mounds and family grave yards surrounded by trees. The harvest is all nearly in and they have begun ploughing - most primitive ploughs drawn usually by an ox and ass. At 7.30 we arrived here (the capital of Shantung) and were met by a charming Consul General Mr Tours. He carried us off to his lovely house where we wallowed in deep hot baths and then ate a huge breakfast. Our train ought to have gone on almost at once but it hasn't arrived from Pekin yet, so goodness knows when we shall get started on the third and last stage of our round about trip! It is about another fourteen hours - but though the train is called the 'Blue Express' I gather the engine is liable to breakdowns or the whole train to be pushed into a siding while Northern War Lords go down the line! I hope now we shan't start until this evening as I should hate to arrive at the Lampsons at 2 or 3am!

It is really a most interesting trip and I am astounded at the cleanliness and comfort and general efficiency of the Chinese railways. I can't tell you how kind everyone has been to us. China is a grand place for two lone females to travel in as one is just handed on from one consul to another - with cables going ahead and always someone to see after the luggage!

However I hope we shan't be stuck here too long as there isn't much to do. The place was evacuated some months ago when the Cantonese were expected and all the furniture from this house removed. Mr Tours has just begun to get it back again - but so far he and about five other people are the only inhabitants.

British Legation
24th September 1927 Pekin

We are safely here now and very glad to be at the end of our adventurous journey though it was great fun.

I wonder if you will have got the letter I wrote from Tsinan - anyway up to there it was a most calm comfortable trip. We ought to have gone on at 8.30 but the train failed to put in an appearance until 2 o'clock when a heated messenger arrived to say the train from Pekin had just arrived and was going out again - so we went helter skelter to the station and bundled into the train which we were told had been kept waiting for us ½ an hour! Then we found we had no tickets as the boy Mr Tours had sent to buy them was not there - he was subsequently found unconscious with two cuts on his head - the story being that he had fallen under the train in his hurry to get to us with the tickets - which we eventually received covered with gore! Mr Tours bore him off to the hospital where he recovered - and meantime the train showed no signs of movement and we eventually heard that the engine had broken down! So until 5 o'clock we sat in the hot dusty coupe in the very smelly station and then the train suddenly started. A few miles from Tsinan we crossed the Yellow River and then entered the great Plain - a most depressing place - as flat as a board for hundreds of miles - every inch cultivated and only occasionally broken by a mud walled village of squalid mud houses or a few clumps of trees and the toiling figures of men and women in blue clothes. At 6 o'clock the engine chucked its hand in again and we sat at a way side station for two hours - it was rather unpleasant as the place was full of soldiers who came and looked at us through the window and three awful looking desperadoes who must have been Russians - also we couldn't hear when we were to go on - no one could talk any English except the train 'boy' and he didn't know much. We went along and ate a bad dinner and then returned and then retired to our sleeping berths - at 8 o'clock the train moved on much to our joy - but it was short lived for at 10 we once more came to a full stop and saw our engine career off by itself! We also heard a lot of shouting and excitement and there were swarms of soldiers and really we were both pretty frightened![34] We sat in our hot little coupe with all the blinds down and the electric light was very dim and kept on getting worse. The only other Europeans were a German girl (who was very calm and rejected our offer of company) and a dour little Scotchman who was rather a comfort to us in theory though in practice the only time we saw him was at dinner. I tried not to think of that vast desolate plain all round us and how helpless we should be if bandits appeared or if the soldiers wished to rob us. I had about 70$ on me and Phyllis about 900$ as she took all her money in cash rather unwisely (I have a letter of credit) However all our fears were of our own imagination as eventually the soldiers produced an engine and at 11.30 we rattled off again - worn out we both slept until we reached Tiensin at 7am and from there the journey was quite uneventful and rather attractive - sunflowers and trains of camels and lots of trees. We were rather upset at finding no one to meet us as Mr Tours had telegraphed and we were feeling guilty at arriving two days before they expected us though I had said in my last letter that the ships were so erratic that we might arrive any time between the 24th and 27th but would telegraph. We bundled into an awful old Ford with all our luggage scattering in all directions and several vagabonds on the running board. They first of all drove us up to the back door of the Legation and then to some offices - we eventually arrived at the front door to be told that Lady Lampson was away until Monday! We were just going off in a dispirited way to the hotel when Sir Miles[35] appeared very genial and kind and said Mr Tours' telegram had only just arrived and so he had expected us that night and that was why no one had met us - and that Lady Lampson had gone to their country bungalow while the boiler was being mended as they had expected us by sea when they would have had twenty-four hours notice of our arrival. However he seemed to think it very enterprising of us to have come overland and we are to go out to the bungalow tomorrow and Lady Lampson is returning on Monday. We feel we have rather planted ourselves on them - but they are so kind and nice. If only we could have got a sea passage we should have arrived on Monday for a week instead of for ten days as we are now. However I can't say I'm really sorry because I shall want every minute here. It is <u>wonderful</u> like a Fairy Story - but mixed with a good deal of dirt and squalor.

The Legation itself is beautiful - an old palace with a green tiled roof and courtyards with plants and red pillars and green and blue and gold ceilings - also of course frightfully comfortable.

We lunched with Sir Miles who is quite charming - huge and beaming (his nick name is Sir Miles and miles of Lampson!) Then he went out and two secretaries took us in rickshaws to the Temple of Heaven, a marvellous blue tiled roof and surrounded by fine trees.

The Forbidden City is all orange tiles and red wall. The Legations are inside the Tartar City which has a huge wall and lovely gates - outside the Chinese City is squalid and filthy and with the dustiest, bumpiest roads I have ever met - but it is all fascinating.

As the Lampsons aren't here we are dining with some Legation people who have a charming house in the grounds - the man Mr George has such nice pictures - Brangwyns, Sheringhams and Mr Lumsden's etchings - also beautiful lacquer and screens and T'ang horses - and though he is rather a forbidding person we have 'clicked' at once.

As you may imagine I am fairly weary after two disturbed nights

British Legation
September 27th 1927 Pekin

There is so much to say that I don't know where to begin - so I'll just give you an outline diary - on Saturday afternoon we went out to the Temple of Heaven in Rickshaws accompanied by one of the secretaries and a nice Captain Harding who we subsequently dined with as the Lampsons were out in the country. On Sunday we went up on to the Tartar Wall and we were to have gone out to tea and dinner with the Lampsons but a thunderstorm had made the road impassable so instead we were taken round some shops (Jade Street and Lanthorn Street etc.) by a charming couple called Benet who live in the Legation and we dined with them. Yesterday Lady L returned. She is quite delightful and very much your style - she took us out to the Forbidden City in the car and after tea she and Sir Miles (who is as nice as she is) took us shopping - oh I forgot-we lunched with a Mr Aveling (the 1st Secretary) who gave us Pekin Duck and a most marvellous pudding made of real fruits covered with brittle sugar and chestnuts and cream inside! There was a dinner party here in the evening and mild Bridge and today the Lampsons went off to some mines so we are once more in sole possession of the Legation (and Legation car!) but Lady L returns on Thursday. On Monday we've been asked to a dinner party at the Belgian legation and on Tuesday we depart. I really feel awfully guilty at having planted myself here for nine days - but the Lampsons have been too kind for words - and we really couldn't help arriving four days too soon! And in the East people don't mind because they don't have to consider their servants! Today we shopped (to some tune as I bought a fur coat! It cost 135$ -the dollar being 1/10 - it is full length and is made of baby leopard[36] - very light and soft and not too startling - it has a delicious marmot collar and cuffs and a lining of yellow Chinese brocade - really a bargain I think and it will be very warm and useful for motoring.)

Mrs Poland bought a white fur cape for her daughter for 60$ - she also bought a lot of Pekin coloured glass (fingerbowls and dessert plates etc.) and I got some meretricious glass flowers - rather nice and very cheap and we got little jewelled trees -·3$ a pair - the flowers all made of turquoise. You may think them horrid or else quite enchanting. I may get you a royal blue bowl for the centre of the table to go with your blue glass, but they hadn't the right size and shape today.

The shops here would go to your head and I'm sure you'd find bargains - I'm a bad shopper as you know. I'd hoped to find lacquer but that is hard to come by, the Lampsons have some lovely pieces but had to pay for them.

This afternoon we took the car out to the Summer Palace and Jade Fountain and the chauffeur drove us back round the Western Hills - Captain Harding came with us. Tomorrow we are shopping and lunching with the wife of the Captain of the Legation Guard and going to see the rest of the Forbidden City. On Thursday we are lunching with Mr Fitzhugh who has a curiosity shop and doing some more sights - I can't tell you how kind everyone is and we have met some delightful people and it is most interesting seeing life in Diplomatic Circles! The Legations are all huddled together inside a glacis and the Quarter is full of guards of every nationality.

I don't think I can begin to describe Pekin - it has gone to my head and I would give anything to live here for a year and do nothing but paint. This house itself is like a fairy palace and the Forbidden City is more romantic and breathtaking than anything I've ever imagined - it is planned on a ten times vaster and grander scale than Versailles and the colour is superb - the yellow huddle of roofs against the blue sky - the rose red walls and eaves painted jade and blue and gold - marble terraces and bridges over canals that are designed to give the best reflection and great golden jars and urns. It really is the Palace of Kubla Khan and to get to it you have to go through gate after gate - and we haven't yet penetrated right inside. The Summer Palace is rather awful - but the lake and the jade fountain and pagoda are charming and coming home we met strings and strings of great shaggy, laden camels! We also met a grand funeral with priests in yellow robes - but every street has its own sight and my eyes were popping out with trying to take it all in! The Chinese City where the shops are is unspeakably dirty and squalid but very fascinating.

British Legation
1st October 1927 Peking

I had a long letter from you forwarded here yesterday - I was so pleased. It is sweet of you to be sending me £10 for my birthday and will be much appreciated as for the first time in my life I am being really extravagant! Also travelling in Peking and Japan is a pretty expensive ploy even when we are being put up at the British Legation.

You will be relieved to hear that the £20: you told me to spend for you - at least £10 will be refunded! I've got you a long string of blue agate beads (sizes from peas to small cherries) they are more grey than blue but rather a charming colour - and I've not seen any really blue though I've looked at dozens. They were l6$ (32/-) I hope you will like them - I also got a carved bobble of blue agate and seed pearls to hang on the end - that was 4$ - if you don't want it I'll buy it back as it will come in for a wedding present. The earrings weren't pretty - but I'm still hoping to get some for about 10$ with seed pearls. I also may get Eleanor a necklace of jade and seed pearls, little balls of real seed pearls very light and pretty - they are 30$ - but he hadn't one in stock though I've seen one belonging to someone else which I loved, of course not the best jade but a lovely pale green.[37]

I looked at hundreds of mandarin coats till I got quite bewildered! The genuine ones were mostly falling to bits and dirty and none under 4£ and £5 but their lovely colours put you out of conceit with the new garish coats - so in the end I got what .I think will be very useful to you. It is a soft thick black crepe de chine coat embroidered in white and with a border of blues and black and white - very uncommon and so like you. The lining is a very poor quality white silk so I think I will get it really nicely lined in Hong Kong with blue crepe de chine. It is a very graceful shape and so soft and comfortable and would do to wear in the evening or as an opera coat. Of course it is quite new and you will have to pay duty but it was only $22 - Lady Lampson liked it enormously - but I hope you won't be disappointed at it being more useful than decorative. I've bought lots of mats etc. made out of old embroideries and a fascinating red pigskin box with gold on it (destined as a wedding present for Jack, but can I bear to part with it!) I'm hoping to find some more - I've also bought several jewelled trees - I'm not sure if they are fascinating or rather 'horrors' the flowers and leaves are all made of little bits of jade and amethyst and agate and they stand about 6ins high in soapstone pots. I thought they'd be nice presents but I'll have to bring them not send them. I'm very pleased with my leopard coat. I hope you won't think it too spotty! I've also bought some amusing toys for Eleanor at the Chinese Woolworths - a jewelled sword for 6d and a complete Forbidden City with ancestral tablets and all for 1/- in a box!

Mrs Poland has been trying to get red lacquer - but it is very expensive though perfectly lovely - we ran some down in an awful little alleyway called the 'Courts of Miracles' but it was beyond us.

Yesterday we spent the entire day shopping - the day before we went to the famous Hall of Classics and the Confucian Temple - we had tea with Mr Southcott who took us to the 'Peihai' (Winter Palace) and we went on the Lake in a boat. The day before we had lunch with a charming Major and Mrs Bray and tea with the Fitzhughs and saw the place where the Ex-Emperor lived (part of the Forbidden City) but it was rather decayed and squalid. Of all the sights the Halls of Audience and the Temple of Heaven are far the finest and the view from the top of the Peihai. I long to go off sketching - but I can't go alone and we always seem to be doing things every moment.

By the time you get this letter I imagine you will have had a cable from me - as I am now over a fortnight overdue. I'm awfully pleased - except I shall hate leaving Ian. I feel so frightfully well and normal that I can't really believe it - I am trying not to do too much though. Any time after the 25th May - it can't be before that date - I shall start home about the end of January or beginning of February unless there is a troopship going earlier that I can get a free passage in!

British Legation
3rd October 1927 Pekin

Yesterday was a divine day - clear as crystal and a blazing sun and cool wind - the hills were like jewels and we motored out to the Emperor's hunting park beyond the Summer Palace in the Western Hills. We climbed up and walked for miles to a lovely temple where we had lunch. The guest room was so clean and nice that I wouldn't have minded sleeping there. In one of the temples was a mummified Emperor - rather grim! We walked on over a hump backed bridge to another temple and picked the car up eventually having done a round of over ten miles. The views from the hills were gorgeous and on the way back we met strings of camels with their wild looking drivers which are very picturesque. The party consisted of Mr and Mrs Bennett and Mr Beer and ourselves.

Today Lady Lampson wanted me to ride with her in the country - but I nobly refused as I'm taking no risks this time.

The drawback to Pekin is the awful dust - in the spring I believe it becomes a fog and everything gets filthy. We have just been to have our hair washed in consequence and I had a Marcel wave in honour of the Belgian dinner party tonight. It is a huge one of thirty people - I feel my French won't stand the strain! Some Chinese came to tea - the Lord Li and his wife and son and daughter-in-law all in Chinese dress - the ladies were shingled and very got up but rather attractive - they talked very little English so we just smiled at each other and murmured "Very nice" at intervals.

Tomorrow we take train for Tiensin where we spend the night and we are dining and dancing with nice Major and Mrs Wade - Our ship goes the next day at noon and we get to Kobe on the 9th. I heard from Ian today - he had reached Nagasaki safely - I'm longing to be with him again.

I can't tell you how I've enjoyed my visit here and how kind and friendly the Lampsons have been - I only hope they don't think we've taken advantage of it by staying so long!

I think it is almost certain now that there will be a baby at the end of May or early in June and I am so pleased - the only thing is I shall hate leaving Ian so soon - the more we are together the more dependent we get upon each other - and I feel sorriest for him in this case - because I shall have all the joy and excitement of seeing you and Eleanor.

> Osaka Shosen Kaisha
> 7th Oct 1927 On board S/S Chojo Maru

This is one of the nicest ships I've ever been in. · It is quite small but brand new and charmingly decorated - little dwarf trees and Japanese pictures and we have such a nice cabin with two little beds instead of bunks one on top of the other. The food isn't good - but I think 3 or 4 days starvation will be very salutary after all the good food we ate in Pekin! Most of the other passengers are Japanese but there is a killing Armenian - American who calls herself 'Mamma' and plays execrable bridge - one youth who refers to himself as 'yours truly'!

I'm afraid my letters from Peking were very scrappy and unsatisfactory but I never seemed to have a spare moment and there wasn't a writing table in my bedroom. I think I told you about our wonderful day in the Western Hills - that was Sunday - on Monday we did some shopping and saw about our tickets and money etc. In the afternoon Lady Lampson had a Chinese tea party and in the evening we went to a big official dinner at the Belgian Minister's. It was rather interesting as there were ten different nationalities present from German to Japanese. I was a little disconcerted by having my hand kissed by the French and Italian attaches. I sat between the American Secretary (a nice man) and a rather genteel Italian. It was the best dinner I have ever eaten - and I wished that like Sir Miles I could have let my waistcoat out! We felt very proud that Sir Miles was our representative in that gathering. He is over 6ft 4 and broad in proportion - a very fine figure of a man - he is also so genial and kind and calm and I can't imagine any man more suitable to his job. I hear the Chinese all admire him and he puts them into a good humour and makes them laugh and gets things done. After dinner we went on to the Hotel de Pekin and danced.

Tuesday morning we packed and I paid a farewell visit to the Imperial City with the yellow roofs. Then we all went to lunch with Mr Newton (the Councillor to the Legation) He is a bachelor with a wonderful menage and once again I overate. Then we paid a series of farewell visits in the Legation and at 4·30 departed by train, Mr Beer coming to see us off. I don't think I have ever met so many nice people in the course of one week.

We arrived at Tiensin at 7·30 and went straight to the Hotel and changed and then dined with Major and Mrs Wade - they had a party consisting of the Colonel and his wife - a Major from the Border Regt. and a perfectly charming Subaltern from the East Yorks. We all went on to the Country Club and danced - it has a marvellous floor on rollers and a very good band. When that shut at 12 we went on to a sort of night club until 2. We should have sailed early next morning - but got a message saying the ship was delayed 24 hrs. (China is the most maddening country to travel in as nothing ever keeps up to time table) So there were we stuck in a very expensive hotel in Tiensin which is a deadly hole. We weren't allowed to go to the Chinese City and the Concessions are just like an ugly European suburb built on a salt marsh. However the Wades were very kind to us and took us to the Country Club to tea and to the pictures in the evening. I wasn't feeling at all well - a cold in the head and very sick and bilious (are you surprised after all our lunch and dinner parties?) However I'm quite well again now - but I felt the visit to Tiensin was £3 wasted - the only thing is we are now certain that the 'Titania' will arrive first at Kobe and Ian will be there to meet me.

We eventually left Tiensin yesterday morning - the train very late and crowded with refugees (I think we only just got away from Pekin in the nick of time - as we hear the gates are to be shut!) Owing to the river having silted up you can no longer sail from Tiensin but have to go by train to Tangku (like sailing from Gravesend instead of London) We had several hours to put in at Tangku, a most desolate spot, but fortunately we had met in Pekin the man who lives there in charge of the railway - so they had told us to look them up. They live in a bungalow in a railway siding but keep cows and even bees! and we had a delicious tea with scones and honey and cream and they presented us with a large bottle of fresh milk which is making all the difference to this journey as condensed milk always makes me sick. We sailed at 7 and so far it is lovely and flat calm. We pass dear Wei Hai Wei at 4 o'clock this afternoon and we reach Moji on Sunday morning and then go through the Inland Sea which I believe is beautiful - though I fear a lot of it we go through at night. We arrive at Kobe early on my birthday and there I shall see Ian. I think we shall go straight on that evening to Kyoto - as there is nothing to see in Kobe and the hotel is ruinous - and Ian and Mr Lipscombe join us at Kyoto on the 14th or 15th for the five days leave - We may go for one night to Nara. 'L27' goes down to Hong Kong on the 20th - I shall have to either leave on the 19th by P and O spending two days at Shanghai - or else wait until the 25th and go direct to Hong Kong in a China Navigation Co's boat. It rather hinges on whether the Lushington's friend (the Head of the Kyoto Girls' University) comes up to scratch and asks us to stay! If she doesn't I think we shall be so broke by the 19th that we shall have to leave. We hear Japan is awfully expensive and of course this is the Tourist season.

The Miyako Hotel
13th October 1927 Kyoto Japan

Up to date Japan has proved a bitter disappointment - I don't know how much it is the fault of the place or how much it is that I'm rather fed up with travelling and hotels and was thoroughly spoilt in Pekin. Also I've begun feeling sick though otherwise very fit.

The voyage from Tiensin was very calm but I was as sick as a cat all the time and hated it - even though the passage through the Korean Islands was lovely - fantastic rocks and wooded Islets. We got to Moji early on the 9th and went ashore - a foul place - we sailed again at noon and the only bit I did enjoy was the next few hours through the Inland Sea - really calm and lovely little islands and fishing boats etc. We got to Kobe at 7am on the 10th. Ian met us - but owing to the agents having told him the ship wasn't coming in until 8 he was rather late and I was beginning to get very fussed. He had a car ready and we drove out to an hotel at a place called Takaralzuka about twelve miles outside Kobe which the British Consul had recommended as the hotels in Kobe are so frightfully expensive. This one was very nice and half the price and with pine woods and orange groves all round and an electric train which only took thirty-five minutes to get into Kobe. We went and had tea with the Glencrosses (I do admire her travelling about with three children under eight - a Russian governess and a Filipino nursemaid!) and we explored the shops - but Kobe is another foul place - like a ramshackle English town (rather like the awful bungalow suburbs that are springing up everywhere) and the people wear a depressing mixture of European and Japanese costume (a kimono - a bowler hat and elastic sided boots is a favourite combination! Or pink Jaeger pants sock suspenders and a coolie coat!) Some of the little ladies are attractive but give me the Chinese every time - also I think the Chinese are more intelligent - these people are like educated apes.

It poured all night and we went into Kobe armed with mackintoshes in the morning - there we looked at gold screens which are rather lovely but cost £4 pounds each - Phyllis Poland wants one for her house. I sent you a cable which I hope will thrill you! (I wonder where you were when you got it?)

After lunch Ian got back and we went for a walk in the pine covered hills. Very nice - but just like Surrey - the only amusing thing we saw was a party gathering mushrooms. They go about twenty or thirty complete with children and make a regular annual holiday of it and when we saw them they were drinking tea and a lady was singing to a sort of guitar and it was rather picturesque.

This morning Phyllis and I went in to Osaka and took the train here - our hopes running high that we were really getting into Japan proper. We were very dashed to arrive at a vast railway station situated in a beastly looking town - it got slightly better as we drove up here in a rattly Ford car. We had heard much of the beauty and comfort of this hotel and how they gave special naval terms and we had an introduction to the manager - but it has all ended in my having to pay £1 a day for an almost squalid back bedroom furnished in aged blue plush and looking out on to a timber yard - Phyllis couldn't bear hers and is paying 24/- a day for one not much better - anything at all nice is 30/- to £2. The lounge is like a station waiting room the bathroom etc. Victorian to say the least of it - the whole thing not a patch on the Hotel de Seine! Ian comes on Friday for his four days leave and I think he will hate it and the worst thing of all is that it has suddenly turned bitterly cold and is very grey and inclined to rain. We went down to the shopping district - bits of it are attractive little canals and wooden houses with lanthorns outside - but everywhere there are clanging trams and Ford cars and even the nice bits are more like the White City than a real place. The shops are very attractive but wickedly expensive and the trail of the American tourist is over all the land. I don't think I shall buy anything and I hope you won't be disappointed at my spending so little of your money.

The nicest thing that has happened was finding two batches of letters from you awaiting me - I loved the account of Eleanor's birthday and I am glad she liked the Chinese dolls.

Are you pleased about the baby? Funnily enough I think I really want another girl - Ian to my surprise is awfully bucked about it but I think would prefer 'John Ambrose'.

October 13th

Things are brighter today- the sun is out and Japan is more attractive - we spent the morning at a bewildering kimono shop helping Captain Richardson and Mr Norrison from the Titania buy Haoris - I got a kimono for Eleanor - powder blue with large pink peonies - very thick silk lined pink - it is the proper kind that the Japanese children wear, printed silk not embroidered. I got you a scarf (knowing your passion for them - white and blue) and when Ian comes I am going to get him to give me a Haori - We are just off now up to a lake and walking back over the hills. So Goodbye.

Inland Sea
21st October 1927 P and O.S.N.Co SS Kashmir

Here am I on my way down to Hong Kong. Ships fitted very well as Ian left yesterday morning and is going direct and so will arrive three days before I do which will enable him to fix up rooms etc.

We are really looking forward to being settled for a bit in Hong Kong and I hope Ian finds nice rooms. I'm sick of hotels and living in my suitcases.

Mrs Poland was so disappointed in Japan that she fled back by the first ship and I should certainly have accompanied her if Ian hadn't been there - as it was we thoroughly enjoyed his four days leave. The first day we went out in a very crowded tram to Lake Beiva and then up a mountain in a funicular railway. From the top we got a really glorious view and there was rather an interesting monastery. The hotel had provided a most excellent picnic lunch all packed in little wooden boxes (butter in one - salt in another, salad in another) and a wooden knife and fork and when you've finished you just throw away the lot.

On Sunday Tim Taylor joined us and Mr Lushington (who is Japanese interpreter) and the Glencrosses came to lunch. We all went by train to a place Kameoka where we hired a boat and proceeded to shoot the rapids. It was quite exciting and we went through some lovely scenery very reminiscent of Scotland. In the evening Mr Lushington took us to dinner at a Japanese restaurant with two friends of his. One talked English quite well and he was very interesting as he was the man who arranged the Japanese print collection at the S. Kensington Museum - he knew Mr Binyon and Mr Waley.[38] I can't say I enjoyed the food much - it consisted largely of eels and fungus! The next day we lunched at a private house with a Mr Kita, a curio dealer. He couldn't talk very much English - but the serving man talked French! The food was much nicer though too much of it (it lasted from 1 until 3) and I quite liked the national drink of Sake which you drink hot out of a little tiny bowl. We got pretty weary squatting on the floor for two hours - but I managed my chopsticks most successfully. It was rather charming, the room with its paper windows and spotless matting (you always have to take your shoes off before entering a Japanese house) and we each had a little low lacquer table with a tray with different coloured bowls. Then Mr Lushington took us to see a most interesting thing called the No dances - they are very old and have never changed since classical times. The stage is quite bare except for a conventional pine tree painted on the back - the orchestra consists of a drum a sort of flute and a stringed instrument - the chorus all kneel at one side and chant while the principals in gorgeous and very ancient robes and masks go into very slow and stately posturings - the hall itself is only used for these dances and only the better class Japanese attend - instead of chairs each party has a square of matting with a little fence round it and a brazier in the middle where they make tea all the time.

The next day we went to the Nijo Palace - a fortified 16th century castle belonging to the Shogun. It is moated and quite fine outside, and inside it is quite the loveliest interior that I have ever seen - each room is surrounded by sliding screens covered with gold foil and painted most exquisitely with pine trees or peonies or bamboo or birds - the effect is rich and mellow and altogether entrancing like a fairy palace - the floors are spotless matting or mirror like polished boards - the upper panels of the passages are parchment colour with gold and silver blown on to them so that it gives the effect of clouds - the ceilings are carved - there is no furniture. The windows are paper covered and you slide them back to see the little conventional gardens. We saw another palace, the Awata - smaller but equally fascinating. It was rather funny, we found that to see the Nijo we had to get a permit from our Ambassador at Tokyo and of course there wasn't time - but as the whole thing is a mere formality we got in on two old permits - but I felt rather guilty signing my name as Miss O'Brien from the U.S.A! Still it was worth temporarily losing one's nationality and forging in order to see those screens!

On Tuesday we spent the day at Nara which ought to be a lovely place but is quite spoilt by Japanese trippers - horrid little booths and postcard shops everywhere and paper and banana skins etc. We returned by train with a party of merry mushroomers - very tight and behaving just like an English bank holiday crowd. On Wednesday we came back to Kobe and dined in the 'Titania' and there was a dance afterwards. Ian was sailing early in the morning so I spent the night alone at the Oriental Hotel (14/- for a room which I shared with a rat!) and I embarked at noon next day. Ian took all my heavy luggage in L27. So I am travelling like a perfect lady with two neat suitcases. This is a small ship but I have a three berth cabin to myself on B deck and it is beautifully calm so far. The Glencrosses are on board and a very nice brother and sister we have made friends with - the brother went through that Hankow show[39] and it was most interesting hearing a first hand account of it.

I am awfully glad to have been to Japan - but I quite feel I may have misjudged it - for one thing it was bitter cold weather which I always hate and I had a liver chill most of the time in consequence. We were too early for the maple trees and the place struck me as singularly lacking in colour. Also we hadn't time to get right away off the beaten track - and that again is difficult not knowing the language. It is abominably expensive (you could live for a month in China for the cost of ten days in Japan - we compromised by living at the cheapest rate which was pretty uncomfortable and for the same expenditure one would have got deluxe accommodation anywhere else) The shops were either very trashy (like Beales' Oriental basement!) or else rather lovely and very expensive and like Liberty. The one thing that wasn't a disappointment is that the trees in Japan really do all grow twisty like a Japanese print - and some of the little houses and gardens are charming. It is an amazing mixture of exquisite cleanliness and neatness and filthy squalor and worse smells than China or Venice.

Japan is the only place that I have done as a complete tourist and Ian and I have come to the conclusion the only possible way to be a tourist is to have unlimited money and be able to take cars everywhere etc. China I have seen from the point of view of the resident which is far the nicest way of seeing a place and Pekin and Singapore and Colombo from private houses or Government Houses which is perhaps the nicest and cheapest way of all - so I daresay I've been spoilt. Still of all the places in the East my allegiance is still faithful to Wei Hai Wei.

P and O S N Co
27th October 1927 S.S.Kashmir

We got to Shanghai early on Sunday morning and kind Mrs Napier came off in the tender to meet me - I also discovered afterwards that Mrs Macmicheal had sent to meet me too - but as I didn't know she knew I was passing through I wasn't looking out for her car. Anyway as I wasn't feeling very well I think staying with Mrs Macmichael might have been too hectic and my clothes wouldn't have been up to her Shanghai standard - as even in Wei Hai Wei she always looked like Paris! but it was very kind of the old bird to think of putting me up. As it was I went off rather in fear and trembling with Mrs Napier who is quite the oddest looking creature you have ever seen. Imagine Mrs Sumner or Mrs Lovell of the moated grange but 6 feet tall and crowned with golden hair - arrayed in grass green tweeds and a mangy feather boa and smelling of moth balls and there you have a slight idea of Mrs Napier - but it is a shame to write this - because never in my life have I met anyone so kind. Do you remember I told you how she'd come up to me and said "I'm sure we should find friends in common" and I not having been attracted by either of them had been pretty standoffish and detestable - but of course what completely changed me was à propos of Edinburgh - she said "I read a most delightful book of reminiscences the other day written by a wonderful old Edinburgh lady called Mrs Sellar" and she nearly hugged me when I said I was Mrs Sellar's granddaughter.

Anyway she drove me out to her house in the French Concession - a tiny little house in which the nursery had been turned into a spare room for my benefit. They have a little girl aged five, Mr Napier (who I don't think I really liked - rather odd) is years younger than she is and is quite a junior in the B.A.T. Firm (a branch of your Imperial Tobacco's) and they are not at all well off according to Shanghai standards - but they have a car and a chauffeur and everything was very comfortable and nice and she insisted on my having breakfast in bed and thoroughly spoilt me.

I was also motored out to the Golf course and generally shown round Shanghai. One can't go into the Chinese City just now and the Concessions are almost like London - huge buildings and dense traffic and wonderful shops from Paris and London and heaps of Russian shops. I found a shop where you got lovely all silk stockings for 3/6 a pair and laid in a large stock - I would have sent some to you but for this infernal silk duty.

On Monday I rang up the old Dents who asked me to tiffin. Old Vyvyan hadn't changed a day since I last saw him seven years ago nor had the house which was still like a dusty museum. It is full of priceless stones out of the Imperial Palaces - pictures 1000 years old - rare hangings and carvings etc. and then awful old yellow plush chairs and countless dusty ornaments and five rampageous dogs who are very much spoilt children. We had a quite excellent and recherché lunch and afterwards the old gentleman played the organ and 'Cubby' the piano and they have a marvellous gramophone.

I felt a great deal better for my two days ashore - but yesterday was rough and I stayed in bed and was awfully sick. I'm a bit groggy today but thank goodness we get to Hong Kong at dawn tomorrow. I hope Ian will have found somewhere for me to live - I am so sick of hotels and my boxes.

After this taste of it I rather dread the long journey home alone - but it is a great thing getting two evils over together as under either circumstance separately I feel pretty sick. I read Mrs Erskine's book the other day 'Sex at Choice' and she says the sicker you are the less chance of a miscarriage and the more likely it is to be a girl - so I imagine I'm for another daughter.'

Chapter Eight

1, The Albany
28th October 1927 Hong Kong

Few places have I been more glad to leave and few places more enchanted to return to than Hong Kong! I am being much chaffed at having remarked in all seriousness, "If you want to really appreciate Hong Kong go to Japan". Anyway of course this is the perfect time of year here - enchanting weather and sunshine and that awful fog we had all spring quite gone - and everything is looking green and lovely after the summer rains. We got in at 7am on Friday and Ian came to meet me in the motor boat and we came straight up here to breakfast. That nice Mrs Harker had kept a room for me - refusing several people who wanted it and only letting it for short periods until I arrived. We were very thankful as Hong Kong is <u>crammed</u> and I don't know where we should have gone - Mrs Hutchinson and Mrs Hooper arrived last week and were only able to get back downstairs rooms at Lauriston for which they are paying double what we do for a front room here - so we are very lucky.

I found the most glorious budget of letters from you awaiting me. Three fat ones with lots of enclosures as well as masses of papers. I simply love your letters - they just tell me all the things I want to know about Eleanor and the garden etc. and seem to bring you so near.

It is rather thrilling about Wong Wing Wu[40] and I must finish Ginger which is a nicer story I think. We seem to be quite successful authors at the moment but without making a penny out of it!

Thank you most awfully for your princely birthday present - it was angelic of you and will be most useful as I must get a lot of new clothes as all the ones I brought out here have fallen to bits, but the silks here are so cheap and so lovely that one is glad to have the excuse to buy! And I shall lay in stocks of brocade shoes and things like that. We are not quite as bankrupt after Japan as we expected to be. I can't quite think why not - except that we didn't buy much as things were so dear - also Ian has had a rise of pay (2/6 a day)

I don't quite know what to do about Xmas presents. I'm giving you the silk coat I got in Pekin and I feel if I bring it with me I might get off with less Customs duty, the same with Eleanor's dressing gown.

We seem to have plunged straight into a whirl of gaiety and such a lot of new people belonging to the ship have arrived or are just about to arrive that I forsee having to have many parties. I haven't had time to unpack yet and my clothes after five weeks knocking about are too awful. I went yesterday morning to see Ailine Nicholl off in the 'Kashmir' then went and had my hair washed and waved at a Japanese barber where I sat surrounded by Chinese ladies in beautiful brocade gowns!

In the afternoon the Polands had a tennis party. I'm still playing mild tennis - I really think the exercise is good - but of course I won't go in for tournaments or anything really strenuous. Now that I am on dry land again I'm feeling as fit as anything and not even sick and just revelling being back in the warmth again and sun. How I hate cold.

We went out to dinner and on to a dance at Government House which was great fun as we saw all our friends there. I also saw Mr and Mrs Allen - he was with Ian in the 'Revenge' and is now in the 'Frobisher' which goes back to Malta next week. She only arrived two days ago - isn't it sickening for her - however she says she thinks it will sound rather amusing to talk of her 'weekend' in China! Several other wives have also only been out here for two or three weeks.

Jim and Grace[41] arrive on Friday - we hear that he will probably get a very nice house out at Lymoon (about ten miles away at the entrance to the harbour where his battery is): the Colonel is not married and though at present it is occupied by a married subaltern Jim can presumably turn him out as he is senior. It will really be rather fun having them here - especially ten miles away! (for heavens sake don't send this letter on to my mother-in-law)

We are so pleased with our quarters - the old French landlady is so kind and nice and it is the ideal position in the whole of Hong Kong as we are well up the hill and look on to the botanical gardens and there is a garden in front where Bobjohn lives (Yes thank you he is very well and going like a bird and none the worse for his travels!)

We have a very big bedroom one end furnished like a sitting-room and with two wardrobes and lots of room for clothes - we have a bathroom of our own (very primitive) and we also have a very big verandah - half closed in and with electric light - so we always sit there and in the morning I have my breakfast there with the sun pouring in. It looks out on to grass and palms and other exotic trees and you can't see another house and with the birds singing you'd never know you were in a town, the only snag is that being on the ground floor the verandah is shut off with iron bars which look a little like a monkey's cage but I dare-say that is better than midnight visitors. The Albany is one of the oldest houses in Hong Kong and features in all the old prints. The food is plain but very wholesome and good and it is all delightfully un-hotel-y. The best feature of all is that we only pay 150$ (£15) a month for everything light - room - attendance - and all my food - and Ian pays just for his food extra about 3/- a day - there is an amah who does all our washing for 10/- a hundred pieces and also does ironing etc. - just as well as we have a lot of entertaining to work off. However drink is very cheap here practically no duty and Mrs Harker is very good about providing special dinners and one can get the use of a sitting-room - so really we've fallen on our feet. As it is as nice and half the price of anywhere else in Hong Kong it is naturally very difficult to get in to. I've got quite a lot to do in the way of making curtains etc. as the present ones are a revolting shade of pink which swears with my orange and jade green cushions etc. I seem to spend my life making rather gaunt looking rooms inhabitable but it is rather fun and I think I'm better at it than I would be at making a real house nice.

4 The Albany
3rd November 1927

Hong Kong is really very pleasant. just now - a perfect temperature - hot but fresh and lovely sunshine and a clear atmosphere - (so different to what it is in the Spring!) On Sunday Ian and I went out to Big Wave Bay - which more than lived up to its name - as there were huge rollers coming in and we had a lovely bathe - the water was quite warm and it is such a pretty place a little white sanded cove surrounded by grassy hills and one might be hundreds of miles from any town and there were hardly any other people there - You can't get at it except by car - that is where little Bobjohn is so useful. The end of the expedition was somewhat marred by the discovery that we'd left the tea behind!

On Monday Ian played hockey and I went to the monthly meeting of the Hong Kong Art Club - a lot of tea and gossip and not much art! I've really only joined so as to be able to exhibit at the December Show. Tuesday Ian had a day on. I was very busy making curtains and cushions etc. And I went out to tea and dinner.

The garden outside is so pretty and you see all sorts of lovely butterflies and exotic birds and there is a frangi-pangi tree outside the front door which sheds enchanting smelling flowers. The food is just like what you would get in a Pension in France or Italy - I suppose because the place is run by a French-woman - the 'Boys' are quite good and the wash amah excellent. The bathroom with its grey cement walls and floor and scullery tap is not very attractive - but I suppose you can't expect marble bathroom for £15 a month any more than a silk umbrella in a 10 cent hash! The room looks quite nice now with the Wei hai orange curtains and apricot bedspread and blue and green cushions and a Chinese embroidered hanging that I bought and my own pictures! The walls are pale grey and the floor polished and I have got lots of pots of chrysanthemums. It is worthwhile trying to make a gaunt room look nice because Ian appreciates it so and he is very easy to please!

4 The Albany
5th November 1927 Hong Kong

Will you send me two copies by <u>book</u> post of No 5 Joy Street as soon as you can - one can't get it here and anyway would have to pay double for it - but I'd like to send one to the Napier child as they were so kind to me in Shanghai and one to the Lampson children - I thought of it before but thought I could get it at Kelly and Walsh.

Yesterday was Mr Allen's wedding, It was very quiet and took place at 11 o'clock in the Cathedral - No one there except the people belonging to the ship and a few outside friends of his - she looked charming in a lovely dress - but terribly nervous - Captain Poland gave her away and Tim Taylor was best man. Ian was in charge of the arch of swords and afterwards the crew of the submarine dragged the bride and bridegroom down to the jetty, the coxsin acting coachman! The reception was on board the Ambrose - a very good home made wedding cake and lots of champagne - It was a gorgeous day and everything was very simple and friendly and nice. They went off in the Commodore's barge with the whole ship cheering and letting off crackers. Poor things there is no where here to go for a honeymoon - so they are just out at Repulse Bay where we shall see them when we go to dance there tonight!

The French Hospital
7th November 1927 Hong Kong

I'm afraid I've got a dreadful disappointment for you - I've just had a miscarriage. I'm most awfully sad about it and everything seems very flat - but of course it isn't so bad only having known about it for six weeks - but I had begun to look forward so much to the summer and I knew how pleased you would be. And now we shall both have to wait another year, as the Dr. says I mustn't start again out here as this is such a bad place for keeping babies (though good for starting) but he says several patients of his who have had one or two mishaps out here have been quite all right at home and there is no reason why I shouldn't be especially if I go to bed for a few days at the 2nd and 3rd month. I don't anticipate any difficulty in starting a baby it merely seems to be a case of saying the word 'go'! but I hate the thought of having to wait again.

I asked the Dr. if I had been doing too much (I felt rather guilty at having played two games of tennis last week) but he said he thinks it was quite unavoidable - an irritable uterus - probably upset by my having been so sick in the 'Kashmir' combined with the place. The same thing happened to Mrs North ten days after we got to Wei hai wei after she had been very sick in the 'Hunchow' and that was two and a half months too (she has bravely - though I think unwittingly - embarked upon another already!) It was unfortunate my travelling about at that time, but of course I didn't know about it until I got to Pekin - or for dead certain until Japan.

It started on Saturday a propos of nothing - as all morning I had been writing letters and doing up Xmas parcels and only went out to the Post Office - Ian was playing cricket so I sat on the veranda and sewed and read until teatime when I was going out to tea with Mrs North and to see the match - I had just changed my dress and was starting out - when I felt something happen. I lay down and went to bed - We got hold of Dr Fitzmaurice (who lives at the Albany) but as he is Fleet ophthalmic specialist. he wasn't much help - though very kind - he told us of a civil Dr. who came up on Sunday morning and said if I lay on my back for a week all might be well. However on Monday it got so much worse that we summoned him again and he said I must go straight to hospital and sent his car for me. We had a nightmarish time as directly I put a foot out of bed it all began to happen. Ian had to wrap things round me and carry me out and Mrs Fitzmaurice packed my bag. I don't know how I survived the quite long motor drive and Ian carried me in and then everything happened - but no pain at all. Unfortunately at about 8 I began to bleed violently so the Dr was summoned and he said there was still a clot to come and he had better take it away - so I was wheeled away to the Operating Theatre (a most terrifying experience) and given chloroform and knew no more about it - and this morning I'm perfectly all right - no temperature - no bleeding and you can see how well I am by the fact that yesterday they said I should be here for eight or ten days and now the Dr. says I can go in three or four days and do anything I like in a fortnight - but it all seems a terrible waste of time and money and worst of all in hope and joyful anticipation.

I think Ian is very disappointed - he has been perfectly adorable - doing the part of sick nurse while I was laid up at the Albany and so upset and sympathetic. Fortunately he hasn't been very busy - he went to sea today - but came here at 7·45 to find out how things were and then back when he got in from sea.

This is a most comfortable place - I have a large light room to myself and the food is excellent (I'm already on 'full diet') The sisters are all gentle white robed French nuns and the nurses funny little coffee coloured people but very efficient and they have Chinese amahs to wait on them. I believe they charge £1 a day - which is cheaper than the Peak Hospital and anyway I'd never have got there in time. There aren't any private nurses or Nursing Homes here.

4 The Albany
18th November 1927

Your letters do make me so sad to think that you are still looking forward to June. It seems such a long time to wait until I can start again as now it is pretty definite that Ian is to bring one of the old 'L' boats home and they can't start before the middle of September because of the typhoons and heaven knows how long they will take to get home - with luck before Xmas. Ian's refit has been put off again until the middle of December but 'L27' has ceased to run as her engines are so wonky, so I suppose Ian won't go on the Southern Cruise at all now even if there is one. So I shall come home when he goes north unless I came by Trans Siberian railway! (Lots of people in Pekin go that way taking children and I heard it was most comfortable and reliable! and only ten days from Pekin and £60 - but I'm afraid Ian won't let me. Mrs Poland is rather keen to go back via Canada for a change and as I shall probably throw in my lot with her as she wants also to go home in the spring.)

I've done very little this week except have lots of visitors and Ian took me out a run in Bobjohn most evenings and I could walk as far as the 'Helena May' (The Women's Club and library) and one day I played Bridge. Next week however I hope to be active again

– but I am being very careful as I am so anxious to pave the way for next time.

4 The Albany
13th November 1927   Hong Kong

It nearly broke my heart getting your letter which you had written just after my cable - and I shall go on getting them now for seven or eight weeks and all the time knowing what a bitter disappointment there is for you. I'm still absolutely miserable about it as I just long for another baby. I can't really reproach myself very much about not having taken enough care - I was far more careful than I was before Eleanor's arrival and short of leading an invalid's life I could hardly have done less.

Anyway there is no good now having vain regrets - the great thing is that I have quite recovered and have at least 10 years ahead of me in which to have others - and one can't possibly afford to ever have more than three children all told so now if Ian gets his promotion in the next three years we could perhaps have two close together to be companions to each other.[42] I'm going out for my first walk today. Mrs Fitzmaurice is coming with me and I am going to change my books at the library and read the papers there and come back in a 'chair'. Yesterday and the day before I went for a drive in Bobjohn - we made a sort of divan of cushions so that I could lie almost flat - it was lovely getting out into the sun again.

This veranda is a very nice place to lie out in and we had fortunately bought one of those long cane chairs so I am very comfortable and from now onwards I shall be able to do more every day - but oh dear it is all very flat and sad it is like some dreadful game where one has always to be going back to the beginning.

I was thrilled to get No 5 Joy Street and I think they have reproduced the picture most awfully well.

We are delighted with the £7.7 which I really don't consider too bad pay - as I should only have charged f3.3 for the picture (and after all I've still got the original) and £2.2.0 a story is about ordinary magazine rate.

Ian has written a nice new story and I'm going on with 'Ginger' again having got back into the right atmosphere.

It was rather funny - I turned to Ian and said 'Isn't it exciting that's the first money you've ever earned' (meaning by your pen) whereupon he retorted indignantly 'I like that and me in the Navy man and boy for 20 years!'

I suppose now you will go abroad in the spring? Couldn't I send my luggage by sea and hop off with a suitcase at Marseilles and meet you at either somewhere in N. Italy or Provence (very handy for Marseilles and it did look so attractive, and then return via Paris?) I can't tell you yet when I shall arrive as it all hinges on Ian's refit - but they usually go north in April so that is probably when I should be starting - anyway I should arrive at Marseilles probably sometime in May. You can't find anyone who would like to 'present' me[43] this summer? It seems a good opportunity as next summer I hope to be otherwise engaged and after that we shall likely be abroad again. I should like to go to Scotland in the summer or autumn and Ian is due to be back by October or November but it might be earlier or later according as to whether he has to take one of the derelict submarines home (they are vaguely starting in the summer or autumn and goodness only knows hew many breakdowns they will have en route.) I'm making all these plans to try and fill the blank I know we shall all feel when the summer comes, though I shall be very excited to get back to you and Eleanor.

4 The Albany
26th November 1927 Hong Kong

What a fascinating book you have sent us![44] Ian and I are glued to it and find our average is about 50% - not very good! We are taking it out to supper with Jim and Grace tomorrow and I feel they will be far better at it. They are surprisingly well read and intelligent - but it doesn't seem to give them much pleasure so to speak - I mean I don't feel they enjoy life as much as a lot of our friends who are totally uneducated! I feel I am getting to like them better. I went to see Grace the other day and arrived rather early before she came in - so I looked at her books - they were Trevelyan's History of England, a novel by Johan Bojer, a book of Essays by Middleton Murray and Blackwoods magazine. That doesn't somehow conjure up one's idea of Grace at all - but I'm beginning to feel she is really much nicer than I thought. She loves Sylvia Warner books. There is a strong vein of crank in both of them which has the effect of making Ian and me aggressively Philistine - but especially in the Hong Kong atmosphere it is nice to meet people who are not just to the usual pattern. Incidentally we don't see much of them at present as the water divides us - but will see more of them when they go to Lymun. We took them down Cat Street the other day and they came back to supper - but Jim of course has been out in camp.

The heavenly weather continues and I can enjoy it now though I'm not doing anything very active as I'm still a bit sore (no wonder when I believe they scraped my inside and then treated it with iodine) but I'm feeling very well - only still dreadfully disappointed. Yesterday the Hutchinsons came to dinner and we went on to a dance at Government House. .Today Ian is 'day on' and I am lunching with the Glencrosses and going to the races with them and having tea with the Lakes in the KOSB's box. Tomorrow we are going to a meet of the 'Stag and Boar 'ounds' taking Bobjohn over to the Mainland. On Thursday we dined in the Titania with Tim and went to an amateur rendering of Bulldog Drummond, quite good.

We have shifted our room and are now upstairs and the view is a constant joy. You look through a foreground of palms and bamboo and mimosas across the ship dotted harbour to the Kowloon hills. We are nearly 400 ft up and perched right on the side of a hill. At night from the veranda (and it is still hot enough to sit out there) the harbour lights through the trees look like fireflies. It is a very big room with two French windows and a curtain goes down the middle - so that you can make it into two separate rooms as well as the veranda.

4 The Albany
1st December 1927

Sunday was a heavenly day so we went for a picnic to Big Wave Bay and had a lovely bathe - we got back at six and went to Evening Service in the Cathedral - a congregation almost entirely sailors and a few soldiers - and then went on to supper with Jim and Grace. Monday I took Grace to the monthly Art Club meeting. Next month is the annual Exhibition I am sending in eight pictures - but half are not for sale as I want them to take home. Tuesday we went to a tennis party and Maurice came to supper and we went to the 'pictures' and yesterday was the St Andrew's Ball. We danced reels and schottisches until the room rocked! and then we ate a huge supper. The K.O.S.B. pipers played and it was a great show and very crowded.

We had great excitement here two days ago, we woke up at 2am to hear galloping hooves in the garden - both of us instinctively thought 'someone has left the Beacon Corner gate open and the ponies have got in![45] However when we were properly awake we remembered that alas! 1100 miles divided us from Beacon Corner.

In the darkness we could see nothing and Ian suggested it must be the tame stag escaped from the Botanic Gardens - However next morning from our veranda we saw a huge grey water buffalo in the garden! They are very savage brutes and can't stand the smell of Europeans though they are generally fairly docile with the Chinese. This one however was very fierce and evidently had a great sense of humour - as it hid behind a clump of palms - and then whenever a coolie appeared down the path - pounced and charged - the coolies fairly nipped over the wall into the Botanic Gardens. The police were telephoned for and about a dozen arrived - Sikhs and Chinese and an English sergeant - they approached warily but the old buffalo fairly scattered them off the premises! It was most amusing to watch from above - but we were a little anxious about Bobjohn parked in the garden and Ian couldn't get near it. He asked one of the Sikh policemen what they intended doing and received the reply 'Have sent for dog catcher!' For about two hours nothing happened except tentative approaches of police and coolies and rushes by the buffalo who knocked over a good many flower pots and broke the fence and once nearly got a coolie who fell down. All the windows downstairs were barricaded and we were properly besieged. At 11am a man appeared with a rifle (the dog catcher?) and after four or five attempts succeeded in killing the animal just under our window - the corpse was then removed by sixteen coolies and some bamboo poles.

4 The Albany
13th December 1927

I can't remember when I wrote to you last - the days seem to go so quickly though one has no duties or responsibilities of any kind - yet I find I have to get up early in the morning in order to get through all I have to do in the day! One thing of course is that Ian is more at a loose end with 'L27' going into dock - but that is delightful. I've also been busy getting pictures ready for the Art Club Exhibition. I've sent eight - of which six you haven't seen. I rather hope they won't sell. I put 'not for sale' on two of them and pretty high prices on the pastels of Wei hai - I did some copies of them in water colour as a commission for Mrs Poland. Grace has sent some really charming oil paintings - I'd never seen anything finished of hers before and I think they are very good - much more professional than mine. The Exhibition opens tomorrow and goes on for two days.

Darling Eleanor

I thought it would amuse you to see the way people go about in Hong Kong. On the flat roads they go in a rickshaw which is rather nice. But up the hills they are carried in a chair which is very bumpty-bump.

Aunt Grace gave me your message. Did you like No. 5 Joy Street and Daddy's story and Mummy's picture?

I hope you will have a very happy Xmas and that next Xmas we shall all be together again.
Your Loving
    Mummy.

4 The Albany
18th December 1927

It is difficult to believe that it is only a week until Xmas, it has turned warm again and all the leaves remain on the trees and there is nothing to show the change of season. In Flower Street the roses and sweet peas have begun to come in again.

We had a lovely day out at Fanling on Tuesday and on Wednesday we had a tennis party. Thursday was the Art Club Exhibition. I enclose you a cutting from the local paper about it. Grace's pictures were much admired by all the critics and she got very good notices, but didn't sell any. I sold three out of my six that were for sale, and I made 75$ - the only sad thing was they were my two best pictures and I'm so sad you won't see them.

On Friday we had some people to dinner and went on to an amateur opera which was very good though too long. In the afternoon Jim and Grace took me to an auction. I'd never been to one before and it was most thrilling. I feel one could very easily lose one's head! We got a pair of little cupboards for 14$ 50 cents - and took one each - they are modern red lacquer - but very attractive all covered with amusing figures and a lot of gold. (in the meantime we are using it as a sort of cellar having nowhere else to keep drinks!) but eventually it would make a charming medicine or nursery cupboard. For $5 I got a Chinese ladies' dressing case - blackboard bound with brass - the lid lifts up and has a mirror and the front opens and shows lots of little drawers with brass handles - it would do for a man's dressing room. I think it is old - or oldish - and it is in quite good condition and the ship's carpenter is going to polish it up for us. Ian insisted on bidding for a terrible Chinese picture of a horse! It is about six foot long and painted on silk and being the only bidder we got it for a dollar.

Did you see the article 'Bobjohn becomes Bobjonah' in the November 4th Number of the 'Light Car?'[46] We think it reads rather well! The local Sunday paper here reproduced it last week - we didn't see it but the storekeeper in the Dockyard saved it up to show Ian. I must try to get a copy for you.

'L27' went into dock on Thursday and is being rapidly reduced to a heap of wreckage which nearly breaks Ian's heart and she had been looking so nice and smart beforehand. I doubt whether he will take her to sea again though she is supposed to be finished in April - but they usually take at least twice the time anticipated. The latest buzz is that the Ambrose and submarines may leave for home in July or August, but owing to typhoons I should say September was more probable.

4 The Albany
20th December 1927

Things are rather hectic up in Canton[47] just now there are ghastly photographs in the papers and refugees are pouring in here. All the English have been collected in Shamian[48] and are protected by a company of K.O.S.B's. This time it appears to be more anti-Bolshevik than anti-British - but its a 'distressful' country. However Hong Kong seems very prosperous and peaceful and Shanghai even more so to the casual eye at any rate.

The Ambrose is having a 'dressing up' dinner party to which we asked Jim and Grace who however refuse to come on the score of being too old and staid for such foolishness and Jim made the insulting remark that the Welsh blood in Ian must be stronger than the Scotch to enable him to enjoy it! but I think it is more a question of profession - sailors remain so extraordinarily young and light-hearted in many ways - while many of the soldiers here are rather 'mouldy' though not the K.O.S.B.'s who are a particularly nice lot and there is a great Entente between them and the submarines. I'm getting to know a few of the civilians and they are very nice when you do get to know them - but we envy them their beautiful flats and houses. All the bank clerks have superb flats with two modern bathrooms and every luxury.

<u>Boxing Day</u>

P.S. How awful - this letter has never been posted - so I'd better go on with it.

The children's party in the Ambrose was a huge success. The children were handed over by their parents on the jetty and all numbered! I went off with the first boat load. When they got on board there were swings and seesaws and a lovely shute and a most realistic aeroplane. It was a beautiful warm afternoon and most of the children were blissfully happy. Two or three were shy and unhappy and Mrs Poland and I looked out for them. The next entertainment was a simply marvellous Punch and Judy Show - a real Chinese one and much more exciting than the English variety though with points in common, but no English Punch and Judy has a grinning tiger! nor do its characters do juggling with plates and bowls! A huge tea followed in the wardroom and then Father Xmas came through the skylight and about 6 o'clock the parents arrived to collect their young - I forgot to mention a very thrilling pirates cave and an Aunt Sally with real heads to shy at! and Ian dressed up in his Amoy Cat suit and was chased all over the ship by children trying to pull his tail! I did long for Eleanor to be there as you may imagine.

On Saturday we took Bobjohn over to the Mainland and motored out to the Fanling steeplechases - we forgathered with the Hutchinsons and Glencrosses - had a picnic lunch - We picked one winner - our other two fancies refused to jump! Duncan and Margaret however were very lucky and picked three winners. We dined with the Maclarens and went on to a cinema 'The Last days of Pompeii'

I enjoyed Christmas day much more than I expected to - I'd never spent a Christmas on board before and it was really rather fun. We went off at 9·45 to Church - first of all a stand up service with all the Christmas hymns on deck and then the second service down in the little chapel of St Ambrose in the depths of the ship. They have a carved wooden Altar front with St George and the dragon - St Nicholas patron saint of sailors and St Ambrose clasping a submarine to his bosom (I wasn't quite sure if the latter was slightly profane or not!)

At 11 o'clock we started a tour of the decorated mess decks - Signalmen - torpedomen - daymen etc - all most beautifully done and evidently great competition in each mess - cigars and chocolates and cake etc. were pressed upon us! Then we went to the submariners mess decks - 'L27' had two magnificent cakes worthy of Ninny - Ian cut one and I the other and Ian had to drink everyone's health in a mug of beer then they gave three cheers too - After that we went to the Galley and inspected the turkeys (the officers always present the crew with turkey) and then to the store rooms - ship's office and Sick Bay - all awfully interesting. Everywhere were placards 'Where will the Ambrose be next Xmas?' and Captain Poland wrote on all of them 'Home' and signed it. Then we went to the W.O's mess and had cocktails and finally to the Wardroom and champagne! and ended up by having to go and watch the Rum[49] issued (out of a cask with 'God Save The King' in brass letters round it - this is the thing that always tickles the American Naval Officers!) Personally I preferred the Rum to all the other sips that I had had to partake of! At 12.30 we embarked in a motorboat and went over to pay our respects to the Titania and then back to the Ambrose to lunch in the Captain's cabin, in the afternoon we all played tennis (very creditable tennis too considering the awful mixture of eats and drinks we had partaken of in the morning!) In the evening Jim and Grace came to dinner and we all went on to a Chinese theatre - entertaining but not as nice as the theatrical performances in the Wei hai temples.

4 The Albany
1st January 1928

I tried to send off the parcel containing the mandarin coat - Eleanor's kimono and Ninny's silk - but as it was going to cost 20$ (£2) in duty, postage and insurance and then probably give you trouble at the other end - I didn't think it good enough - I'm sure I shan't have to pay so much if I bring the things - certainly not postage anyway - but I think I must send you the blue agate to keep you going.

I enclose a chatty snippet[50] for the 'Glasgow Herald'. I tried to write a more ambitious article on a Chinese Festival at Wei hai - but it was incredibly dull and full of (probably inaccurate) information - so in despair I reverted to the colloquial and I'm afraid I haven't even made a 'fair copy' of it. I'll do a funeral next!

What a week we've had - never in bed before midnight and yesterday and the night before not until 2am. On Wednesday we went to a small dance given by the C in C in the 'Hawkins' which was quite amusing - Thursday was a frightful day. It poured all day so we kept the house until the evening when we dined with the Hewitts (He is the Naval Padre - we don't much like him). It was a very unclerical party with two tables of bridge - Ian being odd man out had a dull evening looking on. On Friday I made Ian's fancy dress - it is fatal having achieved a reputation for being rather good at them as Ian is expected to appear in something new and original every time! I also went to lunch with Mrs Hackforth Jones and to see Grace who is laid up with a broken vein in her leg which she got escaping from a water buffalo!

I think the 'Ambrose' fancy dress dinner dance was a great success and both Duncan and Margaret enjoyed it - There were about seventy people all told and some very funny dresses. I wore Janet's Victorian dress which is the most becoming costume I have got and the bonnet is very useful in keeping one's hair tidy as there was a good deal of dancing on deck. Ian went as a Victorian gentleman (Edwin and Angelia) he wore his uniform frock coat to which I added a plum coloured velvet collar and cuffs which hid the stripes - I added a frill to his shirt and straps under his shoes to his white duck trousers - a black satin stock and a fob and long dundreary weepers and a borrowed top hat (rather small) It was really very effective - he might have been a daguerro type of his own grandfather. The Hutchinsons came as an old farmer and his granddaughter - Duncan wore a fancy kilt with a sporran made out of a sponge bag and shaving brushes etc. and Margaret had a Victorian dress with pantalettes made of some of your genuine antiques!

Yesterday Ian played cricket and I went for a ride with Duncan and Margaret and young Richardson. We went along an awfully pretty path across the hills from Happy Valley to Deepwater Bay - about four or five miles. First through market gardens all full of marigolds and dahlias and then along the hillside among bushes of cistus and other shrubs. There was one place where we could canter - but mostly it was very steep. At Deepwater Bay we got off and the ponies all had a good roll in the sand - then we came home the same way. I had a very well behaved pony and thoroughly enjoyed it and I am not so very stiff today either. In the evening we dined with the Pearsons and they took us to a Fancy Ball at the Peak Club - Once again I wore the Victorian costume - but Ian couldn't as the frockcoat had to be ready for him to wear today - and I couldn't face sewing on medal ribbons at 2am so he wore the Amoy Cat costume with great success. Mrs Pearson looked charming in a venetian dress - and the Commodore was to have gone as a Chrysanthemum but at the last minute said he didn't feel well and so didn't come at all - sheer funk I think really!

We knew very few people outside our own party - but it was amusing to see the 'Taipans' at play - but thank heaven I can go to bed early tonight! Ian has a day on. I went to church in the morning and then on to lunch with the Maclarens. The whole of next week is booked up which is sad as I want to go out sketching.

I hope you haven't been fussing about my not being well - I've never felt better in my life than I do just now and I've got quite a good colour again. The doctor's bill has just come and is only $50 - which I think is very little as it included the operation and anaesthetic and about half a dozen visits. The hospital was just over £4 - so the whole thing was less than £10 and I had a lovely room and couldn't have been better looked after. I think it is considerably cheaper to be ill here than at home.

Aren't these 'howlers' rather nice:-

'Christians are only allowed one wife - this is called monotony.' and 'Contralto is a low sort of music which only ladies sing!' I culled these from Dean Inges 'Lay thoughts of a Dean.'

4 The Albany
6th January 1928 Hong Kong

The most thrilling news! A cable came from the Admiralty yesterday to say that the 'Ambrose' and six submarines are to be home by the end of June! Isn't that wonderful and Ian is almost certain to take one of the boats - probably his old friend L7! Of course one never really dares to rejoice too much as it may all be changed next week - but this really does seem pretty definite and they will be leaving at the end of March. I hope to possibly get a passage in the troopship 'City of Marseilles' which goes in March - otherwise by whatever ship I can get in to. I shan't know about the trooper until the last moment so I will have to cable you the name of the ship and then you can follow its movements in the paper. If I can't get a passage in a British ship I may have to come Nordeutcher Lloyd or Tristino Lloyd and get out at Venice or Genoa. Anyway I should be home by the end of April or early in May six weeks or so before Ian which is perfect as I shall have that time alone with you and then the excitement of going to meet the flotilla and rather fun all our friends coming at the same time - then seven weeks leave in July and August (and buying a car!) and then in September I can settle down to try and have another baby! I-don't know what job Ian will get next - quite on the cards to build an 'O' boat and bring it out here in a year or so!

4 The Albany
8th January 1928

My darling Eleanor

Her is a little English girl going for a walk with her Chinese Nanny who is called an Amah. She must come from Canton or South China because she has big feet.

It is just a year ago today that I sailed for China - but very SOON NOW I shall be sailing for home. Isn't that glorious - and I hope Daddy will come very soon after that and we shall all be together again - Won't we hug you ?

I have got an umbrella like the one the Amah is carrying. Do you like it? It is raining such a lot here just now. I wonder if you had snow at Burley and if you played in it?

4 The Albany
12th January 1928

We went a most interesting expedition yesterday - out to an island Lantao. We started at 9am going in the police launch with nice Mr Wynn Jones the district officer who had business to transact there. A Captain Doyle (R.E.) and his wife came too and another couple and an old archaeologist whom we put ashore on a desert island to look for fossils (which he didn't find!) It was a grey rather chilly day and we got somewhat bored by the three hours in the launch though cheered up at the end by an excellent picnic lunch. But I'd go double the distance to see again a place as fascinating as 'Tai,O' the principal village of the island. No Europeans live there except two police sergeants and it is utterly unspoilt and Chinese. First of all we watched two men on a bamboo raft hauling in fish out of a net which was worked by another couple of men sitting on a hill with a primitive winch. The fishermen wore bamboo hats and palm leaf cloaks and the fish in the net looked like tiny pieces of silver and the whole scene was most uncommon and attractive. Then we walked, to the village which is like a Chinese Venice - all built on piles. Each house is different from its neighbour and leans crazily upon its stone supports and is reflected in the water - each has a bamboo ladder and a rickety veranda with pots of plants from which the inhabitants sit and fish. The roofs are thatched with shaggy leaves and above are poles on which flutters the family washing - Across this species of Grand Canal there is no bridge but a sampan ferry goes continually from side to side where there are stone steps. For this ferry you pay a cash (1000 to the dollar!) Then we went to the market - a very gay scene where all sorts of fish were being sold and mandarin oranges and gay paper toys and kites - I bought a back scratcher for 2 cents! All the women seemed to be wearing very smart new varnished hats with pink strings and the people looked very prosperous (It is the great fish place which supplies Hong Kong). There was also a large open square and a temple dedicated to the War god. In the corner was stabled his life size paper horse with a beautiful grin which I longed to acquire for Seton! Then we went down a long narrow cobbled street hung with gay signs. At one place some old women were making biscuits in wooden moulds, in another a little girl was treading a primitive mill for grinding rice. At another place we went in to a hovel occupied by an old man and there saw an opium divan. Mr Wynn Jones said he had run him in two or three times - but this time though he searched everywhere even in the thatch of the roof he couldn't find any smuggled opium. We returned in a sampan down the creek and in and out of the houses. I'd have given anything to have had a week there to sketch - but there is no way of getting to the place except by launch or anywhere to stay. We took photographs but the light was not very good and I did some hurried scribbles. With the exception of Pekin it is the most attractive place that I have seen out here. We went back on board at 3.30 and had tea and arrived back at 6.30 when we had hurriedly to change and go out to a dance in the 'Tamar' which was very good fun.

Hong Kong is a most hectic place - one is always booked up at least a week ahead for every minute of the day and I've even got engagements for February! The difficulty is to see enough of the people you do like and not get involved with people you don't. I had a disastrous lunch party the other day - two females I hardly knew and who disliked each other at sight - one gushed all the time and the other snubbed her so badly that I felt quite shy though she had my full sympathy!

Ian is very happy because Tim has lent us his gramophone and his vast selection of high class records - so we dress to the strains of Bach and Schubert and are consequently always late - but I'm beginning to acquire quite a taste for music.

4 The Albany
20th January 1928

Isn't it exciting that it is all settled (as far as anything is ever settled in the Navy!) and that Ian is going to take L8 home and they start upon March 23rd.

The Naval Transport Officer is being very kind and helpful and is full of hope that he will get passages for Mrs Allen, Mrs Drinkwater and Mrs Hutchinson and myself in the 'City of Marseilles' sailing sometime between March 3rd and 17th - so by the time you get this letter I may be just starting - I'll cable as soon as I know - but it will probably not be until the last moment.

It has been a week of lovely weather - like a perfect September at home - We spent the whole day out at Fanling on Tuesday and the mauve hills against the blue sky were a dream. Mrs Fitzsimmons and I played in a competition in the morning on the short course while Ian played Tim - then we had a picnic lunch and a foursome afterwards. On Monday I had Mrs Maclaren and Margaret, Mrs North and Phyllis Poland to lunch and Ian and I went a nice picnic in the afternoon in BobJohn. On Wednesday we played our mixed doubles in the tournament and after a very exciting game were knocked out. We won the first set 10-8 but rather went to pieces after that. Ian and Jim are still in the men's doubles and are playing this afternoon while I go out and see Grace in their new house and have tea. Then we are dining with the Hutch's and going to see the Chinese New Year stalls and hope to pick up bargains!

Yesterday Ian was playing in the tournament and I went with Margaret and nice Mrs Percival out to Fanling to practise for the gymkana. It is lovely to be riding again and I get on well on the straight - but I'm not very good at the 'bending' race. There were about ten females all pretty indifferent horsewomen except two, and Major Lake and a delightful Scotch sergeant were in charge of us! We had tea at the 'Hunters Arms' and a very hilarious train journey home. I picked Ian up at the U.S.R.C. and we went to visit our friend 'Canton John' to see if he had any New Year bargains. He is a cheerful old ruffian of a curio dealer and we bought a very nice opium table and a mandarin's bead box and another fan case for $19. He started at $24 for the three and it took nearly an hour to get him down and I got so hot and exhausted in the process! I got Seton[51] a lovely pink horse Chien Lung (18th century) I got it from one of the big dealers Komor who guarantees his stuff - but of course not cheap.

4 The Albany
23rd January 1928 Hong Kong

My darling Eleanor

I wish you had been here to see all the streets before Chinese New Year. They look so pretty with great big lanthorns and heaps of lovely flowers and branches of flowering almond etc. Everybody buys a plant - here is a little Chinese girl carrying hers home.

There is a great deal of noise too as everybody lets off crackers and rockets. Then all the houses and junks are decorated with red 'joss' papers and peacocks feathers as well as the flowers. In one street they sold nothing but goldfish - such funny looking ones with bulging eyes and feathery tails - rather like a Pekinese dog. I wanted to buy you some - but I was afraid they would die before we got to England. But I got you a toy Chinese cooking stove in which you can light a real fire! Here are two trees I bought for my room - a tiny pink camellia and a tiny orange tree in a green pot with lots of real oranges growing on it!

These are joss papers and are supposed to bring good luck - and here is one of the funny goldfish!

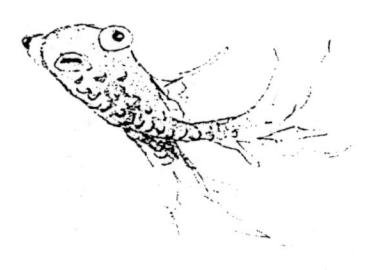

Isn't it lovely to think how soon I shall be able to give you a real hug!

Here the letters end; the last few from Hong Kong and from the 'City of Calcutta' on the homeward voyage are missing. My grandmother took me to meet the ship at Southampton; with the callousness of a six-year old I quite took my mother's return for granted, and was more interested in the present she had brought me.

   Ian and Ruth never returned to China. My brother did part of his National Service in Hong Kong in the late 1950's, when it was not possible to visit China, and in 1987 I was able to take a holiday in China and Hong Kong and see the place of my origin 67 years earlier.

Notes

1. Ninny was Ruth's nanny, Mabel Wilkinson from Herne Bay, who had stayed on as companion to her mother.
2. 'The Black Heathens' - the branch of the Dent family who lived in Blackheath.
3. 'Ambrose' was the submarine depot ship which supported L7 and the rest of the flotilla.
4. Miss Duff was the daughter of the widowed Admiral Duff, and was acting as hostess for her father in the official yacht 'Alacrity'.
5. K7 was Ian's previous (steam) submarine.
6. This was unfair to Ian, who wrote verse all his life, but Ruth was presumably thinking of 'arts and crafts'.
7. Iris Ryder and Muriel Clogstoun were childhood friends of Ruth's: Muriel became my godmother.
8. Ian had survived most of the major naval action of the 1914-1918 war. He had served in the 'Inflexible' in the first battle of the Falklands islands (1916), and his photographs of the battle, the sinking of the Scharnhorst, Port Stanley etc. were given after his death to the Naval Museum in Portsmouth 1982, when they were of particular interest in the light of the current conflict.
9. T.B. was still a major scourge in the 1920's
10. Ruth's anti-American prejudices (mainly acquired from distant views of groups of tourists) were only dispersed when she came to know USN officers and their wives.
11. Ruth was born in Dumfriesshire (at Maxwelton, where the braes are bonny).
12. Ruth always referred to her mother-in-law as 'Mrs Macnair' until she was able to call her 'Granny'. Janet was Ian's sister.
13. 'Aunt Carlo' was Nellie Sellar, May Dent's unmarried sister, who lived in Edinburgh and 'knew everybody'. Her

introductions to various diplomatic acquaintances around the world were of great service to Ruth on her travels. I remember her as a kind but rather formidable elderly lady in her gas-lit house in Rosebury Crescent Edinburgh.
14. Sic. This may mean 'before he finishes his sea time'.
15. Newcastle in Northern Ireland, where Ruth had been on holidays with her grandmother.
16. Voelas - a house near Aberdovey rented by Ian's mother.
17. 'Hurl' a jaunt (Scots).
18. Basil Blackwell, the Oxford Publishers, had agreed to publish stories and poems by Ian, illustrated by Ruth, in their children's annual 'Joy Street'. This was a distinguished publication, whose authors included Compton Mackenzie, Walter de la Mare, Hilaire Belloc, Eleanor Farjeon, etc. Ian and Ruth were contributors from Number 5 (1927) to Number 11 (1933), the first story being 'Six Green Parrots', and the last 'The Celestial Dog'.
19. Later Admiral Roddy Miles. He and his wife Marjorie (née Sellar) were cousins of Ruth's.
20. 'Bobjohn' was originally a bright yellow two-seater with a dicky seat behind, known as 'The Flying Banana'; Ian had reconstructed it with a body covered with rubberoid roofing and green American cloth. I remember riding in Bobjohn on Ninny's lap in the front seat, while Mother rode behind in the dicky. One of my earliest memories is of Bobjohn down on a steep Devonshire hill and Mother getting out to push; the car suddenly started and she fell flat on her face. I thought this hysterically funny.
21. See 'Old Ah Chong and his windy weather'
22. Chiang Kai Shek.
23. 'Ginger' was published by Blackwell's in No. 9 Joy Street, and as a separate children's book.
24. David Garnett.

25. 'Tim' Mark Taylor and Ian remained close friends for the rest of their lives, and were still corresponding in verse in their 80's. Tim became my sister's godfather.
26. Ian eventually wrote a poem to complement Ruth's picture of the lady in the chair, published in No. 6 Joy Street. (1928).
27. Ian's comic poem 'Caractacus Adolphus Brown was published in a Blackwell's Girl Guides' annual, and subsequently in No. 7 Joy Street (1929).
28. This was a predecessor of water-skiing, but with a single board attached to the motor boat.
29. Puss = Eleanor. Ian's allowance of £100 p.a. from his mother was being paid to my other grandmother for my keep.
30. 'Six Green Parrots' when published in No. 5 Joy Street had a coloured illustration by Ruth, but black and white illustration by someone else.
31. Mlle Suzanne Lenglen, the French tennis champion, impersonated by Ian at the fancy dress dance.
32. Janet Macnair - Ian's sister.
33. Sir Miles Lampson was ambassador in Pekin (one of Aunt Carlo's introductions).
34. Ruth later discovered that the noise and excitement had been due to the train crew cutting down trees to fuel the engine.
35. Sir Miles Lampson.
36. No ecological scruples about rare furs in the 1920s - but Ruth lived to be rather ashamed of her baby leopard coat.
37. I remember the jade and seed pearl necklace with delight - also the model of the Forbidden City. Ruth's purchases were part of the background of my childhood, and many of them we still possess.
38. Lawrence Binyon, 1869-1943, poet, art critic and historian, especially the art of China and Japan. Arthur Waley, 1889 - 1966, oriental scholar, translator of Chinese and Japanese poetry, cataloguer of oriental art in British Museum.

39. Hankow had been the scene of various Communist uprisings, and had been in the forefront of the general strike of 1923.
40. Wong Wing Wu was published in No. 10 Joy Street, and as a separate children's book by Blackwell's.
41. Ian's elder brother, J.L.P. Macnair, was a regular officer in the R.A. (Later Director of the Military College of Science, Shrivanham, and a member of the Ordnance Board.) His wife Grace (nee Atkins) was an artist, and Jim had musical and scientific interests which were unusual for an army officer of the period; also they held more sophisticated political views than many of their Service contemporaries. Ruth was nervous of her brother and sister-in-law: she suspected them (unjustly) of being intellectual snobs, and of despising the rather frivolous pleasures (such as fancy-dress dances) which she and Ian enjoyed. At first she was very much on the defensive, but her prejudices began to melt during this Hong Kong spell, and when she got to know them better they became great friends.
42. Owing to two still-births, Ruth's family was more spaced out than she had planned. My sister Dionis was born in 1930, and my brother Miles in 1937.
43. At court.
44. A general knowledge quiz book.
45. Ponies getting into the garden remain a hazard of life in the New Forest.
46. See page 237
47. Sun Yat Sen had set up his Kuomintang Government in Canton, at first supported by the Communists, in opposition to the military rule of Yuan in Pekin. Chiang Kai Shek succeeded Sun Yat Sen in 1925, and in 1927 (the year Ruth is writing) he broke with the Communists and declared war on them, imprisoning and executing many in Canton. Later he advanced North, defeated Yuan and occupied Pekin, and in 1928 set up a national government in Nanking. The Communists under Chou

En Lai and Mao Tse Tung subsequently undertook the Long March, regrouped in North-west China, and after the defeat of the Japanese took over the country, forcing Chiang Kai Shek and his followers to flee to Taiwan.
48. Shamian Island, once the foreign consulate area (and now the site of an excellent hotel, the White Swan).
49. The daily issue of rum in the Navy was stopped in the 1960's.
50. This article and the one on the Chinese New Year are missing.
51. Seton Thomson, a distant cousin of Ruth's, collected model horses of every age and material, from Tang porcelain to Woolworth plastic. The valuable items of his collection were left to the Kelvingrove Museum, Glasgow.